Mark Piggott, a native of Phillipsburg, NJ, enlisted in the US Navy in 1983 and began a 23-year career. He served on three aircraft carriers and various duty stations as a Navy Journalist before he attained the rank of Chief Journalist. He retired from active duty in 2006. His first novel, *Forever Avalon*, was published in 2009, followed by his second novel, *The Dark Tides*, in 2014. He and his wife, Georgiene, live in Alexandria, Virginia. They have three children.

To my heroes: My dad, William Piggott, and my grandfather, William Davis.

Mark Piggott

THE OUTLANDER WAR:
BOOK 3 OF THE FOREVER AVALON SERIES

AUSTIN MACAULEY PUBLISHERS™
LONDON * CAMBRIDGE * NEW YORK * SHARJAH

Copyright © Mark Piggott (2020)

The right of Mark Piggott to be identified as author of this work has been asserted by him in accordance with section 77 and 78 of the Copyright, Designs and Patents Act 1988.

All rights reserved. No part of this publication may be reproduced, stored in a retrieval system or transmitted in any form or by any means, electronic, mechanical, photocopying, recording or otherwise, without the prior permission of the publishers.

Any person who commits any unauthorised act in relation to this publication may be liable to criminal prosecution and civil claims for damages.

A CIP catalogue record for this title is available from the British Library.

ISBN 9781528920889 (Paperback)
ISBN 9781528963237 (ePub e-book)

www.austinmacauley.com

First Published (2020)
Austin Macauley Publishers Ltd
25 Canada Square
Canary Wharf
London
E14 5LQ

I would like to thank my friend and fellow writer-editor, Michael Stettes, for helping me edit my novel. It always takes another writer to point out the spelling errors and grammar mistakes you missed. I also want to thank Adam Aldrich, a talented young artist who helped to inspire the design for my book cover. He was able to capture what was in my head through a conversation over 'Twitter'. That's just incredible.

Prologue
The Battle of Camlann

The field was strewn with the dead: Warriors felled by sword, axe, spear and shaft. Blood pooled on the ground like an open wound, but there were no winners this day. Only death triumphed. Camlann sat near the western coast of Wales in Britain. This was the last stand by Mordred and those forces loyal to his sorceress mother, Morgana le Fay, against King Arthur and the Knights of the Round Table.

The Battle of Camlann was the final conflict between King Arthur and Mordred. The two combatants lay side-by-side on the ground, both men mortally wounded by the other. Morgana's spell may have kept her son young and beautiful, but the power of *Excalibur* had cut easily through that enchantment.

As Sir Percival ran to his monarch's aid, Mordred crawled away, not wanting to wait for the last of the Knights of the Round Table to finish him off.

Percival dropped his sword and lifted Arthur's head onto his lap. "My liege," he cried. "I am here, Your Majesty."

"Percival, listen to me," King Arthur groaned. "Take *Excalibur* to the Lady of the Lake. It must not fall into the wrong hands!" He gave the sword to Percival, placing the hilt firmly in his hands. "You must do this for me."

Percival nodded his head as tears began to roll down his face. "I will, my King! I will," he assured him. Arthur smiled, his mind at ease, then coughed violently. Blood spewed from the King's lips and spattered across Percival's breastplate.

"Find Mordred, Percival," Arthur choked out. "He must not be allowed to take the throne of Camelot. You must…" King Arthur coughed again and gasped for air. Percival did his best to comfort his dying friend.

"Do not fear, milord. For if there is breath in my body, he will never sit on the throne. This, I swear!"

King Arthur took one last breath and became still, his eyes staring into the stars above as he died in the arms of his most loyal knight. Percival cried and closed the King's eyes before setting him gently down on the ground.

He looked over to *Excalibur* and knew he had a promise to keep. Percival reached for the sword, but it was suddenly scooped up by the hands of Merlin the Magician, who had approached unnoticed during the King's passing. The sorcerer and advisor looked regal in his flowing robes and long white hair and beard. He took the sword and, without a word to Sir Percival, walked steadily toward the top of a nearby hill.

"Merlin, what are you doing?" Percival screamed, as he leapt to his feet. "I must return *Excalibur* to the Lady of the Lake. It was the King's final command."

Merlin said nothing. He quickened his pace to the reach the hilltop, walking past the bodies of the dead knights. Percival became infuriated. He ran up and grabbed the wizard by the arm.

"Dammit, Merlin, answer me!" he commanded. Merlin spun around and pointed his staff at Percival to ward him off. The twisted shaft of Wyche elm had three branches at its top, resembling a trident, with crystals of rose, smoky and white quartz embedded in them respectively. The crystals glowed, magical energy flowing among them, warning the knight to stay away.

"We don't have time, Sir Percival," said the wizard. "I must act quickly to save us all."

Merlin turned away, his beard swaying with each step, as he continued his pace. Percival was confused by Merlin's statement. "Time for what? Merlin, what do you mean?" he shouted, as he chased after him.

"The age of magic is coming to an end, and so is our world," he explained. "With Arthur's death, the magic that fills our realm is already starting to fade. I must act quickly if I am to stem the tide."

"But how?" Percival asked. "How can you do that?"

"There is a spell, one of the first ever written," Merlin explained. "If I focus that spell through *Excalibur*, it will summon and collect all world's magic together in one place."

"But where, Merlin? Where are you sending it?"

Merlin stopped at the summit. "To Avalon, my boy! To Avalon! There, I will hide all magic, all magical creatures, beings and objects from the rest of the world."

The wizard raised his staff high before slamming it into the ground in front of him. He took *Excalibur* and situated the hilt between the branches, allowing blade to hang down from the staff. Then Merlin stood behind his creation and began chanting an ancient spell in a language unknown to this day and age. He repeated the words over and over into a perfect rhythm and soon, magic began to pour from the ground around him, swirling into a vortex of magical energy.

Percival stood back and watched the ritual unfold before him. The magic around Merlin grew brighter and brighter as the spell reached its zenith.

"No!" shouted a voice from behind. Percival drew his sword and spun around to see Mordred charging up the hill, bloodied and wounded from his fight with

King Arthur. His blonde hair was dirty and matted, but his golden armour—a gift from his mother to protect him from harm—shone flawlessly in the glow of Merlin's magic.

"I will have *Excalibur*," Mordred shouted. "By birthright, I am now King!"

Percival stepped forward. "You will never be King, Mordred. My descendants and I will always stand between you and the throne."

"You will not stop me, Percival," Mordred said, bristling with anger as he drew his sword. "No matter where you go, I will take *Excalibur* in my hands. I will sit on Arthur's throne. *I will be King!*"

Percival leapt at Mordred, swinging his sword down in a crushing blow, but Mordred blocked the attack with surprising strength given his injuries. As steel clashed, Merlin maintained his concentration chanting until the magic that surrounded him exploded in a brilliant flash of light. Instantly, the three men disappeared. And they weren't the only ones. Across England and around the world, everyone and everything touched by magic vanished—just as Merlin had intended—and over time, faded into myth and legend, never to be seen again.

Or so he thought.

Chapter 1
Avalon Returns

Captain Larry Rich sat in his chair on the bridge of the *USS Theodore Roosevelt*, savouring a fresh cup of coffee as he watched the flight deck crew scrambling to get ready for the first launch of the day. As the captain of an aircraft carrier, he commanded more than 6,000 sailors on one of the largest warships afloat.

Rich reflected on this past year. He recently had taken command of the warship, back at sea for the first time after an extended shipyard overhaul and carrier qualifications. The ship was operating in the Caribbean as part of 'Global Triad', a joint exercise with combined US and South American forces. This was the first major exercise of combat readiness for the ship and Captain Rich wanted to make sure there were no hiccups on deck. As a former 'Air Boss' of an aircraft carrier, he knew what it took to keep the action on deck moving, so he expected the same from his crew.

The only thing Larry hated about the exercise was its location. Call him superstitious, but he never liked flying or sailing anywhere near the Bermuda Triangle. This notorious stretch of ocean had long plagued mariners and pilots due to reports of countless, strange disappearances happening there.

For Larry, it was personal. He lost a good sailor—and the sailor's family—to the Triangle. Chief Bryan Drake worked for Captain Rich as Air Boss on *USS George Washington*. He mentored and moulded Bryan into being one of the top sailors in his command. During a particularly bad storm, Chief Drake saved a sailor from going overboard and ended up in the soup himself. Less than a year later, his wife and children disappeared near the same spot while paying their respects. Only his oldest daughter, Ashley, had survived the ordeal.

"Captain, the Air Boss says he's ready to go." An officer's voice returned Larry's thoughts to the present. "Request permission to turn the ship into the wind to begin flight operations."

"Permission granted," Captain Rich said. Within minutes, the aircraft carrier turned and its speed increased to give the flight deck perfect conditions to launch aircraft. As soon as the recovery helicopters lifted off into the air, the first aircraft were lined up on the catapult, ready to launch. Captain Rich took another sip of coffee and sat back in his chair to watch the action unfold.

Without warning, a loud, inhuman roar pierced the air, causing the Captain to spit out his coffee. He looked out the window, forward and aft, thinking maybe it was an explosion on deck, but everything appeared to be normal, aside from the flight deck crew being just as stunned by the unexplained sound. Suddenly, a wave of luminous energy cascaded toward them from the west, flooding the air as it swept across the ship, sparking off the deck and aircraft like static electricity. Every instrument on the ship and in the aircraft—on deck and in the air—shut down for a split-second before flickering back to life.

Captain Rich opened his mouth to request a status report from the nearest officer when he noticed a wall of water, more than 200 feet tall, rushing toward his helpless ship. There was no time to react before it was upon him. It lifted the carrier into the sky, rolling it out and about, before rushing past.

Miraculously, the ship and its crew were safe. Everyone on the bridge watched as the wave headed east toward the coast of the United States. Captain Rich knew the potential devastation it could cause. "Get on the horn to Fleet Forces Command and warn them about that wave."

"Aye-aye, sir!" the officer acknowledged.

"Captain! Look!" one sailor shouted, as he pointed out the window. Captain Rich turned around, and his eyes grew as wide as hen's eggs. He couldn't believe what he saw. Out in the ocean, an island had appeared from nowhere. It sat more than a mile from the carrier and its coastline stretched southeast beyond the horizon. To make matters stranger, a second island, this one smaller with a towering mountain in the middle, hovered in the air just off the larger island's coast. Waterfalls flowed out of the mountain and into the clouds below that formed a ring around the base.

"What the hell is that?" someone asked, as shock settled in.

"Sound General Quarters! This is not a drill!" the Captain ordered, as he rushed out onto the bridge wing with a pair of binoculars in hand. As the clanging bells and whistles sounded the general alarm across the ship, sailors rushed to get to their battle stations. Captain Rich stared at the floating island through the binoculars, trying to comprehend exactly what he saw.

As he examined the floating land mass, he saw something even more extraordinary. Flying about the central peak were creatures of myth and legend that half of his brain recognised immediately, and the other half rejected outright. He blinked several times and the creatures didn't disappear. They were dragons. He couldn't deny it. They moved in and out of various cave openings in the mountain as if it were their home.

"Captain!" the nearest officer shouted. "Contact South, Southwest over that island!"

"What is it?" Captain Rich asked.

"Unknown, sir. It's something no one's ever seen before, and it's moving very slowly!"

Captain Rich looked through his binoculars and was equally as stunned as his crew. A wooden ship, like an old, Spanish galleon with full sails and canvas wings, soared through the air toward the floating island. The surprises kept getting bigger and bigger, and Captain Rich didn't need any more surprises.

"Tell CAG to put a Hawkeye in the air immediately. I want to know how big that island is. Send up a couple of Hornets as its escort. Also, shut down all external communications. I don't want somebody's pictures or video ending up on *YouTube* or *Facebook* until we know what we're dealing with."

The captain's orders were quickly relayed. The CAG, or Carrier Air Group commander, helped air operations get the right planes into position and ready to launch, along with its fighter escorts. Even with all this, Captain Rich knew he needed some more guidance from his chain of command on how to deal with this.

"Get me Fleet Forces Command, now," he shouted. "This is completely beyond me."

***

Lord Bryan MoonDrake, the Gil-Gamesh of Avalon, looked out at the aircraft carrier sitting off the coast of Emmyr. Standing on a rocky outcropping, the Half-Elf Lord of Avalon couldn't believe what he saw and didn't understand how it had happened.

For 3,000 years, Avalon had existed apart from the normal world, hidden by a magical barrier created by Merlin the Magician to protect the island, its inhabitants, all of magic from the changing world. Only small fluctuations in the barrier allowed people from the outside onto the mystic isle. The Gil-Gamesh had been one of those people. In the outside world, he was Chief Bryan Drake, a sailor in the United States Navy. Once he arrived on Avalon, he became something more.

Now the barrier was gone, Avalon was once again in the outside world, and he—the champion and protector of this realm—was not sure how to protect it from this.

A Navy aircraft carrier carried enough firepower to level entire countries. What would they do if attacked by dragons or one of the flying airships? He knew he had to stop this from getting worse than it already was.

Standing next to the Gil-Gamesh, in awe of the modern warship out on the water, was Captain Rhona McLoughlin, Captain of his Dragon Guard. In all her years as a Shield Maiden of Avalon, the blonde Valkyrie had never seen anything like it before. Rhona stared at the aircraft carrier, as the planes buzzed around its deck like bees on a hive.

Bryan pulled out a lens from his pocket and held it up to look out at the carrier. *"Video Visum!"* he commanded, enabling the lens to zoom in and out like a telescope. He saw an E-2C Hawkeye, a propeller-driven plane with a spinning dome on top, lined up on the catapult, ready to launch, with two F/A-18 Hornets standing by right behind it.

"They're getting ready to launch a Hawkeye…probably to get an overlook on the island," he said.

"Launch? Launch what, Milord? What's a Hawkeye?" Rhona asked.

"There's no time to explain, Rhona, listen to me. I need you to get a message out to all ships in the air and to every city across the four corners of Avalon. Tell them the barrier is gone and we are back in the outside world. I need every available knight to make their way to the coast to prevent anyone from coming ashore," he ordered. "Tell them to capture and contain any Outlanders but do not kill them. Order our airships to stick to the coastline, but do not venture any farther than normal beyond the shores. We don't yet know if magic will work outside Avalon."

Suddenly, their attention was focused on the sound of a sputtering engine. The Hawkeye was flying toward the coast of Avalon as its engines suddenly failed. The plane began to descend rapidly, coming in for a crash landing.

"Is it going to crash?" Rhona exclaimed. "But that means—"

"Part of the barrier is still intact," Bryan interrupted. "Avalon still has its anti-technology barrier which means only magic works inside our shores." Part of Merlin's spell that protected Avalon for centuries also kept technology, like machines, electronics, etc., from working on the ancient island. On Avalon, the laws of science deferred to the laws of magic.

The Gil-Gamesh focused his lens and watched as the Hawkeye crashed hard in the meadow across from Emmyr on the Avalon coast. It was a miracle that it didn't explode on contact.

"Rhona, get that message out now!" the Gil-Gamesh exclaimed. "Tell Edan to bring the *Avenger* down to the crash site and to have Doctor Bonapat with him. There's going to be injuries. I'm going down to check on the crew. Do it, now!"

Captain McLoughlin turned and quickly ran back toward Port Charles to relay the orders. "And tell Lady Stephanie to get in touch with Ashley," Bryan shouted after her. "Ask her to see if word of Avalon returning has made the news in the outside world."

The Gil-Gamesh looked up in the air and whistled until one of the dragons flying by heard his call and landed next to him. As the Lord of the Dragon Isle and a DragonMage of Avalon, Lord MoonDrake had a special rapport with the dragons. He jumped up on then flew down toward the crashed airplane. He hoped he wasn't too late.

***

Any crash landing you could walk away from was a good crash landing in the eyes of many pilots, including Commander T.J. 'Bullfrog' Johnson, who breathed a sigh of relief at surviving his first. He couldn't believe his luck in getting his plane safely down to the ground. His body ached from the impact, but he was no worse for wear. He turned to check on his co-pilot and flight crew.

"Is everyone all right?" he spoke into his microphone, but there was no power at all. "Can you guys hear me? Is everyone all right?" he shouted this time.

"I'm okay, T.J.," his co-pilot Lieutenant Dave 'Smarty' Hillsdale groaned.

"Skipper, I think Janice broke her leg!" came a voice from the back of the aircraft.

"Dave, try to raise the carrier while I help them out," T.J. said, as he quickly unbuckled his seatbelt and climbed out toward the rear of the aircraft. Ensign Janice 'Hairspray' Longwood was pinned underneath one of the radar consoles that broke free during the crash, pinning her left leg under the heavy panel. The other two flight crewmen—Lieutenant Kevin 'Poe' Byrd and Chief Petty Officer Harry 'Bigfoot' Bigelow—were trying to lift the console up to free her.

The darkness inside the aircraft hampered their efforts. "Poe, pop the hatch so we can see what we're doing?" T.J. ordered. Poe rushed over to aircraft door and opened it. He looked out across the expansive field and stared up at the floating island behind them.

"What the hell is this place?" he asked aloud.

"Don't worry about that right now and get over here," T.J. shouted. They worked together to lift the console up just enough to pull Janice free from under the mangled wreckage.

"No go on the radio, T.J.," Smarty shouted from the cockpit, as he stepped out. "Everything's dead."

"Okay, let's get outside and shoot up a flare. That should get their attention."

The crew worked their way outside, helping Janice as she limped along, cringing in pain with each step of her broken leg. They moved far away from the wreckage, in case a stray spark from the flare hit the leaking fuel and caused an explosion. Chief Bigelow pulled out a flare from the emergency supply kit and set it off, sending a green ball of fire into the air, signalling their position.

"What happened, Commander?" Chief Bigelow asked. "We just lost power, all at once. It was almost like an EMP."

"An EMP wouldn't affect our hydraulics, Chief. Those failed, too. Everything did," T.J. explained. "I don't know what it was, but it wasn't like anything I've ever experienced before."

"T.J., I think you're in for another new experience," Poe said, pointing in the air. They all looked up to see a dragon gliding down to the ground with a single rider on its back. The rider, dressed in an armoured breastplate and a leather waistcoat, looked like he just stepped out of a renaissance fair. His hair was pulled back in a ponytail, black with a streak of grey at the temples. His face showed age, but not that old, with hints of grey in his neatly trimmed beard. The thing that was strangest to them was his pointed ears; like those on Santa's elves.

The Gil-Gamesh assessed things as soon as he landed, and he sensed the urgency of the situation. He turned to the dragon and patted it on the neck as he spoke to it in a strange language. The dragon nodded its head and roared loudly as it took off into the air, back toward Emmyr.

"Is everyone all right?" he asked the crew in English, catching everyone by surprise.

"No, one of my crew members has a broken leg," T.J. answered. "Where the hell are we and who the hell are you?"

Bryan said nothing but walked toward the injured officer. T.J. and Poe stepped up and blocked him from getting near her. "Please, let me pass," Bryan said politely, "I can help her."

"Not before you tell me who you are and where we are?" T.J. said, standing firm.

"Commander, if I don't treat your injured crewman and get you back to your ship immediately, more pilots are going to die when they cross over into Avalon and their electronic and mechanical systems fail, just like yours did."

"How do you know our systems failed?"

"Because I do," the Gil-Gamesh said. "Your technology doesn't work here and anyone else trying to reach our island will experience the same thing you did, but they might not be as lucky as you. Now, I am here to help, not to hurt you. If I wanted to hurt you, I would have. So please, let me help."

T.J. realised he had no choice but to let him help. He nodded to Poe and the two men stepped aside. The Gil-Gamesh kneeled next to the injured crewman, reached into his belt pouch and pulled out a small vial with a pink liquid. "Here, drink this," he said, as he handed her the vial.

"Whoa, wait a minute, what is that?" T.J. asked, grabbing the Gil-Gamesh's hand.

"You wouldn't believe me if I told you," Bryan responded calmly. "It'll help with the pain and start healing her injuries."

Janice looked up at T.J. and gave him reassuring nod. He pulled his hand away and Janice took the vial, drinking it all down.

"Tastes sweet. Do you have a name, stranger?" Janice asked.

Bryan drew a dagger from his boot to cut away her flight suit and expose the wound. The tibia bone was protruding out from her leg and bleeding.

"Lord Bryan MoonDrake, Gil-Gamesh of Avalon."

"Gil-Gamesh? Is that a title of sorts?" Poe interrupted.

"It is," Bryan replied. "Now, this is going to—" In a sudden motion, he braced Janice's leg and pushed her tibia bone back into place. She screamed, biting her lip at the excruciating pain. "…hurt." Bryan took a scarf from his pocket and tied it around her injured leg to slow the bleeding. Janice cringed, as he tightened it down.

"So, Avalon," she said through gritted teeth, trying to take her mind off the pain, "you said this is Avalon, like King Arthur's Avalon? But that's a legend and a fairy tale."

"Well, behind every myth, there's always a bit of truth, wouldn't you say?"

"So, what, you're telling me this is a fantasy land?" Poe asked in disbelief. Before the Gil-Gamesh could answer him, the whiny roar of a dying jet engine reached them from over the water.

They turned and saw an F/A-18 Hornet falling from the sky, smoke billowing out of the engine, as the pilot tried to glide it in, but it was going too fast.

Bryan jumped to his feet. "Everyone get behind me!" he shouted, as everyone jumped back, looking for cover. "*Acheron Draconis!*" he yelled, and his body erupted with magical energy that swirled around him and took the form of a giant dragon. The crew stared in awe and disbelief at his arcane abilities.

"*Defendo!*" the Gil-Gamesh commanded, and the dragon form spread its massive wings in front of them. The jet hit the ground hard, exploding on impact. Fire and debris hurtled toward them, but the magic held firm, the heat and shrapnel battering against the dragon form alone, rendering the explosion harmless to the crew.

Poe and Chief Bigelow started to run toward the wreckage, but T.J. stopped them. "You can't help him," he ordered. "He died on impact."

"Why didn't he eject? He had plenty of time," Chief Bigelow wondered, as Bryan dissolved the dragon form and turned his attention back to Ensign Longwood.

"I told you; technology won't work here. Your engines, ejection seats, weapons systems, communications…none of that will work on Avalon."

"Oh, don't give me that bullshit," Smarty exclaimed. "You expect me to believe this is some magical fairy land? And what are you supposed to be? An Elf wizard?"

"Half-Elf, actually. On my father's side," the Gil-Gamesh joked. Trying to explain his transformation into a Half-Elf by Lord Baldrid of the Elves of Alfheimer would take far too long. "And what would you call what I just did to protect you or the dragon I flew down here on, Lieutenant? A figment of your imagination?"

"For someone from a different world, you seem to be knowledgeable on our military ranks, Lord MoonDrake," T.J. interjected.

Bryan smiled again, that devilish smirk he's known for. "People have been coming to Avalon from the outside world for centuries," he explained. "Trust me, we are well informed about your world."

Another loud roar. This time, that of a giant dragon flying past overhead. It landed near the crash site, with scales glittering with a gleam of metallic gold and green and a wingspan that was just as long as the Hawkeye's. Horns and spikes protruded from its head and down its back. In the middle of the beast's forehead, a large golden gemstone glowed dimly.

The dragon growled and huffed at the flight crew, who could only stare and tremble in fear. "That's no illusion, Smarty," Janice said.

"Don't worry. Gamorg won't hurt you," Bryan reassured them.

"Gamorg? That thing has a name?" Chief Bigelow asked.

"Yes, he does. And I would ask you to be a little more respectful in your tone if I were you. You're in the presence of the King of the Dragons."

"King? Did he say King of the Dragons?" Poe asked in disbelief. Bryan walked up to Gamorg and greeted his old friend reverently. He spoke to him in dragon tongue, a strange and garbled language to the flight crew listening nearby.

"The barrier is down," Bryan said. "Tiamat took away the protective barrier that hid Avalon from the outside world, but the magical barrier is still intact. How is that possible?"

"I warned you this might happen, my friend," Gamorg growled. "I don't know how the Great Mother took down the barrier, but she did. Magic still exists here on Avalon, and that can never be destroyed."

"But why did she do it? I didn't summon her at the battle of Idlehorn. She killed Morgana le Fay of her own volition. That should have been sufficient to satisfy her hunger."

More than a year ago, the Gil-Gamesh and the forces of Avalon defeated the sorceress Morgana le Fay and her army from spreading the Dark Tides, a spell of anti-magic that destroyed everything it touched. Bryan had been tempted to summon Tiamat, the Dragon God, to help defeat Morgana should the need arise, but he never needed too. Nevertheless, Tiamat came and destroyed the sorceress forever by swallowing her whole.

"You threatened her, Gil-Gamesh, and she does not take threats lightly," Gamorg explained. "Taking away the barrier was her way of getting back at you and the rest of Avalon." Gamorg stared at the flight crew with curiosity. "Who are they? Outlanders who fly inside a metal bird?"

Bryan looked back and chuckled. "Yeah, something like that," Bryan said. This didn't go unnoticed, especially by T.J.

"What are you telling him?" T.J. asked the Gil-Gamesh.

"Nothing important. Don't worry, he's as curious about you as you are of him," Bryan answered without looking back, then pointed in the direction of the aircraft carrier. "Do you think you can fly beyond the barrier to the ship out there?" he asked Gamorg.

"Yes, we have tested the borders of Avalon," Gamorg explained. "Since magic once existed in the outside world, we can travel beyond our shores. It's their infernal machines that won't work here."

Bryan patted Gamorg on the neck, as he heard a warning horn coming from above him. He looked up to see the *Avenger* gliding down from the sky above. The flight crew was amazed once again at the site of a flying, wooden, sailing ship swooping down from the sky. Its sails billowed in the wind and its large canvas wings heaved to capture the air underneath.

"What in God's name is that?" Chief Bigelow asked.

"The *Avenger*. It's my flagship," Bryan said.

"I thought you said technology doesn't work here?" T.J. asked.

"The only technology on my airship is pulleys and gears. Everything else is pure magic."

"It's like something right out of *Peter Pan*," Janice said with a child-like smile.

"You four, get ready to grab the lines to steady the ship as it lands," Bryan ordered the flight crew. They looked at T.J. to see if they should listen to the Gil-Gamesh. He nodded his head and they all moved into position under the airship. Lines were dropped over the sides, both forward and aft, as Captain Edan

O'Brian shouted orders to the crewmen on what to do to help the airship land. In the meantime, Bryan checked on the injured officer.

"How are you feeling, Ensign?" Bryan asked.

"Much better, sir, thank you," she replied. "Whatever you gave me is working wonders."

"Glad to hear it, but just in case, I'll have Doctor Bonapat look you over once the *Avenger* is secured."

"Is everyone here as kind as you are?"

"Most, but not all," he answered with a smirk. "Just don't move around too much. That elixir may make you feel better, but your leg is still broken."

Within minutes, the ship was close enough to the ground to lower the gangplank. Sailors rushed off the airship to take over for the crewmen holding the *Avenger* in place. Captain O'Brian followed with Doctor Bonapat close behind. To the crewmen, these sailors and their Captain, looked like old-world mariners in their dress and style, like something out of a Douglas Fairbanks movie. Doctor Bonapat stood out as the only black man amongst all the people they've seen so far. He immediately walked over to the injured officer. The Gil-Gamesh sidled next to him.

"I gave her a healing elixir and set her broken bone a few minutes ago, Allain," Bryan said. "She seems to be doing better but you might want to splint her leg, so she can travel."

"I will do what I can, Gil-Gamesh," he said with a thick Haitian accent. "Now, my dear, how are you feeling?"

"Much better, thank you, Doctor," she replied, as Allain set his bag down before he checked her wounds. With the injured officer in good hands, Bryan walked over to Edan.

"Peter, get my cloak!" he ordered a young sailor. The curly-haired young man took off below decks to retrieve the Gil-Gamesh's cloak while he talked to Edan.

"I'm going to take the senior officer and fly out to their ship on Gamorg," the Gil-Gamesh explained. "Once Allain has the ensign well enough to travel, you'll bring her and the remaining crewmembers out to the ship. Gamorg said magic works beyond the barrier so you should be all right. The deck is high enough for you to pull right alongside, about amidships and extend the gangplank over to drop them off. Don't linger about… Just drop them off and get back to Emmyr. Understood?"

"Yes, milord," Edan said confidently with a salute. Just then, Peter returned with the Gil-Gamesh's grey cloak. He flipped it across his shoulders and fastened it in the front before pulling up the hood.

"Commander, you're with me. I need to get you to back to your ship. Captain O'Brian will follow us with the rest of your crew as soon as Doctor Bonapat ensures your injured crewman is well enough to travel," he said, as he turned and started to walk toward Gamorg.

"I'm not leaving my crew behind, Lord MoonDrake," T.J. insisted.

Bryan sighed in frustration, as he walked up to the pilot to talk, face-to-face. "How many more of your aircraft have to crash before you understand what's happening here? I have to warn them to stay away from Avalon," Bryan said with a firm, even tone. "I can't just fly out there on the back of a dragon and convince them of what's happening here. I need you there to help me explain exactly what happened to you and the other aircraft, so they'll understand the urgency of the situation. Do you understand?"

T.J. thought about it for a moment until his co-pilot placed a hand on his shoulder. "Go ahead T.J.; we'll be right behind you," Smarty said.

T.J. acknowledged his co-pilot with a reassuring nod. "I have your word they'll be safe, Lord MoonDrake?"

Bryan nodded his head. "Absolutely."

The Gil-Gamesh led T.J. over to Gamorg and climbed aboard. When Bryan reached down and helped the Navy pilot up, sitting right behind him, T.J. felt his stomach lurch. "Oh shit, I'm going to regret this," he said quietly. Bryan laughed and spurred Gamorg into the air. The ride was rough at first as Gamorg pumped his wings to get lift and speed, but soon smoothed out as he flew out toward the carrier.

"What's the best place to land?" Bryan asked, feigning ignorance about the aircraft carrier.

"Right alongside the island—the structure there—in the middle of the deck! Next to that!" T.J. shouted back.

"Think they'll fire at us?" he asked.

"I don't know," T.J. answered. "Is this thing bulletproof?"

"Can't say. He's never been shot at before, at least not with bullets." Both men took a deep breath and hoped for the best as they glided down toward the carrier.

***

Captain Larry Rich looked out toward the mysterious island at the billowing smoke from the downed aircraft. He didn't know what happened to them; no one on board did. There were no signs of weapon's fire detected from the island. Both aircraft suddenly lost power and went down. He ordered the other F/A-18 Hornet away from the island, just to be on the safe side. He awaited further instructions from Fleet Forces Command before doing else.

"Captain, CDC has a contact coming in from the island," the OOD relayed from the Combat Direction Centre or CDC.

"Where is it?" Captain Rich asked.

"North, northwest, sir—it's barely registering on the radar."

"Lookouts have them in sight, sir," said one of the sailors in a headset. "They say it looks like a…dragon, ah, sir…carrying two men. One of them appears to be one of the pilots."

"Where away?" Captain Rich asked, as he stepped off the bridge and onto the bridge wing with his binoculars.

"Off the stern, Captain, at about two o'clock," Captain Rich looked up and finally saw them. One of them was the pilot, but he couldn't make out the other one. He was cloaked with a hood pulled up over his head.

"Sir, CDC has the CIWS locked on, ready to fire," the OOD said. The CIWS or Close-in Weapons System was a phalanx Gatling gun capable of firing 4,500 rounds per minute.

"No, tell them to hold their fire," he ordered. "Tell the Air Boss to clear the deck, give them plenty of room to land. Have security send up a detail, just in case, but I think they're bringing back one of our pilots. Maybe now we'll get some answers."

The OOD quickly relayed the orders as the Captain watched the dragon glide in and land on deck in front of the island. He rushed down to meet this stranger and get some information about this mystery island.

Gamorg landed on deck, his claws tearing through the non-skid surface, as his massive weight buckled the steel structure. He grunted at the Gil-Gamesh at the weird feeling of the surface of the deck, but all Bryan could do was try to keep him calm. He didn't want to set anyone off with an angry dragon.

Bryan helped Commander Johnson down, as he looked around deck. Though he'd only been gone from the outside world for two years, more than 20 had passed on Avalon. Time moved differently between Avalon and the outside world, at least it did while the barrier was in place. He wasn't so sure about that now.

For Bryan, it was almost like a homecoming as he jumped down off Gamorg and onto the flight deck. The last time he was on one, it was during a storm when he fell overboard after saving the life of one of his shipmates. That accident led him to Avalon and his life as the Gil-Gamesh. When his wife and children came out to where he was lost at sea, they also came through the barrier to Avalon. Only his daughter, Ashley, decided to return to her life in the outside world, so she could be with her husband, Andrew.

The flight deck crew looked on in disbelief at the dragon and medieval knight that just landed on deck. A photographer snapped off dozens of pictures, as his camera whirred in rapid succession. Chiefs and officers kept the men and women back, not allowing them to get too close.

A metal hatch suddenly swung open as armed sailors filed out, guns pointing at Bryan and Gamorg. Commander Johnson tried to wave them off, but their threatening stance only angered Gamorg, who snarled and growled at them, ripping into the deck as he stomped his feet and dug his claws into the steel surface.

"At ease, weapons down! Weapons down!" came an order from the island, as Captain Rich stepped out on the deck. Bryan immediately recognised his old boss and was happy to see a familiar face, but he quickly changed his expression. He couldn't reveal who he really was to anyone here... Not just yet.

The Captain was accompanied by his second-in-command, Commander Tim McReynolds, the ship's Executive Officer or XO. His high and tight haircut and gruff exterior highlighted this African-American's former life as an enlisted

Marine. T.J. walked over to the captain, as the Gil-Gamesh jumped down off Gamorg. The master-at-arms lowered their weapons but kept an eye on the cloaked stranger and the dragon. Gamorg breathed in deep, and huffed at them, flaring his nostrils.

"They smell of fear, Gil-Gamesh," Gamorg growled. "Their courage is absent behind their puny weapons."

Bryan couldn't help but laugh. "They're just not used to seeing something like you, my friend. Don't let it bother you."

T.J. brought the Captain over to the Gil-Gamesh. One of the sailors followed close behind the skipper. "Captain Rich, this is Lord MoonDrake, the Gil-Gamesh of Avalon. Lord MoonDrake, Captain Larry Rich, Commanding Officer of the *USS Theodore Roosevelt*."

Captain Rich held out his hand the Gil-Gamesh. Bryan just stared at him, being cautious and aloof so as not to reveal his identity to his former mentor and friend. "You are the senior officer in this area, yes?" Bryan asked.

Captain Rich pulled back his hand, a little confused. "I am…I was hoping you'd be able to tell me what's going on?"

"First things first. My airship will be coming alongside in a few minutes with the four remaining crewmembers. I would appreciate if you would give them permission to fly in and have some of your sailors standing by to assist with lines."

"Four crewmembers? What about the Hornet pilot? What happened to him?" McReynolds quickly interjected.

The Gil-Gamesh was silent but Commander Johnson spoke up. "He died on impact when his plane went down. He wasn't able to eject."

"What? Why the hell not? Will somebody please tell me what's going on?" Captain Rich shouted, his anger getting the best of him.

"I'll explain it to you as best as I can, Captain; you'll need to act fast to prevent any more deaths," the Gil-Gamesh stated plainly. "But first, I need your permission to bring my airship in, so we can return your crewmembers, and I would recommend you get some medical help up here as well. One of the crew has a broken leg. My doctor is tending to her, but she will need further care."

"Yes…yes, of course. XO," the Captain said to his executive officer, "get a medical team up here ASAP and post some sailors amidships to help tie off their vessel and someone tell the CDC to stand down any weapons against an incoming contact."

The crew responded quickly to the Captain's orders, as they scrambled to get everything ready for the arrival of the *Avenger*.

"Thank you, Captain. Now, to answer your questions. I am the Gil-Gamesh, Champion and Knight Eternal of Avalon and I represent His Majesty, King Bowen Arthur Gregory Bartholomew Pendragon, ruler and monarch of Avalon. First and foremost, I must ask you to respect the sovereignty of our island. No one, and I mean no one, is permitted to enter Avalon—by land, sea or by air—without the express permission of the King. Not that your technology will aid nor allow you to reach our island anyway."

"What do you mean by that?" Captain Rich asked.

"Avalon is governed by the laws of magic, Captain, not science. Nothing electronic or mechanical will work there as Commander Johnson can attest to."

"He's right, sir. I lost power, hydraulics, everything as soon as we got close to the island," T.J. explained. "That's what happened to the Hornet too, sir."

"It is imperative you establish a blockade around Avalon; nothing in and nothing out. I cannot allow any further breaches of Avalon's sovereignty to occur until I have conferred with the King and the other Lords of Avalon."

The XO laughed under his breath at the Gil-Gamesh's comments, which infuriated Bryan.

"Did I say something funny?" Bryan asked him directly.

"You can't expect us to believe this magical fairy tale of yours, do you?"

"Ask the two-ton dragon standing behind me," Bryan replied. Gamorg snarled and stepped toward the group and the smile disappeared from the XO's face. Everyone jumped back, and weapons were raised at the threatening beast.

Bryan said something to Gamorg in dragon tongue that calmed him down before he turned back to the officers.

"I don't care what you believe. I'm here to tell you the facts. And the fact of the matter is that Avalon is a sovereign nation and, as the representatives of another sovereign nation, I'm asking you to respect our laws. Avalon is off limits to Outlanders and that means you!

"We will not be responsible for any more of your aircraft crashing into our island. You have been warned! Additionally, anyone coming to our shores without permission will be captured and detained until such a time as we can return them to the proper authorities. Anyone taking aggressive action toward Avalon or the people of Avalon will be dealt with equally deadly force."

Once again, Commander McReynolds chuckled under his breath. Captain Rich glared at his XO for his rudeness, but Bryan was the one who interjected. "Is this a joke to you, Commander?" he asked.

"I'm sorry, but what are you going to do? Shoot at us with arrows? Attack us with magic swords?" McReynolds quipped.

The Gil-Gamesh instantly drew *Twilight*, the blade blazed with dragonfire, and sliced through the weapon of one of the master-at-arms, cutting it clean through before pointing the tip of the sword directly at McReynolds. Armed sailors moved in quickly to protect the commander. Gamorg moved behind Bryan, roaring fire and smoke into the sky in defiance.

"Stand down!" Captain Rich yelled. "Stand down!" The sailors stepped back and lowered their weapons. The Captain turned his attention to the Gil-Gamesh. "That was uncalled for, sir!"

"I am a Lord of Avalon, Captain, and as such, I expect to be treated with the proper respect and courtesies, not to be questioned and mocked for it!"

"I'm sorry, Lord MoonDrake. It won't happen again." Captain Rich looked at his executive officer to follow suit. "XO…"

McReynolds swallowed his pride. "I'm sorry, Lord MoonDrake," he said reluctantly. Bryan sheathed his sword and decided to ignore the executive officer's ineptitude.

"You seem to know a lot about us for being so isolated from the modern world, Lord MoonDrake," Rich offered.

"As I told Commander Johnson, Avalon was hidden from the outside world, but it was still accessible. People have been coming to Avalon for centuries. We learned a lot about the outside world from them through books, stories and such. In fact, my best friend was a Navy pilot. He was my—"

Before the Gil-Gamesh could finish his sentence, a tiny creature swooped in and hovered next to him. It appeared to be a small dragon, less than three feet long, with wings like a dragonfly, hovering in the air like a hummingbird would. The creature chirped and tweeted strange sounds to the Gil-Gamesh before landing on his shoulder and, as it sat there, continued to talk to him. Bryan's face was grim.

"What the hell is that?" McReynolds asked.

"This is Maverick, he's a fairy dragon," Bryan explained. "He just informed me that a large 'metal bird' fell from the sky into a field near New Camelot, the capital of Avalon. From the description, I would think it was a passenger airplane."

"Were there any survivors?" the Captain asked.

"None have been found yet, but they're still searching the wreckage. I'm very sorry," Bryan said. "I will try to return the remains of anyone we find there, and those of your pilot." He looked at Maverick and spoke to him in dragon tongue before he brushed him away. The little dragon snapped at him before flying back toward Avalon.

As Maverick flew off, the *Avenger* arrived, sliding right next to the aircraft carrier. The airship slowly edged forward, matching speed with the warship. Once their speeds were matched, lines were tossed across to the sailors waiting on deck. The sailors held them fast and secure, so a gangplank could be stretched across from the *Avenger* to the deck of the carrier. Once in place, sailors helped the remaining flight crewmen across to the carrier.

"Captain, with your permission, sir, I want to check on my crew," T.J. said, as he excused himself to meet his returning shipmates. He paused for a moment to shake the Gil-Gamesh's hand. "Thank you, Lord MoonDrake, for being true to your word."

Bryan shook his hand and gave him a courteous nod before turning his attention back to the Captain. "I will return within the month to meet with you again, Captain. That should give me enough time to speak to the King and sort things out. In the meantime, I must insist you establish a no-flying zone over Avalon before any more lives are lost. I suggest you keep your distance from the island. You wouldn't want to run aground if you stray too close to our shores."

"I will do what I can, Lord MoonDrake, but it won't be easy convincing my superiors of this. I promise you I will try," he said, holding out his hand. This time, Bryan took it in appreciation. "Pardon me for asking this, Gil-Gamesh, but I get the feeling we've met before."

Bryan was afraid of this. "I doubt that, Captain," Bryan said, as he turned his head and pulled back his hood, showing him his pointed Elf ears. "I'm a Half-Elf on my mother's side," Bryan added with a smirk.

After the last of the crew were transferred over to the carrier, the gangplank was pulled in and the lines released as the *Avenger* soared away, back toward Emmyr. The Gil-Gamesh leaped on the back of Gamorg. The dragon took a few steps back, away from the sailors, and spread his wings open. The dragon beat its wings furiously, causing hurricane-like downdraft as it took off and flew back toward Avalon. Captain Rich and the others just watched with awe and curiosity.

"Mac, let's stand down from General Quarters but maintain security alert. We don't know what could come off that island," Captain Rich ordered.

"Aye-aye, sir!" the XO replied, as he ordered the crewmen to disburse just as the medical team carried Ensign Longwood toward the elevator to take her down to medical. The captain stopped them before they moved on.

"How is she?" he asked T.J.

"She's doing good, sir. Their doctor took excellent care of her. Whatever they gave her is working miracles."

"Commander, I want you and your crew to make a detailed report to Washington on everything that happened to you and everything you experienced and saw on there. We need to know what we're dealing with."

"I understand, Captain, I'll see to it," T.J. said, "but I have to tell you, sir, I don't think they mean us any harm."

"Do you think they're hiding something?" Captain Rich asked.

"Oh, absolutely, sir. They're hiding something, but what it is? Who knows?"

"Yeah, that's what I'm afraid of."

***

Gamorg brought Bryan down into the heart of Port Charles. The port was already buzzing with the news of the re-emergence of Avalon into the outside world. Some people were afraid while others were delighted at the news, but all were concerned about how this revelation would affect them.

Once he was down on the ground, Bryan jumped off Gamorg and sent him off to his mountain home while he looked around for his port manager, Captain Jasper Hawke. Hawke looked like a typical sailor with a long-tailed waistcoat, a tricorn hat covering his stringy, black hair and knee-high boots. He had been running the port of Emmyr since the Gil-Gamesh first established it. As much as he hated the constant rush of business through the port, he founded and cherished it, and he would never turn it over to anyone else.

People gang-rushed the Gil-Gamesh to ask him about the return to the outside world, but Bryan shooed them away to get to Jasper.

"Jasper, as soon as the *Avenger* is tied up, tell Edan to get the ship ready to sail to New Camelot," he ordered. "Also, get a crew down to the crash site on the beach to look for remains of the pilot. If you find any, please be respectful. Place the remains into a coffin and seal it until we can take it back to the ship off the coast."

"Yes, milord, it will be done!" Jasper snapped, as he saluted before he hurried to relay the Gil-Gamesh's orders. Bryan started walking back toward his home at the Dragon's Veil. People continued to crowd around and pelt him with questions. He knew he needed to calm them down.

Bryan stepped up to on some crates to get above the crowd. *"Vox Vocis,"* he said, placing his hand over his throat to increase the volume of his voice. "Listen to me, all of you!" he shouted. Immediately, the crowd quieted down to listen. "The rumours are true. Avalon has returned to the outside world. There are modern military warships sitting off our coast as we speak; however, they cannot approach our shores. The barrier that prevents technology from functioning on Avalon is still intact."

Upon hearing that, many of the gathered people breathe a sigh of relief. "I have already spoken to their senior military commander and I have been assured that they will stay away to give me time to confer with the King and the other Lords of Avalon," he continued. "In the meantime, stay alert. We must do what we can to protect our home and our people, but we must not be the aggressor. With any luck, we will be able to sort this out and restore the barrier, one way or another."

As the Gil-Gamesh stepped down from the crates, most of the people had been reassured but some were still concerned as to what this meant for Avalon. Bryan made his way up through the crowd and continued home. Halfway there, he was met by Captain McLoughlin.

"Milord, the word has been spread across Avalon. All the coastal cities are calling out every available knight to protect the shores. Extra support is coming from inland cities to the coast," she explained.

"And our ships? Where are they?" he asked.

"Ten ships are in the air right now on patrol. They are being rerouted to the coasts, except for the *Serenity* and *Defiant*. I am keeping them on the main trade routes in case any pirates or Brood decide to take advantage of the situation."

"Tell Captain Hawke to get the *Prometheus* and *Nostromo* underway to join them as soon as possible," Bryan ordered. "And try to see if Master Dinius and the Elves of Alfheimer can provide some additional coverage for the coastal patrols."

"I'm sure Master Dinius and the Dwarves will help out, but Lady Lyllodoria has turned down every request I've made for assistance."

"Well, keep trying, she can't ignore this," Bryan replied. Since the death of her husband, Lord Baldrid, and her son, Eonis, at the hands of Morgana le Fay, Lady Lyllodoria and the Elves of Alfheimer had retreated to their home, not mingling in the affairs of Avalon. Bryan had to find a way to spur her out of her grief.

"Also, Rhona, I want you to make it clear to all the ship's captains that any airship trying to leave Avalon and head to the outside world will be shot down immediately. I don't care who they are. No one can leave Avalon, period. Is that understood?"

"Understood, milord," she said, bowing in respect and turning toward the port to carry out his orders. Bryan continued walking. His mind was jumbled with thoughts about the implications of Avalon's return to the real world. His heart raced thinking what it could mean for them. Lost in these anxieties, it took a while before Bryan realised he had been running. He slowed the pace of his stride and tried to calm his mind.

The Dragon's Veil was not the largest castles in Avalon but was adequate for the Gil-Gamesh and his family. They were never one for the opulent lifestyles like some of the other Lords of Avalon, mostly due to their humble upbringing from the outside world. In any case, it still stood as an imposing structure with towering spires and a sizable central keep.

Bryan made his way through the castle to his private chambers at the top. From there, he entered a secret passageway up the tallest tower to his conjuring room. It was here that he honed his magical skills as a DragonMage. It was also where he kept a special magical artefact…the Ring of Eluned.

This magic ring was one of the 13 Treasures of the Island of Britain. The ring had a magical stone in it that, when covered by the wearer's hand, made the wearer invisible. It was one of many artefacts in the collection of Merlin the Magician.

Through the ring, the Gil-Gamesh could confer with Merlin through an ancient magic called the Thaumaturge Effect. When a wizard uses a magical item over a long period, like a wand or staff, it became imprinted with their magical essence—part of their spirit or soul. When Merlin died more than 1,000 years ago, essences of his spirit could be found in the many magical items he used over the years, but Merlin had centralised his spirit in one item—his spell book—while the other items could be used as conduits to reach him.

The Gil-Gamesh possessed one of these artefacts as did his oldest daughter, Ashley, in the outside world. This allowed them to communicate from time-to-time while giving Merlin a chance to peer into the modern world.

Bryan entered the room and saw his wife, Stephanie, sitting by the room's solitary window, the Ring of Eluned resting in her open palm. Her eyes were closed, as she sat in a trance-like state while communing with Merlin. Bryan knelt next to her and placed his hand on top of hers to join her. He closed his eyes and focused until he could smell old books and pipe smoke. When he opened his eyes, he found himself standing in Merlin's private library, the spiritual representation of the wizard's spell book where Merlin's spirit now resided.

The library appeared to be over a hundred feet tall with five levels of bookshelves filled with every book imaginable. Staircase spiralled to each level and hanging ladders glided back and forth across the bookcases for easy access. The only furniture in the room was a couple of thick, comfy chairs in front of a roaring fireplace.

Merlin and Stephanie were standing in front of a large mirror that hung on the wall. The two were opposites of each other. Stephanie was dressed prim and proper in a flowing dress of Elven silk, her long, red hair neatly braided and wrapped around her head, held in place by a jewelled tiara. Merlin, on the other hand, wore an old, ragged—yet comfortable—robe. His long, white hair and beard were dishevelled and unkempt.

Bryan stepped up to the mirror to see what they were watching. Through Ashley's eyes, they could see into her home in Virginia. She watched the news, occasionally flipping networks. Avalon was the top story on every channel. The sudden appearance of a mysterious, yet unnamed island in the middle of the Atlantic had everyone in a state of shock. Though the massive wave mysteriously dissipated before it hit the coasts of the United States and Africa, it did incredible amounts of damage to Bermuda, the Bahamas and other islands in the south Atlantic. Missing airline flights that were in route over the ocean before the island appeared also raised concerns. From space, satellite images of Avalon were being taken, showing its massive bulk where open ocean should be.

Scientists were already theorising about where it came from and what implications it would have on the Earth, from weather patterns to ocean currents and migration routes. Historians and conspiracy theorists were postulating the island was everything from the legendary Atlantis to Hyperborea and even Lemuria. A little over an hour had passed and already, chaos spread across the world with Avalon's arrival.

Stephanie finally saw that Bryan had joined them and took him by the arm. She knew he'd probably felt guilty about this and the ramifications weighed heavy on him.

"It's official," she told him. "The world has gone completely mad."

"Merlin, please tell me you know of some way to fix this?" Bryan asked.

"I'm sorry, my boy. But, for once in my life, I don't know what to do. The barrier was created when I cast the original spell that brought magic from the outside world to Avalon. It was a side effect of the spell, not something I intended to do.

"I warned you that making a deal with Tiamat would have repercussions," Merlin scolded Bryan.

"Merlin, I'm not going to rehash that argument over-and-over again. Again, I never summoned Tiamat, she came of her own accord," Bryan retorted. More than a year ago, the Gil-Gamesh led the armies of Avalon against a resurrected Morgana le Fay and her followers. Morgana had resurrected a powerful spell—The Dark Tides—for the sole purpose of destroying all magic and wiping out the line of Pendragon once and for all. Bryan contacted the dragon god, Tiamat—a five-headed beast the size of an aircraft carrier—in case his plan to stop Morgana failed. In the end, Tiamat came anyway and devoured Morgana, ridding the world of her evil once and for all. The Gil-Gamesh stood up to the dragon god when he refused payment, but it seemed Tiamat had the last laugh.

"It doesn't matter who's at fault, we need to deal with things here and now," Stephanie interjected. "Bryan, did you talk to someone on the ship out there?"

"Yes, I did, and it was Larry," Bryan said, referring to their family friend.

"Captain Rich? Did he recognise you?"

"Fortunately, no. I think I threw him off with my Elven looks, but that may not help next time we meet."

"What do you mean next time?" Stephanie asked.

"I told him I would confer with the King and the other Lords of Avalon and get back to him within the month. I told him in was in their best interest to set up a naval blockade and no-fly zone to keep everyone out," Bryan lamented. "Eventually, we will need to establish some sort of diplomatic relations with the outside world. That's why I'm heading to New Camelot. I need Ocwyn."

"Bryan, you can't leave at a time like this," Stephanie scolded. "You're needed here, on Emmyr. The people need you to lead them, especially with that ship sitting right off our shores."

"Steph, I'm responsible for all of Avalon, not just Emmyr."

"Yes, but Emmyr is your home, Bryan," she pointed out. "Your place is here. Besides, I think they're already reaching out to you from New Camelot. That table in your study started glowing shortly before I came in here."

Bryan knew there was no arguing with her. "Merlin, try to find some way of restoring the barrier. If you need to, ask Ashley to help you. She loves research, and I will ask the Wizard's Council to join in as well."

"Very well, Gil-Gamesh, I will do my best," Merlin said. "It'll be nice to have her company again."

"In the meantime, Steph, tell Ashley and Andrew to go away, somewhere secluded where no one would think to look for them," Bryan insisted. "If Larry or anyone else recognises me or figures out who I am, they could find themselves in dire straits. For the time being, I'd rather they be somewhere safe."

"Ashley mentioned a cabin Andrew's grandfather left to him in his will," Stephanie interjected. "I remember him saying the paperwork for the transfer of the property hadn't gone through yet, it's still under his grandfather's name."

"Good, so while you do that, I'll get in touch with Ocwyn and the other Lords of Avalon." Bryan closed his eyes and returned to his body in his conjuring room. Bryan took a deep breath to regain his senses after coming out of his trance. His mind raced with the images of Avalon on the television and the opinions of so-called experts. He knew the can of worms this opened and that their presence in the real world would have major implications on everything from the world economy to religion and political strife.

Chapter 2
A Gathering of Forces

The Gil-Gamesh moved quickly down through the Dragon's Veil to his own private library. In here, the knowledge and history of the past Gil-Gamesh's were preserved, passed down from one generation to the next. One of the more unusual items in the study was a stone table or at least a part of one. It had once been part of a much larger table that had been cut into sections. Centred on the table was a single, carved rune that glowed like a soft, magical ember.

Bryan knew it meant he was late to the gathering and wasted no time, placing his hand on the glowing rune. *"Adsecatio!"* he chanted. Immediately, the Gil-Gamesh was transported to a room within Castle Pendragon, standing around a round table along with the other Lords of Avalon. This was the original round table built by King Arthur himself that allowed him and his knights to confer with one another as equals. Through the rune stone, the Lords of Avalon are connected to the mystical table, able to gather together to discuss urgent matters without leaving their homes.

The Gil-Gamesh looked around the table at all who were present. Master Dinius Oddbottom, Lord of the Gilded Halls of the Dwarves. Sir Cuthbert Nottingham, Duke of Nottinghamshire. Sir Olaf Ericksson, Baron of the North Highlands. Sir Robert Devereaux, Earl of South Essex. Sir Vanark Elderson, Duke of Eldonshire. Grand Master Hugo Courtland of the Wizard's Council of Avalon. T'Ronga, Great Chief of Togo. Dame Sarafina, Headmistress of the Shield Maidens of Avalon. Sir Cedric Octavian, Captain of the Knights of the Round Table. The Lords of Avalon circled the table, each standing before a different rune. Across from the Gil-Gamesh stood King Bowen, ruler of Avalon, though the seven-year-old boy could barely see above the tabletop. He was flanked by Chamberlin Ulric Ocwyn and Sir Hunter MoonDrake, the Gil-Gamesh's son.

Unknown to the other Lords of Avalon, King Bowen was his grandson, conceived through a sweeping romance between Hunter and Bowen's mother, Queen Cadhla Pendragon. Cadhla was one of the first victims of Morgana le Fay's resurrection. Only a selective few, close to the Gil-Gamesh, knew Bowen's true heritage.

Bryan noticed one person missing from the gathering, the Lady Lyllodoria of the Elves of Alfheimer. Her reluctance to be involved in the affairs of Avalon since the death of her husband and son has made Bryan's job even harder. He used to count on the Elves of Alfheimer to assist him without question. Lately, however, Lady Lyllodoria stayed in the Elven capital and rarely allowed the Elves to venture out.

Bryan bowed politely to King Bowen and Chamberlain Ocwyn. Bowen just smiled at his grandfather, while Ocwyn returned the courtesy. Hunter just nodded his head, recognising his father's presence.

"Are we expecting Lady Lyllodoria or has she bowed out of our gathering again?" Bryan asked, clearly frustrated.

"I'm sure the Lady Lyllodoria has a good reason for not answering the call," Ocwyn started.

"Don't make excuses for her, Chamberlain. She has withdrawn like a turtle in its shell since Lord Baldrid and Eonis died. It's been over a year. She needs to come out of her funk."

"That's the difference between humans and Elves, Gil-Gamesh," came a voice as Lady Lyllodoria emerged from the shadows. Her beautiful face glowed, draped by flowing, blond hair that fell about her dress of white, elven silk, adorned with silver jewellery encrusted with precious gems. "You humans mourn loved ones who lived but a scant number of years while we Elves have a thousand lifetimes to reflect on."

She stared at the Gil-Gamesh. The room quieted quickly. Bryan knew he stepped out of line and bowed respectfully to the Elf Queen. "Please forgive me, milady. I meant no disrespect toward you."

Lyllodoria bowed her head in acceptance and turned her attention back to the King. Ocwyn cleared his throat before addressing the assembled Lords of Avalon.

"Now then, onto the matter at hand… Gil-Gamesh, would you please provide everyone with an update on the situation?"

"As you all know, Tiamat destroyed the barrier that protected Avalon from the outside world," he began. "We are back in the real world with a group of modern military warships sitting off our coastline. The good news is the anti-technology barrier is still intact, so none of their machines will work on Avalon. I've spoken with the senior military commander and advised him to set up a naval blockade and a no-fly zone around the island for their protection and ours. This will help keep people out, but some are bound to get through."

"Some already have," Sir Olaf interjected. "One of those warships appeared right on top of my fishermen, destroying two boats. It's anchored in the middle of our fishing grounds because it can't get any of its damned mechanics working to move further out to sea."

"I'll send Rose out with some dragons, Baron Ericksson. They should be able to tow them out beyond the barrier."

"We experienced a similar problem in Lake Ouroboros, Gil-Gamesh," Lyllodoria added. "A sailing boat appeared in the middle of the lake. The people aboard were almost eaten by the Leviathan when they started shooting at it with those contraptions you call guns."

"Where are they now?" Bryan asked.

"We brought their ship to our piers on the lake. They are currently our guests in Alfheimer."

"I've had similar reports from knights out along the shoreline," Sir Cedric noted. "A few boaters here and there and a pilot from one of those flying planes glided down to the ground on something he called a parachute, right into a nest of newly hatched griffins."

"Did he end up as lunch or did you rescue him from the hungry little beasties?" Dinius joked.

"This is no time for jokes, Master Dinius," Ocwyn scolded. "We are in danger of being overrun with throngs of Outlanders who think Avalon as nothing more than a place of fantasy where they can live out their dreams like *Harry Potter* or *World of Warcraft*."

"I'm not worried about those people, Chamberlain," the Gil-Gamesh conceded. "I'm worried about those warships sitting just off our coast. Those ships carry enough firepower to turn the entire island into a pancake."

"But the barrier prevents that, right?" Sir Cuthburt said. "I mean, their technology won't work here on Avalon."

"But for how long, Cuthbert," the Wizard Courtland stressed. "With one part of the barrier destroyed, I can ascertain that the secondary barrier will slowly begin to disintegrate, and magic will soon disappear from Avalon and return to the outside world. I have foreseen it."

"Which is why I need you and the rest of the Wizard's Council help to find some way of restoring the barrier," Bryan interjected. "You must pool all of your efforts into this, Hugo."

The Wizard Courtland just nodded his head, as if the idea was a foregone conclusion, but not everyone was sure.

"We have no time for research; Avalon is completely vulnerable. We must do something right now," Sir Robert lamented. "This is your fault, Gil-Gamesh! You should never have contacted Tiamat!"

"My father did what he had to do to stop Morgana le Fay, Earl Essex," Sarafina interjected. "I don't remember seeing you there to help fight against her and her minions." The adopted daughter of the Gil-Gamesh stood firm to protect her father's reputation.

"Hold your tongue, shield maiden. You do not address a Lord of Avalon that way!" Sir Robert fumed.

"Then I will," Chief T'Ronga growled. "You cowered in your homes, praying for victory while the Gil-Gamesh led the army of Avalon against the *mchawi* le Fay. He did what he had to do. Otherwise, you would all be dead or enslaved by the Dark Tides."

"Now see here, Chief T'Ronga…" Sir Cuthbert shouted, coming to the defence of Sir Robert. The arguments grew louder and louder until the boy King had his fill.

"That's enough!" shouted Bowen, as loud as a seven-year-old could. Everyone stopped arguing and looked down, sullen and embarrassed by their monarch. "It doesn't matter how or why it happened, what matters is that we protect the people of Avalon from the threat of the outside world."

"Well said, Your Majesty!" Ocwyn concurred. "The question remains, what are we to do next?"

Everyone turned and looked at the Lord MoonDrake, seeking his leadership. Bryan knew what his role was in the affairs of Avalon: Champion of the Realm and Commander of the Knights of the Round Table.

"First off, all Outlanders are to be brought to Emmyr," he said. "I will hold them here until I can return them safely to the command ship off the coast. Second, we need to strengthen our forces along the coastline. Right now, as far as we know, there are only American warships off our coast, but more countries will be sending ships down to test their abilities against us. This means Russia, England, France, Germany and African nations too. We have to be ready for them."

"I agree with the Gil-Gamesh's assessment, Your Majesty," Chamberlain Ocwyn said. "We should send the word out to all the interior towns and villages to send every available man to the coastal area within their lands to defend us from possible incursions."

"Yes, make it so, Chamberlain," King Bowen ordered. "Dame Sarafina, how many shield maidens can you provide?"

"I can send an additional 100 shield maidens to each of the Lords of Avalon to augment their forces," Sarafina replied.

"I'll pull my Dwarves out of the mines for the time being to protect the Gilded Halls while I send an additional 1000 of my finest warriors to each of the Lords of Avalon," Dinius proudly proclaimed.

"Excellent. Thank you, Master Dinius," King Bowen said, beaming with pride before turning to the Queen of Alfheimer. "Lady Lyllodoria, can you provide some of the Elves to add to our forces?"

Lyllodoria was silent for the moment, not looking at the King as fear overcame her sensibilities. She had not the heart to turn away the request of King Bowen. "Your Majesty, I am reluctant to send my Elves on an errand away from their home in Alfheimer," she started, but before the Gil-Gamesh could interrupt her, she continued, "however, I will send a ship with a full complement of the *Hildrägo Boquè* to Emmyr to assist the Gil-Gamesh with the defence of the dragon isle and the coastline where the main warship sits."

"Thank you, milady," King Bowen acknowledged. "Is there anything else, Gil-Gamesh?"

"Yes, Your Majesty, I need Chamberlain Ocwyn on Emmyr to join me in negotiations with the Outlanders," Bryan stressed. "We will be meeting with them by the month's end. Also, Dinius, I would like Pombur to join us, representing the Dwarves of the Gilded Halls and if you could send someone with your complement to represent the Elves of Alfheimer, Lady Lyllodoria…"

"Not to worry, Gil-Gamesh, he'll be there," Dinius proclaimed. Lyllodoria just nodded her head politely to the Gil-Gamesh. Bryan took her silence as a slight for his insult from earlier. He knew he had to mend fences with her if they were ever to be allies again, but that would have to wait.

"Ocwyn and I will let you know how these first rounds of negotiations go, Your Majesty, but in the meantime, everyone must stay alert and keep each other informed of any transgression against our sovereignty.

"And for God's sake, keep an eye on the dark forces out there in Blackbriar Forest and elsewhere," Bryan added. "Something like this might just be enough to bring them out of their holes and take advantage of."

Everyone nodded their heads in agreement before letting the King have the final word. "Then it's settled," King Bowen concluded. "We will meet again after the initial negotiations with the Outlanders to get a full report from the Gil-Gamesh and Chamberlain Ocwyn."

With that, the assembled Lords of Avalon bowed and, one-by-one, faded from the roundtable until all that remained was King Bowen, Sir Hunter and Chamberlain Ocwyn. "Well, that went better than expected," Ocwyn stated, then noticed that the King looked confused and unsure. "What's the matter, Your Majesty?"

"I'm worried about Grandpa," he said, referring to the Gil-Gamesh. "He looks scared. I've never seen him scared before, not even before the battle with Morgana le Fay." Ocwyn admired the little King for how he was more worried about his grandfather than anything else.

"I don't think it's fear you sense, Bowen," Hunter interjected to help explain things to his son. "He's torn between the world he left behind and the home he made here on Avalon. He knows some of the people on those warships out there; he fought beside them for more than 20 years. You can't just ignore the fact that he may be forced to fight against people he once considered his brothers-in-arms."

***

The light flickered as the damp, musky air prevented the flame from burning any brighter. The torchbearer descended the winding stairs into the dark dungeon. He had traversed the staircase many times, but he always did so carefully, given the slanted, narrow steps. This slowed him greatly, which he knew could be just as dangerous to him as a fall—his Master hated tardiness.

Underneath the shadows on his hooded cloak, his features were barely visible. His face was covered in dark runes—some tattooed, some branded, all put there very recently—the scars and burns still healing. He was bald except for a long ponytail, knotted at the back of his head.

Johan Ulrich was once a prominent member of the Wizard's Council of Avalon, head of the House of Dark Magic, but he sided with Morgana le Fay in her attempt to destroy Avalon. Though he wasn't captured after the battle of Idlehorn Mountain, his punishment was justly severe. He was ostracised by the council and disowned by his family, and for that reason, he wore a simple, black onyx stone on a pendant around his neck.

The Ulrich clan were a large part of the upper class of Avalon society. Their forebearers could be traced back to the first people brought to Avalon more than 3,000 years ago, when it was created. To have someone dishonour the Ulrich name by siding with the evil sorceress was reprehensible beyond measure.

When Johan went home to try and explain himself, the elders of the Ulrich's would hear nothing of it. Without a word, they disowned him in one single action. He was given the black onyx stone by his father as he turned his back on him. For centuries, this tradition was carried out against anyone who betrayed the honour of their clan.

Lost, alone and hunted by the Gil-Gamesh, he was forced to take refuge in the deep recesses of Blackbriar Forest. He had to take on a new name, one that would signify that he wore his dishonour with pride and be a slap in the face to the line of Pendragon—Artūras Blackstone.

Blackstone reached a single, solitary door. The door had no handle or lock, just an ornate metal scrollwork of lizards that looked like they were sleeping in a nest. He waved his hand across the pattern. "*Domum Accrescat!*" he shouted.

The lizards began to move until, one-by-one, they entered the keyhole previously hidden by their sleeping forms. Gears whirred to life, grinded together and the door opened. Blackstone entered the room, and the door shut, the lizards scurrying back into place to lock it.

Inside, the room was lit by thousands of candles. It was a simple room, furnished for one to live comfortably. One corner of the room was set up for conjuring with a cauldron over a low fire and a table filled with various components for a variety of incantations.

A man with golden-blonde hair in a dark robe stood over the table, assembling an ornate gold amulet with a dark red ruby in its centre. He mumbled softly, chanting his spell, as he hung the amulet on a hook over the cauldron, inches above the bubbling liquid. Blackstone stood there and watched quietly so as not interrupt the spell.

"*Ligare Tuam Animam Anima Mea!*" chanted the blonde man in a continuous melody, as he tossed various components into the cauldron: a dragon scale, the hair of dead witch, a sprig of wolfsbane and the cobwebs from a mausoleum. As each one hit the bubbling liquid, wisps of smoke popped from its surface and infused into the amulet causing the ruby to glow, brighter and brighter, until the brilliance engulfed the room in a blinding light.

The light soon faded, and Blackstone rubbed his eyes to clear the spots from them. The amulet pulsed softly now, as tendrils of magical energy swirled around it. He smiled, realising the success of his master's spell, but that was soon interrupted.

"You're late, Artūras," growled the Master, not turning around. "Explain yourself!"

"My apologies, but I wanted to be sure of the news before I came to you. It has happened just as you predicted. The barrier is down. Avalon has returned to the outside world."

"And what of the Gil-Gamesh? What is he doing?"

"My sources in New Camelot told me that he is leading a delegation to negotiate with the Outlanders," Blackstone added. "Meanwhile, they are sending every available knight to the coast to prevent Outlanders from broaching the shores. It couldn't be more perfect, my Master. The time has come for you to reclaim your rightful place on the throne of Avalon."

"Patience, Artūras. First you must seek out our allies while I assemble an army to retake New Camelot and capture the Twin Swords of the Dragon Knight from the Gil-Gamesh." The dark wizard took the amulet off the hook and held it in his hands. "I have waited more than 3,000 years for this…what's a few days more?"

***

Captain Rich kept his crew aboard *USS Theodore Roosevelt* on high alert while they sailed just off the mysterious island of Avalon. His orders were to maintain position near the floating island while using aircraft to survey the coastline, pinpointing defences and strength of the forces. This type of surveillance had to be done manually, as satellites proved inadequate to pierce the veil surrounding the island. The so-called 'anti-technology barrier' that the Gil-Gamesh mentioned extended miles into the upper atmosphere, causing overflights impossible.

They had already seen an increase in troop presence along the coastline all around Avalon. There were dozens of sightings by pilots of strange creatures flying along the coast. He had to find sailors familiar with the *Dungeons and Dragons* game to help identify them. He also had to move the fleet further away from the coast because of strange sightings in the waters off Avalon; everything from mermaids to enormous sea creatures were spotted by the lookouts. It seemed that maybe the sea stories from long ago were true.

Increased campfires were visible all along the coast as more troops moved in daily. Rich knew they were well within in their right to protect their borders, but this was a little extreme. He was grateful for their assistance in rescuing the crew of the E-2C Hawkeye and in aiding the destroyer *USS Farragut* in getting back to sea after drifting too close to the island; though, he wasn't sure how to include 'towed by dragons' in his report.

The situation had grown even more complicated was the addition of ships from other foreign navies to the area. Russia was sending a heavy missile cruiser and two destroyers in addition to a British Royal Navy helicopter ship and two the French frigates. Not to mention, the numerous submarines in the area, pinging away at the coast, looking for some way inland from the sea.

Captain Rich sipped his cup of coffee while reviewing the latest news articles about the mysterious island. Though they hadn't officially named it, the speculation about what it was and where it came from were rampant across the news media. This was going to get worse before it got better, and Rich wanted to stay one-step ahead.

"Captain, SMO needs you down in medical, ASAP," the Officer of the deck relayed. The SMO, or Senior Medical Officer, was responsible for the health and medical needs of more than 6,000 sailors aboard the aircraft carrier.

"Did she say what it's about?" Rich inquired.

"No, sir, she just said she needed you to come down to medical and that she couldn't talk to you about it over the phone."

Rich didn't like it to leave the bridge during flight operations, but if the SMO insisted that he talk to her in person, it must be serious. "All right, tell the Air Boss to keep flight ops going and to let me know as soon as the COD arrives from Bermuda."

The COD, short for Carrier Onboard Delivery, was a transport plane used to carry people and supplies to the ship at sea. Captain Rich was expecting a representative from the State Department for the negotiations with the Gil-Gamesh later this week, but the Navy wouldn't elaborate as to who would come.

As he made his way through the ship, sailors moved aside so the Captain could make his way to Sick Bay on the lower deck. Listening to the crew as he walked past them, he heard everything from grumblings about email and the internet being down, to excited conversations about being at the forefront of this incredible discovery. Overall, attitudes and morale were positive, which was just how he liked it. Rich needed his crew to be ready for anything.

As he walked into Sick Bay, one sailor yelled out, "Attention on deck!" Sailors stopped what they were doing and snapped to attention as the Commanding Officer stepped in.

"Carry on," Rich ordered, letting everyone get back to work. As he made his way toward the SMO's office, he spied Ensign Longwood, still recovering from her broken leg. She sat in her bed, talking with her squadron commander, acting as if her leg wasn't broken at all. Her spirit was upbeat as she insisted on getting up and back to duty.

Captain Rich knocked before stepping into the SMO's office. "Okay, Coop, what's so important that you can't talk to me on the phone about it?" he asked, as he closed the door behind him. He called her 'Coop'—a nickname she got for her choice of vehicle, a Mini Cooper, complete with the British flag on the rooftop.

"It's something I can't believe myself and I wasn't about to start spreading the latest scuttlebutt," said Coop, aka Commander Carolyn Gerwien. Her brash,

Midwestern upbringing was something Captain Rich liked about her. She had a thriving medical practice in Iowa when the attacks of September 11, 2001, led her to enlist in the Navy. The grey streaks in her hair came from numerous combat tours in Iraq and Afghanistan. She hoped this tour would be less stressful, but that's not happening.

Gerwien punched some keys on her computer and turned the screen around for Captain Rich to see. It was an x-ray image of a broken leg. "This is an x-ray of Ensign Longwood's leg taken right after she arrived back on board from your mysterious island."

"Okay, she has a broken leg. We knew that, so what?"

Gerwien punched some more keys on her computer. "Here's an x-ray we took just an hour ago," Carolyn said. The image changed to show a fully healed leg, no broken bones.

"It's only been a little over a week. How is this possible?"

"She said that this Gil-Gamesh, whoever he is, gave her something to drink. Whatever he gave her, it started to heal her broken bone in days. I've never seen anything like it, but that's not all."

"What do you mean?" he asked.

"Did you know Ensign Longwood was diagnosed with ovarian cancer her senior year in college?" Captain Rich shook his head, anticipating the doctor's next revelation. "She opted for surgery to remove her ovaries instead of chemotherapy, so she could continue to pursue a Navy career." The Commander punched more keys on her keyboard. "She gave up the possibility of children for her career." The image on the computer screen changed again. It was another x-ray but that of a perfectly healthy woman. "Until now. Her ovaries have regrown and there is no sign of cancer anywhere."

Captain Rich was shocked and couldn't believe what Carolyn had told him, but the proof was right there in front of him. "So, you're saying this miracle cure-all not only heals wounds, but it also regenerates body parts and cures cancer?"

"It would seem so, but I can't be 100% sure," she added. "I've requested her complete medical record from Portsmouth Naval Hospital to make comparisons, but I don't have the right equipment here to exam her blood and tissue thoroughly to make an accurate diagnosis. I recommend sending Ensign Longwood to back to Portsmouth Naval Hospital or maybe Bethesda to confirm everything."

"Have you told anyone else about this?"

"Are you kidding? Whom could I tell about this without someone sending me off to the looney bin or revoking my license to practice medicine? Why do you think I asked you to come down here?"

"Okay, let's keep it that way for now. I may need you to brief this State Department bigwig they're sending in from Washington."

There was a knock at the door. Before either of them could react, the door opened and the XO burst in, breathing heavy as if he was out of breath. "Sorry, skipper, but we just got word the COD's 30 miles out," he huffed out between breaths.

"Okay, Mac, but there's no need to bust in unannounced just to tell me that," Captain Rich admonished.

"Yes, sir, but we also got word who was on board from the State Department; it's Secretary of State Barry."

Captain Rich jumped to his feet at the mention of Secretary of State Clinton Barry, the top diplomat for the United States. The two men rushed out of Sick Bay as fast as they could. There were a million things to do and not enough time to do them in when a dignitary the calibre of the Secretary of State was coming aboard.

***

Bryan and Stephanie MoonDrake rarely got time alone, but tonight was quite different for them. With their son, Hunter, away at New Camelot, his adopted daughter, Sarafina, at Glennish Hills with her children Thomas and Meriel, and their daughter, Rose, either training with Sarafina or off with her love, Edan O'Brien, they sat down to a quiet dinner for two. The two of them had been going non-stop since the barrier came down. Stephanie gave much of her time to reaching out to Ashley for updates from the outside world. The magical trance was quite taxing on her mind and spirit and had left her exhausted. The Gil-Gamesh, on the other hand, was busy preparing defences and following up on reports from all-around Avalon about incursions by Outlanders.

The two sat quietly while eating a delicious meal of roast duck, fingerling potatoes and mixed vegetables, served with a rare Elven wine—over 1,000 years old. Stephanie looked across at him, as he ate his food without even looking up from his plate. She knew something was bothering him and, as usual, Bryan bottled it up deep inside him so not to burden others with his problems. After more than 30 years of marriage, she could read him like an open book.

She decided her best option was to work her way in slowly to find out what's bothering him. "When do you expect Ocwyn and the others to arrive for the negotiations?" she asked.

"By the end of the week, I hope. It'll give me time to work out the details so we're not heading into things unprepared," he replied.

"And the additional forces from Lady Lyllodoria and Sarafina? When can we expect them?" she pushed further.

"Soon…"

"Good, then maybe you'll be able to relax," she replied curtly, looking down at her food like him. Bryan looked up and stared at her with a bemused look on his face. Stephanie finally stopped eating and looked back at him, her face unchanged but deep down inside; she was smiling because she knew she had him. "What?"

"I know what you're doing, Steph, but there's nothing bothering me, okay?"

Stephanie shrugged her shoulders, as she wiped her mouth with her napkin. "I really don't know what you're talking about."

"You're poking and prodding just enough to get me to open up," Bryan stated. "Well, it's not going to work this time. Nothing is bothering me."

"Really? Because you could have fooled me," she bantered back at him. "First off, you blame yourself for all this and you shouldn't. You did what you had to do."

Bryan started to argue, but she pushed on. "And secondly, you think that you need to solve this problem all by yourself, but you don't. Let me tell you something, Lord MoonDrake, Gil-Gamesh of Avalon, there are people more experienced and a helluva lot smarter than you on this island. Let them carry the load for a while. You just need to worry about protecting the people and advising Ocwyn and the others about what those idiots out there may do next.

"You have a group of incredibly talented people who will do whatever you ask them to do and yet, you feel the need to do everything yourself. But you can't, Bryan. You can't do it all by yourself because if you continue on like this, you'll be dead before the end of the month."

Bryan sat there in awe of his wife. She knew him so intimately and perfectly that there was nothing for him to rebut. He always said they were soul mates and this proved it again. And she was right. She was right on every level. All he could do give her that devilish grin he was known for—the one that Stephanie hated so much.

"Don't you smirk at me like that, you misbegotten—" she started to say, but before she could finish, Bryan took her by the hand pulled her onto his lap, wrapping his arms tightly around her. He kissed her passionately and she returned it, knowing that it was his way of telling her she won the argument.

He rested his head against hers, comforted by her concerns for him. "I can't live in the past," Bryan said. "What happened did so for a reason. I can't worry about what the Lords or anyone else thinks about it. I just have to do my job and protect Avalon."

Stephanie smiled and brushed the hair out of his face. "How in the world did you survive for ten years here without me?" she joked.

Bryan laughed and kissed her again. "God only knows, my love."

Just then, Amelia Pomodoro, the Gil-Gamesh's shield maiden, burst through the door. Though only 5'2", she carried herself as if she were a giantess. Her red hair and freckles poked visibly from underneath her massive helm gave her a youthful appearance, but underneath, she was a seasoned warrior.

Amelia was trying to catch her breath when she noticed Lady Stephanie sitting on the Gil-Gamesh's lap. She quickly turned away, embarrassed and afraid she had interrupted an intimate moment between them. Unlike most others on Avalon, Bryan and Stephanie were known for the occasional public display of affection.

"Please forgive the intrusion, milord. I didn't know that—"

"There's no need to apologise, Amelia," Bryan said, "Lady Stephanie was just collecting her reward for winning another argument." The couple laughed at the joke, but Amelia didn't. She wasn't in a laughing mood.

"Begging your pardon, milord, but Captain McLoughlin requests your presence immediately. We've captured some Outlander spies."

"Where at? Somewhere along the coast?" Bryan asked, as Stephanie got off his lap.

"No, milord, here on Emmyr."

Bryan jumped to his feet and followed Amelia, with Stephanie close behind, down to the main hall. Captain McLoughlin and other members of his Dragon Guard surrounded a group of five men, kneeling on the floor with their hands behind their heads. They were dressed in black combat gear with camouflage makeup covering their faces. They varied in height and weight, but all were in excellent physical condition. Bryan knew immediately they were Special Forces, but whose?

The Dragon Guard had spears and swords pointed at the captured men, watching them closely, especially with the Gil-Gamesh and Lady Stephanie present. Rhona walked over to brief Lord MoonDrake on their capture.

"We captured them near the northern ridge of Emmyr, milord," she stated. "They ran into a group of dragons and when they realised their weapons wouldn't penetrate a dragon's hide, they ran toward Port Charles. That's when we captured them."

Bryan looked away from the soldiers and began to examine the cache of weapons and equipment Rhona confiscated from them while she continued her briefing. "The only thing I don't know is how they arrived on Emmyr. They shouldn't have been able to fly their damn machines past the magical barrier."

The Gil-Gamesh spied something among the equipment that answered that question. It was a small oxygen tank attached to a hose, but the mask was missing. "Oh, they flew all right, just not in the way we're used to," he said. "They did a Halo jump."

"Halo jump, Gil-Gamesh?" Amelia queried.

"High Altitude Low Opening… Halo," he explained. "They flew near the island, high in the atmosphere and parachuted down to Emmyr. The mask is missing from his oxygen tank, probably because he had to rip it off as they got close to the island. The pressure valve likely failed once they crossed the magical barrier.

"Send some men further up the mountain, past where you captured them," Bryan continued. "I'm sure you'll find some more of them there; probably dead from asphyxiation, am I right?"

Bryan addressed his last remark toward the captured soldiers, but none of them spoke up. They said nothing, just continued to stare straight ahead. While Rhona sent Amelia to relay orders to one of their patrols as to where to search, Bryan picked up one of the weapons to examine the make and model. "An AK-74N…Russian made," he said, as he took out the magazine and cleared the chamber, ejecting a single round. "*Spetsnaz*? Am I right, comrade?"

They continued to stay silent, which infuriated Rhona. "Answer the Gil-Gamesh!" she shouted. They remained quiet until one of the men spat on the ground at her feet. Rhona stormed at the man as she drew her sword. She grabbed him by the collar and lifted him in the air with ease, shocking the captured soldiers at her incredible feat of strength. She laid her sword under his chin and across his throat.

"I have killed men for less, dog," she threatened. She saw fear in his face and watched his blood trickled down her blade, the tip of her sword puncturing his skin, but only just.

"Rhona," Bryan said. It was all he needed to say. The Captain of the Dragon Guard never removed her gaze from the soldier and slowly lowered him until his feet touched the ground. Once she released him, Bryan stepped up next to Rhona.

"*Spetsnaz?*" he asked again but the man stayed silent.

"What is *Spetsnaz*, milord?" Rhona asked.

"Russian Special Forces," he explained, "cold-blooded assassins as far as I'm concerned, and you don't come armed to the teeth like this to gather intelligence. So, let's find out what their mission really was."

When Bryan said that, the *Spetsnaz* soldier braced himself, as if he expected to be tortured. "Oh, don't worry, no one's going to hurt you," the Gil-Gamesh assured him. "Your cooperation is guaranteed to be painless."

With that, the Gil-Gamesh reached out and touched him on his head. Instantaneously, images begin to flood his mind through the dragon sight—an innate ability he possessed that allowed him to see the past, present and even future of someone through touch.

Images of the man as a young boy appeared. A father drinking heavily. A father beating the boy with a belt in a drunken tirade. The father being arrested for killing the boy's mother. The boy being raised by the state. The boy attending a military academy. The boy excelling in marksmanship and hand-to-hand combat, driven by rage.

As the images got more intense, Bryan concentrated so he could focus on recent events. He saw a briefing by high-level Russian officers being conducted, highlighted by satellite images of Avalon and its position in the Atlantic. Emmyr was pinpointed by the target circles around it. One officer held up a picture of Bryan, taken on the flight deck of the *USS Theodore Roosevelt*. He saw flashes of Russian Navy ships coming toward Avalon. He watched as the men loaded into a transport plane, wearing their full jump gear; as the back door of the plane opened, the men jumped out one by one. As they fell through the clouds, Avalon and Emmyr came into view. The soldier suddenly began to gasp for air. He ripped off his mask and took a deep breath just as he opened his chute, before landing hard on the mountainside.

Bryan let go of the Spetsnaz soldier; he had seen enough. The two men shared the images, but the soldier was dazed and confused by the exchange. He breathed heavy as his eyes grew large, unsure of what just happened to him. Bryan saw enough to know what they were doing on Emmyr.

He walked back over to their gear and started rummaging through their bags until he found what he was looking for: a targeting laser for long-range missiles. "Son of a bitch," he cursed, "they were going to light us up, paint Emmyr as a target for an enemy attack."

"You mean laser-guided missiles, like the ones used in Iraq and Afghanistan?" Stephanie asked.

"Exactly, they must not have believed the reports that technology won't work on Avalon. These men were an advanced team, to provide intelligence to the Russian Navy ships on their way here and, just in case the Russians aren't happy with negotiations, target us for an attack."

"How do you know this?" the Russian soldier asked, his thick accent coming through his English.

"Because I was once like you," Bryan began. "I was a sailor serving my country proudly until fate brought me here to Avalon, but I'm also a knight. I've been fighting against the likes of you for all my life and if you think you can come to my home and threaten my people, you are sadly mistaken. Now, you'll face Avalon justice."

"Put them in the cages until we transfer them back to the Outlander's ship," the Gil-Gamesh ordered Rhona, "and stow all their weapons and gear in the armoury."

Bryan spun on his heels and marched out of the main hall, targeting laser in hand, with Stephanie close behind. Rhona bowed and left with the Russian soldiers in tow. Beneath the island of Emmyr was iron cages, hung from chains, where criminals were sent to contemplate their wicked ways.

Stephanie tried desperately to keep up with Bryan's pace, but he was angry, rushing headstrong until he stepped outside. "Bryan, where are you going?" she asked, almost breathless.

"I'm going to deliver a message to these Outlanders who think they can invade our sovereignty without consequences," Bryan huffed, as he whistled in the air, sounding out a special call to summon his ride.

"Bryan, I know you're upset by this invasion of our home, but you can't let it endanger any chance for a peaceful outcome," Stephanie pleaded. "They're scared, you know that. That's why they're reacting this way. You can't lash out like this."

"I'm not lashing out, Steph, I'm sending a warning, one that they'd better listen to! Avalon is defended!"

A loud roar echoed from above as a Wyvern flew down and landed next to the Gil-Gamesh. The dragon hybrid was unique, unlike the dragons of Emmyr. The Wyvern had a muscular body with strong legs and oversized wings for arms, covered in iridescent scales. It had a long neck with a smaller head, adorned with plumes of black and white feathers. Tabby, as the Gil-Gamesh called her, was his hunter.

Without saying another word, the Gil-Gamesh leaped on the back of Tabby and spurred the creature into the air. Stephanie was nearly knocked over by the powerful downdraft created by the flying beast. She watched, as Bryan steered Tabby around the island and out to sea, toward the military warships.

"Please be careful, my love," she whispered, as she watched him fly off.

***

Captain Rich watched the C-2 Greyhound come in for a landing on the flight deck of the aircraft carrier. The COD was carrying Secretary of State, Clinton Barry, to represent the United States in the initial negotiations with Avalon. The boatswain's mate rendered honours over the ship's announcing system as soon as the plane touched down.

This past week had been one headache after another. A dignitary the calibre of the Secretary Barry just added to the burden Captain Rich was carrying on his shoulders.

Still, he preferred someone like the Secretary here to handle these negotiations. Captain Rich was never one for politics, even if being a naval officer sometimes called for operating in political avenues. Rich was a sailor, first and foremost, and he liked it that way.

"OOD, tell the Boss to keep recovering aircraft while I go down to greet our guest," he ordered.

"Aye-aye, Captain," the Officer of the Deck concurred.

"Captain, sir, lookouts are reporting that Gil-Gamesh fellow is flying toward us from the floating island," a sailor on sound-powered phones relayed. "He's coming in on some sort of dragon again from the northwest."

"Dammit, why now?" Rich cursed. "OOD, tell the COD to hold everyone on board, do not disembark and keep the flight deck clear until I find out what he wants."

The officer relayed the order while Rich took off down the island to the flight deck. "Make a hole!" he shouted, as he slid down the ladder rails. Sailors quickly moved aside as he traversed down several flights of stairs until he reached the flight deck. He stepped out on the deck just as the Gil-Gamesh landed. This creature was not as big as the massive dragon he rode in on before, but its giant wings created a downdraft equal to that from a helicopter.

Bryan saw the Captain waiting for him and jumped down off the Wyvern. Just as before, sailors stood in awe of the magical creature, who squawked and snapped at everyone in the strange surroundings. Rich saw the Gil-Gamesh without his hood for the first time, but he still didn't recognise his former Chief standing before him.

"This is not a good time, Gil-Gamesh," Rich said. "I wasn't expecting you for a couple more weeks."

Bryan said nothing. He just handed Captain Rich the laser-targeting box he took off the *Spetsnaz*. "What's this?" Rich asked.

"You tell me," Bryan said, feigning ignorance. "I took it off a group of soldiers who somehow made their way into my home. I warned you about invading our sovereignty without permission, Captain."

"I had nothing to do with that, Lord MoonDrake," Rich insisted. "If you bring these men to me, I'll get some answers for you."

"They'll be spending the next few weeks in my dungeon as punishment for their incursion," Bryan snapped back. "They belong to something called *Spetsnaz*, I believe. Does that mean anything to you?"

Captain Rich was genuinely shocked when Bryan mentioned that name. "Are you sure about that?" Rich asked. Bryan just nodded his head. "*Spetsnaz* are Russian soldiers. Special Forces. There are Russian Navy ships heading into the area. I'll speak with their commander once they get here and straighten this out. Whatever you do, please don't do anything rash to further aggravate the situation."

"Rash? Outlanders assault my home and you don't want me to do anything rash?" Bryan argued. "Answer me this, Captain. These *Spetsnaz* had a picture of me that was taken here on your ship. How did they get that, hmm?"

This was yet another revelation that left Captain Rich dumbfounded. "I suggest you get your things in order before you tell me how to handle mine. I will return those men to you, unharmed, when I return with the delegation from the King, but in the meantime, they will submit to Avalon justice."

Bryan turned and walked away without another word. He climbed on the Wyvern and quickly took off, heading back toward the floating island of Emmyr. As Captain Rich watched, the XO came up behind him.

"Sir, I escorted Secretary Barry down to your stateroom," he relayed to the Captain. "He was a little airsick from the flight out here." McReynolds saw the laser-targeting box in the skipper's hands. "Where the hell did that come from?"

"Russian *Spetsnaz* got on their floating island somehow. The Gil-Gamesh captured them, with this," Rich explained. "But that's not the worst of it. The Russians had a picture of the Gil-Gamesh, a picture that was taken right here on this flight deck."

McReynolds couldn't believe it. "Tim, I want every camera in the photo lab checked; I want every cell phone of every sailor who was on deck that day gone through, and I want every email sent off this ship since that island appeared reviewed. If we have a spy on my ship, I want to know about it yesterday, is that understood?"

"Yes, sir, I'll take care of it personally," he responded.

"I'm going to brief the Secretary," Rich said. "This mess just got a whole lot worse."

***

Captain Rich informed Secretary Barry on the entire situation from the moment Avalon suddenly appeared in the ocean to today. Though he read all the reports prior to flying out to the carrier, Barry wanted to hear it personally from the commanding officer.

A career diplomat, Barry had served in every position imaginable with the State Department for more than 30 years. The 58-year-old had just a little grey hair on his temples, showing his even keel in handling stressful situations that he was known for. He slowly sipped his coffee, as he tried to quell the queasiness in his stomach from the bumpy flight out to the carrier. The emergence of the mysterious island was creating havoc to weather patterns across the Atlantic. Turbulence and rough seas hampered travel across the ocean from East to West.

Once Captain Rich finished his briefing, he sat back in his chair, waiting to answer any questions the Secretary might have. "I should also tell you, sir, my Senior Medical Officer will have further updates on Ensign Longwood to brief you about as soon as she receives her medical file from Portsmouth Naval Hospital and completes her diagnosis," he added.

"If I didn't see it for myself, I wouldn't believe any of this," Barry rebutted. "Do we know anything more about the *Spetsnaz* soldiers they captured?"

"No, sir. The only thing I can surmise is that they parachuted on the island. It must have been a Halo jump because I've had no reports of unusual contacts in our area in the past 48 hours except for a Russian transport that said they were enroute to Bermuda with supplies for the ships coming into our area. It had to be them!"

"Why the hell would the Russians do that? It makes no sense. We've been sharing information about the island with anyone who's asked."

"Does that include photos, sir?" Captain Rich asked.

"Photos? Photos of what?"

"The Gil-Gamesh told me that the *Spetsnaz* had a picture of him taken here, on my flight deck, when he came aboard previously," Rich explained. "I know we submitted all information on Avalon, including photos, to Washington. I'm having the XO check things out on our end here, but could they have gotten a photo from what we sent to you?"

"No, absolutely not. We only gave information, no imagery. We didn't want to create hysteria by showing people these knights, dragons and flying ships. I need to know how they got those pictures, Captain."

"I'm working it on it, sir," Rich assured him. "But with three Russian ships on their way here, they aren't going to be happy when they find out their men are being held prisoner by the Gil-Gamesh."

"No, they're not." Barry said and took another sip of coffee. "Tell me, Captain, what's your opinion of this Lord MoonDrake, the Gil-Gamesh?"

Captain Rich thought for a minute, reflecting to his conversations with the Gil-Gamesh. "I stand by my original assessment, sir. I think he's an honourable man. He demonstrated that with the care he showed for my Hawkeye crew, but I think he's hiding something. There's something very familiar about him but I just can't place my finger on it."

"What do you mean?" Secretary Barry asked.

"I feel as if I know him as if I met him before, but I don't see how that's possible. He said he's a Half-Elf on his mother's side."

Barry became confused. "I read in Commander Johnson's statement that he said he was a Half-Elf on his father's side. It would seem, the Gil-Gamesh is either a comedian or a liar."

"He reminds me of a Chief Petty Officer I once knew who died at sea during a Nor'easter, but it couldn't be him," Rich explained. "The Gil-Gamesh must be over 50-years-old. Chief Drake was in his late 30s when he fell overboard two years ago. I'm sure it's just a coincidence."

"I have found, Captain, that there are no such things as coincidences. See if you can get me this Chief Drake's personnel file. There may be more to this than he is letting on, and I prefer to go into negotiations fully armed, not shooting blanks."

***

Bryan and Stephanie waited underneath the statue of Sir Charles Taylor, the port's namesake, at the head of the piers with Rhona and Amelia as the dwarven airship *Fullangr*, flagship of Master Dinius Oddbottom, arrived on Emmyr. The ship carried two of the negotiators for Avalon. Chamberlin Ulric Ocwyn walked off the ship with Chancellor Pombur. Their positions and mannerisms were nearly identical, but that where their similarities ended.

Chamberlin Ocwyn's appearance distinguished his role as advisor to the King of Avalon. His robes were regal red and gold with dragon-themed embroidery on the back and sleeves, a distinction for serving King Bowen Pendragon and the Gil-Gamesh, who was considered by many as the Lord of the Dragons. Beneath his robes, he wore a frock of blue and silver, a gesture of loyalty to his former position as Chancellor of Emmyr. He walked long strides, and with every step, was sure to pound the ground with the edge of his staff—a marvellous thing of gold and precious gems with an orb of black marble sitting atop, which was said to be a piece of the stone that once encased *Excalibur*. His long black hair flowed off his head from his distinct receding hairline. Bryan swore it had receded even farther since he took on the position as Chamberlin of Avalon.

Chancellor Cornelius Pombur was unique in his position as advisor to the Master of the Gilded Halls of the Dwarves. He stood almost a foot taller than most Dwarves, with a multi-coloured robe embroidered with the symbols of the Dwarves—gems, gold, hammer and anvils. The brightly coloured garment was meant to take your eyes off the stark white beard that went all the way down to his feet, as it was the only hair on his head. His beard and hands were adorned with jewellery made from precious metals and gems, signifying his status. His strides were much shorter, and his staff was a unique blend of metals with a spiked hammer head on top. Like all Dwarves, Chancellor Pombur was always prepared for a fight.

As the two walked down the pier toward the Gil-Gamesh, the Elven airship *Aerdrie Faenya* arrived at the port, right next to the *Fullangr*. As the crew worked to moor the airship, Bryan saw who was on deck and his demeanour turned sour almost instantly. "You've got to be kidding me. Lady Lyllodoria sent her?"

"Sent who, milord?" Amelia asked.

"Eileanora, the Assassin of Alfheimer." They all looked down the pier to the Elven airship to see whom he was talking about. On the bridge of the airship, shouting orders to the crew, was a beautiful female Elf. She was dressed in green, black and brown leather armour covered in mithril scales that resembled leaves.

Her long, black hair was pulled back into a ponytail, braided neatly down her back just past her torso. At the end of the braid was an ornate metal spike that she occasionally used in combat.

Around her waist hung a long sword called *Çîsilæri* in Elvish but known to most by another name, *Whisper*. The enchanted blade was infamously quiet, making no noise whatsoever when drawn or swung. A perfect weapon for the perfect assassin.

Rhona and Amelia looked on in awe of this legendary warrior rarely seen outside Alfheimer. "The Dark Lady! The *Dubh Bhean*!" Rhona exclaimed, rattling off the assassin's nicknames. Eileanora was Alfheimer's dirty little secret known only to a few on Avalon. When problems arose that endangered the sanctity and security of the Elves of Alfheimer, Eileanora was sent to deal with it. She was ruthless, cunning and practically invisible when she carried out her missions. Being out in the open like this was out of character for Eileanora, and that troubled the Gil-Gamesh.

"Why in the world would Lyllodoria send her to join the negotiations?" Stephanie asked with contempt.

"Spite," Bryan said, "she knew I would object to Eileanora being part of the negotiations and when that happens, she'll take the company of Elves and head back to Alfheimer. She can appear to help without helping whatsoever and blame it on me. Problem solved."

"So, what are you going to do?"

Bryan smiled. That smirk again. "Be the adult in the room and not fall for it."

As Ocwyn and Pombur reached the end of the pier, they bowed courteously to the Gil-Gamesh and Lady Stephanie. They both ignored protocol and greeted the two with a hearty handshake and a hug respectively. Ocwyn was visibly concerned.

"I'm sorry, milord, I did not know that Eileanora would be Lady Lyllodoria's representative. Truly, I didn't."

"It's all right, Ocwyn. I don't blame you. This is her way of getting back at me for my remarks about her withdraw from the affairs of Avalon."

"It would appear, that the Lady Lyllodoria has a sense of humour," Pombur added.

"Yes, but not a very good one," Bryan remarked, as Eileanora and two members of the elite Elven Guard known as the *Hîldrägo Boquè* approached. These Elves are chosen at birth to be trained as warriors in defence of Alfheimer. Bryan called them the Elven Special Forces, trained in every form of combat imaginable. The *Hîldrägo Boquè* have never known defeat in the face of their enemy.

"*Salüs dai Tulafáir*, Gil-Gamesh," she greeted, as she placed her hand over her heart and bowed in respect. "I bring you greetings from the Lady Lyllodoria of Alfheimer. I have 200 of the *Hîldrägo Boquè* under my command to assist you in the defence of Emmyr."

Lord MoonDrake returned the traditional Elven greeting by bowing with his hand on his heart. "*Salüs dai Atrémar*, Eileanora. I welcome you and the *Hîldrägo Boquè* to my home. You remember my wife, Lady Stephanie MoonDrake," Bryan said, as he presented his wife. Both Stephanie and Eileanora exchange courtesies, though you could sense the coldness between them.

"It's been a while, Eileanora. Three years ago, on the Hirule Trail through the Fenris Mountains, I believe," the Gil-Gamesh remarked. "You and I were both after the alchemist Albertus Critch, but you found him before I did."

"He murdered the Elven Silk Trader Aindreas, a close friend of Lord Baldrid. Your methods were slow and unproductive. In the end, he met Elven justice."

"I don't consider putting a man's head on a pike justice," Bryan retorted. The silence between Eileanora and the Gil-Gamesh was deafening until Rhona cleared her throat and brought them back to their senses.

"Yes, this is Rhona McLoughlin, Captain of the Dragon Guard, and Amelia Pomodoro, my shield maiden," Bryan said, as he continued the introductions. The two bowed in respect to their guest. "Rhona will escort the *Hîldrägo Boquè* to where they will be staying while on Emmyr. Captain, if you please!"

Rhona motioned for the two members of the *Hîldrägo Boquè* to follow her, as they moved off to gather the rest of their company.

"And where will be I be staying, Gil-Gamesh?" Eileanora asked coyly.

"In the Dragon's Veil, of course. We would be honoured to have you as our guest, along with Chamberlin Ocwyn and Chancellor Pombur. I would like to discuss the upcoming negotiations with everyone tonight at dinner. Mrs Thurgoode makes an excellent *Perfügio undá Dulcîse*."

"I look forward to our discussion," she replied with a bow. "Please allow me to retrieve my things from the *Aerdrie Faenya*."

"Of course, Amelia will escort you up to the Dragon's Veil and show you to your room," the Gil-Gamesh replied. She bowed again before heading back toward the airship. Amelia moved up next to the Gil-Gamesh, confused and a little scared.

"Milord, please don't leave me alone with the *Dubh Bhean*," she pleaded. "Who knows what she may try?"

"Oh please, Amelia, she's not going to anything to anyone. At least not yet," Bryan contended. "Just be polite and courteous in everything you say or do. Don't give her any opportunity to insult or demean you."

Amelia got the message and headed down the pier, passing a group of Outlanders being escorted off the two ships. These are the people who unexpectedly arrived on Avalon when the island returned to the outside world. They are mostly tourists with one Navy pilot mixed in with them. They looked at their surroundings, confused but in utter amazement at the sight of a floating island and everything associated with it.

Bryan glanced at them curiously and he knew he needed to handle this personally. "Stephanie, why don't you take Ocwyn and Pombur back to the Dragon's Veil," he insisted. "I need to get these people secured until we return them to the fleet."

Stephanie said nothing and gave her husband a peck on the cheek before leading Ocwyn and Pombur toward an awaiting carriage. The Gil-Gamesh walked up to the Outlanders being guarded by some Dwarves and Elves from the two vessels. He motioned for members of his Dragon Guard to take over from them.

"We'll take them from here, you can all return to your ships," he commanded. The Dwarves and Elves bowed respectfully before leaving their charges to the Gil-Gamesh and his men.

"Ladies and Gentlemen, my name is Lord Bryan MoonDrake, the Gil-Gamesh of Avalon. I would like to welcome you to my home of Emmyr. From here, you will be taken to a secure location, given food and drink, a place to sleep and freshen up. As soon as feasible, we will be taking you out to a military ship that is sailing off the coast. Until then, I ask that you do exactly what my people tell you to do without question. I understand how confusing the situation is, but don't make it any worse by disobeying their orders. Is that understood?"

Everyone spoke out at once. Anger, frustration and fear came through in their voices, hammering Bryan with question after question until he had just about enough.

"Do not tempt my patience!" he shouted, quieting down the Outlanders almost immediately. "Things are far dire than you could possibly realise, and I have more pressing matters to deal with than your trivial banter. This is Avalon and you will abide by Avalon law or you will be dealt with severely!"

"Don't talk to me about the law, mister," said one man. "I happen to be a lawyer and, no matter what fantasy-land this is, you must adhere to international law."

Bryan walked up to the man and stared him down. "What is your name, sir?"

"Harold T. Cartwright, Esquire." he replied. "I want you to tell me how you're going to return my $25 million-dollar boat to me. It's sitting docked in that lake next to your pointy-eared friend's place."

"Ah, so you're the one who tried to kill the Leviathan with a gun," Bryan surmised. "Mr Harold T. Cartwright, Esquire...if you like, I can return you to your boat and place you back on the lake and let you take your chances with the Leviathan. Is that what you want?"

Cartwright quickly backpedalled as he was at a loss for words. "Well no, I don't... It's just that I expect to be compensated for my property, by the rule of law."

"That's the problem, Mr Cartwright, Avalon does not follow the laws of the outside world. We have no treaties, no legal agreements of any kind with your world, and until such a time as those diplomatic matters are settled and I am under no obligation to treat you anyway except by the laws of Avalon.

"So, until that time, I suggest you do as I say, or you can spend the night in my dungeon for disobeying the command of a Lord of Avalon. Which will it be?"

Cartwright swallowed hard and took a step back away from the Gil-Gamesh. "No, that won't be necessary, sir. Your hospitality will be just fine. Thank you."

Bryan stepped back to allow the guards to escort the Outlanders away. They looked at him in awe and in fear as they walked by before spotting something totally out of character for this medieval world. Chancellor Henri Beauchamp walked briskly down the pier toward the Gil-Gamesh, brushing past the Outlanders.

As one of the few Frenchmen on Avalon, Henri lived up to his reputation as both an efficient organiser and an outlandish dresser. His flowing frock, wide-brimmed hat, complete with a feathered plume, and neatly waxed moustache made him look more like something from *The Three Musketeers* than the court of Avalon.

Bryan relied heavily on Henri with the delicacies of diplomacy and the affairs at the court, something the Gil-Gamesh usually handled with the sword rather than the pen. Henri stopped just short of Lord MoonDrake to offer a courteous bow. "I was told by *Capitaine* Rhona you wanted to see me, milord?" Henri asked.

"Yes, Henri, I want you to take charge of the Outlanders that just arrived," he commanded, as the two began to walk back down the pier. "I want you to make sure they are provided food, drink and any other necessities within reason. Call in Allain if anyone has an urgent medical issue, but I want you to keep them separated from the rest of Emmyr. Make sure the guards keep any onlookers out too!"

"*Mais bien sûr*, Gil-Gamesh, I will see to it personally," Henri acknowledged with his usual vim and vigour.

"Turn on your charm, Henri, be reasonable yet firm," Bryan said. "I don't want any problems until they depart the island and are out of our hair."

"And what should I do if they start asking questions about us, milord?"

Bryan thought for a moment. He didn't want to give too much away to be spread virally on the internet and television once they got home. "Stick to the basics, Henri. A little bit of history, something about the mythical creatures, but nothing more than that. Avoid any talk of Outlanders on Avalon… Dumb it down for them. I don't want to give too much away before the negotiations."

"*Excellente,* Gil-Gamesh; I will keep them guessing yet thoroughly informed."

"I'm sorry you won't be part of the negotiations, Henri, but I need to keep the party as small as possible."

"*Je comprends*. Milord. I will just wait my turn until the French delegation arrives. Then, you will call on me, *n'est-ce pas?*" Henri joked. Bryan shook his head and laughed. Through all his overstuffed ego and garish clothes, he could always count on Henri to cheer him up.

Chapter 3
Negotiations Between Worlds

Dinner was quiet and quite formal, something rarely done at the Dragon's Veil. Mrs Emily Thurgoode was nothing short of a tyrant when it came to formal dinners for the Gil-Gamesh, because he so rarely had them. She ran that household with an iron fist and Stephanie, for one, was grateful. She kept everything organised and proper, ensuring every protocol was adhered to with military precision and dinner was no exception. From the main course to dessert, she orchestrated course after course brought from the kitchen to the table by the staff.

Normally, conversations were abundant and joyful during one of her dinners, but not tonight. The dining room was as quiet as a church. Everyone seemed focused on their meal, not willing to talk about anything. The mood was especially uncomforting with Eileanora at one end of the table and the Gil-Gamesh at the other, with Ocwyn, Pombur, Lady Stephanie and Rhona between them. Amelia stood directly behind Lord MoonDrake, not taking her eyes off Eileanora for one second.

She sat there eating her food quietly, flanked by two members of the *Hîldrägo Boquè*, cutting each morsel into a tiny bite that she ate with quiet precision and speed. She ate as if to nourish herself, not to enjoy the delicacies before her. Ocwyn, ever the politician, was first to break the silence.

"Emily, you have outdone yourself," he complimented. "If there's one thing I miss about Emmyr, it's your cooking. I shall have to steal you away, so you can properly train the cooks in New Camelot."

"Yes, indeed, Mrs Thurgoode," Chancellor Pombur added, not to be outdone by Ocwyn. "It was an absolutely stellar meal."

Emily blushed from the compliments. "Well, thank you both very much, it was my pleasure," she said with a curtsy. "But I wouldn't get any ideas of taking me away from Emmyr, Chamberlain," she stated to Ulric. "You'd have to fight Lady MoonDrake for me, and I doubt you'd win."

"No, they wouldn't," Stephanie said good-naturedly. A snicker came from the other end of the table. Everyone turned to look at Eileanora, who just sat there and continued to eat without even looking up from her plate. The Gil-Gamesh was frustrated to no end at the rudeness of Lady Lyllodoria's representative. He knew he needed to put her in her place as quickly and diplomatically as possible.

"Emily, would you please give us some privacy?" Lord MoonDrake asked. "We have some important matters to discuss."

"Of course, milord," Emily replied with a quick curtsy, as she motioned for the staff to follow her out.

"First and foremost, I want to be up front with all of you," Bryan started. "I know the commanding officer of the ship off Avalon."

Everyone was surprised to hear this, including Eileanora who stopped eating and looked up for the first time.

"His name is Captain Larry Rich. He was my officer-in-charge during my military duty in the Navy. He was, in many ways, a mentor for me as a young sailor."

"Did he recognise you?" Ocwyn asked.

"No, I don't think so," the Gil-Gamesh assured him. "I think my ears and older features threw him off. In any case, I wanted you to know that before we go out to the ship."

"And are there any other surprises you haven't told us?" Eileanora asked curtly.

"As a matter of fact, I do. I have several captured Outlander soldiers in my dungeon," Bryan replied without missing a beat. Pombur spat out his food and drink across the table.

While Stephanie tended to Pombur, Eileanora jumped out of her chair and slammed her fist on the table. Rhona cautiously placed her fingertips on the hilt of her sword, glancing back to the Gil-Gamesh, as if waiting for a command. He just quietly shook his head, which Rhona took to mean she should be patient.

"Who are these Outlanders and how did they breach Avalon?" she demanded. Bryan just sat there, calm and collective, which infuriated Eileanora even more.

"They are called *Spetsnaz*, special forces for the Russian Federation," he explained. "I guess you could say they are comparable to the *Hîldrägo Boquè*."

"Nothing is comparable to the *Hîldrägo Boquè*!" Eileanora exclaimed. "Do not liken these Outlanders to the 'Army of Ten Thousand Years' ever!"

The Gil-Gamesh simply nodded his head in understanding. "In any case, they arrived on Emmyr via a parachute from high altitude. Some of them didn't survive the jump because their equipment failed as soon as they crossed the barrier. Others died when they ran into some dragons on our northern edge.

"I already informed Captain Rich that I was holding them prisoner until we arrive for our first negotiations. Then I will turn them over to him for dispensation."

"What? Is this what you call justice on Emmyr?" Eileanora fumed. "They should be publicly executed for their transgressions."

"That is not for you to decide, Eileanora," the Gil-Gamesh snapped back, his tone now more commanding. "I am Lord of Emmyr and the decision is mine and mine alone. In the hope of forging peaceful negotiations with the Outlanders, I will not shed first blood."

"Of course, you won't Gil-Gamesh, because you do not care about Avalon or the interests of Avalon. All you care about is your precious Outlanders!"

"Now see here, Eileanora! Lord MoonDrake has defended Avalon since the day he arrived on our shores," Ocwyn retorted. "He has taken arms against every enemy that threatened Avalon, saving countless lives in the process."

"Not everyone," Eileanora snapped back.

"Ah-ha!" Bryan shouted, as he leaped out of his seat. Everyone looked at the Gil-Gamesh with a confused glance, unsure of where he was going with this. "I knew it! Lady Lyllodoria didn't ask you to come to Emmyr; you volunteered, didn't you?"

Eileanora said nothing and Bryan pressed on.

"You jumped on the chance to come to Emmyr, but not for honour or duty to Alfheimer. You did it for revenge, to get back at me."

"You're mad. I don't know what you're talking about," she stammered, as sweat trickled down her brow. The *Dubh Bhean* was unaccustomed to sweating,

"Yes, you do! *Uêvos cadtis quäsli ebriðs stùlt!*" Bryan cursed at her in Elvish, calling her a lying, drunken fool. Eileanora gritted her teeth as she leaped at the Gil-Gamesh. She jumped on the table and sprinted toward him. Then, in one quick motion, she whipped her hair around and snapped it toward him as the poison spike on the end arched right at Lord MoonDrake. This was a move she'd done thousands of times in battle, one that had never missed. Until now.

Bryan caught the spike just before it reached him. He used her momentum and pulled her down to the table, face down. In one swift motion, he pinned her to the table by placing his foot on her braid and drew *Twilight*.

The two *Hîldrägo Boquè* drew their weapons to defend Eileanora, as did Rhona and Amelia, getting between them and the Gil-Gamesh. Bryan didn't want anyone else involved in this.

"*Tǽnèru!*" he shouted in Elvish. "*DeÞoscõ iush Pugnǽ!*" The Elves stopped their advance and sheathed their weapons. Bryan had declared his right of challenge and since Eileanora attacked first, the Elves had no choice but to accept it. It was a matter of honour for them.

Rhona and Amelia kept their weapons drawn and ready, waiting for the Gil-Gamesh to command them. He nodded at the two shield maidens. They immediately sheathed their weapons. Everyone's attention was now focused on Bryan and Eileanora.

Bryan brought *Twilight* close to the base of her scalp. She struggled against his weight on her hair, pinning her to the table. She didn't even try to draw her sword as the positioning was awkward and she would be instantly disarmed.

"At least let me draw my sword," she exclaimed. "You have declared the right of challenge. I must be allowed to defend myself!"

"In a minute, in a minute. I'm going to say a few things first, and if you make any more aggressive moves, I'll give you a pixie cut like you'll never forget. Did you honestly think you could assassinate me without any repercussions to yourself? Or is it that you just didn't care if you lived or died?"

"You have no idea what you're talking about."

"This is about Eonis, isn't it?"

A quiet hush fell across the room at the mention of Bryan's long-time friend, Eonis. He was the first Elf the Gil-Gamesh met when he arrived on Avalon. He was a fierce warrior and a good friend to all who knew him. Eonis was killed more than a year ago, at the hands of Morgana le Fay. She demonstrated the power of the Dark Tides, reducing Eonis to dust by destroying the magic within him.

Eileanora's demeanour changed immediately, as the pain of his death rushed over her. "It was your fault," she screamed. "You cared nothing about saving him. You only cared about your whore Outlander daughter!"

Out of nowhere, a dagger plunged between Eileanora's braided hair and into the table. Lady Stephanie, still gripping the dagger in her hand, leaned her face close to the Elf's.

"Call my daughter a whore again and I'll be the one giving you a haircut!" she whispered to Eileanora.

Bryan pulled out the dagger and gave it back to Stephanie before releasing his weight off Eileanora's hair. She quickly sprang to her feet and drew her sword, ready to fight the Gil-Gamesh, but Bryan sheathed his sword and stood there before her, arms wide in a non-threatening stance.

"Let's finish this, Gil-Gamesh. You have declared *iush Pugnæ* and it must be answered."

"Oh, don't worry. I will, just not right now."

"What? Are you afraid to fight me now that I am ready for you? Who's the *ebriðs stùlt* now?" she bantered on.

"Eileanora, I will give you the right to face me in one-on-one combat, just not right now. Right now, we must deal with the fact that Avalon is sitting in the middle of the Atlantic Ocean, surrounded by a fleet of ships with enough firepower to kill everyone here. That's why I need you to get past whatever vendetta you have against me and focus on the mission at hand."

Eileanora was confused and bewildered by his statement as was everyone else in the room. "Why do you think I goaded you into attacking me? I knew you had to have some ulterior motive for being here, but I need you focused on what's best for Avalon, not killing me."

"And why should I care about what happens between Avalon and these Outlanders? My only concern is Alfheimer."

"See, there you go lying again. I know you don't feel that way, Eileanora."

"You know nothing, Gil-Gamesh. What makes you think I care about any of you?"

"Because Eonis told me about the two of you," Bryan revealed. Eileanora's face remained stern, but her cheeks reddened. "You were his *Verś Datûim*, his one true love. He described you as a warm, loving person, but you kept it hidden so people would fear you instead of like you."

"Eonis would never have betrayed me by telling you my most intimate secrets! You're just saying all this to confuse me, so I won't take my vengeance on you."

"Really? You love to get up early every morning and watch the sunrise. It's your favourite time of day because it reminds you that the new day has begun. You have a curiosity about the religion of man. You secretly attend regular Sunday worship service whenever you're near a church. You wanted to find out if someone like you, who has done so many horrible acts, can be redeemed in the eyes of God."

Bryan continued, as Eileanora stood there, stunned at the level of knowledge the Gil-Gamesh detailed from his time with Eonis.

"You have a particular weakness for caramel confections. He said you would go to New Camelot regularly, to the Hammer Schmidt Candy Company, I believe, to get a fresh supply whenever you're off on a mission. You prefer the sugar rush from caramel to drinking efion tea."

A tear gently rolled down her cheek. "Why would he tell you all this about me?"

Bryan walked up to Eileanora. She resisted his approach at first but then lowered her sword, allowing Bryan to reach out and grab her by the shoulders. "Because he was my best friend," Bryan explained. "When Charles died, then Thomas, I was inconsolable. I felt like I had lost my family all over again. Eonis was there for me. He opened up, to me, about his relationship with you to show me that you can always find friendship and love, even in the most unexpected places.

"I knew it was true love," he continued. "He always spoke about you with a loving, caring tone in his voice. He loved you, even though Lord Baldrid and Lady Lyllodoria disapproved of your relationship. That didn't matter to him. He believed in you, Eileanora. Don't you think it's time you believed in yourself as something more than a killing machine? Come on now, he didn't want you to be alone and unloved."

Tears rolled down her cheeks as if the death of Eonis has happened all over again. "But I *am* alone and unloved, he's gone. My love is gone from me forever."

"And that's my fault, Eileanora," Bryan admitted. "Please believe me that I still can't forgive myself for the lives we lost to Morgana le Fay: Eonis, Archie, Cadhla, Kragmar and Nihala, Lord Baldrid and hundreds more. Someday, I may come to terms with it, but I can't afford that right now. Tiamat has destroyed the barrier and returned Avalon to the outside world. The only way we can protect Avalon, and Alfheimer, from any potential Outlander threats is by working together. It's what Eonis would have wanted."

Eileanora thought for a minute. Finally, she sheathed her sword and wiped the tears from her eyes. She walked past Lord MoonDrake and bowed to Lady Stephanie.

"Milady, I apologise for my rude behaviour tonight," she said. "Please tell Mrs Thurgoode that her dinner was exceptional."

Stephanie nodded her head, accepting her apology. Eileanora turned back to the Gil-Gamesh, her eyes glanced downward away from him. "I will think on all that you have said, milord. I would…"

She paused for a moment to gather her thoughts. "… I would like to talk to you more about your conversations with Eonis. Perhaps they would help me, help both of us, move forward."

"I would be happy to, Eileanora," Bryan said. "I have a 2,000-year-old Elderberry wine that Lord Baldrid gave me. I was saving it for a special occasion. I think this merits it."

Eileanora smiled slightly and nodded her head, as she turned and walked away with her *Hîldrägo Boquè* guard close behind. The room was silent for another minute until Pombur picked up his flagon of ale and drank it down in one gulp.

"My, that was exhilarating!" he declared. "I rarely get away from the Gilded Halls. Is it always like this?"

***

The bridge of an aircraft carrier is a disciplined, well-oiled military machine and the *USS Theodore Roosevelt* was no exception. No one entered the bridge without the express permission of the commanding officer and then, only on official business. No sightseeing is allowed, even when you're steaming a few miles off the coast of a magical island like Avalon.

Captain Rich sat in his chair, reading over the daily intelligence reports from Operations. The flights around the island continued to survey the coastline regularly. The troop build-up continued to grow anywhere the island was accessible by the shore. *They really don't want us venturing inland*, he thought.

Besides the troubles from within Avalon, Captain Rich was dealing with the added headache of militaries coming from around the world to get a glimpse of this enchanted island. There were more than 50 ships from several nations that had joined in the blockade, and coordinating this massive fleet fell upon his crew. Fortunately, for Rich, the Navy was sending the *USS Harry S. Truman* to take over operating the fleet, so he can concentrate on communication with Avalon.

Then there were the tourists: Cruise ships, private yachts, sailboats, along with every type of small plane trying to get as close to the island as possible. One company out of Bermuda was even offering a flying tour of the magical island for $500 per person. The world knew the name of the island was Avalon.

The identity of Avalon was made public when an internet gossip site posted 'exclusive' photos of the Gil-Gamesh and the dragon on the flight deck of the carrier; the same pictures the Russian *Spetsnaz* were briefed on. It seemed an enterprising, young photographer on board had emailed the photos to his brother to sell to the highest bidder. Rich knew he would eventually have to discipline this sailor, but he was focused on more pressing matters. The fact that this Gil-Gamesh may, in fact, be his dead friend, Chief Bryan Drake.

The prospect that his friend and his family may be alive was great, but the fact that the same friend may have lied to his face like he did was another thing. He didn't know if the Gil-Gamesh was telling the truth about his lineage, but Rich intended to find out.

"Request permission to enter the bridge," came a voice from behind. Commander Maxine Bacon, the Aerographer aboard the TR, waited for a polite nod from the OOD before stepping on deck. She had her long, blonde hair wrapped neatly in a bun, per military etiquette. She was known for being laid back as an officer, but Rich knew her as the most accurate and reliable 'weather guesser' in the Navy.

Max, as she is called by the Captain and only the Captain, walked over to hand the skipper the weather forecast for the week. "Here you go skipper, calm seas and sunny skies for the next week, maybe longer," she said with a smile.

"Still?" Rich queried, as he snatched the forecast from her hand. "What the hell's going on, Max? We're in the middle of hurricane season. The Atlantic should be a cauldron of bad weather by now."

"Well, I think you can thank your magical island for that one, at least that's what the 'big-wigs' at NOAA are telling me," she explained. "That island has caused a major lull in the Atlantic storm season, and that's affecting weather patterns around the world. They're worried that the jet stream may shift. This could be a major shift in the climate as we know it."

Rich sensed a pause in her voice, something he's come accustomed to. "And?"

"And there are some who are saying that this is the way the world was, a long time ago."

"What do you mean?"

"By all accounts, from your conversations with this Gil-Gamesh character, we think that Avalon existed in the world once before, right?" Rich just nodded his head in response. "We don't know what the weather was like thousands of years ago, but some educated speculation indicates that it wasn't as bad as it is today.

"Perhaps Avalon returning to the real world has restored balance to the climate, maybe for the better."

Rich scoffed at her wild theory. "Do you really think this island controls the weather for the entire planet? Come on, Max, I thought you didn't go in for unproven scientific theories."

"I don't, skipper," she said, throwing her hands into the air, "but sometimes you have to believe in…" Max inferred as if to leave, but something caught her eye on the bridge wing. "…Magic!"

Maxine looked out through the porthole to see a tiny dragon, hovering in the air, holding a scroll of parchment in his hand. Its iridescent wings beat as fast as a hummingbird's, making them practically invisible to the naked eye. Her long pause caused Captain Rich to turn around and see Maverick, the little faerie dragon of the Gil-Gamesh.

He jumped out of his chair and opened the hatch, allowing the tiny creature to fly onto the bridge. Maverick landed on the Captain's Chair and set the parchment down. Everyone on the bridge was in awe of the little dragon. As Rich approached him, Maverick nudged the parchment toward him.

Captain Rich picked it up and broke the wax seal, as he unrolled the scroll until he saw the bridge crew wasn't paying any attention to their duties. "As you were!" he ordered. The sailors snapped to and went back to work. Maxine, however, was enamoured by the little creature.

"Oh, my God, he is so cute!" she cooed, as she reached out to touch him. Maverick loved the attention being showered upon him and allowed her to stroke his head. The faerie dragon just purred as he adjusted his position to let her scratch him in just the right spot.

"Please, Max, don't feed into it," the skipper complained, as he unrolled the parchment and read its contents. "The Gil-Gamesh is bringing out the representatives to negotiate the day after tomorrow," he declared, "along with some stranded Outlanders, as he calls them, and prisoners."

"Prisoners?" Maxine exclaimed, causing her to stop petting Maverick. This little faerie dragon growled softly from the loss of attention.

"It's a long story, Max, for another time," he said, setting the scroll back down in front of Maverick. "Tell the Gil-Gamesh I understand and accept." He spoke to Maverick as if he was talking to one of his sailors, but the dragon didn't move.

"Maybe he doesn't understand English?" Maxine asked.

"No, he responded to the Gil-Gamesh, I'm sure he does," Rich replied, unsure of what to do. Maverick nudged the parchment toward him, only this time, the little dragon mimicked writing with a pen.

"Oh, he wants me to write down my answer, is that it?" the skipper asked, to which Maverick just nodded his head. "I can't believe I'm reduced to having a conversation with a dragon."

The bridge crew chuckled, as did Commander Bacon, but when the Captain turned and looked at his crew, they shut up and went back to their duties. He snagged the scroll and set it down on a clipboard, writing his response under the Gil-Gamesh's with a ballpoint pen. When he finished, he handed the scroll back to Maverick.

The faerie dragon beat its dragonfly-like wings and hovered in the air over the chair before zipping out the open hatch and back toward Avalon. Captain Rich and Maxine watched as the tiny creature disappeared as fast as it arrived.

"Guess who's coming to dinner?" Maxine joked, but Captain Rich wasn't amused. It only left him with more questions. Maybe now he'll find out just who the Gil-Gamesh is.

***

New Camelot was buzzing with excitement and fear since Avalon returned to the outside world. Security around the capital city was on high alert. The Knights of the Round Table had a solemn duty to protect King Bowen and his people from Outlander threats—that seemingly fell from the sky—while keeping a close eye out for anyone or anything within Avalon that tried to take advantage of the situation. The thieves' guild couldn't pickpocket a single purse with the tight security on display throughout the city.

Sir Hunter MoonDrake kept a watchful eye, as he patrolled around the city. As knight attendant to King Bowen, his duty was to answer to the King's commands. Today, the King asked him to find out how his people were dealing with the situation at hand. Hunter knew his report would not be a good one.

He sensed the fear, bewilderment and unease from everyone he met. While some met the news with delight and curiosity, most of the people were afraid—afraid that their way of life was coming to an end. Over the past centuries, Outlanders coming to Avalon have told stories of the modern world, machines and technology as well as political strife, religious persecution, war and social unease. These were things totally unfamiliar to the average citizen of Avalon and that frightened them.

Although Hunter grew up in that world, he hasn't been a part of it for more than 12 years. Like the rest of his family, he missed his favourite things at times: Video games, television, movies, NASCAR races and hockey. Those things have given way to long nights at the pub, listening to minstrels play music while bards recited poetry, jousting tournaments and Highlander games.

Most of all, he enjoyed the time he had with his son. Bowen may be the ruler of Avalon, but he's still a seven-year-old boy. Hunter has a chance to bond with his son, mould him into a great king the way his father moulded him into a knight of the Round Table. He wanted to be there for Bowen, especially with his mother gone now.

A hand touched his shoulder, startling the young knight out of his thoughts.

"Sir Hunter, didn't you hear me calling for you?"

Hunter turned to see Lady Brigida Olafdotter, daughter of Baron Ericksson of the North Highlands. Her long, blonde hair flowed from underneath a long, red scarf that rolled around her head and neck, framing her beautiful face. As the daughter of a Highland Baron, her heritage showed through in her leather armour with overlapping metal rings and leather vambraces and leggings. Around her waist hung an *Ulfberht*, a traditional Viking sword.

The people of the North Highlands of Avalon were known as both fierce warriors and skilled fishermen. Though they keep to themselves, they are an integral part of Avalon society. Hunter knew Brigida and many of the other children of the Lords of Avalon. They were their own social group as the heirs of the future of Avalon.

"I'm sorry, Bree," Hunter apologised, calling her by her nickname, before giving her a friendly hug. "My mind is wandering today. When did you arrive in New Camelot?"

"Just this morning," she replied. "My father asked me to talk to the markets to let them know we won't be sending our usual quota. The fishing has been very strange since our return to the outside world."

"What do you mean?" Hunter asked and motioned for her to join him on his walk back to Castle Pendragon.

"These aren't our normal fishing grounds anymore," Bree started. "The waters are much warmer than usual, and the quantity and quality of fish dropped off drastically. We're catching fish no one has ever seen since our clan began fishing the waters, off the coast of Avalon."

"That makes sense. We're not a contained climate like we once were. The ocean surrounding Avalon is different from the climate we're used to and it's creating an imbalance in our ecosystem."

"I don't understand? What's an e-co-system?" Bree queried, sounding out each syllable. Hunter chuckled, not realising who he was talking to for a moment.

"Sorry, Bree, it's something I learned in school in the outside world when I was a boy," he explained. "An ecosystem is a group of living organisms—like people, fish and animals—who live in conjunction with the uh, sort of, non-living components of their environment, like air, water and soil. Together, they interact as one system."

"An ecosystem?" Bree answered.

"Yes, exactly. Our ecosystem was contained in our pocket universe under the barrier."

"And now?"

Hunter sighed, trying to put the right words together. "Now, we've rejoined the ecosystem of the whole planet, putting our world, our way of life, in jeopardy."

This troubled Bree deeply. "But, your father is trying to find a way to restore the barrier, isn't he?"

"That, on top of fortifying Avalon's defences and leading the negotiating team out to form a kind of diplomatic status quo with the military warships sitting off our coast."

"You've seen these ships before, yes? You know what they're capable of?"

Hunter paused again to try to explain it to her as easy as possible, but also so as not to scare her any more than she already is. "When I was eight, my father took me and my family out on what they called a 'family day cruise' on his ship," he said. "It was a way to show the family members of the sailors what their job was like when they were at sea. For an eight-year-old boy, it was exhilarating…but for you, it would have been terrifying," Hunter continued. "Those ships have more firepower than a hundred wizards combined. I'm just glad the anti-technology barrier is still in place."

The two stopped just outside the gateway into Castle Pendragon. Hunter looked at Bree and saw a far-off look in her eyes. He realised he may have gone too far in telling her about the might of the US Navy.

"Bree, you mustn't worry yourself about these things," he assured her. "The United States of America isn't about to go to war with Avalon, and my father knows that. He'll set things right. You'll see."

Bree's frown turned into a smile of relief when she gave Hunter one last hug before he excused himself to go inside, but as soon as he was gone, her frown returned. She was uneasy about the threat of the outside world and what it meant to her people and her family.

As she turned and headed back toward the markets, she stopped but for a moment at the entrance to a local tavern, the *Slaughtered Lamb* as if she was considering having a pint. "All right, I'm in," was all she said, seemingly to the air itself, before she continued walking. After she was gone, Artūras Blackstone stepped out from the doorway, his hood pulled low to hide his face. He smiled.

***

The one good thing about distinguished visitors coming aboard an aircraft carrier is that there are plenty of people around to help get things ready. Anyone who was not on watch or part of flight operations was scattered about the *USS Theodore Roosevelt* sweeping, mopping, dusting and polishing. These were the first diplomatic talks between the world and the island of Avalon, and Captain Rich wanted to ensure that nothing was out of place.

The visiting dignitaries from Russia, Great Britain and NATO were already aboard and awaiting their arrival in the Captain's inport cabin along with Secretary Barry. Many other nations wanted to participate in the talks but since it was being held on United States territory, the US government had the last word. Too many mouths at the table would leave everyone hungry.

Captain Rich waited on the flight deck patiently, keeping an eye toward the floating island of Emmyr. The Gil-Gamesh said they would be arriving at midday, so he ensured flight operations were completed by 1000 hours. He was flanked by armed US Marines, a recent addition to his security forces with their proximity to Avalon and the potential danger it represented. Two companies of the Marine Corps Security Force Regiment were now stationed on the carrier.

The deck was cleared except for sailors acting as line handlers, awaiting their arrival with security personnel manning every entrance on deck. No one was allowed anywhere near the visitors from Avalon when they arrived.

The hatch behind the Captain opened and the XO stepped out on deck, radio in hand. "Captain, contact coming toward us from the floating island," McReynolds informed him. "I think they're on their way."

"Thanks, Mac. Go down and inform the Secretary that our guests are arriving."

McReynolds nodded his head and turned back inside, closing the hatch behind him while Captain Rich and his security detail walked across the deck toward the line handlers. The sailors snapped to as the Captain approached. Normally, he would have a junior officer or chief take charge of a simple detail like this, but he didn't want to risk it.

It's not that he doesn't trust his crew, he just didn't want to expose his sailors to potential danger. He didn't know what to expect from the Gil-Gamesh and his delegation from Avalon and he wasn't taking any chances.

The *Avenger* glided in, just like before, and manoeuvred alongside the aircraft carrier, matching speed with the warship by adjusting it sails. Captain Rich was impressed with the way its captain handled the small, wooden ship next to the massive American warship. He looked across to see a young, man commanding the airship, impressing him even more.

Just as before, the sailors grabbed the lines and secured the *Avenger* as a gangplank was extended across. When everything was secure, a signal was sent and a pair of large doors below the airship's wheel opened. Instead of the expected dignitaries, a long line of civilians and military personnel stepped out and proceeded to the gangplank.

The ship's captain led the group across to the carrier flight deck. He was dressed like the Gil-Gamesh, though his appearance was more *Pirates of the Caribbean*. He wore a long-armoured waistcoat with plate chest armour underneath, a bicorn hat on his head and knee-high boots. A single sword hung around his waist; a cutlass with skull and crossbones on the hilt.

The captain of the *Avenger* led the group across the brow. One-by-one, they were helped across by men on the *Avenger* and handed off to one of the Roosevelt's sailors.

"Captain, sir, I am Edan O'Brien, Captain of the *Avenger*," he said, saluting Captain Rich by tipping his hat. "The Gil-Gamesh sends his regards. He instructed me to bring these guests and prisoners to you."

Rich didn't like the delay in starting these negotiations, but he saw no alternative at this moment. "Take them to the XO," Rich ordered two of the Marines. "Escort them down to the wardroom for debriefing." The Marines acknowledged the order and led the group across the flight deck to Commander McReynolds.

"When can I expect the Gil-Gamesh and your King's negotiators?" he asked Edan.

"They'll be along shortly, sir. I will return within the hour with the remains from the two plane crashes on Avalon," Edan explained. "Please have some men and equipment standing by assist with the offload. I think your modern conveniences will be better equipped to handle it."

"Yes, of course, I'll see to it," the Captain said with a salute of his own. Edan returned the salute before returning to the *Avenger*. Once aboard, the gangplank was lifted, the lines were released, and the airship headed back toward Avalon.

Rich gave orders to the line handlers to stand by and await their return. As he turned back toward the ship's island, an energy vortex appeared in front of him and four people suddenly appeared. Standing alongside, the Gil-Gamesh was a small party of three very different individuals. Their dress was as ornate and unique as the next.

One was tall, with long hair flowing off a baldhead, wearing an elaborate robe adorned with jewellery of gold and precious gems, carrying a golden staff.

The other was also as eloquently dressed but quite short, only about four feet tall, but he walked with stature. The one woman amongst the group was strikingly beautiful and equally terrifying in her appearance. She wore armour that resembled leaves on a tree, armed with a long sword that hung at her waist. She made Rich feel quite uncomfortable, even from a distance.

"Good afternoon, Captain," Lord MoonDrake announced. The Marines reacted quickly, raising their weapons and stepping in front of the Captain, but he immediately ordered them to stand down.

"Forgive our sudden appearance, but I thought it best that we give you time to get the people on board prior to our arrival," the Gil-Gamesh asserted, but the Captain didn't buy it. For now, though, he let it go.

"That's quite understandable, Lord MoonDrake," he remarked, his voice edgy with discontent. "I think it best we move inside before introductions are made."

"Of course, sir, please, lead the way," Bryan motioned. Captain Rich led the party toward the island with the Marines following close behind. The group looked around in awe at their surroundings, noting the foreboding aircraft and their weaponry as well as the impressive size of the steel ship.

As Captain Rich opened the hatch to lead them inside, one of the Marines stepped up to stop them. "Excuse me, sir," the Marine stated, "but it's against regulations to allow armed personnel aboard the ship. They must be disarmed."

Captain Rich cursed under his breath. He knew the Marine was correct, and only doing his duty by pointing that out, but the Captain knew this wasn't the right time for this. Before he could answer the Marine, the Gil-Gamesh spoke up.

"A knight would never allow himself to be disarmed," he proclaimed. "I give you my word, as a Lord of Avalon, that we will take no hostile action while we are guests aboard your ship."

Rich was pleasantly surprised at the diplomatic tone taken by the Gil-Gamesh. "They will be allowed to carry their weapons, Sergeant," he ordered. "I take the Gil-Gamesh at his word."

The Marine acknowledged the Captain's order and stepped aside. The party was led down one flight of stairs to the deck below the flight deck. Ocwyn and Pombur stepped lightly as the tight stairwell was not meant for long robes. Once down, they were taken directly to the Captain's inport cabin.

The Gil-Gamesh could not help but notice all the security around them. There was an armed sailor or Marine at every hatch, crossway or door. Either they didn't trust them, or they wanted to ensure the crew wouldn't snoop around. Either way, it was a little unnerving, Bryan began to second-guess himself in arranging this meeting.

Inside, the cabin looked just as Bryan remembered from other carriers; an office with a small lounge area for meetings, greeting dignitaries, etc. Quite roomy for a ship built for 6,000 sailors. There were four others waiting for them, all in uniform except for Secretary Barry. They looked shocked at the guests from Avalon, as if they just stepped out of a renaissance fair.

"Lord MoonDrake, may I introduce Secretary of State Clinton Barry, representative of the United States of America," he introduced. The two men sized each other up.

"Lord MoonDrake, it is an honour to greet you on behalf of the President of the United States," Barry said, extending his hand.

Bryan returned the handshake. "Thank you, Mr Secretary," he said, then paused for a moment to focus on images he was seeing through the dragon sight. When he realised his awkward silence, he released the Secretary's hand and turned toward Ocwyn.

"If I may begin the introductions, Chamberlain Ulric Ocwyn, representing His Majesty King Bowen Pendragon of Avalon." Ocwyn bowed to the assembled group, as the Gil-Gamesh continued his introductions.

"Chancellor Pombur, representing the Dwarf Lord of the Gilded Halls of Avalon, Master Dinius Oddbottom." Pombur bowed politely as well as the Gil-Gamesh moved on.

"And Eileanora, representing the White Lady Lyllodoria, Queen of the Elves of Aflheimer," he stated, as Eileanora just nodded her head politely, never taking her eyes off the others, nor her hand off the hilt of her sword.

"I am Lord Bryan MoonDrake, Gil-Gamesh of Avalon, Knight Eternal of the Realm and Commander of the Knights of the Round Table."

"Well, gentlemen and lady, if I may…" Barry began, "let me introduce General Piotr Garasimov of the Russian Federation," The big, burly Russian looked menacing with his narrow eyes and large head as he acknowledged the introduction with a simple nod.

"Representing the North Atlantic Treaty Organisation, an alliance of countries in Europe with common defensive goals, Admiral Francois Charbonne of France." The admiral bowed politely to the distinguished visitors. His crisp, clean uniform and sharp appearance matched his precise, military behaviour.

"And lastly, from Great Britain, His Royal Highness, Prince George, the Duke of York," Barry introduced the young prince, dressed in his RAF uniform. His blonde hair and good looks made him a paparazzi dream, but his quiet, reserved demeanour spoke to his royal upbringing.

The prince bowed to the guests from Avalon, but they surprised everyone when the four dropped to one knee and bowed their heads to the young royal. Everyone was confused, especially the prince. "No please, that's not necessary," Prince George responded.

"With respect to your Royal Highness, it is," the Gil-Gamesh said, as they all returned to their feet. "We are a monarchy and we respect all royalty, especially yours."

"Mine? I don't understand?"

"At one time, Britain was home to many of us on Avalon," Ocwyn explained. "Our shared lineage can be traced back to Arthur Pendragon, King of the Britons. You are part of that lineage, your Highness, maybe not directly, but you're still a part of it. We respect that common bond between our two Kingdoms." Ocwyn bowed once again to the prince, who was embarrassed yet honoured by the people of Avalon.

There was a strained, uncomfortable silence for a moment until Secretary Barry jumped in. "Yes, well, why don't we all sit down and get comfortable. I think we would all like to hear a little more about your history if that's possible."

"It is, sir, but first, there is something that must be attended to," the Gil-Gamesh interrupted. "I would like an apology from General Garasimov." Everyone was stunned by the sudden request, except for the four from Avalon.

"An apology? For what may I ask?" General Garasimov said, his thick, Russian accent slurring his words together.

"You ordered your *Spetsnaz* to invade my home, sir, that is an affront not only to me but to all of the people of Avalon," he announced. "Before any negotiations can begin, I demand an apology from you."

"I don't know what you're talking about. I gave no such orders to—"

"Don't lie to me, General!" Bryan interrupted, his voice growing loud and demanding. "My magic's revealed everything to me. I saw you briefing those men before they left on their mission.

"I will only ask this one more time and then we are leaving. You invaded my home without cause or reason and I demand an apology, General!"

Silently, they waited while Garasimov squirmed in his boots. The General took a deep breath then finally relented. "I apologise to you and your people, Lord MoonDrake," he choked out. "We never meant any hostility toward you. Please accept my humble apology."

Bryan stood there for a moment, letting the General sweat it out just a little bit longer until he finally extended his hand to him. The General straightened up and took his hand wholeheartedly. "Thank you, General," Bryan acquiesced. "Your men have been turned over to Captain Rich along with the other guests of Avalon. I assure you, no harm came to them."

"*Spasibo*, Gil-Gamesh," the General said with another bow of his head. Everyone took a deep breath and sat down on the sofa and chairs. While Lord MoonDrake, Ocwyn and Pombur were seated, Eileanora stood behind them, defensively, keeping a watchful eye on everyone.

Ocwyn began by regaling the long history of Avalon, from the death of King Arthur to present day. He included some detailed history of the first Outlanders arrival on Avalon as well to try to explain the 'Bermuda Triangle' phenomenon. Pombur added in some colourful history of the Dwarves, from the first Dwarf Lord Dvallin to Master Dinius. Everyone got quite the education that afternoon as they soon came to realise that all the stories of myth and legend were true.

Curiously, Eileanora remained quiet through the entire dissertation. "Lady Eileanora, could you please tell us a little about your people's history?" Secretary Barry asked. She just stared at him with a blank expression, no emotion whatsoever.

"If I were to try and tell you even a tenth of the history of the High Elves of Alfheimer, it would take me half the night to do so," Eileanora exclaimed.

Most of them were left dumbfounded by her statement. "I'm sorry, but I don't understand?" Barry inquired.

"How old do you think I am?" she asked coyly.

Secretary Barry shrugged his shoulders, trying to guess her age. "Oh, I don't know, 30 years old, maybe?" Eileanora scoffed at him while Bryan and the others laughed under their breath.

"I am 2,394 years old," she said. General Garasimov spat out his coffee.

"That's impossible. How?" Barry asked.

"Elves are beings of pure magic," Bryan tried to explain. "They don't age like the rest of us. The same for Dwarves, though not as long-lived as the Elves. Pombur here is a young 487, am I right, Pombur?"

"You are indeed correct, milord. I turn 488 next month," he pronounced. "We Dwarves have an average lifespan of about 600 years. If we're lucky that is."

"And what about humans," Prince George interjected. "What is the average age of a human on Avalon?"

"Humans have been known to live between 130–170 years of age, depending on their profession, location and level of activity," Ocwyn explained.

"But how is this *le possible*?" Admiral Charbonne inquired.

"As we've said, magic," the Gil-Gamesh said. "All the magic in the world was brought to Avalon. The longer you live on Avalon, the more magic your body soaks up. It makes us live longer and feel more energised. People don't die of disease or sickness on Avalon, our magics have seen to that. People die from goblin raids or troll-hunting parties or whatever dark creature gets loose on the population."

"So, can everyone on Avalon use magic?" Secretary Barry asked.

"In some form or another," Ocwyn explained. "Most people can do every day simple things like lighting a candle or moving small objects, but only adepts of the arcane arts can wield true magic."

"May we see an example of this?" General Garasimov asked. The Gil-Gamesh looked over to Ocwyn who nodded his head in approval. Bryan reached into his coat pocket until he pulled out a small lump of charcoal.

He held it out in the palm of his hand, then crushed it into dust. "*Tenebris!*" he yelled. The dust began to swirl until it shot out in every direction, covering the room in complete darkness. Not even the electric lights could illuminate through the pitch-black fog that enveloped everyone. It was like being in the deepest, darkest cave without a candle or torch.

The others were impressed and a little frightened by the darkness. They couldn't see their hands in front of their face. "*Luminarium!*" the Gil-Gamesh yelled and four glowing lights appeared from a small gemstone in his open hand before they began to dance around the room. The lights spun faster and faster until the darkness was completely dissipated. They disappeared as the Gil-Gamesh closed his hand around the gem.

"That was *incroyable!*" exclaimed Admiral Charbonne. "*Un écran magnifique, Seigneur* MoonDrake!"

Bryan nodded his head, acknowledging the compliment, as he put the gemstone back in his coat. Secretary Barry saw this as an opportunity to find out more about their magic elixirs. "These magic's you speak of, does that include potions, like the one you gave to our female flight crewman who broke her leg?"

Bryan didn't like where the question was going but decided to follow along anyway to see where it leads. "It does, why do you ask?"

"Ensign Longwood was previously diagnosed with ovarian cancer, one that had to be surgically removed," Captain Rich chimed in. "Your potion not only healed her broken leg, but it also regenerated her organs and destroyed any traces of cancer in her body."

Bryan and the others were taken aback by this revelation. He looked over to Ocwyn who was pondering over what he just heard. "It's not supposed to do that," Bryan asserted. "Our healing elixirs mend broken bones and heal wounds; they do not regenerate limbs or organs."

"Unless," Ocwyn interjected, "unless the complete absence of magic in her system caused the magic of the potion to have a concentrated effect, wholly healing her body. That is something we never expected."

"Perhaps if we had a sample of your healing elixir, we could try to replicate it using our modern technology," Barry asserted. "It could save a lot of lives."

"It doesn't matter if you could replicate the potion, Mr Secretary, it still wouldn't work outside of Avalon," Bryan exclaimed.

"Oh, and why not?"

"Alchemy is much more than a simple science," Bryan said. "Alchemy combines science and magic. Our best alchemists take months, sometimes years, to perfect their formulas using both chemistry and magic. You can't duplicate that outside of Avalon."

"Also, some of the plants and herbs are found only on Avalon," Ocwyn interjected. "You would not be able to find anything like them in the outside world."

"Even more reason for us to come to a mutual understanding so we can begin to share between our two worlds," Secretary Barry stated quite diplomatically.

"I'm sorry, Mr Secretary, but that's not possible," Bryan stated. "Our presence here is causing more harm than good."

"That's not true," Captain Rich chimed in. "My meteorological officer tells me that we have already seen a dramatic improvement in global weather patterns, all thanks to your return to the world."

"That may be, Captain, but it's had quite to opposite effect on ours," the Gil-Gamesh said. "It's affecting everything from winds patterns in our shipping lanes to the fishing off our shores. The sooner we leave, the better."

Everyone in the room was thoroughly confused. "Excuse me?" Barry exclaimed.

"As we speak, our Wizard's Council is endeavouring to find a way restore the barrier and return our home from whence we came, hidden from the outside world," Ocwyn explained.

"But why?" Barry pleaded. "We both have so much to offer each other, so much to learn. You have healing practices that could help thousands currently suffering from diseases and other maladies, and you've missed out on thousands of years of technological advances. Think of the benefits for your people from our modern conveniences."

"We have benefited quite well without your technological advances," Eileanora interjected. "All your machines have done is make humans lazy and weak."

"I think what the Lady Eileanora is trying to say is, we have a simpler way of life on Avalon," Ocwyn said to ease the tension. "We do not require the 'machinations' of your world, as it were, beyond those we already use."

"Simply put, Mr Secretary, your technology has no place on Avalon," the Gil-Gamesh affirmed.

"Then why are we having these negotiations if not for the establishment of relations between your world and ours?" Barry postulated, his voice growing tense with anger.

"That was never our intention," Bryan said. "All we wanted to do was to make you aware of who and what we were, so you would understand the dire urgency of the situation and why it is necessary to keep people away from Avalon."

"Do you know how much it costs to keep ships and their crews out here 24/7?"

"If it's compensation you want, I'm sure we can come to an arrangement," Pombur interjected. "The Dwarves of the Gilded Halls of Avalon would gladly make payment in gold or jewels, whatever you require."

"I think perhaps that's a discussion for another time, Chancellor Pombur," Prince George asserted. "I still don't understand why you have to leave our world again. It would be wonderful to have magic a part of our world again, wouldn't it?"

"You have to understand, Your Highness, that magic is contained on Avalon, all magic in its various forms," Ocwyn delicately explained. "If it were to leave Avalon and spread across the world, we would be putting the entire planet in danger."

"I'm sorry, I don't follow you," Secretary Barry said.

"Magic, like everything else in life, has two sides, a light and a dark," Bryan explained. "There are many evils and dark powers associated with dark magic. It's contained on Avalon and 'policed' by myself and the Knights of the Round Table. We keep the darkness in check. It's hard enough to maintain order on an island the size of Avalon; think how hard it would be to do that across the entire planet."

The room fell eerily silent as everyone contemplated just to that.

"Plus, we would lose our way of life, something the people of Avalon would never accept," Ocwyn said. "No, it is better that we return from whence we came, back into the myths and legends of old."

"I doubt that people will ever forget your island and its appearance in our world," Captain Rich said. "You can't just go away and think people will just forget what happened."

"Perhaps," said General Garasimov, "there is something they don't want us to see on Avalon. Perhaps Avalon has its own secrets."

The general's tone infuriated the Gil-Gamesh, but remained calm. "Is that why you sent an assault team of armed soldiers to invade my home General? To spy on us? Or was it to set us up for an attack?"

General Garasimov jumped to his feet, his fists clenched, his face fuming. "How dare you? After I apologised to you, you have the audacity of accusing my country of what amounts to guerrilla warfare!"

Bryan got up and stood toe-to-toe with the General. "Well, if you weren't plotting an attack, then why the hell were your men carrying a laser-guided targeting system?" Everyone's eyebrows raised slightly, and Bryan realised he had said too much.

Ocwyn reached out and touched the Gil-Gamesh on the hand. "I think it is best that we return to Avalon. I think we all have a lot to dwell on before our next meeting."

As the four turned to leave, Captain Rich stepped forward.

"It's you, Bryan," he said plainly. "Chief Bryan Drake, it's you, isn't it?"

The Gil-Gamesh said nothing, as he turned and looked at Captain Rich with a straight face. "My name is Lord Bryan MoonDrake, Gil-Gamesh of Avalon."

"Right. And 'Lord MoonDrake' just happened to recognise a laser-guided targeting system. No, you are Chief Aviation Boatswain's Mate Bryan Drake, United States Navy. I know it's you, Bryan."

The Gil-Gamesh just continued to look at the Captain with a blank expression on his face. He cursed himself internally for letting his temper get the best of him. He made sure to show no emotion and continued to stare.

"Chief Bryan Drake died at sea, Captain Rich," the Gil-Gamesh said. "You won't find him anywhere on Avalon." He took a deep breath. "*Migro-transit Emmyr!*" he chanted and the four disappeared in the same energy vortex they appeared in earlier on the flight deck. Captain Rich and the others were left dumbfounded by the revelations. Most of them were confused, but Rich and Secretary Barry knew the truth about the Gil-Gamesh now.

"So, what do we do now?" Rich asked Secretary Barry.

"I think we are going to have to take some more drastic measures," he sneered. "Tell me everything you know about his daughter."

Chapter 4
Evil from the Shadows

On Avalon, South Essex was known as a city of artisans. The finest craftsman could be found in South Essex of all mediums—wood, metalwork or canvas—as well as exceptional tailors, tinkers and tradesmen. It was a town full of the finest shops you could ever find, outside of New Camelot.

In South Essex, the *Black Swan* was one of the most reputable taverns, with the best food, wine and spirits in the city. But even the best places can attract unsavoury characters.

Inside, the tavern was brightly lit with the glow of candlelight and roaring fires. The rooms were decorated in the finest silk drapes and tapestries of red and black. The décor lived up to the name, with as swans could be seen represented in various shapes and sizes from statues to wall sconces.

While the rest of the tavern was crowded, as usual, the back of the room was empty, save for one guest. The owner arranged this at the request of the guest, but also, so the other patrons wouldn't be subjected to his company.

He sat alone with his back to the wall, gorging himself on rare roasted beef and bottles of 500-year-old Aldinian Whiskey. He appreciated spirits, especially rare ones, and he always came to the *Black Swan* whenever he was in town because they carried the best.

His name was Abdel Ben Faust, a mercenary by trade and considered by most as the finest swordsman on Avalon. His skin was reddish-brown. His long, black hair was pulled back tightly in a ponytail, exposing his pointed ears and long face. A scar ran from his left temple, across his nose and down his right cheek—a reminder of being cut from his mother's womb. His moustache was long and thin, hanging down below his chin, which was where his true heritage showed through.

From there grew horns that resembled a goatee, twisted like braided hair. Abdel Ben Faust was a half-demon, the son of a witch and an Incubus, conceived during a blood moon in a magical ritual. His mother died while giving birth to him. He had to be cut from her womb by the same clerics that killed his demon father.

Faust was raised a slave, tormented regularly for his demonic form, but in his torment, grew strength and resolve. He moulded himself from slave to mercenary warrior, becoming a master swordsman available to the highest bidder.

He had avoided conflict with the Gil-Gamesh since his return to Avalon thanks to an innate ability from his demonic lineage. Faust could conjure 'demon holes' to move from place-to-place, unseen. Demon holes were doorways of black smoke, fire and brimstone. Only binding him in iron prevented him from using his power.

Faust came to South Essex to indulge his tastes while the Gil-Gamesh and the rest of the Knights of the Round Table moved to the coast to protect Avalon from the Outlanders. He knew there would be no trouble, coming to the *Black Swan* and drinking his fill, before moving on to his next job.

The curtain to the back room was pulled aside as young Finnick Devereaux, son of the Earl of South Essex, stepped in. The young man was nearly 50, young for a noble of Avalon. His dirty, blonde hair, dashing good looks and fine clothes endeared his upright lineage. He pulled a handkerchief from his inside pocket and waved it in front of his face, as he tried to dispel the stench coming from Faust.

"He is here, milord, just as I said," Finnick said to someone behind the curtain. A robed, hooded figure stepped through, walking right past the young noble.

"Good. Leave us, Finnick, and make sure we are not disturbed," the hooded figure said.

"Are you sure you want to do this, milord?" Finnick asked. "The last man who interrupted Abdel Ben Faust while he was eating had his head chopped off and tossed into a stew pot."

"Not worry, I've come bearing gifts," said the stranger, as he pulled a bottle from out of robe pocket. Finnick bowed and left the room, closing the drapes behind him.

The stranger walked up to Abdel's table but stopped when the half-demon drew his sword and chugged down the last of the whiskey, resting his blade across the table. It was a broadsword, nearly four feet long, with a jagged edge etched along the top edge of the blade. Wisps of smoke curled from the sword, as if it were burning, and the runes etched deep into the blade glowed softly. This was *Deathsong*, a cursed blade that only Abdel Ben Faust could wield, and he did so very well.

"I'd think twice before sitting down," Faust warned, as he finished his drink. The stranger just placed the bottle down in front of him. Faust dropped his own bottle to examine the gift.

"Can it be?" he exclaimed. "*Panaque*, distilled from the vines of the dryads of Meliai, over 4,000 years old!" He popped the cork and smelled the delicate bouquet of the fine spirit. He looked up at the stranger and nodded his head to the chair in front of him. The hooded figure sat down as Faust sheathed his sword and poured himself a drink.

"So, to what do I owe this honour and whom do I have to kill to keep this bottle?" he asked, as he took a sip of the delicious liquid.

"The bottle is yours, Abdel Ben Faust, a gift for listening to what I have to say," he began. "But first, I have a question for you. Last year, when Morgana le Fay was resurrected, why were you not part of her forces at the Battle of Idlehorn Mountain? Surely a swordsman of your calibre could have turned the tide in her favour."

Faust was insulted by the stranger's accusation but let it pass. "Her cause was lost from the moment she began," he scoffed, as he took another sip.

The hooded man seemed irritated by his answer but just sat back and listened. "Go on."

"She let the Gil-Gamesh live," he said. "You don't give someone like the Gil-Gamesh any glimmer of hope. She should have killed him when she had the chance. That's always been the problem with despots like Kraven Darkholm and Morgana le Fay. They want that power, but they want to gloat about it in the process. That's what got them killed.

"I don't side with losing causes," he concluded, as he downed the last of his drink. "I've answered your question, now you answer mine. What do you want?"

"I want you to lead an army to take Avalon out of the grips of the Pendragons and the Gil-Gamesh," the stranger said without skipping a beat.

Faust just laughed under his breath. "Well, if you wait long enough, the damn Outlanders with all their technological weapons will do it for you."

"Oh, I doubt that," the stranger impugned. "If the Gil-Gamesh is as resourceful as you say, then all I should do is wait until he restores Avalon as it was before, hidden from the outside world. Then, we tear Avalon apart, taking the throne and killing him in the process."

Faust was not convinced by the hooded stranger's plan. He laughed again, as he poured himself another drink. "Well, in the first place, you'd need an army at least 10,000 strong," Faust calculated. "Hell, the goblins don't even have half that number anymore, and the trolls are all whipped lackeys for that shield maiden now. So where is this army you speak of?"

The stranger reached into his robe and pulled out a ruby amulet, still glowing from the strong magic he had imbued within it. Faust barely glanced at it, "What's that supposed to be?" he asked.

"The key to controlling the most powerful army in creation, the Wraith Legion of Purgatory!" Abdel Ben Faust was stunned, aghast at the stranger's claim. The Wraith Legion was an army of fallen knights, trapped in purgatory because of some dishonour or shame that fell upon them in life. They served a penance, keeping the demons of the underworld in check until they earned their place in Heaven.

Faust rolled his eyes. "No one can control the Wraith Legion. It's impossible."

"You can with this," the stranger said, dangling the amulet. "With this amulet, they will follow your every command. You will be their General, Abdel Ben Faust, and you will conquer Avalon for me. In return, I will give you the Twin Swords of the Dragon Knight as payment, for your collection."

It was well known that Abdel Ben Faust had, over time, collected the weapon of every knight, warrior and monster he bested in battle. He kept his collection hidden from prying eyes. He liked to savour every victory by looking at the weapons of his fallen enemies hanging on the walls of his vault. The swords of the Gil-Gamesh would be the centrepiece of his collection.

The stranger had intrigued Faust with his offerings but wasn't convinced completely just yet. He needed to know something more. "Who are you?" the half-demon asked.

The hooded figure stood up and peeled back his hood. Faust recognised the face almost immediately. "You? You've been dead for centuries, millennia even! It can't be!"

The stranger pulled the hood over his head and sat back down. "I assure you, it is me, Abdel Ben Faust. I have many machinations at work, but I need a general to lead my army. You are the one man I can entrust with this task because I know that you will only accept my offer if you believe it can succeed.

"So, will you join me?" he asked. Faust sat there, stroking his chin in contemplation. After a few moments, he raised his glass.

"When do we get started?"

***

At the Dragon's Veil, the Gil-Gamesh sat with his head between his hands, overwhelmed with guilt over his outburst at the negotiations. He let his anger get the best of him and, for that, he may have lost hope of securing peace for Avalon.

Ocwyn and Pombur sat across from him as Mrs Thurgoode poured them both some wine. Eileanora just paced quietly behind them, shaking her head in disbelief. "I do not understand why you are so upset, milord," she started. "You stood your ground against the Outlanders unreasonable demands."

"Which is why you're a better warrior than a diplomat, Eileanora," Ocwyn chirped. "The Gil-Gamesh may have stood up to them, but he made an incalculable error in revealing his identity."

"It was bound to happen sooner or later, Chamberlain Ocwyn," Pombur interjected before drinking down his entire goblet of wine. He held out his empty goblet to Mrs Thurgoode, who brought him more. "We should explore the possibility of using this to our advantage."

"Were you even in the same room as the rest of us?" Ocwyn asked angrily. "We have no advantage against the Outlanders. Their weapons have us outgunned and outmatched."

"Yes, but if the barrier remains intact, they can't use their weapons against us," Eileanora said. The arguments went on until the Gil-Gamesh's patience wore out.

"Enough!" he shouted, standing up and yelling at them like a teacher scolding their students. "This was my mistake. I take full responsibility for what happened today. There's nothing more we can do right now."

Lady Stephanie entered the room with an entourage following close behind her, including Chancellor Beauchamp, Captain McLoughlin and her daughter, Rose. Bryan paused for a minute to look at his wife and knew something was wrong.

"Ocwyn," Bryan said, "I suggest you and Pombur leave in the morning. You can inform the King and the other Lords in person back in New Camelot."

The two men were stunned by the Gil-Gamesh's assertion that they should abandon the negotiations. "But, milord, shouldn't we present a counter to their demands?" Ocwyn queried. "I know that the first round didn't go as well as we would have liked it, but that doesn't mean we should just abandon all hope of coming to terms with the Outlanders."

Bryan sighed, as he shook his head. "Ocwyn, there will be no more negotiations. My friend, I think you greatly underestimate their resolve in this," Bryan said. "They want something we told them wouldn't work for them and they couldn't have, and yet, they still insisted on having it…our healing elixirs!

"Our magic works miracles on them and they want to make sure everyone in the world can benefit from it," he continued. "But that's not what'll happen. Once they discover that they can't replicate our elixirs, they will give out what they want to the highest bidder, ensuring that only rich, the powerful and the corrupt can take advantage of its magic, not everyday people.

"And then, ultimately, Avalon will no longer be an enchanted isle. It'll become an attraction, a novelty like *Disneyland*. People will come here for the chance to ride a dragon, pet a centaur or take magic lessons from a real honest-to-goodness wizard. We'll become a sideshow for the masses."

"Milord, I think you are exaggerating," Pombur said. "We would never allow that to happen, no one would."

"We won't have any choice!" the Gil-Gamesh shouted, startling everyone with his outburst. "You don't get it, do you? If the last barrier fails, nothing will prevent the Outlanders from coming to our shores and we will have no choice but to acquiesce to their demands."

"Bryan, how do you know all this?" Stephanie asked.

Lord MoonDrake sighed and took a deep breath before he looked at his wife. "Because, I saw it. I saw it all through the dragon sight once I shook hands with the Secretary of State. That's our future if we don't restore the barrier."

The room was silent at his revelations. Everyone was left dumbfounded until Lady Stephanie finally spoke up. "No, I refuse to accept that," she stated. "You once told me that fate had no control over our lives, even after we arrived on Avalon, that we exacted our own destiny. I refuse to believe that everything we have built here was all for naught."

"Steph, it's just not that simple," Bryan said.

"Yes, it is, Bryan. We have to stop trying to negotiate with these people and focus our efforts on restoring the barrier," she said, as she grabbed him by the face, forcing him to look at her. "We have some of the smartest minds in all of Avalon here in this room. If anyone can fix this, we can."

Bryan's heart leaped at the enthusiasm and confidence displayed by his wife. It was moments like this that made him appreciate her more and more; it's probably why he married her. He kissed and hugged her for bringing him out of his funk.

"Gil-Gamesh, do yourself a favour and don't lose this woman," Pombur jested. "Because if you don't, I just might ask her to marry me!" Everyone laughed at the old dwarf's joke, breaking the tension in the room.

"All right, Bryan, Pombur and I will leave for New Camelot in the morning. Then, I'll put a fire under those lazy bastards at Strongürd Keep," Ocwyn assured him. "In the meantime, I suggest you keep an eye on the Outlanders and make sure they stay right where they are."

"I will stay with the Gil-Gamesh, Chamberlain Ocwyn, and help him with the defence of Avalon," Eileanora interjected. Bryan bowed his head in appreciation.

"We have two more ships coming to Emmyr with an additional 500 men by the end of the week, Gil-Gamesh," Henri piped in. "Captain McLoughlin and I have already made the necessary arrangements for their *arrivée, n'est-ce pas?*"

"They're from Sir Cedric, milord, with his compliments," Rhona added. "They're volunteers from New Camelot. We'll have them ready to fight soon enough."

"You see, Daddy? You have all the help you need. There's nothing to worry about," Rose said, as she latched onto her father's arm.

Bryan kissed his daughter on the forehead, as she rested her head against his arm. He appreciated everyone's efforts; he hoped this was a step in the right direction, but the images from his dragon sight still bothered him. He knew it wasn't going to be that easy. Sacrifices must be made.

***

Merlin's library was a maze of stacks upon stacks of books. Ashley normally loved getting lost in here. When she wasn't teaching the special education students at her hometown middle school or spending time with Andrew, she loved to climb through the towering bookcases. She's learned more about the Middle Ages in this past year than she did in four years of college.

But this puzzle was really testing her patience. With the barrier gone, they needed a powerful spell or incantation to restore Avalon from whence it came. There were tons of references to Merlin's original spell, but nothing concrete, and he was no help either.

The great wizard of Avalon sat in his overstuffed easy chair, puffing on his pipe as he racked his brain. A shadow of his former self, the thousands of years spent inside here has diminished his mind and memory.

Ashley languished in her own frustration but forgot all about it when she looked down at the old man. He fidgeted in his chair, angry at feeling helpless for the first time in his storied life. Ashley couldn't help but feel sorry for him. She climbed down the spiral staircase and sat down across from him. She let out a big sigh, flopped her head back and propped her feet up.

"There was nothing in the books of Jannes and Jombres," Ashley lamented. "I don't know, Merlin. I feel like we're missing something and its right in front of our face."

Merlin said nothing. He continued to puff on his pipe in rapid succession as if he was hyperventilating on the sweet smoke. Ashley looked over at the wizard, concerned more for his sanity than his health.

"Merlin, are you all right? Merlin? Yoo-hoo, Earth to Merlin!"

"I'm sorry, my dear, did you look through the works of Jannes and Jombres? There may be something there. They were the sorcerers that challenged Moses and Aaron in the court of the Pharaoh Ramses. They—"

"Merlin! I just told you I looked through there and didn't find anything."

Merlin didn't reply. He just sat back in his chair, distressed and dejected. "Merlin, what's the matter?" she asked.

"What's the matter? Everything's the matter!" he exclaimed. "I spent my entire life protecting and preserving magic to Avalon and it could very well be destroyed, right before my eyes, and there's nothing I can do about it."

"Merlin, my dad didn't know that Tiamat would take away your spell like she did, you can't blame him for that."

"Oh no, of course I don't, my dear. It's not that," Merlin explained. "For centuries, people came to me for my wisdom and guidance to protect Avalon. Now, when I'm needed the most, I feel completely worthless…impudent as a senile, old man."

Ashley got up out of her chair and knelt next to him, placing her hand on his. "Merlin, you are far from impudent or senile. I can barely remember what I ate for dinner last week. You have over 3,000 years of knowledge to reflect on and yet, you can still recite for me the exact words you said to King Arthur when he pulled the sword from the stone.

"I know you won't let Avalon down, not without a fight," she concluded. Merlin smiled and patted her hands, grateful for her encouraging words. He rose to his feet, placed his hands behind his back and faced the young woman.

"Ashley, I would like to ask a favour of you."

"Of course, Merlin, anything."

"I want you to become my apprentice," he asked. Ashley was taken aback by his offer.

"What, me?"

"Ashley, I have lived a long life, half of it spent here, alone except for a new apprentice once every hundred years or so, but I've grown tired. There're spells in here dating back to Methuselah, the very first wizard. I think it's time I pass that knowledge on one last time."

"But why me, Merlin?" she questioned. "I'm nobody special. I have no magical talent whatsoever."

"That's not true and you know it. You held up, on your own, against the will of Morgana le Fay, and that's no easy feat. In the time we've spent together, I witnessed in you a strong, capable mind. I want to pass onto you all my knowledge, all my skill and all my wisdom. I think I've earned my place in paradise," he continued, "and I want to pass on knowing that my legacy is in good hands. I can't imagine better hands than yours, my dear."

Ashley was stunned and flattered that Merlin thought her worthy of this honour, but she didn't share his confidence in her. Plus, she didn't know how she could study under Merlin and stay in the outside world. Then it hits her, something Merlin said.

"Wait a minute, did you say Methuselah?" she asked.

"Hmm? Oh yes, well you see, Methuselah was the first one to discover the magic in our world and how to weave it into spells."

"That's it, Merlin!" Ashley exclaimed. "Could one of Methuselah's original spells could be powerful enough to restore the barrier?"

The old wizard scratched his head for a minute until he realised what Ashley was telling him. "Ashley, you're brilliant. Brilliant, I say!" he yelled. "There should be some of Methuselah's original spells in here. I acquired them from Baba Yaga, a witch from the steppes of Russia; a positively dreadful woman. I won them in a game of Mancala."

"Well, come on then," Ashley said with a new enthusiasm, but before she even reached the steps, music started playing throughout the library. It was loud, obnoxious, head-banger music, something Ashley hated.

"What on Earth is that horrible racket?" Merlin shouted, covering his ears to drown out the noise.

"It's Andy," Ashley explained. They saw it in a movie and thought it might work to get her attention in case of an emergency. "Merlin, I'll be back in a little bit to help you look for Methuselah's spells. Do me a favour and keep an eye on things for me. If this is something serious, please let my dad know what's going on."

The old wizard nodded his head in agreement. Ashley gave him a peck on the forehead before she closed her eyes. When she opened them again, she was back in the cabin with Andrew. She was wearing headphones plugged into his iPhone, playing that loud music.

She pulled them off and shook her head, trying to clear the cobwebs. Transitioning from Merlin's library back to her body was taxing, but she was slowly getting used to it. She looked up to see her husband, Andrew St Johns, as he stared out the door through the tiny window. His eyes shifted from side-to-side as he tried to see as much as he could without being seen.

"What is it, Andy? What's wrong?" she asked, her voice wavering with concern.

"I went down to Ebner's Market to pick up a few things while you were off in Merlin's library," he explained. "There was a black SUV with a government license plate parked out front, so I got a little concerned. I went next door to Toby's Restaurant and talked to Jordan. He said they were passing around photos of us, asking if anyone had seen us recently. Jordan tried to throw them off, said we hadn't been up since last spring, but I don't think it worked."

"Well, who are they and what do they want?"

"I don't know, and I don't care to find out. We need to get out of here Ash, and fast before they discover where we are!" he exclaimed, as he grabbed her by the elbow. "You go throw everything in the suitcase while I hang the shutters."

"Do you have time for that?" she asked.

"I'm not going to leave my grandfather's cabin open for some hippie hitchhikers to come along and camp out in it," he crowed. "Now come on, we haven't got much time."

As Andy reached for the front door handle, he quickly opened the door and darted outside, but he was stopped in his tracks looking down the barrel of an automatic weapon. Andy looked up at the man pointing the gun, who stared back from behind his sunglasses.

"Federal agents, put your hands up!" he ordered. "Get down on the ground, now!"

Andy dropped down to his knees, keeping his hands above his head as two other armed assailants entered the room. The three men were dressed similarly, in black pants and leather jackets with dark sunglasses. They quickly searched the cabin, forcing Ashley out from the bedroom.

"You, too! On the ground!" one of the agents barked, shoving her down next to Andy. "Hands behind your head, both of you!"

The two of them placed their hands behind their heads as ordered. Ashley seemed more afraid of them than Andrew, who was mostly furious. "You want to tell what we're being charged with or show me a warrant because otherwise we've got nothing to say and I want to call my lawyer."

"Shut up, asshole!" one agent said, as he punched Andy in the stomach, causing him to double over in pain, wheezing as he tried to catch his breath. He clutched his side, fearing he may have cracked a rib.

"Andy!" Ashley cried, as she reached out to help her husband.

"Knock it off J.J., we're supposed to detain them, not hurt them!" the team leader ordered. "Search them, then sit them up on the sofa."

J.J. grunted in agreement and helped the leader do exactly that. The leader brought in a chair from the dining room and turned it around in front of them and sat down with his arms folded across the back.

"Mr and Mrs St Johns, my name is Special Agent Foster." He took out his ID and badge from the Central Intelligence Agency and flashed it at them before tucking it away. "I have been ordered to find and detain you. Do exactly what my men and I tell you and everything will be fine. Do anything stupid and, well, you've seen what happens when J.J. here gets angry."

"What the hell does the CIA want with us?" Andy demanded. "You can't assault me and hold us here against our will without cause, this is illegal and a load of—" Andy was interrupted, as J.J. pummelled him across the face, knocking him down into Ashley. Ashley helped Andy up, caressing his face and making sure he was all right.

"I told you not to do anything stupid," Foster said. "Any other questions?"

"Yeah, do you have health insurance?" Ashley asked, as her anger boiled up inside.

Agent Foster smirked at her weird question, glancing over at his other men. They all laughed. "Yeah, I do...why?" he asked.

"Because when my dad gets here, he's going to kick your ass!"

"I thought your father was dead?" Foster snapped back. "Is there something you're not telling us, sweetheart?"

Ashely was dumbfounded. These men knew a lot more than they were letting on. She just bit her lip and tended to Andy.

"Harry, check in and let them know we found them," Foster ordered. The other agent put away his firearm and pulled out his cell phone, moving it around the room, looking for a signal.

"There's no reception here," he said. "I'll have to go down to the hotel and make the call."

"Well, make it snappy, and pick us up something to eat while you're at it. We're going to be here a while," Foster shouted. Harry left the cabin.

"So, got anything good to watch?" J.J. joked.

"Go check the perimeter J.J., make sure no one else is around," Foster barked at him. J.J. reluctantly walked outside as ordered while Foster just sat back and kept his eyes on the two of them.

Hours passed, and night had fallen when Harry finally returned, carrying bags of fast food from the local restaurant. Foster and J.J. were quite irate with him as he walked in the door.

"What the hell took you so long? I'm starving!" J.J. cursed.

"Sorry, but this place is hard to get to, especially at night," Harry complained. "I'm from Brooklyn, man, I'm not used to these country roads, okay?"

"Forget it, what did they say?" Foster said.

"They said to sit tight and wait for further instructions, but check in every two hours," Harry explained. "We should hear something by tomorrow. Barry's supposed to talk to them again by then."

Ashley's ear piqued up when she heard them mention Secretary of State Barry. Her mother told her about the negotiations on the aircraft carrier, how they discovered her father's identity. He must be trying to get some leverage for the next time around.

"Can we please forget about it for now and eat already? I'm starving!" J.J. complained as he ransacked the bags for something to eat. Suddenly, there was a loud thump outside. The three agents immediately drew their weapons and moved over to the door. Foster peered out the tiny window and looked around, seeing nothing.

He nodded to J.J. and Harry as he reached for the door handle. The two men stood ready, weapons pointed at the door. Foster quickly opened the door as the two jumped out onto the front porch, checking both sides to see if anyone was there. They found nothing on the porch, and, to their surprise, nothing in the driveway as well.

"Where's the car?" Henry yelled. The car suddenly fell from the sky smashed into the ground upside down, collapsing the roof and spraying glass everywhere.

Before the three men could recover, Gamorg dropped down on top of the car, crushing the roof down under its massive weight. The dragon roared at the three agents as acidic drool oozed from its mouth. They started firing at it, but the bullets bounced off its thick hide. Gamorg inhaled before unleashing a blast of dragon fire right at them. They dove for cover behind the door as the fire incinerated the back of the cabin, starting a fire inside.

The Gil-Gamesh dove at the agents swinging *Twilight* at their weapons. The blade burned with the same dragon fire, cutting guns in half. He held *Twilight* at Foster's throat and *Dusk* at J.J.'s.

Fear gripped Harry as he quickly turned to run away, but he ran right into Eileanora, holding her sword to his face. "Take one more step and it will be your last!" she asserted. "Now drop your weapon!"

Before he could respond, Dee Dee, being ridden by Rose, landed on the ground behind the Elf assassin, quickly followed by another dragon. Harry dropped his gun and slowly raised his hands. Foster and J.J. glanced at each other before they looked over at the Gil-Gamesh.

"Do I need to ask, or do you want to discuss it with the two-ton dragon that's crushing your car?" he asked. Both men dropped the remains of their guns and raised their hands reluctantly as Bryan stepped back, keeping his swords raised.

"Ashley, are you and Andy all right?" he asked without taking his eyes off them.

"I am now, Daddy," Ashley replied, as she helped Andy move out the door, away from the fire. "But Andy's hurt. I think they might have broken some of his ribs."

Bryan quickly raised his swords back across their throats as his anger swelled back up inside. "You've got three seconds to tell me what you're doing here before I feed you to Gamorg!" he commanded.

"And I would answer quite quickly, especially since he hasn't eaten all day," Eileanora added. The three men looked over at the dragon, terrified as the gigantic beast bared its teeth, snarling at them.

"I heard them mention Secretary Barry," Ashley chimed in, as she helped Andy down the porch. "He said they had to sit on us until he talked to you tomorrow."

As Ashley and Andy reached the bottom of the steps, J.J. shoved Andy to the ground and grabbed Ashley around the head and pulled her tight against him. He whipped out a butterfly knife and placed it tight against her throat.

"Andy!" Rose shouted and tossed him a Lancer. Andy caught the weapon and aimed it right at J.J. The Lancer was a magical carbine rifle, of sorts, that

Andy helped Hunter design during the Morgana le Fay affair. The weapon fired spell shots—specialised alchemical mixtures that fired magical rounds at enemies. It resembled an over/under shotgun with a short blade above and below the barrels to help contain the magic until fired. He kept the weapon aimed at J.J., determined to protect his wife.

Eileanora pushed Harry and Foster back against the burning cabin, keeping her blade against both men. The last thing she wanted was either of them trying something like their companion. When the Gil-Gamesh saw Eileanora had the two under control, he turned his attention and his swords at J.J.

J.J. was breathing heavily, nervous but determined to get out of this alive. Ashley said nothing. She was scared but brave.

"If I see that monster make any move toward me, I'll cut her throat, I swear to God I will…" J.J. ranted on and on, making demands to be met before he'd let Ashley go. Ashley stared off, as if in a trance. Her eyes rolled back in her head and the world was gone. J.J.'s voice grew quieter and then silent altogether. After a moment, she opened her eyes, turned her head and lightly touched J.J. on the face.

"*Somno*," she whispered. J.J. dropped the knife and fell to the ground, fast asleep. Everyone was amazed at what Ashley just did, including the Gil-Gamesh. Ashley looked up to see everyone staring at her.

"Merlin's been teaching me a few things," she said nonchalantly, then ran past her father to Andy, worried about his broken ribs. Rose came over to help them both.

Lord MoonDrake knew he needed answers quickly, so he decided to try the direct approach. He grabbed Harry—the one Bryan thought was more intimidated—and dragged him over to Gamorg. He flipped him onto the undercarriage of the smashed vehicle, so he could stare up at the immense dragon.

Gamorg just looked down at the little man and continued to grimace at him. Harry had never been more frightened in all his life. "All right, all right, I'll answer anything you ask, just don't let him eat me, please!" he whimpered.

"What were your orders from Secretary Barry?"

"We were supposed to find the girl and her husband and sit on them until we heard back from him, that's all!" Harry cried.

"How did you know to look for them here?" Bryan asked.

"From the picture we were given!" Harry shouted, as he reached into his pocket. Bryan raised his sword and Gamorg growled at him. He pulled out a photograph and handed it to Bryan. He looked at it and felt his heart sink.

Ashley saw his face and came over to look. She gasped. It was a picture of her and Andy with Captain Larry Rich, outside Toby's Restaurant. Ashley remembered it was taken at the rehearsal dinner for her wedding, more than two years ago. As a close, family friend, Rich agreed to stand in for her father and walk Ashley down the aisle.

Bryan couldn't believe how the man he considered his mentor and friend betrayed him. He tucked the picture inside his pocket as he sheathed his swords.

He grabbed Harry and threw him effortlessly into Foster, causing both men to cry out in pain.

"Is Andy all right to travel?" he asked.

"He'll be all right, Father, I gave him a healing elixir," Rose said.

Bryan turned to Eileanora and held out his hand. "I need to borrow your chameleon stone."

The Elf looked shocked, unsure of how the Gil-Gamesh knew of her possession. She was quite unwilling to part with such powerful magic.

"I will return it to you when I get back to Emmyr," Bryan swore. "I would not deny you your most prized possession."

Eileanora nodded her head; she knew the Gil-Gamesh was a man of his word. She reached into a pouch on her belt and pulled out a small stone. It was pink and shimmered with a multi-coloured hue. She handed it to the Gil-Gamesh who immediately tucked it into his coat pocket.

"Ashley, you ride with Rose. Eileanora, you take Andy and head back to Emmyr. I'll meet you there," he ordered, as he climbed up on the crushed car and onto Gamorg's back.

"Where are you going, milord?" Eileanora inquired.

"To pay my respects to an old friend," he said stoically, as he spurred Gamorg to take flight.

Eileanora sheathed her sword and walked over to Andy, helping him up to his feet. "Are you better, Andrew?" she asked.

"Yeah, a lot better," he groaned as he grabbed his side. "I'll be all right."

"What about them?" Rose asked, motioning to the fallen agents.

"It's more than ten miles to the nearest town with any decent cell service," Andy said. "They won't be going anywhere tonight unless they want to get eaten by bears. Besides, they've got a nice fire to keep them warm." He watched as his family cabin slowly burned to the ground. "Sorry, grandpa."

"Good, we'll be back on Emmyr before they can contact the authorities," Eileanora affirmed. "Let's get going then."

"No, wait a minute," Ashley whined. "We can't go to Emmyr. Andy's got to get back to work soon and school's starting in a few weeks."

"Come on, Ash, you can't stay here anymore," Rose insisted. "They know who you are and will keep coming after you until they get Dad to give them what they want."

"She's right," Andy added. "They've given us no choice. We have to go to Avalon with them."

"But what's to stop them from going after your parents or my grandparents? We can't just leave them like this. They don't know anything about what really happened to us."

"Which is exactly what will protect them from your country's machinations," Eileanora asserted. "We have no time for arguments, Ashley. Your father will see to things, you must trust in that."

"I'm sorry, but I don't know who you are or why I should listen to you," Ashley snapped back at Eileanora. The Elven warrior stepped up and got right in Ashley's face.

"Your father placed his trust in me to get you back to Emmyr, so if I have to put you to sleep to get you on that dragon, believe me, I will!"

Ashley swallowed hard and quietly nodded her head before giving Andy a quick peck on the lips. She climbed up behind Rose. As Eileanora helped Andy up on the dragon's back, Ashley whispered to her sister. "Who is that woman?"

Rose laughed softly. "When I tell you, believe me, you'll be happy that you didn't mess with her."

***

The Gates of Purgatory were as foul as any of the myriad levels of the underworld. Bones littered the ground from countless battles between the demons and undead of the underworld trying to escape. Only the Wraith Legion stood between them and the world above.

The wraiths were fallen knights given penance to guard the gates for one thousand years to earn their place in paradise. They each wore an armoured shell of plate mail, and a ghostly visage of a skull hovered over it. It was a faceless reflection of their human life. Across their heart sat a fiery, red gem—a heart stone. The gem beat with the blood of the wraith; powerful magic imbuing life into the soulless creature.

Beyond the gates lies the Wretched Wasteland, a vast desert that separated the real world from Purgatory. The dark wastes burned from the fires of Hell below instead of the sun above. Anyone who made it past the wraiths usually found themselves lost in the dark recesses of the Wretched Wasteland.

Away from the watchful eyes of the wraiths, a demon hole opened above the Wasteland and from it dropped Abdel Ben Faust and Artūras Blackstone. Once through, the demon hole closed behind them as quickly as it opened. Faust was impressed with himself, as he scanned the terrain around him.

"I never knew I could use my demon holes to move between realms," he boasted. "The Master said it would work but I didn't believe him. For the first time in my life, I'm glad to say I was wrong."

"Don't doubt the Master," Blackstone retorted. "His wisdom is undeniable."

"I don't deny that. I just don't fawn over his every word like you do. Abdel Ben Faust worships no one and nothing."

"Except yourself." Artūras might have said more, but was cut off when Faust grabbed him by the throat. He gasped for air as the half demon's grip tightened.

"Let's make one thing clear, 'Black Sheep'. Mock me again and I'll rip your throat out. Understand?"

Blackstone nodded his head, anything to get Faust to release him. Abdel let go, leaving small cuts in his throat from his long nails. Artūras dropped to one knee, coughing for every gasp of air. He glared at Faust, thoughts of revenge filling his mind, but he curbed his anger. He believed in his master's plan for dominion over Avalon and Faust was an essential part of that. He would bide his time.

Faust turned his attention away from Blackstone and to the Gates of Purgatory. He looked around the gates for any signs of a guard, but none were to be found. "Where are the guards?" he asked. "Why would they leave the gates unguarded?"

"The guards are there to prevent something from getting out of Purgatory, not from getting in," Artūras explained. "They will not challenge us until we step in through the gates."

Faust smirked as he drew this sword; he liked the docile side of Blackstone. "Well then, let's go say hello!" he jested.

"Remember, you must best the Wraith General in battle to gain control of the Legion," Blackstone warned him.

"I know what to do," he answered. "I am more than capable of killing an undead knight."

"Were you not listening to the Master? The General of the Wraith Legion is no fallen knight. He is an angel, answerable only to God, who volunteered to lead the Wraiths and bring them to paradise."

Abdel turned to Blackstone and scowled. "He died once before, he can die again…" Faust asserted, as he twirled his sword in his hand, causing it to whistle in the wind, 'singing' its *Deathsong*.

He trotted through the gates, straight ahead into Purgatory. Artūras was cautious, looking all about as he followed close behind. The terrain was as barren as the Wretched Wasteland, strewn with rocks and ruins of ancient battlements, decimated by millennia of war. The sounds of sword and steel against claw and bone could be heard from the moment they stepped in through the gates.

Faust kept his head on a swivel as he stepped through Purgatory. His senses were quite keen, sharpened by years of battle. He stopped, positioning himself into a battle stance, anticipating an attack.

Out of nowhere, wraiths leaped at Faust and Blackstone. Faust pared their blows easily, as *Deathsong* cut through their armour like a hot knife through butter. The burning blade ruptured their heart stones, causing the wraiths extreme pain as their souls are ripped apart. The armour became an empty shell as the wraith's soul dissipated into nothing.

It was something very few had seen before. When a wraith died in Purgatory, their soul had nowhere to go, scattered like dust in the wind across eternity. Faust was not concerned with that; he was focused on the fight and relished more.

More wraiths appeared and surrounded them. They circled them, not moving against them but rather containing them. Faust was anxious, his blood boiling for more action. "What are they waiting for?" he growled.

"It's not what but who," Blackstone replied. "I think your actions may have piqued the interest of just who we're looking for."

The wraiths rank parted as the General of the Wraith Legion stepped through. He appeared larger than the others, but main difference was his wings, armoured and broad with blades of pulsating energy instead of feathers. He carried a huge claymore which glowed with the same energy as his wings.

His ghostly visage shone with an unnatural light, indicating his heavenly origins. The time spent in Purgatory reflected on his face, peeled back from time-to-time, showing the horrors of war. He stared down at Faust, and frowned.

"Abdel Ben Faust. What brings at murdering scum like you to Purgatory? Surely someone with your reputation earned himself a one-way ticket to Hell."

"Do I know you?" Faust asked.

"The heavenly host knows you quite well, half-demon," he asserted. "As for my name, you can call me Uriel. Now, what business do you and this sorcerer have in Purgatory?"

"I have need of your army, Uriel."

"Speak plainly, demon spawn, before I send you to Hell myself!" Uriel demanded.

"It's quite simple, I'm here to challenge you for command of the Wraith Legion," Faust provoked.

"Are you mad, Faust? No one can command the wraiths but by the command from God on high," Uriel announced. "Now leave this place before you become a permanent part of it!" The General of the Wraith Legion turned his back on Faust to leave.

Abdel was not only insulted but also irritated by him. He opened a demon hole and dropped through, landing in front of Uriel, his sword raised at him. "I didn't say you had a choice, Uriel!" Abdel screamed, as he thrust his sword at the angel. Uriel countered almost immediately with a shining sword of his own. It was a long, curved blade that glowed with pure starlight.

He pushed Faust back, throwing him to the ground. "You had your chance to leave, half-demon. Now you will die here with your demon brethren!" Uriel proclaimed. "Keep the wizard contained, I don't want him helping Faust!"

The wraiths surrounded Blackstone and levelled their weapons at him. Blackstone just stood there and watched the battle ensue, hoping that Faust knew what he was doing.

Steel clashed as the two warriors matched each other blow-for-blow. Faust tried a different tactic and opened a demon hole to get behind Uriel, but the wraith general anticipated this and countered with a vicious backhand just as Faust came through, sending him sprawling.

"Don't try your tired tricks on me, Faust," he said. "I've dealt with demon holes from millennia of battles with your brethren!"

"I am no ordinary demon!" Abdel screamed, as he struck back at Uriel. "I am Abdel Ben Faust, the greatest swordsman in Avalon, and I am more than a match for you, angel!"

Faust swung like a man possessed, lashing blow after blow against Uriel. The pace was too fast for the angel, so he slowed the battle by pushing back against Faust, locking swords together to overpower him.

Abdel saw this as an opening. He scraped the jagged edge of *Deathsong* down along the angel's sword, causing sparks to fly into his face. Uriel was momentarily distracted. Faust disappeared through a demon hole, and reappeared behind the angel almost instantly, then dismembered the angel's wings in two quick strokes.

Uriel screamed, as his wings dissipated into thin air as wisps of energy seep out of his wounds. Abdel stood behind the fallen angel as Uriel fell to his knees. Faust brought his sword across his neck, ready to deliver the final blow.

"Go ahead, take my life, but it will serve you not," Uriel choked out in pain. "Upon my death, I will ascend to paradise and a new general will take my place."

Faust smiled, as he leaned down to whisper in Uriel's ear. "Who said I was going to kill you?" He pulled the amulet from the Master and placed it over the wraith general's heartstone. "I don't mind telling you, this will hurt a lot!"

"*Liberate Animam Eius!*" he yelled and the amulet began to glow, slowly beating to life as faded from existence, screaming in terror until he disappeared completely. His heartstone stopped pulsing and the light inside faded as well. The armour dropped to the ground, an empty shell clanging against the rocks.

Faust took the amulet, now glowing with the power absorbed from the heartstone, and placed it over his own heart. The amulet beat to life as it bonded itself to the half-demon. It burned through his armour and fused to his skin. The smell of his own cooking flesh thick in his nostril. Faust gritted his teeth and smiled, relishing the pain his victory brought him.

The amulet sat where the heart stone does on the wraiths. It burned through his armour and attached to his skin, beating with the pulse of a heart stone, but inside the gem, you could see the torment of a trapped soul—the soul of an angel inside the heart of the scion of a demon.

Faust turned to the wraiths, their weapons pointed at him, but it didn't frighten him one bit. "I am Abdel Ben Faust, General of the Wraith Legion," he announced. "Kneel before your commander!"

One-by-one, the wraiths lowered their weapons and knelt before Faust. The half-demon smiled at the army now under his command. He reached down and picked up the sword of Uriel. It burned to the touch, attributed to his demon heritage touching an angelic weapon. Like the amulet, Faust relished in the pain as the price of victory. He had a new prize for his collection and an invincible army under his command.

He glanced over at Blackstone, who nodded his head in approval of Faust's victory, but the half-demon didn't care. All he cared about was the next fight, against the Gil-Gamesh, and he was going to win.

"The Twin Swords of the Dragon Knight are as good as mine!" he gloated, looking ahead to his next challenge, his next victory.

Chapter 5
A Prelude to War

Captain Rich moved down from the bridge with some urgency, clearing sailors out of his way as he made his way down the ladder wells. "Make a hole! Make a hole!"

He has spent more time away from the bridge than on it during this extended deployment, something he has really come to despise. Unfortunately, when you're hosting a dignitary like the Secretary of State, he had very little choice.

Barry had orders from the President to make one more attempt at negotiations. If he wasn't successful, the fleet was to back off and maintain the blockade while Barry returned to Washington, DC. In his entire diplomatic career, Barry never failed to deliver successful negotiations, and he wasn't about to start now.

Rich knew he crossed some ethical boundaries by providing information on Bryan's daughter and son-in-law to Barry, but it's very hard to say no to someone in his position of authority. As hard as that was for him to do, he was more upset that Bryan pulled this charade over him, hiding in plain sight behind his knightly persona. Much of this would have been easier if he had just been straightforward with him.

Rich knocked on the door to his inport cabin before entering. He spied the Secretary on the phone as he closed the door quietly behind him. Even from a distance, he could tell that something was wrong. After a few more 'uh-huhs', he hung up the phone.

"You wanted to see me, sir?" Rich stated, the impatience quite evident in his voice.

"Has anything come off that island lately?" the Secretary asked. "Anything at all?"

"Nothing within the past 24 hours, Mr Secretary," the Captain replied. "A few of those dragons fly out beyond their borders from time-to-time, but they always turn back. Why do you ask?"

"The men I sent to track down the Gil-Gamesh's daughter haven't checked back in like they were told," he explained. "I was wondering if there was any chance they might have gotten to them from Avalon."

"Let me check with CDC, sir, and see if there are any reports from the rest of the fleet," he answered, as he stepped over to a 'Squawk Box' on the wall next to his desk. It's a basic grey box with buttons connecting to various parts of the ship and a large microphone/speaker in the centre.

Captain Rich pushed the button marked 'CDC' and held down the talk lever. "CDC, this is the Captain, any reports of activity from Avalon during the past few hours?"

After a moment, the Tactical Action Officer or TAO responded back. "Three contacts were tracked returning to the floating island from the North-Northeast at 2147, sir!"

"North-Northeast? Why the hell wasn't I notified?" he screamed at the TAO.

"They were following a regular flight pattern we've been tracking for the past few weeks," the officer responded. "They track northwest and do a loop, following the shoreline until they return from the North-Northeast. It's been their routine for weeks, sir."

"Anything else 'routine' you care to report, Lieutenant?" the Captain snapped at the TAO. There was a long pause before he finally answered.

"Well, sir, one dragon just overflew us about five minutes ago. I was about to report it to you, but you had already left the bridge."

Before the Captain could respond, the door to his inport cabin opened and a young sailor stepped in, quickly closing the door behind him. Rich was confused and slightly irritated that the sailor dismissed all protocol, entering the Captain's cabin without knocking.

"Can I help you, sailor, or do you have a good reason for entering my cabin without permission?" The sailor said nothing to the captain. He locked his gaze on Secretary Barry. Without a word, the sailor leaped at Barry, knocking him over the back of the sofa and onto the floor, kneeling on his chest with his full weight.

He motioned and drew a sword, a golden burning blade, as his appearance changed from a young sailor to the Gil-Gamesh. Bryan kept his sword pointed at the secretary. Rich jumped in to stop him, but he anticipated that.

"*Repellere!*" he yelled, hurling Rich back against the wall, stunning him. Bryan returned his attention to Secretary Barry. The man stuttered as he tried to speak, but the fear was just so overwhelming.

"P-p-please, Lord MoonDrake, I didn't—"

"Shut up, you snivelling worm!" he cursed. "You think that kidnapping and assaulting my daughter and son-in-law would get you leverage against me?"

"I-I-I didn't mean to—"

"Oh, yes you did, coward. Who were they? CIA? Black bag operatives from your embassy days in Libya?"

Secretary Barry was shocked when Bryan rolled off his resume with ease. "Are you surprised, Mr Secretary?" Bryan asked. "Well, you shouldn't be. You can learn a lot about a man through magic and a single handshake. And you," he continued, as he stood up and walked over toward Captain Rich. "How could you betray the trust Stephanie and I placed upon you as Ashley's godfather?" he gritted angrily, as he reached into his waistcoat. "Did you get your thirty pieces of silver?"

Bryan tossed the photo he took from the agents at him. Rich regained his senses and jumped to his feet. "All of this could have been avoided if you had been up front with me, Bryan! You forced our hand!"

"By what? Lying to you about who I was?" he retorted. "I lied to protect my family because, deep down, I knew they would try something like this if they found out who I was."

"If you didn't trust me enough to tell me who you were, then why should we trust you in anything else regarding Avalon?" Rich snapped back at him.

"You want to know everything about Avalon?" he asked. "Fine, I'll show you everything. Then maybe you'll understand."

Bryan grasped the pendant hanging around his neck—a silver dragon with a single, amber coloured smooth gem coiled in its tail—resembling the coat of arms of the house of MoonDrake. It was a dragon stone, given to him by Nihala, the dragon queen, shortly after he arrived on Avalon.

He wrapped his hand around the stone and closed his eyes. *"Astral Visio,"* he said. Suddenly, the room around him began to change as images flowed by as if you were flying.

It started over Emmyr, soaring above the dragon isle, watching as the dragons fly in-and-out of their caves; while just below them, the city of Port Charles was a bustle of activity. Flying airships came in and out of the port as merchants moved cargo from one to the other as they are shipped out across Avalon.

The images swirled again as they were taken out across Avalon, over dense forests and flowing meadows. They come to a large village of centaurs, home of the Northern Tribe of Kéntauros. The sight of centaurs amazed both Rich and Barry, to see them interact with each other just as anyone else would. Children played while the parents worked hard; friends gathered to eat, drink and laugh. The normalcy of their lives surprised them.

The images changed again as the flight took them on a rolling tour across Avalon, from the beautiful city of Alfheimer, home to the Elves of Avalon, to towering Strongürd Keep, the bastion of knowledge of the Wizard's Council. They continued their journey from the dark recesses of Blackbriar Forest, where they saw goblins munching on a dead deer, to the sprawling city of New Camelot, the capital city of Avalon and seat of King Bowen Pendragon, ruler of the enchanted isle.

The two men were mesmerised by the beautiful images that flowed by them, from the wilds of Togo to the mines of the Gilded Halls and high atop the Fenris

Mountains. When their journey came to an end, the images faded. Bryan took a deep breath to regain his composure.

"That was amazing!" Secretary Barry exclaimed. "Why in the world wouldn't you want to share that with the outside world?"

"Because bringing the outside world to Avalon means an end to our life as we know it," Bryan asserted. "The longer we stay here, the more magic seeps out across the globe. Magic is the lifeblood of Avalon and its people. Without it, we lose everything we hold dear."

"Oh, come now, you don't know if that will happen."

"You seem to forget, Mr Secretary, that many on Avalon, including myself, have some precognitive ability. It has been foreseen by myself and others that, if we don't return Avalon to its proper place, it will mean the end for all of us."

Rich was dumbfounded. He was beginning to understand why Bryan kept his secrets so tightly against him.

"The people of Avalon can adjust to the new world," the Secretary intoned as respectfully as possible, "and people like you and your family can assist them in that. We cannot ignore the unique opportunities of having magic back in the world. We have to put the needs of the millions who can benefit from it first, don't you think?"

"So, you want me to sacrifice what's best for my people for what you think is best for the rest of the world?" Bryan countered. "That's the same argument they used to justify slavery, war, eminent domain and even genocide for Africans, Native Americans, Muslims and Jews… I will not trade the life of any Human, Elf, Dwarf, Gnome, Centaur, Jotunn, dragon, goblin or troll for you or any nation on this planet." Bryan brought his face close to the Secretary's. "Avalon will not be dictated terms to surrender our way of life by you or anyone else!"

Just then, the door blew open and armed Marines, led by McReynolds, burst in. They immediately took defensive positions to subdue the Gil-Gamesh. "Drop your weapon now!" he ordered, pointing his own 9mm automatic pistol at him.

Bryan never turned to look at them. He kept his gaze fixed on Secretary Barry. "I said drop the weapon or we will open fire!" McReynolds repeated.

"I can't drop it," Bryan explained. "It would burn a hole through the floor until it went through the bottom of the ship."

"Sheath your weapon then. Bryan, please!" Captain Rich pleaded. Bryan thought for a minute then he sheathed his sword. The Marines quickly moved in to restrain him as McReynolds put his pistol next to his head.

"Not so cocky without your dragon or your swords, are you Chief?" he scoffed.

"That's your second mistake, Commander McReynolds," Bryan responded.

"Oh? What was my first one?"

Bryan didn't say a word. As they went to put handcuffs on him, he swatted at a pitcher of water sitting on an end table, spilling it everywhere. "*Frigidus Aqua!*" he shouted. The water quickly froze as the ice spread everywhere, covering everything and everyone in the cabin, into the passageway, freezing everyone but Bryan in a layer of ice.

The Gil-Gamesh turned to McReynolds and punched him in the face, breaking the ice away. The cocky officer was stunned and shivering, unable to move anywhere.

"Your mistake was thinking I was helpless. A wizard is never unarmed," Bryan said. The XO glared at him as his teeth chattered relentlessly from the cold. He couldn't even talk back or cry for help.

Bryan went over to Captain Rich and broke his head free from the ice, though a little gentler than the punch he gave McReynolds. Rich was shivering cold as well, his teeth chattering away. "I'm telling you this as the man that was once your friend, Captain," Bryan stated. "You need to convince him to forget about assimilating Avalon because it will only end in death and destruction. You don't know and are not prepared for the evils that live on Avalon. Do yourself a favour and stay away."

Bryan turned, not even waiting for a response. He walked over to the outer bulkhead of the Captain's inport cabin. He drew *Twilight* and he began to cut through the steel frame until it fell outward into the ocean, leaving a gaping hole in the ship. He sheathed his sword before jumping through the hole. Within seconds, he appeared again on the back of a dragon as he flew away, back toward Avalon.

It took almost an hour to break everyone out of the ice. Most of them were suffering from mild hypothermia and were immediately taken to sickbay. Commander Gerwien and her team worked quickly to get everyone treated and warm.

Once she finished her rounds, Carolyn checked in on Captain Rich. He was wrapped in a blanket, sipping on a cup of coffee, still shaking from the cold. She hated to see the commanding officer looking so helpless.

"How are you feeling, Captain?" she asked.

"Frozen!" he quipped, chuckling a little bit. "God, I don't think I will ever see that movie in the same light again." He took another sip of the coffee to gather his thoughts. "How's my crew?"

"For the most part, they've held up good," she replied. "Mild hypothermia, like you. It'll take some time to get your temperature up. You were in that ice for quite a while."

"And Mac, how's he doing?" Rich asked.

Carolyn's face turned sad before she said a single word. "I don't know if it's because he was closer to the Gil-Gamesh or maybe because it was directed at him, but he took the brunt of it," she explained. "He has severe frostbite on six of his fingers, which he's probably going to lose, but he's not the one you should be worried about."

Captain Rich didn't understand her at first until it hit him. "Secretary Barry? Is he all right?"

"Oh, he's fine," Carolyn assured him, "it's not that." She moved in close to speak softer. Gerwien knew how 'scuttlebutt' can spread on a ship and she didn't want anyone else hearing her. "He's been on the phone in my office with Washington since he was thawed out. He said this was an out-and-out attack on the United States and their response has to be appropriate."

Larry couldn't believe what Carolyn was telling him. "He's gearing us up for war... War with Avalon!" she said.

***

The Gil-Gamesh sat in his library, sipping a 700-year-old whiskey. He drank in the silence of his study, preferring the darkness at times like this.

When he returned to Emmyr, he said nothing to no one, not even Stephanie, about what transpired on the carrier. He walked down to the library and closed the door behind him. Stephanie knew when to give Bryan space.

Ashley told her about the photo and evident betrayal by Captain Rich. As hard as it was for her to comprehend, she knew it was even harder for Bryan. He looked up to Rich, more than just a mentor, but as a friend.

The Gil-Gamesh continued to sip his whiskey, hoping a drunken stupor might wash away the pain. He remembered all the lectures he told his children and his sailors about not using alcohol to excess, but he ignored all that. All he wanted to do now was forget.

"That's not going to help you, Bryan," a voice said. Bryan looked up to see a ghostly apparition of Sir Percival Peredyr sitting across from him. Percival never appeared to Bryan like this before, but the Gil-Gamesh was too drunk to wonder how and why.

"Percival, I'm in no mood for a lecture tonight," he said, as he gulped down the rest of the whiskey in his glass. He reached over for the bottle before pouring himself some more.

"I would never dream of lecturing you. I thought you could use a friend."

Bryan scoffed, as he took another sip of whiskey. "I had a friend and he turned his back on me."

"Then he really wasn't a friend, was he?"

Now Percival was starting to irritate Bryan. "Did you know that when Stephanie was pregnant with Ashley, I was at sea," Bryan said. "She went into labour a week early, with no one around to help her. The only number she had, in case of emergency, was Captain Rich.

"He not only drove her to the hospital but stayed with her through 22 hours of labour until Ashley was born."

"It sounds to me like maybe he was a friend after all."

Bryan knew where Percival was going with this, and he wouldn't have any of it. "Friends don't turn their friend's daughter over to 'goose-stepping' secret police!" he yelled at the spirit.

"Did he? Did he actually know what they were going to do with the information he provided to them about Ashley and Andrew?" Percival inquired. Bryan thought for a minute and then realised he never asked Rich if he knew what Secretary Barry was doing.

Before Bryan could answer, a knock echoed in the library. The door slowly opened as Hunter stepped inside. "Dad?" he asked, as his eyes adjusted to the dark room.

Bryan looked at Hunter, then turned back to the chair where Percival sat. The spirit of the first Gil-Gamesh was gone. Bryan shook his head to regain his senses, wondering if Percival had even been there, or not. "*Ex Flamma,*" Bryan murmured, lighting the candles and illuminating the room. He walked over to his son.

"Hunter? What are you doing here? Where's the King?" Bryan reached out and took Hunter by the hand, grasping him on the shoulder.

"He's in Alfheimer with Ocwyn," Hunter explained. "After Ocwyn briefed the King on the negotiations, Bowen sent every available knight from New Camelot to the coast. Ocwyn thought he would be safe in Alfheimer, surrounded by an army of Elves until the barrier was restored."

Bryan couldn't help but be impressed with his grandson's demeanour. He was really coming into his own as the King. "The King ordered me to come to Emmyr to help you in any way I can," he added. "He said 'a father and son would be a formidable team' in times like this."

"Well, he would know," Bryan joked. "Come on, sit down. I've got some 700-year-old Aldinian whiskey."

The two sat down as Bryan poured Hunter a glass. They toasted each other, clinking the cut-crystal glasses, before taking a drink. "Not to pry, Dad, but I thought I heard you talking to someone before I knocked," Hunter queried.

Bryan chuckled, afraid Hunter would think him either drunk or crazy. "Percival paid me a visit," he explained. "I think he was trying to help me through my funk."

"Mom said you came back from the carrier, but no one really knows what happened."

"Oh, not much," Bryan said. "I just attacked the Secretary of State, hurled the Captain into the wall, froze them in ice, and cut a gaping hole in the side of the ship."

Hunter was aghast at his father, almost spilling his drink. "You did? What happened?"

"Secretary Barry tried to convince me that the needs of the rest of the world are more important that Avalon," Bryan said. "He said the people of Avalon would learn to adjust to the new world."

"Yeah right, I don't think so. People are scared enough as it is."

"What do you mean?" Bryan asked. "What have you heard?"

"Mostly from my conversations with the other sons and daughters of the Lords of Avalon, you know Bree, Finnick, Jaeger and Tomas. They told me that the old fears of the technocrats, the modern technology of the Outlanders, would bring an end to our way of life."

"You seem to be fitting in quite well with the other 'young guns' of Avalon," Bryan said. "Do you think you're ready to become a Lord of Avalon?"

"Oh no, not me. Not yet anyway. Bree and the others, they've been waiting for a lot longer than I have. They're ready to step up. I still have a lot to learn."

"Speaking of learning, I heard through the grapevine that you are now an apprentice in the arcane art of alchemy?"

"Yeah, my friend Ollie is my mentor plus Julianna's been teaching me whenever I come home to visit."

"What made you choose alchemy if I can ask?" Bryan asked.

"Well, I helped develop the GunStars and the Lancers," Hunter explained. "I wanted to be able to develop the spellshots too, to give a little more ownership to the weapon I helped create. Besides, it's really a blast, like being a kid in the candy store."

"Believe me, Hunter, you're not a boy anymore. You've grown so much since you got here, I don't even recognise the little boy I once knew. Only the man I see before me now."

"I appreciate that, Dad, but I don't know if I'll ever be ready to be Gil-Gamesh."

"You think I was?" Bryan shot back at him. "I had less time to train and prepare to become the Gil-Gamesh than you will. You must believe in yourself, Hunter.

"I'll tell you this," he continued, as he raised his glass to toast his son, "I truly believe that you will be a great Gil-Gamesh."

Hunter blushed, raising his glass to return the toast. The two men drank the whiskey but were abruptly interrupted by a strange buzzing noise. It's a sound neither of them had heard in years.

Hunter put down his glass and reached into his pocket. He pulled out Ashley's cell phone and it was vibrating.

"Where did you get that?" Bryan asked and snatched the cellphone from him.

"Ashley gave it to me. She told me to give it you for safekeeping," Hunter explained. "How is this possible? It shouldn't be working."

Bryan thought for a minute as he opened the flip phone and looked it over. Ashley preferred the old fashion tech to modern smartphones. The screen was flashing that the battery was almost dead. He closed the phone and then he realised what had happened.

"The magical barrier is beginning to fade," Bryan assumed. "Emmyr sits just off the coast of Avalon, so that means we're now outside the barrier."

"But Emmyr is an island of pure magic. Without magic, what will happen?"

Bryan sighed. He knew the answer and it wasn't pretty. "The island falls and we all die. Come on!" Bryan tossed the cell phone on the floor as the two took off.

They made their way through the Dragon's Veil, ignoring everyone's questions as they ran out of the castle. Bryan and Hunter move down through Port Charles, as Bryan led them to the southern tip of the floating isle, where he first saw the aircraft carrier off the coast of Avalon.

They made their way around the tip as far as they could go. Bryan wanted to get a good look at the western face of Emmyr. He set his gaze up and down the rock face, looking all around. Hunter joined him in his search, but he wasn't sure to look for.

"What are we looking for?" Hunter asked.

Bryan kept looking until he finally spied what he was looking for. "That!" he shouted, pointing down toward the base where the rock started to go under the isle. "Look there, see how the rocks are starting to break off."

Hunter glanced down and saw what his father feared. Sections of the island started to crack and break away, falling into the water below. Piece by piece, it was clear to see that Emmyr was in danger crashing into the sea.

"What are we going to do?" Hunter asked, but Bryan didn't have an answer for him. He was speechless.

The two men were interrupted by the roar of a dragon from above. Gamorg swooped down and landed next to them. Bryan could tell immediately that his old friend was not happy.

Gamorg roared again, his voice filled with pain. Bryan walked up, as Gamorg lowered his head. The Gil-Gamesh hugged him around his head, placing his head against his. The emotion they shared was overwhelming, even for Hunter standing just a few feet away.

"I am so sorry, my friend," Bryan said, a tear rolling down his cheek. "This is all my fault."

"I don't blame you for any of this, Gil-Gamesh," Gamorg said. "But I must look out for my dragons, so as much as it pains me to say, I have to ask you to leave Emmyr."

Bryan was confused by his request. "What? I don't understand."

"To save our home, we must move Emmyr inland over Avalon. We cannot do that with your people on the island. You have no choice, you must leave."

Bryan hated to think to leave what he has called home for more than twenty years, but it had to be done to save Emmyr from falling into the sea. "I understand, Gamorg. How much time do we have?"

Gamorg closed his eyes as the stone in the middle of his forehead glowed. When he opened his eyes, his sadness turned to rage. "We have less than a day before they attack," he snarled, looking out at the ships of the coast.

"What? But why would they attack Emmyr?" Hunter asked.

Before Bryan answered him, he realised that his son understood Gamorg. The two of them spoke in the dragon language, an ability Bryan discovered when he arrived on Avalon. It seemed to be an inherent ability in his family.

"Once they see that Emmyr is starting to deteriorate, they'll take advantage of it and make their move."

"So, what do we do?" Hunter asked.

"We evacuate the island as quickly as possible." Bryan and Hunter jumped into action and headed back to Port Charles to get the ball rolling. He didn't hesitate and sounded the alarm as soon as they reached the port.

"To arms lads, to arms!" he shouted. The men of the port rallied to the Gil-Gamesh. "Go out to every house, every tavern and every shop in the city! Get everyone to the square immediately! Get to it men, there's not a moment to lose!"

No one questioned his orders. Each man went from door-to-door, passing along the Gil-Gamesh's instructions. Soon, everyone was making their way to the square in front of the Dragon's Veil. The square was filled with people, confused and concerned. Never had Lord MoonDrake called the entire town together like this.

While his father rallied the town, Hunter rushed into the Dragon's Veil to get his family as well as the entire staff out to the square. As much as they pressed him, Hunter didn't want to tell them anything before his father did.

The Gil-Gamesh stood on the base of the statue at the centre of the square. The statue was a 50-foot representation of his wife and children he had made shortly after he began construction on Port Charles. It had always been a proud representation of the heart and spirit of the city.

Bryan looked out over the throngs of people that filled the square. They came to Emmyr, to Port Charles, on the word of the Gil-Gamesh, about the new city above Avalon that would become the heart of commerce for the magical island. His heart sank at the thought of having to tell these people that they must now leave their homes forever. *"Vox Vocis,"* he said to cast his spell.

"My friends…" he began to say, but the words escaped him. He paused for a moment and took a deep breath. "My friends, the time has come when we must leave Emmyr, our home in the clouds, and return to Avalon."

The crowd gasped in disbelief, talking amongst themselves while the Gil-Gamesh continued to speak. "The barrier has started to retreat toward Avalon and we are no longer protected by its powerful magic.

"Without magic, Emmyr has started to break apart. Soon, we will all be in danger of falling into the sea. We have no choice but to evacuate as quickly as possible."

The voices of concern grew louder as the people began to panic. "Listen to me!" he screamed, as he tried to get their attention. "Listen to me!" he shouted again until everyone finally quieted down.

"We don't have time for this!" he continued. "Gamorg has gazed into the future. He must move Emmyr inland to save the dragon's home, but not with us on it. We have less than 24 hours to depart, so we must act quickly to save as much as we can.

"We'll bring in as many airships as needed, taking people from Emmyr to Steinfisk in the North Highlands. I'll send word to Baron Ericksson to aid in your arrival. Pack light, take only what you need. Remember, you can't take everything with you.

"The Dragon Guard and other warriors will join the shore defences down below. We must be ready in case the Outlanders try to take advantage of the situation." Bryan wanted to tell them more, but he knew better than to start a panic.

"I can't begin to tell you how much you have all meant to me and my family. I consider all of you, my family. You have been with me through the good times and the bad, through the best and the worst that Avalon had to throw at us. We came through it together and we'll get through this too.

"Above all, we mustn't panic, we mustn't despair. We will survive this, but we must first think of the dragons. They are the heart of the magic that is Avalon and we must do everything we can to save them. Without them, we would all fall into the abyss."

Bryan looked out at the people of Port Charles and saw their fears fade away. He wanted to inspire them into action and he saw in them the pride and spirit he always knew was there.

"Come now, everyone, we haven't a moment to lose," he concluded. "Let's take our leave of our home and do so with the strength, courage and love she has given us."

The people of Port Charles rallied around the inspiring words of the Gil-Gamesh, and began the painful task of leaving their home. As Bryan stepped down from the statue and walked over to his family, bringing the leaders of Emmyr with them, he looked to each one of them to do their best in this desperate hour.

"We don't have a lot of time," he said, "and we must act fast if we're to save everyone and what remains of Emmyr."

"*Je ne comprends pas?*" Chancellor Beauchamp asked. "What are you not telling us, milord?"

Bryan sighed, not wanting to say anything aloud, but he realised that, to make this mass evacuation go as easy as possible, he must tell them.

"Gamorg said the Outlanders will attack Emmyr in 24 hours," he explained. "We have to get everyone off the island to safety before the attack begins.

"Listen to me very carefully, I know you all have your own belongings to pack, but I need you to help make this go as quickly and efficiently as possible. I will not sacrifice a single life for some mere tokens or wealth.

"Jasper, keep the ships moving in and out as quickly as possible," he directed Captain Hawke. "The people come first, then the merchants can empty their warehouses, but not before. Henri, you go with him to make sure the merchants understand that!" Jasper tipped his hat in salute while Henri bowed, as the two men headed down toward the piers.

"Captain McLoughlin, I want every knight, shield maiden and warrior alike sent down to shore defences below," he ordered the Captain of the Dragon Guard, "but leave a small contingent on Emmyr until the very end, just in case of looting or panic."

Rhona acknowledged the order with a salute and took off with Amelia to carry them out. "Edan, get the word out to all the captains in the air to make for Emmyr post haste!" he commanded. "We need them here to help with the evacuation and to be ready to fight back against an Outlander attack."

Captain O'Brien tipped his hat in salute before following right behind Jasper toward the pier. Stephanie thought Bryan was finally going to talk to her, but instead, he addressed Eileanora. Lady MoonDrake felt she was rudely dismissed by her husband.

"Eileanora, I want the *Hîldrägo Boquè* to join the shore defences, but I have need of the *Aerdrie Faenya*," he stated. "I need it to take my family to Alfheimer."

"What?" Stephanie asked. "Why Alfheimer, Bryan?"

"King Bowen is already there with Ocwyn, Mother," Hunter interjected. "It's the safest place for you to be right now."

"Steph, I don't have time to argue this with you," Bryan said. "You have a lot of packing to do and very little time to do it."

He went over to his wife, took her by the shoulders and gently kissed her. "Please, do this for me. I need to know that you, Ashley and Andrew are safe, especially Ashley. I need her to continue her work with Merlin on finding a way to restore the barrier."

Stephanie took his hand and kissed it in understanding.

"We think we found something, Dad," Ashley said. "Before those federal agents took us, Merlin and I were about to begin looking through the spells of Methuselah. Merlin is confident that they may be the key to restoring the barrier."

"But, sir, I want to stay here with you and help you defend Avalon," Andrew interjected, hoping to prove himself to his father-in-law.

"I know you do, Andrew, but you're a duel citizen of the United States and Avalon," Bryan explained. "I don't want to take a gamble at ruining any chance you and Ashley might have in returning to your lives in the outside world."

Andy nodded his head. He knew that the Gil-Gamesh was looking out for his and Ashley's best interest. Lastly, the Gil-Gamesh turned to his other two children. "Rose, Hunter… I need the two of you flying around the island to monitor the deterioration and keep an eye on the fleet.

"Rose, you take Dee Dee and Hunter, you can fly Tabby. Report back to me if you see anything out of the ordinary, understand?"

The two nodded their heads, happy that their father placed such faith in them for an important mission like this. Bryan was happy to have everyone understanding and supportive at a desperate time like this. He could only hope that they were not too late to save Emmyr.

***

The Command Direction Centre, or CDC, on an aircraft carrier was considered the heart of the ship. From there, the ship's defensive and offensive weapons were controlled. In addition, all intelligence was gathered and collated there—from radar, sonar and aircraft and ships in the fleet—giving a minute-by-minute representation of the surrounding area. The room was dimly lit by the glow of the various screens illuminating in the darkness.

Captain Rich and Secretary Barry stepped into the CDC, taking a moment to let their eyes adjust to the dark. They immediately headed over to the Operations Officer, Commander Hank Jefferson, better known to his men as 'Buckshot' because he was an avid hunter. Jefferson liked to smoke cigars, but since the

Navy had a 'no smoking' policy on ships, he couldn't indulge in his favourite pastime. Instead, he kept a cigar in his mouth, rolling it around to savour the flavour.

"What have you got, Hank?" Rich inquired.

"Sir, there's been an increase in activity around that floating island. The flights in-and-out have doubled on the hour. It's as if they're evacuating, sir."

"Evacuating? But why?" Secretary Barry asked.

"Sir, I believe it's because that island is starting to fall apart," Hank informed him. "Newman, pull up the pictures." A sailor next to the Operations Officer clicked on two pictures on his computer, opening them on the large display screen in front of them. It was two photos of Emmyr, displayed side-by-side.

"This image was taken shortly after the island appeared," Hank said, pointing to the picture on the left. "This one was taken less than an hour ago. As you can see, there are large sections of the island missing.

"I asked the Navigator to tell the lookouts to keep a close watch on the underside of the island," he continued. "I've received reports of pieces dropping into the sea below, consistently for the past four hours."

"What's causing this?" Rich asked.

"I haven't a clue, sir, but Petty Officer Newman here has a theory," Hank said, putting his hands on the young sailor's shoulders. "He's one of those geeks who plays *World of Warcraft* and *Magic the Gathering* when he's off duty."

Operations Specialist Troy Newman shrugged off the commander's droll attempt at humour. "Well, sir, we know that the island is protected by a magical barrier that prevents technology from working there," Newman stated. "What if that barrier is shrinking, sir?"

"Newman, you need to explain things a little more clearly for us old men," Rich emphasised.

"Yes sir, sorry, sir. The island is floating due to its connection to the magic of Avalon, but if the magic is fading, the island can't sustain itself for much longer. It'll fall into the ocean."

"That means your missiles, aircraft and other weapons will work close to the island," Secretary Barry surmised. "We can attack them, then they'll come to reason."

"Mr Secretary, I have no orders to engage the forces on Avalon," Rich asserted. "We don't know how far the barrier has receded into the island to ensure our weapons will work there."

"Then I suggest you find out, Captain," Barry retorted. "Send out your reconnaissance planes to test the barrier. In the meantime, I'll phone Washington and get you those orders."

Barry turned on his heel and started walking out of CDC. "We will make those bastards pay for their effrontery on a representative of the United States of America."

Captain Rich sighed at his frustration with Secretary Barry and his vendetta against the Gil-Gamesh and Avalon. Right now, he could only follow orders. "Hank, tell CAG to have a couple of Hornets fly some high-speed passes over the floating island. Tell them to get as close as possible without endangering themselves or their aircraft."

The captain turned to leave CDC himself until he had one more thought. "Oh, and tell the pilots not to engage anything flying around the island unless they are attacked first. Understood?"

"Aye-aye, Captain!" Hank responded, putting his unlit cigar back into his mouth as he turned his attention to his sailors. "All right, ladies and gentlemen, time to earn our paychecks!"

***

Soaring the skies around Emmyr was what Rose loved to do best. When she was up there, flying on the back her dragon, Dee Dee, she was in heaven. Dee Dee was her best friend, ever since she rescued her in the cave-in when Dee Dee was just a baby dragon. Since then, they formed a bond stronger than any magic in all of Avalon.

Rose could fly to the ends of the Earth on Dee Dee and that still wouldn't be far enough. The only exception was when she was flying with Edan, her one true love. That was when she had the two things she loved in most life all at once.

Unfortunately, she was flying around Emmyr with her brother, Hunter, and he was never fun to be with. In her estimation, Hunter got a real 'stick up his butt' ever since he became a knight. She always felt he acted superior to her and Ashley, as the heir apparent to the Gil-Gamesh.

What made it worse was he became the consort to Queen Cadhla and, together, they had a son, Bowen. Not only is he the father of the King of Avalon, he gave Bryan and Stephanie their first grandchild. He always had to 'one-up' them, or so she thought.

Hunter flew next to her on Tabby, a hybrid dragon called a Wyvern. Unlike its dragon cousins, Tabby didn't have forearms, only wings, plus her wings were feathered and much larger than that of a dragon. He kept his head on a swivel, his eyes focused on the island and the fleet just off the coast of Avalon.

Rose, on the other hand, was enjoying the sunset, and Hunter noticed that she wasn't doing what their father had asked. "Rose, keep your eyes on Emmyr or the ships, not the sunset," he shouted at his sister.

"Oh, give it a rest, Hunter," she snapped. "We've been out here all day and it's still the same. Emmyr is slowly breaking into pieces and the jerks are still out there on their ships."

"That could change at a moment's notice, you should be more attentive on a mission like this," he tried to assert the urgency in her.

"Listen to me, Sir Hunter, you're not in New Camelot right now. You're in my domain and here, nothing can compare to the wingbeat of a dragon in the skies over Avalon."

Suddenly, a loud roaring sound started building from behind them. Hunter and Rose turned to see two US Navy fighter jets heading right toward them, catching them both off guard.

"Except for maybe two jets barrelling right at us at supersonic speeds!" Hunter warned.

"How can they be so close to Avalon?" she asked. "They're going to fly right over Emmyr!"

"I told you the magical barrier was rescinding. Or didn't you believe Dad's warning this morning?"

If Rose could reach her brother right now, she'd smack him in the head, but her bigger concern was the approaching jets. "How fast do you think they're going?"

"Close to 700 miles per hour, why?"

"Because their backwash is going to play hell with the air currents, we're gliding through," she surmised. "We need to move away from Emmyr or they're going to throw us right into the rocks!"

"How do you know that?" Hunter asked with a tone of utter disbelief.

"Hunter, for once in your miserable life, will you please trust me? I've been flying around here long enough to know what changing winds patterns can do to a dragon's flight."

Hunter could see the seriousness in his sister's eyes, so he took her word for it. "Okay, sis, you lead, I'll follow!"

Rose spurred Dee Dee on as Hunter got in right behind her. She started taking them away from Emmyr, but a sudden updraft lifted them higher than she wanted. That's when a disaster happened.

The first F-18 zoomed past them at causing a wicked downdraft and a swirling mass of turbulence. Rose was rocked by the force of the winds, but her experience on a dragon kept her in control. Hunter, however, wasn't as lucky. Due to her large wings, the turbulence spun Tabby into an upward spin. She flew right into the underside of the second F-18 Hornet, knocking Hunter from the bridle.

He fell toward the ocean, knocked unconscious from the impact. As the aircraft collided into Emmyr, exploding on contact, Rose took Dee Dee and dove for Hunter. "Come on, girl, we've got to catch him!"

Dee Dee pulled her wings in tight, for a faster dive, as the dragon tried to reach Hunter before he hit the ocean below. "Reach for him, Dee! Reach for him!" Rose shouted, pleading with her dragon to save her brother.

Dee Dee reached out with its claws and grabbed Hunter in the nick of time, as Rose leaned back to help her pull up from the dive, rising in the air back toward Avalon. Rose looked down at her brother, looking for any signs of life. "Hunter! Hunter!" she screamed. "Dammit, mama's boy, answer me!"

Hunter began to stir, as he rubbed his head. "Mom told you not to call me mama's boy, 'Pez Head'!" he moaned, as he tried to shake out the cobwebs. Rose couldn't help but laugh, happy to see that her brother was all right.

Her concern grew again when she heard another explosion as the wreckage of the Navy aircraft fell into the water below. Tabby was falling right with it, killed on impact with the supersonic jet. This wasn't going to help things, Rose thought to herself. In fact, she knew it would only make it worse.

***

"What you mean one of the aircraft exploded?" Captain Rich screamed over the sound-powered phone to CDC.

"As they approached the island, there were two contacts flying below them," Jefferson explained. "After the first Hornet passed overhead, one swung upward and struck the second Hornet from underneath. It pushed the aircraft right into the rocks. Lieutenant Pelly had no chance to eject, sir. The aircraft exploded on contact."

"What about the contact? What happened to it?"

"Well, sir, the dragon must've snapped its neck. It fell right into the ocean," Hank continued. "But the guy riding it was picked out of the air by the other dragon rider. Damnedest thing I ever did see."

"Did they attack the Hornet or was it an accident?" Captain Rich asked just as Secretary Barry walked onto the bridge of the aircraft carrier.

"I couldn't tell, sir, but I wouldn't surprise me if they got caught in the jet wash," Hank concurred. "At that speed, I doubt those creatures ever experienced something like that before."

"All right, Hank, have the other Hornet return to the carrier so we can get a full debrief," Rich ordered before hanging up the phone, not waiting for an acknowledgement of his order.

"What happened?" Barry asked.

"One of the Hornets crashed into the floating island during their high-speed run," Rich began. "It collided with someone riding a dragon, flying around the island."

"So, they were attacked?"

"We can't be sure, Mr Secretary," Captain Rich cautioned. "They could've been caught in the aircraft jet wash. It might've been an accident."

"Maybe it was, maybe it wasn't, but I think this will convince the President to approve orders to attack the island. These transgressions have gone on long enough," he spat out. He turned on his heels and ran out of the bridge.

Rich felt completely helpless. This incident would only make matters worse and bring them one step closer to war.

Chapter 6
Magic vs. Technology

Doctor Bonapat examined Hunter very thoroughly while his mother looked on with concern for her baby boy. Though he may be a grown man, he will always be his mother's son and she never let him forget that.

"I feel fine, Doc, just a little headache, that's all."

"Ramming your head into a military aircraft will cause a lot more than a headache, Hunter," Doctor Bonapat said. "I would prefer that you take it easy in case of a concussion, but since you are your father's son, I know you'll ignore it."

"Oh no, he won't, Allain," Stephanie interjected. "He's going to be with me on the *Aerdrie Faenya* our way to Alfheimer."

"Stop it, Mom, I'll be fine. Dad needs my help with the defence of Avalon."

"Hunter, your father has an entire army of Elves, Dwarves, knights and shield maidens assembled down at the coast," Stephanie dictated to him. "I know you want to fight by his side, but you won't do him or anyone any good if you pass out from a concussion."

Hunter knew his mother was right and just nodded his head, disappointed in himself. When Stephanie left to check on the progress of the packing with Mrs Thurgoode, Rose stepped up to check on Hunter.

"Hey, how are you feeling?" she asked.

"I'm okay," Hunter said, as he tried to stand up, but then the room started to spin, and he had to sit back down. "Okay, maybe not."

Rose knelt in front of her brother, putting her hand on his shoulder. "Look, you need to take it easy like the doctor said," she said. "You hit that jet pretty hard, even for your hard head."

They both enjoyed the laugh together. "What happened to Tabby?" Hunter asked. Rose was quiet, afraid to answer him, but Hunter knew what happened.

"She fell into the ocean," Rose replied quietly. "I think she died on impact with the jet. She took the brunt of it. It likely snapped her neck."

Just then, the two realised they weren't alone in the room. They turned to see their father standing just a few feet away from them. He rushed over and gave both of his children a hug and a kiss, lingering a little longer on Hunter.

"Are you all right?" he asked, cradling his son's injured head. Hunter just nodded his head slightly as he cringed from a massive headache the slightest movement gave him. Bryan turned his attention to Rose for some answers. "What happened?"

"Two jets came right at us at high speed," she explained. "It's as if they were trying to get as close to the island as possible but they got out of there just as fast."

"I was afraid of that," Bryan confessed. "They're testing the barrier, to see how much it's receded back toward Avalon."

"I'm sorry about Tabby, Dad," Hunter said with a great deal of remorse and guilt. "She got caught in the jet's wake, I couldn't get her under control."

"It's not your fault, son. In that situation, I doubt anyone could have done better. Listen, I know you're leaving with your mother, so you need to start heading down to the pier. I'll send Amelia to help you, all right?" He just nodded his head in agreement, though it's not what he wanted to do.

"Rose, I need you to wait for me down by the piers," Bryan ordered. "Gamorg and Dee Dee will be meeting us there shortly."

Rose followed behind her father as the two started to leave the room. "Hey, Pez Head!" Hunter yelled at his sister. It was a nickname he gave her as a child because, when she laughed, her head would occasionally pop back like a Pez candy dispenser.

"Thanks for saving me, sis. I owe you one."

Rose smiled. It was the first genuine compliment he had given her since they arrived on Avalon. "Anytime," she said, then winked, "…mama's boy."

The two laughed at each other's insult, but it was a mutual respect that brought them closer together.

***

Captain Rich peered out from the bridge through his binoculars at the floating island. Even though it was close to eight o'clock, there was a glow coming from the far side of Emmyr. There was plenty of activity from the island while things remained quiet along the coat. Firelights dotted the coastline where he knew there to be defensive encampments, but they haven't changed in weeks.

Rich was worried, more so than before, of the possibility of war with Avalon. Secretary Barry had been on the phone non-stop, trying to convince the Pentagon and the President that attacking Avalon will force them to the negotiating table. It was his pride talking, not diplomacy, being humiliated by the Gil-Gamesh like he was.

"Excuse me, sir, but they sent up your dinner," the OOD interrupted, derailing the Captain's train of thought.

"That's fine, Lieutenant, have them set it up in the at-sea cabin," he said, as he continued to stare at the floating island through the binoculars. The OOD quickly relayed the order while Rich looked out toward Avalon. He wished he had one more chance to talk to Bryan to maybe prevent this from escalating anymore.

Captain Rich finally put down his binoculars and stepped down from his chair. "I'll be in my cabin, OOD. Come get me if there are any changes to the activity on the floating island."

"Aye, aye, sir!" the young lieutenant acknowledged with a salute. Rich headed off the bridge for his at-sea cabin. Inside, he found a tray of food, covered with a metal dome, sitting on his desk. He wasn't hungry, but he knew he needed to eat something.

Rich sat down and removed the dome, but to his amazement, there was no food on the plate. He reached for his phone to call down to the galley and chew out the Mess Captain when he heard a tiny burp behind him.

He turned around to see the Gil-Gamesh's faerie dragon, Maverick, sitting on his bed. The tiny creature patted his stomach, from the feast he just ate.

"What are you…how did you get in here?"

Maverick said nothing. He motioned toward the desk. Rich turned to see a small scroll of parchment sitting next to the tray. He unrolled it and read, "Vulture's Row, now!"

He jumped out and ran up two flights to the top deck of the carrier with Maverick buzzing close behind. The top deck was called 'Vulture's Row' because it was the one place where sailors could watch flight operations from, peering down on the deck like vultures.

He opened the hatch and stepped outside into the night air. His eyes tried to adjust to the darkness but before he could see anything, a hand touched him on the shoulder.

"*Migro-transit Emmyr!*" a voice said, and in the blink of an eye, Rich disappeared from his ship and found himself on the floating island. He immediately dropped to one knee, feeling sick to his stomach.

"Sorry about that, teleportation is nasty the first time around," the Gil-Gamesh said. Bryan was waiting for him on Vulture's Row and teleported him from the ship to Emmyr. "Take a few deep breaths, it'll help the nausea pass."

Rich stood up slowly, as he rubbed his eyes and held his hand over his mouth. When he finally opened his eyes, the sickness went away quickly as he marvelled at what he saw.

They were standing down at the heart of the city, the port. There were several piers jutting out from the island with flying airships moored to them. Passengers and cargo were being loaded onto each ship at a frantic pace. As soon as one was loaded, it left the port quickly, only to be replaced by another airship, then the process started again.

Rich looked up the street from the port through the city. He was amazed at the size and scope of this tiny city built right into the face of the mountain, leading up the hillside toward the castle sitting at the apex of the town.

He also noticed how people were tossing things out windows, trying to get their belongings together and make their way toward the piers. He could feel the sense of urgency, the panic and the fear. They were scared yet a sadness filled the air.

"Bryan, what's going on? Why are you leaving?"

"Oh, I think you already know the answer to that. Your Hornets buzzed the island, almost killing my son in the process."

"Hunter? Hunter was on one of the dragons?"

"Yes, and Rose," Bryan replied. "They were keeping an eye on the slow disintegration of Emmyr and on your fleet."

"My God, Bryan, why on Earth would you let your 15-year-old son fly around on a dragon?"

"Because I'm not fifteen anymore, Captain!" came a voice from behind them. Hunter stood there with his mother, sisters and Andrew. Captain Rich couldn't believe it when he saw Hunter and Rose, how grown and mature they looked.

"Time passes differently on Avalon. Or it did, rather, before the barrier fell," the Gil-Gamesh explained. "It's been only two-to-three years to you, but more than 20 for us."

Before Rich could say another word, Stephanie walked up to him and slapped him across the face. Rich did nothing, but he could see the anger in her eyes.

"That's for turning your back on your goddaughter by turning her over to those mercenaries!" Stephanie screamed, wagging her finger at him. "That is something I will never, ever forgive or forget, Larry."

Captain Rich didn't have a chance to respond back as Stephanie turned her back on him before giving Bryan a kiss and heading down the pier with the others.

"She's not the forgiving kind, Rich, especially when it comes to her children," Bryan said.

"Why did you bring me here? Just to let her work out her frustrations?" Rich demanded.

"No, I brought you here to show you the people you're going to attack in the morning."

Rich was dumbfounded that Bryan already knew what was going to happen, then he remembered. "Precognitive, right? You already saw this in the future?"

"Not me, but Gamorg did," Bryan explained, as he motioned for the captain to follow him up the street. "We have until dawn to get everyone off the island, so the dragons can move it inland, hopefully preventing it from disintegrating any further."

"But why? I don't understand?"

"I told you there would be consequences if all the magic left Avalon and spread throughout the outside world. Dragons are one of the primary sources of magic; they're born with it flowing through their veins.

"As the magic ebbs from Avalon, it begins to deplete those sources, namely dragons," the Gil-Gamesh continued. "This island floats because of magic, and as that magic leaves Avalon, well, you know the rest."

As they strolled up the street, Captain Rich looked hard at the people of Emmyr. They were just normal, everyday people with families, businesses and homes. They glared at him, some bitter and angry, some scared and apprehensive. The last time he saw panic like this was during the evacuation of New Orleans before Hurricane Katrina hit.

"You know, if we could have seen this before, it might have helped sway things better," Rich said to Bryan.

"Yes, well, I couldn't have brought you here before without having to explain this," he replied, pointing toward the statue in the town square of Stephanie and the children. Rich looked at the bronze monolith in awe. "I had it commissioned when the town was established. I wanted something to remind me of them every day."

"I think a painting would've been more manageable, don't you think?" Rich joked. The two men shared a laugh, something they haven't done in a long time. "Bryan, I am so sorry about giving Secretary Barry the information on Ashely and Andrew. I swear to you, I didn't know he was going to send armed thugs after them."

"I know, Captain, and I believe you," the Gil-Gamesh said. "Unfortunately, I don't think it's going to do either of us any good. After tonight, there will be a war between Avalon and the outside world."

"There's got to be some way of preventing this from escalating to that!"

Before Bryan could answer him, Captain Rhona McLoughlin of the Dragon Guard walked up to them. Captain Rich was in awe of the nearly seven-foot blonde-haired warrior woman who resembled a Valkyrie standing before him.

"Milord, we just received word from our lookouts that…" she started to report, until her voice trailed off at the sight of Rich.

"Oh, I'm sorry, Rhona, this is Captain Larry Rich, Commanding Officer of the *USS Theodore Roosevelt*," he introduced. "Sir, this is Rhona McLoughlin, Captain of the Dragon Guard, my own personal guard here on Emmyr."

Rhona nodded her head politely, and Rich returned the courtesy. Rhona turned her attention back to the Gil-Gamesh but was clearly hesitant.

"It's all right, Rhona, you can speak freely," Bryan assured her.

"Yes, milord. Our lookouts report a lot of clamouring on the large vessel," she reported. "Bells and alarms are being sounded all around the ship."

Rich realised it's because he was no longer aboard. "They must have discovered I'm not eating dinner like I was supposed to," he stated. "I think you better get me back there."

Bryan nodded his head and reached out to touch him, but Rich held up his hand to stop him. "Whatever happens tomorrow, Lord MoonDrake, I will do my best to stop the attack."

He smiled and nodded, assured that his friend and mentor would do what he could. "Thank you, Captain, but be forewarned, we will not hesitate to respond to any attack made against us." Captain Rich understood what Bryan said and closed his eyes. "*Migro-transit USS Theodore Roosevelt!*" Bryan yelled, and Rich disappeared again. When the Captain opened his eyes, he was back on Vulture's Row on his ship.

He dropped to one knee and took a couple of deep breaths, as he tried to make his nausea subside. "Sir, are you all right?" came a voice from behind, as a young sailor stepped up to help the captain to his feet.

"I'm fine, sailor. Can you help me down to the bridge?" he ordered.

"Yes, sir!" the sailor replied, as he waved over two others to help him. One quickly opened the hatch while the other got in front of the captain as they moved down the ladder, one in front and one behind, to ensure he wouldn't hurt himself.

Within a few minutes, Rich was feeling better as the sailors helped him onto the bridge. The OOD saw the captain being helped in and went into action. "Boatswain's Mate, medical emergency on the bridge, now!" he ordered, as the duty Boatswain's Mate sounded out the emergency call.

The OOD went over to help get the captain into his chair. "Sir, where were you? We couldn't find you anywhere on the ship," he inquired.

"I know, Lieutenant, I was occupied elsewhere," Rich said, as he sat back in his chair, his stomach still churning from the teleportation. "Would someone please get me a cup of strong, black coffee?"

"Belay that order!" Commander Gerwien shouted, as she entered the bridge with her medical team. She set her medical bag down on the console next to the captain and took out her instruments.

"Coop, I'm fine, just a little nauseous, that's all."

"You made me run all the way up to the bridge and that means I get to examine you, Captain." As one of her corpsman took his blood pressure, Carolyn continued with his examination. "So, you want to tell me what happened to you to help me with my diagnosis or do I have to take you down to sickbay for a full medical exam?"

Rich knew how obstinate his medical officer could be, so he relented. "I was abruptly teleported to Emmyr," he said with as straight a face as he could muster. "The Gil-Gamesh wanted to have a private chat with me."

"Teleportation? You were teleported to-and-from the floating island?"

"Why do you think I'm so queasy right now? It wasn't a pleasant experience," he said, as he looked to the rest of her medical team. "OOD, stand down from whatever alert you started and stand down medical emergency too."

Gerwien turned to her medical team and ordered them back to sickbay. The OOD relayed the order to the Boatswain's Mate to announce it over the ship's intercom. Captain Rich just sat back in his chair, holding his head in his hand, trying to shake loose the cobwebs.

"So, you're the first man to be teleported. I know about 100 doctors who would love to examine you from head-to-toe, including me."

"Yes, well, that's not going to happen tonight," Rich responded. "I need to speak with Secretary Barry ASAP!" Rich started to get out of his chair, but his head started spinning again.

"Captain, let's get you something to eat first, then I'll give you some anti-nausea medicine, all right?" Carolyn chided him. Reluctantly, Captain Rich nodded his head, knowing he wouldn't be able to dissuade her.

In his at-sea cabin, Captain Rich ate a simple meal of soup, salad and toast. When he was finished, Carolyn gave him some medicine to help him beat the queasiness. Carolyn helped the captain down to his inport cabin.

As the two officers stepped inside, Secretary Barry was still railing on the phone. The tone of his displeasure could be heard from a mile away. Carolyn helped him sit down while Barry finished his phone call.

"Captain, are you all right?" he asked, as he hung up the phone.

"I'm fine, sir, just a little sick to my stomach," Rich groaned. "What is the word from Washington?"

"Well, the President wants a response, but the Joint Chiefs are apprehensive," Barry explained, as he poured himself some coffee. "They don't like the idea of planning an attack against an enemy we have no credible intelligence on."

"Well, I can tell you that we're in no danger from the floating island," Rich said. "They're evacuating as we speak."

The captain's revelation caught Secretary Barry off guard. "What? How? Why?"

"With the island falling piece-by-piece into the ocean, they're evacuating the town as quickly as possible," he stated, "That way, the dragons can move the island safely inland. It seems that with magic leaving Avalon for the outside world, it's starting to take its toll on them."

"And how did you come about this information?" Barry asked.

"The Gil-Gamesh teleported me to Emmyr, to show me what was happening to his home and his people. He took me on a walk through the city. I saw merchants, families, women and children, no soldiers; well, except for a seven-foot blonde amazon.

"They're scared, Mr Secretary," he continued. "They are afraid of what we represent, and I think that it's on us to show some restraint. We shouldn't attack Emmyr."

Secretary Barry sipped his coffee, never taking his eyes off Rich. "I have to wonder, Captain, if this is your professional opinion or one voiced out of concern for your former shipmate."

"Mr Secretary, I've been in the Navy for more than 30 years," he started. "I've been part of numerous operations, both military and humanitarian. I've seen people preparing for war and running away from war. These people are running away from it. They are no threat to the United States of America and I will bank my career on it."

Barry looked at him and feigned his best smile. "All right, Captain, I will relay your information to the President. In the end, it's his decision."

Rich politely nodded his head, before turning to Carolyn to help him up. The two left the secretary alone as he finished his coffee. He picked up the phone and dialled another number, waiting patiently until it connected.

"Yes, this is Secretary Barry, can I speak with the President please?" He waited again while he was being connected. "Yes, Mr President, I have some news. Earlier this evening, Captain Rich was taken by the Gil-Gamesh to the floating island…magical teleportation he called it. The captain reported seeing hundreds of armed fighters preparing for war.

"He said the Gil-Gamesh wanted to demonstrate that they weren't afraid to fight. He was gloating, as the captain described before they sent him back to the carrier. They are gearing up for war, Mr President, and I must stress we do an appropriate response that will deter them from ever taking up arms against the United States."

***

As the morning sun rose over Emmyr, the last of the townspeople loaded onto the last airships at the piers. The Gil-Gamesh, Amelia and Rhona just finished a walk-through of the town with a contingent of the Dragon Guard.

They swept down from the Dragon's Veil, checking every residence and business to ensure no one was there. They found a few stragglers, some last-minute looters, but they were dealt with accordingly.

They reached the port, where Rose was waiting with Captain Hawke, Captain O'Brien and Eileanora. Like the Gil-Gamesh, they were all heartbroken and sullen over leaving Emmyr.

"Is it done?" Eileanora asked.

"Yes, no one is left in Port Charles but us," Bryan said. "The last to leave, eh?" Bryan looked up at the statue of his friend, Charles Taylor, the namesake of Port Charles.

Lieutenant Charles Taylor was flight leader of Flight 19 that disappeared in the Bermuda Triangle in 1945. In fact, he and others survived and made it through to the island of Avalon. Charles Taylor was instrumental in helping Bryan transition to medieval life on Avalon. He even helped design the airships and build the port on Emmyr. He died trying to protect the port and shipyard from goblin invaders. Bryan named the port in his honour.

Bryan placed his hand at the base of the statue and looked up at it. "I'm sorry, old friend, I did everything I could to save our home," he said, as a tear rolled down his cheek. Suddenly, explosions could be heard from off in the distance and the island shook as the explosions rang out. His sadness turned to anger as Bryan realised their attack had begun.

"Rose, have Dee Dee get Gamorg for me," Bryan instructed his daughter. "I need him and five other dragons, his best fighters. Now go!"

Rose didn't say another word. She ran down to where Dee Dee was waiting for to carry out her father's instruction. Bryan then turned to Captain Jasper Hawke. "Jasper, I want you to take command of the *Avenger* and get ready to fire off some 'freezing fog' shots on my order?"

"Me, sir? But what about Edan?" Jasper asked, confused about the order as Edan was.

"Edan will be with me, I need you on the *Avenger*, ready to fire. Understood?"

"Understood, milord. What is my target? The fleet of ships?" Jasper asked.

"No, I want you to lay the fog around Emmyr. We must protect the island from aerial assault."

"What aerial assault, Gil-Gamesh?" Amelia asked.

"The one they're going to launch from the aircraft carrier," Bryan explained, as more explosions rattled off from the far side of the island. "Once we take out their guns, they'll launch aircraft to drop bombs on us from above."

"But you're not going to let them, are you, milord?" Eileanora asked.

"Oh, hell no!" he yelled. "We're going to take the fight to them while Gamorg and the dragons move Emmyr inland."

A loud roar came from the sky above as Gamorg descended into the port along with five other dragons and Dee Dee. Bryan walked over and bowed respectfully to the King of the Dragons.

"It has begun, my friend," Gamorg snarled. "We must move Emmyr quickly to avoid further damage. I hope you have a plan?"

"I will take Dee Dee and these five dragons to attack the warships," he began. "Their dragon fire should melt the weapons arsenal on the ships, rendering their ability to attack us inoperable.

"When they launch aircraft to continue their attack on the island, the *Avenger* will lay down freezing fog all around Emmyr. Their aircraft will be unable to penetrate the fog to drop their weapons. That will give you the time to move the island."

Gamorg nodded his head in agreement and roared at the other dragons, speaking to them in dragon tongue. They all nodded and roared back to their King. "We will fly with you one last time, Gil-Gamesh," Gamorg said. "The Dragons of Emmyr will show these Outlanders what true power is."

Bryan turned to the others to relay his orders. "Rhona, Amelia, Eileanora, Edan and Rose, you will join me on the dragons in attacking the ships," he instructed. "You have some experience riding on them, so this should be easy for you.

"Target the open decks on the ships," Bryan continued. "That's where all the weapons systems are mounted and launched from. A blast of dragon fire should melt everything into slag. Stay low and close to the dragon. Their hides are bulletproof, but you're not."

"Excuse me, milord, but are you sure this is a mission for Rose?" Edan interrupted. "Though she is probably the most experienced dragon rider, next to you, I'm just not sure if—"

"Edan, I'm not going to have a discussion with you about Rose right now, especially since you're not married," he snapped at him. "So, until such a time, and as her father, I will ask my daughter to do things you probably won't like."

"Milord, I was only thinking of—" Bryan reached out and grabbed Edan by the mouth, covering it with his palm.

"I know how you feel about her, Captain, but if we don't stop this attack right now, we may lose any chance we have of saving Avalon. Now, before you put your foot in your mouth with another outrageous, male chauvinist comment and piss off my daughter any more than she already is, I suggest you stop arguing with me and get on a dragon."

Edan nodded. As soon as the Gil-Gamesh took his hand away, Edan turned to explain himself to Rose, but she just turned on her heel and headed over to Dee Dee. Edan sighed, knowing he had a lot of apologising ahead of him.

The five climbed on their dragons as Bryan went over to see Gamorg. "Where will you take Emmyr?" he asked.

"Toward the Fenris Mountains, they will shelter us for the time being," Gamorg said.

"Will I see you again anytime soon?"

Gamorg smiled, as best as a dragon could smile, but he didn't answer Bryan. He roared as he spread his wings and took off into the air. The Gil-Gamesh was troubled by his friend's silence, but he had other things on his mind.

He jumped up on the back of the remaining dragon and got ready to fly. "Rhona, you take Rose and Amelia to the left, Eileanora and Edan are with me on the right," he ordered. "I want those guns silenced! We must stop the bombardment to give Gamorg the time he needs to move Emmyr.

"Let's teach these Outlanders that Avalon is defended!" he shouted, as he spurred his dragon into the air. The others followed suit, as the dragons took off into the sky and headed toward the fleet.

***

From the bridge of the *USS Theodore Roosevelt*, Secretary Barry watched the assault on the floating island. US cruisers and destroyers, in addition to Russian ships supporting the attack, were firing on the island. Their guns are peppering the floating island as chunks are falling off into the sea, but the process was proceeding too slowly for him.

"Why are we only using shells, Captain? Why aren't we firing tomahawks or other missiles?"

Captain Rich huffed at the impatience of the Secretary of State. He didn't understand why the President approved this attack, but he had to follow orders. "As I explained, sir, Commodore Denniston was unsure if the weapons would arm prior to detonation, and the Joint Chiefs agreed with his assessment. They don't want to waste multimillion-dollar ordnance on a chance they won't work. It's better to stick with shelling the island for now."

"Captain, lookouts report six contacts coming around the southern side of the floating island, diving toward the water," the OOD reported.

Both Rich and Barry immediately turned their binoculars toward Emmyr to see what the lookouts spotted. They spied the six dragons, with riders, moving toward the fleet.

"Is it him?" Barry asked, as he squinted his eyes, focusing on the dragons.

Rich grinned. "It's him. I told you they would retaliate to any attack, sir," he said before turning to the bridge officer. "Contact Commodore Denniston and the rest of the fleet. Tell them to prepare ship's defences against incoming attackers.

"Not that it'll do them any good," he muttered to himself.

They watched as the dragons broke off into two packs of three, but one took the lead. Rich could see it was the Gil-Gamesh but he wasn't sure what he was doing. He watched as he sat upright on the dragon and poured some liquid into the water with one hand while motioning with the other. Then it became clear to him: he was casting some sort of spell.

Something began to rise from the water directly under the Gil-Gamesh. The water started to form into serpents, creatures made entirely of the water itself. The watery beasts roared as they charged right at the ships firing on Emmyr. They smashed into the warships.

"Dammit!" Captain Rich cursed when he realised what Bryan was doing.

"What? What is happening?" Barry screamed.

"He's hitting the ship's right on the radar and bridge," Rich explained. "He's blinding them!"

Around each of the ship's superstructure were large plates that provided them with a 360-degree view of their surroundings. The water striking the surface caused a temporary wave in the system, effectively blinding them.

The dragons moved in to attack. They laid down dragon fire across the deck, melting the gun mounts and missile launchers into heaps of slag. In-and-around the ships, they flew with speed and grace, disabling the fighting capabilities of the naval vessels.

The Russian ships, however, were a different story. Bryan motioned for Eileanora to follow him in. He directed the watery serpents to strike the ship on the side, causing them to list by almost 45 degrees. Then, the Gil-Gamesh and Eileanora's dragons fired blasts of dragon fire right at their waterline, creating gaping holes.

When the Russian ships righted themselves, water flooded in below decks. Alarms sounded almost immediately as the Russian destroyers were rendered useless—payback for the *Spetsnaz* invasion of Emmyr.

Secretary Barry threw his binoculars on the deck, cursing aloud at the fact that the superior technical might of the United States Navy was laid low by a medieval wizard. "Captain, we can't wait anymore. You need to launch the strike group against that island immediately."

Captain Rich sighed. He hoped that it wouldn't come to this, but he had his orders and he would follow them. He reached over to the sound-powered and hit a button. "Boss, let's get 'strike package alpha' in the air."

He hung up the phone before turning to the bridge officer. "Officer of the Deck, turn the *Roosevelt* into the wind, prepare to launch aircraft!"

***

The Gil-Gamesh and the others flew back toward Emmyr when the guns were silenced. He hovered above the southern tip, watching the activity on the deck of the carrier very carefully through his viewing glass. He watched as the ship turned into the wind and aircraft started moving around deck, getting into position for launch.

The others gathered around him. Awaiting further orders from the Gil-Gamesh. Bryan turned to see if Captain Hawke had the *Avenger* in position. He spied it floating just above Emmyr.

"All right, fly down to the encampment and let the dragons return to Emmyr," he ordered. "Gamorg needs all the help he can get moving the island."

"Even Dee Dee?" Rose whined.

"I'm sorry, Rose! Dee Dee too! Now go!"

As the five headed down toward the shoreline, Bryan flew directly to the *Avenger*. He guided his dragon around to the back of the ship, patted the dragon on the side as a sign of thanks before dropping onto the deck.

"Are we ready, Jasper?" he asked, as soon as his feet touched the deck.

"All guns are locked and loaded, ready to fire, milord," Jasper acknowledged.

"Then let's get to work," Bryan exclaimed. "It's time to make Emmyr disappear!"

The *Avenger* started to circle the floating island while the cannons fired a continuous volley of what the sailors called 'Killer Frost' shells. A dense fog shrouded the island. The mist glistened with ice crystals that formed a protective shell around Emmyr.

When they were done, the *Avenger* took its position directly above the fog bank, waiting for the next attack. Jasper shouted orders, keeping the men on their toes. He hadn't been in command of a ship for some time, and he was relishing in the opportunity to stretch his sea legs.

Bryan stood on the bow, looking out over a fog-covered Emmyr, and to the fleet beyond. Jasper walked up to the Gil-Gamesh, awaiting further orders. "What are your orders, milord? Prepare for incoming attack?"

"No, Jasper, prepare to spring the trap!" he said with a smile. "Have the forward guns loaded with hallucinogens!"

Jasper smiled from ear-to-ear when he realised what he planned. "Yes, sir, Lord MoonDrake!" he replied before he turned to the men and started barking out orders.

As the guns are loaded and readied for firing, Bryan looked ahead through his looking glass. "*Video Visum!*" he chanted, causing the lens to zoom, giving him a bird's-eye view of the skies around him.

He finally spotted the strike group heading in toward Emmyr. It was at least twenty F/A-18 Super Hornets, loaded with as much firepower that they can carry. They were lined up in formation, moving in to strike.

"Ready, Jasper?" Bryan asked.

"Ready to fire, milord!"

"Then by all means, Captain Hawke, fire!" The cannons rang out and showered the sky with sparkles and colours, swirling through the air, expanding outward. The colours began to take shape as various mythological creatures, from dragons to chimeras to hippogriffs.

The hallucinogenic artillery created illusions that appeared real to whomever they're fired at. The pilots saw dozens of mythical creatures flying right at them. The reacted as anyone would, firing recklessly with their 20mm cannons as they swerved, dived and climbed to avoid the monsters. Some of them went into the fog bank surrounding the island, which created a whole new set of problems for them.

The 'Killer Frost' fog surrounding Emmyr froze anything entering it in a thick layer of ice. As the planes flew into the freezing fog, their systems malfunctioned, weapons failed, and engines cut out. They dropped from the sky, straight down into the ocean. Some of them ejected safely and parachuted down, but a few of the planes crashed into the sea, exploding on impact.

The remaining aircraft regrouped and form up for another run. The Gil-Gamesh knew the hallucinogens wouldn't work a second time. He ran over to the rail and looked down at Emmyr. Bryan knew instantly what he had to do.

"Captain Hawke, take us to Avalon, out of the range of their weapons, immediately!"

Jasper didn't delay, as he barked orders to the crew. They responded instantly, as the *Avenger* turned and headed back over Avalon, protected by the anti-technology barrier. Some of the crew thought they were running away, but the older sailors knew differently. They saw it on Bryan's face. Outlanders were in for a big surprise.

***

From the bridge of the *USS Theodore Roosevelt*, Captain Rich and Secretary Barry listened in on the ship-to-pilot communications pumped to the bridge from CDC. They watched in disbelief as the pilots scrambled at the Gil-Gamesh's illusions and then screamed in horror as their equipment froze up in the deadly fog and they dropped from the sky.

Rich couldn't take any more of it as he grabbed the sound-powered phone. "What are you doing, Captain?" Secretary Barry asked.

"I'm recalling all our aircraft. They are no match for his magic!"

"No, no, you mustn't! They must try again! They have to destroy that island!"

"Mr Secretary, my orders were to attack Emmyr, soften them up to force them back to the negotiating table," Rich argued. "By my assessment, we're the ones who've been softened up. They damaged four destroyers and two cruisers, not to mention the two Russian cruisers that are abandoning ship as we speak, in danger of sinking!" he continued. "We've got eight aircraft down and only four pilots to rescue. No sir, I will not sacrifice another airman for your personal vendetta against the Gil-Gamesh!"

"Now see here, Captain Rich, I—"

Before the Secretary could speak another word, the OOD interrupted the two men. "Excuse me, sir, but lookouts are reporting that the flying ship left its position over the floating island and is moving inland."

Both Rich and Barry raised their binoculars to over Emmyr. They watched as the airship with the Gil-Gamesh moved inland over Avalon, behind the protection of the anti-technology barrier that surrounded the island. It may be shrinking, but he was still out of reach of the Navy jets.

"Captain, CDC is requesting new orders," the OOD relayed. "Do you want the remaining fighters to return to the ship or swing about for another run?"

Rich pondered his next move. With the Gil-Gamesh out of the way, the island was still a viable target, if they stayed clear of the fog. He knew he had to satisfy both Secretary Barry and Washington, so there was only one choice in the matter.

He picked up the sound-powered phone again and pushed the selector button for CDC. "Ops, this is the Captain. Tell the pilots to make another run at the island, but to stay clear of the fog bank," he ordered. "Also, tell them not to stray too close to Avalon. Do not, I repeat, do not pursue the Gil-Gamesh's airship. Understood?"

"Yes, sir!" the Operations Officer responded. Rich hung up the phone and looked over at the Secretary. He was not happy that they weren't going after the Gil-Gamesh, but at least his home would take the brunt of the damage.

The jets pulled together, in tight formation and flew directly at Emmyr. The aircraft in front of the formation fired rockets into the fog at the island before veering off, back toward the sea. The others rose high over Emmyr and dropped heavy ordnance over the centre of the island.

They waited patiently, but there were no explosions, no fire, no flash, nothing at all. They watched as the ordnance fell out from the bottom of the fog bank and into the ocean, exploding harmlessly. Everyone was confused and perturbed, especially Secretary Barry.

"What happened?" he screamed. "Why didn't the bombs hit it?"

The fog bank began to lift. The floating island of Emmyr, home to the dragons of Avalon, had been sitting in that exact spot off the northeastern shores of Avalon for more than 3,000 years. Now, the island was gone, moved by the dragons away from the debilitating attacks of the Outlanders.

Rich breathed a sigh of relief. He hoped this would be the end of this folly. He picked up the sound-powered phone to make another call to CDC. "Ops order all aircraft to return to the *Roosevelt*," he ordered before changing the selector button to speak to the Air Boss. "Boss, get the deck ready to recover aircraft."

He hung up the phone and sat back in his chair. "Mr Secretary, would you like me to make the report to Washington, or will you?"

Barry looked down in disbelief and dejection. "If you would please, Captain Rich. I think I need to lie down for a little while."

"Of course, sir, I'll take care of it."

Barry put the binoculars down and left the bridge. As he walked down several flights of stairs, he pondered everything he saw today, and it left him depressed. He failed to bring the Gil-Gamesh back to the negotiating table, and he had never failed in his life.

As he opened the door to the Captain's inport cabin, he was met by the Captain's Secretary, Warrant Officer Ladonna Lucas. The young woman was a perfectionist by nature, something every captain needs to run his ship's office. If a task wasn't right, Lucas sent it back and wouldn't accept it until it was.

She was on the phone and quickly motioned for Secretary Barry to stand by. "Yes, sir, just one minute," she paused, as she put her hand over the receiver. "Mr Secretary, its General Garasimov for you, sir. I called up to the bridge for you, but they said you were on you way down here and that you weren't feeling good. I could have him call back later, sir?"

"No, that's all right, I'll speak with him," he said, holding out his hand for the phone. Ladonna handed him the receiver and quickly exited the room. Barry poured himself some water, as he sat down to take the call.

"Yes, General, this is Secretary Barry," he paused, listening to the Russian military commander. "Yes, I realise that the island is gone, and we've got nothing to show for it."

He paused again, as he listened to more of the general's comments. "Yes, I do believe we still need to strike back, especially for your cruiser crews, but what can we do?" He paused to hear the reply.

"Really, you have the authority to do that?" Barry asked. "How soon can they be here?

"Yes, I think that's a definite possibility, General Garasimov. Let me put a call into the President and I'll get back to you. We may have a chance to strike back at these medieval bastards yet!"

Chapter 7
A Prophecy Revealed

Hugo Courtland's sleep was troubled. The Grand Master of the Wizard's Council tossed and turned as his dreams turned to nightmares these past few weeks. From his bedroom inside Strongürd Keep, he was haunted by visions of death and destruction—his and Avalon's respectively.

He woke up screaming, his lips trembling, his breath laboured and his body covered in sweat. It had been the same nightmare for weeks, but tonight was different. Tonight, he awoke with someone in his room. A robed, hooded figure stood at the foot of his bed.

"It's you…it is you, isn't it?" Hugo asked.

"Yes, Hugo, it's me, but you've known of my return since the death of Morgana le Fay. I have to wonder, why didn't you tell anyone about me?"

"I c-couldn't," he stammered. "If I said anything to change the course of time, my death would be long and painful. I will die tonight, in peace."

"Oh Hugo, you will die tonight, but I'm afraid it will not be peaceful. Unless of course, you tell me what you saw in your dreams? What lies in the future for Avalon?"

Hugo tried to remember the images from his dreams, but they were painful and quite harrowing. He had tried to forget it, but he could never shake the truth from his dreams.

"I saw Outlanders invading our sacred shores, only to be wiped out by the ghosts of Avalon past. I saw Elves, glowing with a light of pure starlight, ascending into the next realm but with their ascension came with a cost— Avalon destroyed, falling into the sea. A broken realm, scattered to the four winds. I then saw an evil moon rising over the House of Pendragon, and you were in that moon, laughing and towering triumphantly over the remains of Avalon."

Though Hugo couldn't see him do it, the stranger smiled with glee. Hugo's predictions were never wrong. "Thank you, Hugo, you have been most helpful!"

"I'm not finished...I also saw the coming of three dragons to oppose you at every turn. Your reign will not be an easy one as they will do everything within their power to depose you."

The stranger grimaced and gritted his teeth. "And who are these three charlatans?"

It was Hugo's turn to smile. "That you will have to discover for yourself."

The stranger had heard enough from the old wizard. "As you said, Wizard Courtland, I will reign over Avalon. It's a pity you will not be here to witness it."

A demon hole opened next to the wizard's bed and Abdel Ben Faust stepped through. Before his feet even touched the bedroom's floor, he had beheaded Hugo Courtland in a single, clean swing of his sword. The wound cauterised instantly from the burning edge of *Deathsong*. The head dropped to the bed. The body shook violently for several moments. Then, it lay still.

Faust looked down as his handiwork and sheathed his sword. "So, what now milord? Surely, he lied about his prophetic dreams to throw you off."

"No, Abdel, he didn't lie. The one thing Hugo Courtland always did was tell the truth, especially when it came to his visions. He was very proud of his remarkable accuracy in predicting future events. We wait," he concluded. "We will strike soon enough, as he told us, when the Outlanders invade Avalon. After all, we must protect our lands if we are to rule them."

***

The *Avenger* came down at the edge of the major encampment for the defence of Avalon. More than 2,000 knights, shield maidens, Dwarves and Elves were positioned less than one mile inland from the coast. At the outer edge of the encampment, airships were moored as crews rotated through patrols along the coastline.

Sailors tossed down lines from the *Avenger* that were attached to winches. The men laboured to winch the airship down as the wings were folded in close to the ship and the sails dropped. As soon as the gangplank was lowered, the Gil-Gamesh and Captain Hawke left the ship and headed straight for the command tent.

Like the homes on Avalon, the tents were constructed tesseracts—pocket dimensions that allowed for larger living areas inside small spaces—every one of them bigger on the inside.

As the Gil-Gamesh approached the tent, guards standing outside the entrance snapped to attention before the pulled back the tent flap. Bryan stepped inside to see Eileanora, Rhona, Edan and Rose leaning over a table, looking over a layout of Avalon. The positions of all the Avalon forces were represented by small figurines as were the Outlander ships surrounding the island.

With them at the table is Sir Frederick Winslow Murdock, knight-errant from Nottinghamshire, or as Amelia called him, a mercenary-for-hire. His dashing good looks, bushy moustache and long goatee fit his reputation as a dashing rogue, but he was also a reliable fighter and a good friend of Lord MoonDrake. That's why Bryan had made him commander of these forces.

The Gil-Gamesh immediately reached out a hand to his friend. "Freddie, it's good to see you!"

"Come on, Bryan, you know I never miss a good fight. I hope you saved some for me!"

"Oh, don't worry, this is far from over. You'll get your chance!" Bryan said, patting his friend on the shoulder. "So, how are the rest of our forces?"

Everyone turned back to the table as Frederick briefed them on the position of the forces of Avalon. "Sir Cedric is positioned on the southern coast with more than 2,000 under his command. Baron Ericksson has secured the north from Steinfisk to the edge of the Fenris Mountains.

"On the west, Master Dinius and Chief T'Ronga have the western shores protected down to South Essex," he continued. "Avalon is ready for whatever the bastards decide to throw at us."

"Rhona, what about Sarafina and the remaining shield maidens?"

"Dame Sarafina has taken position near Candletop Lighthouse. We have every available shield maiden deployed around the island. All the younger trainees are in Alfheimer with Lady Stephanie and your grandchildren."

"They've abandoned the Convent? Why?" Bryan asked.

"With all the forces scattered around Avalon, we had no one to protect the Convent or the young trainees," Rhona explained. "Lady Lyllodoria offered them sanctuary at Alfheimer."

Eileanora chuckled before she caught herself and covered her mouth.

"Is something funny, Eileanora?" the Gil-Gamesh asked.

"No, milord, I'm just trying to imagine groups of human children playing around the ancient city. It is something I could never imagine."

Bryan laughed. "Well, times like these can make for strange bedfellows, wouldn't you say?"

Everyone around the table chuckled, something they hadn't been able to do for the past few days. "So, what's the plan, milord?" Edan queried. "Do we wait for the barrier to shrink some more?"

"No, Edan, not if we can help it. What's the word from the Wizard's Council or Ashley? Any luck finding the spell to restore the barrier?"

"We've been so wrapped up in the defences and evacuation of Emmyr, we haven't had a chance to reach out to them," Frederick explained.

"All right, I'll reach out to Strongürd Keep myself," Bryan said. "Eileanora, I want you to mix in the *Hîldrägo Boquè* with the shore watch. They have better eyesight to keep an eye on the Outlander ships."

"It will be done, milord!" she said with a nod of her head.

"Captain Hawke, I want you to take Rose to Alfheimer on the *Avenger*, and while you're there, get an update from Ashley." The Gil-Gamesh's orders confused everyone at the table, especially Edan. His heart sank at the thought of losing his ship to Jasper Hawke.

But before he could voice his objection, Bryan stopped him. "I know what you're going to say, Edan, but I want you to know this is not a demotion; it's a reassignment."

"I'm sorry, milord, I don't understand?" Edan asked holding back the fear and frustration.

"I need you to head to Cornish and take command of the *Flying Fancy*," Bryan stated. Over a year ago, during the resurrection of Morgana le Fay, one of her allies was Captain John Henry Avery, the legendary Pirate King. Captain Edan O'Brien captured Avery and his ship when they tried to escape once the tide of the battle turned against him. Since then, the ship had been gathering dust at the shipyard in Cornish.

"The Outlanders are a superstitious bunch, especially sailors," Bryan explained. "The sight of a pirate ship will give them second thoughts about attacking Avalon again."

"But, *sire*, Captain Hawke is just as capable of commanding the *Flying Fancy*," Edan argued.

"No, Edan, he can't, because of that!" Bryan retorted, pointing at Edan's sword, *Crossbones*. It was the sword of the Pirate King that Edan claimed when he captured Avery and his ship. "You won that sword from Avery and with it, only you can command the *Flying Fancy*.

"There's a legend of the first Pirate King, Avery's ancestor, Captain Henry Avery," Bryan continued. "It was said that he won every battle he'd ever fought, even after he arrived on Avalon. There were stories written throughout the diaries of the past Gil-Gamesh. They talked about the constant struggle my ancestors had in trying to catch Avery.

"That drive, that spirit, is a powerful magic. The sword and ship were passed down from generation-to-generation of Avery's descendants, just like the Twin Swords of the Dragon Moon were passed down through the line of Sir Percival. Both the sword and ship were passed on when one Captain was either killed or stepped down from command, and with it, the magic of the first Pirate King.

"Just like I am the only one who can wield the twin swords, you are the only one who can command the *Flying Fancy*, Edan. I need you to take up the mantle and be the Pirate King."

Edan thought about everything the Gil-Gamesh said. He hated to lose the *Avenger*, but the fact that he and only he could command the *Flying Fancy* made it impossible to resist. "With your permission, milord, I would like to bring some of my crew with me."

Bryan smiled. He was happy to see that Edan saw things his way. "I'll let you and Jasper work that out. In the meantime, we must stay focused. The enemy is still out there. We've dealt them a terrible loss, but they will not back down. Questions?"

Everyone around the table remained silent, as Bryan scanned the room. They all understood what was expected of them. Just then, Amelia burst in, huffing and puffing out of breath. The disturbed look on her face was enough to tell the Gil-Gamesh that something was wrong.

"Amelia, what is it?"

"Milord," she said, gasping for air. "The Wizard Courtland is dead!"

The room was dumbstruck, save for Bryan. "What? When? How?" he asked.

"He was murdered in Strongürd Keep last night, beheaded by an unknown assailant. The wound was cauterised, Milord."

Bryan knew immediately what she was implying. "Abdel Ben Faust!" he exclaimed. "I thought that son-of-a-bitch was still in South Essex."

"Sir Devereaux doesn't know when he left," Amelia said. "He said people steer clear of him when he comes to town."

"Why in the world do they continue to allow him access to South Essex?" Eileanora inquired.

"He tips good," Frederick quipped. "There are not very many who could afford an assassin of Faust's calibre. They should be easy to track down."

"We'll deal with Faust after the crisis is averted," Bryan said. "Amelia, who has taken control of the Wizard's Council?"

"Wizard Jean-Paul Baptiste has been elevated to Grand Master of the Wizard's Council, milord."

Bryan nodded. He leaned down on his elbows, closed his eyes and tried to gather his thoughts. So much was happening all at once and it gave him an uneasy feeling. His gut instinct told him that this was just the beginning of something bad. "*By the pricking of my thumbs, something wicked this way comes'*," he muttered to himself, quoting Shakespeare.

Everyone looked at the Gil-Gamesh with confused curiosity. "Milord?" Amelia asked.

Bryan chuckled, took a deep breath and stood up. "Yes, sorry. All right, everyone, you have your orders. I need to speak with the new Grand Master of the Wizard's Council."

Without another word, Bryan turned and walked out of the tent at a fast pace. He moved through the encampment, not stopping to talk to anyone as most were accustomed to. He almost made it to his tent, when he heard his name being called from behind.

"Gil-Gamesh!" Edan shouted, as he ran up to him. He'd been chasing the Gil-Gamesh ever since he left the tent. "Lord MoonDrake, a word please!"

Bryan stopped just short of his personal tent, and he gave Edan the chance to speak. The young man's breathing was laboured, but he was finally able to gather himself to talk. "I just wanted to apologise for my—"

"Enough, Edan, you need to stop apologising all the time," Bryan said sternly. "You don't have to be constantly worried if you've said something or did something wrong. If you're not apologising to me, you're being an overprotective male chauvinist when it comes to Rose."

Bryan got right in Edan's face, poking his finger into Edan's chest. "If I were you, I would take this time to set things right with my daughter before you lose her forever."

The Gil-Gamesh turned on his heel, back toward his tent, before he whipped around for one last point. "And Edan, when you return from Cornish with the *Flying Fancy*, I expect the Pirate King, not the apologetic, young sailor I see before me!"

Bryan turned again and entered his tent without another word to Edan. He knew he was harsh with his young Captain, but that was what he needed, especially now.

The Gil-Gamesh spent the next few minutes catching his breath while he gathered the things he needed to contact Strongürd Keep—a water basin and a mirror. It was something he learned from his former mentor, the wizard Archibald Bowbridge, who had died at the hands of Morgana le Fay.

He submerged the mirror inside the basin and set it on the floor. "*Loquere Strongürd!*" he beckoned, as he passed his hand over the basin three times, repeating the incantation until the basin began to glow with a blue light.

The Gil-Gamesh stepped back as the light erupted into a column of shimmering blue. Within seconds, the light changed into the image of an old man in regal robes. His head was adorned with a gold bald cap. A long, thin white beard hung down from his chin to his knees. His face was careworn from more than 1,000 years of service to Avalon. It was Chancellor Ian Talbot, Minister of Magic for Strongürd Keep.

"Ah, Lord MoonDrake, it is good to see you," the wizard proclaimed with a short bow. "What can I do for the Gil-Gamesh of Avalon?"

Bryan was always appreciative of Chancellor Talbot's grace and courtesy. He was once Chancellor to Queen Cadhla but, as his age started to slow him down, he stepped down to return to his home at Strongürd Keep until the end of his days.

"I need to speak with Grand Master Baptiste, Chancellor Talbot," Bryan said. "I realise this is not a good time for you, but it is vital that I speak with him."

"Of course, Gil-Gamesh, give me a moment to retrieve him," Talbot said, as he stepped out from view. When until Grand Master Jean-Paul Baptiste appeared, he was dressed quite differently since the last time Bryan has seen him. His robes were befitting his new position, made of flowing Elven silks of dark blue with black and red embroidered with gold ornaments and gems. His long red hair was braided with gold ornaments to hold his hair neatly in place. A simple crown of gold adorned his tiny head.

Bryan bowed in respect to the new Grand Master of the Wizard's Council. "Jean-Paul, I would offer you congratulations on your ascendance to Grand Master, but I know this is not how you wanted it to be."

"Actually, Gil-Gamesh, it happened exactly as I was told," he replied. Bryan was taken aback. "Yes, Hugo came to me a few days ago and handed me an envelope with his seal. He told me not to open it until after he died. It was his last will and testament, stating it was his wish for me to be his replacement as Grand Master of the Wizard's Council."

"Did he say anything else, about who his assailant was?" Bryan asked. Jean-Paul shook his head.

"I'm sorry, no, but we all know who it was. Abdel Ben Faust's cursed blade leaves a distinctive mark. Besides the fact that the attendants, who discovered the body, said the room smelled of brimstone and sulphur."

"Yes, I know, his demon holes. But how did he gain entry to the Keep? I thought your magical wards would prevent such an incursion?"

"They should, but somehow, he was able to bypass them. That means he must have had help from inside the Keep," Baptiste observed. "Just another mystery to add to my list."

"That's why I was calling. Any luck in finding a way to restore the barrier?"

"We have found some promising possibilities, but we still need the additional spell from Merlin to make it complete. I must say, Lord MoonDrake, that your daughter has been a remarkable asset to Merlin. She has a great acumen for magic, especially for an Outlander. He was wise to make her his apprentice."

Bryan was stunned at Jean-Paul's announcement. He was unaware that Merlin had asked Ashley to be his apprentice, and Jean-Paul realised it.

"My apologies, Bryan, I thought you knew."

"It's all right, Jean-Paul, my family has a habit of not telling me things until the last minute. I'll get back with you when I know more. In the meantime, keep at it. We need to restore Avalon away from the outside world as soon as possible. I have a feeling the Outlanders will try to take advantage of the shrinking anti-technology barrier."

"We will continue our endeavours, Gil-Gamesh. You have my word," Baptiste bowed before the image faded and the light disappeared, leaving Bryan standing in darkness.

"*Ex Flamma!*" Bryan shouted and with a wave of his hand, candles lit themselves all around the room. He sat down and poured himself a goblet of wine. It was the first time that he'd had the chance to rest.

So much is happening at once, he thought. But he knew where his focus needed to be right now. He had to protect Avalon from the next attempt by the Outlanders against him. He knew that Secretary Barry was angry, lashing out at him with the superior might of their military forces.

"They're going to attack, I know it!" Bryan said aloud. "We have to be prepared for anything they might throw at us!"

***

Weeks passed and there had been no aggressive movement by the Outlanders. Their ships remained where they were, off the coast of Avalon. The US Navy destroyers, damaged in the battle for Emmyr, departed when new ships arrived to replace them. The two Russian cruisers were quickly abandoned after the extreme damage they had taken and sank into the sea.

Dotted along the coast of Avalon and sitting atop the raised cliff-face were outposts manned 24/7 by the Knights of the Round Table, shield maidens, the Dragon Guard and Elves from the *Hîldrägo Boquè*. Their job was to keep an eye on the fleet off the coast and report any movement toward Avalon by sea or by air.

At one outpost, located directly across where Emmyr once floated in the sky, sat a small group of men in the third hour of their watch. A small fire kept them warm, but it was of little comfort. It was three o'clock in the morning, the air was chilly and the tedious nature of the watch was already getting to some of them.

Of all the knights there, Sir Eadric Cuthbert was the oldest. At nearly 100 years old, he was still considered by many to be in his prime. He had fought in many battles throughout his career as a Knight of the Round Table, evidenced by the many battle scars on his body. He could have had them healed but he preferred leaving the marks as they were, because to him, each one was a story. His shaggy beard of black and grey was the only hair on his body as the rest had either fallen out or was burned off at one time or another. He leaned against his halberd, a two-handed polearm with a broad axe blade and a pike, and tried to shake off the sleep. He knew he had too much to drink before coming on watch, but the young men kept asking for one more story and he couldn't help himself.

As Eadric dozed, Feredir kept his gaze locked off the coast of Avalon. As one of the youngest members of the elite *Hîldrägo Boquè*, the Elf warrior was always mindful of his duties while on watch. He memorised all the ships situated off the coast of Avalon and took careful inventory whenever he assumed watch. His stark-green eyes and brown hair highlighted his beautiful features, as did his traditional copper-coloured armour of the *Hîldrägo Boquè*. Armed with his longbow and long sword, his normally dutiful attention was interrupted by the occasional snoring of Eadric, a recent bout of which had woken the veteran.

"Are you sure you should be standing the watch when you're so tired, Sir Eadric?" Feredir inquired politely.

"Nonsense, Feredir, why I once stayed awake for four days straight on twenty minutes of sleep at the siege of Kohlwick Hollow," Eadric replied, as he snapped to attention. "I usually need some action to keep my focus, so I don't drift off."

"Well, you're not a young man anymore. You should take it easy on the late-night revelry."

"Speak for yourself, lad," Eadric snapped back. "It's late night revelry that keeps this old man going."

"Lad?" Feredir said, as he glared at Sir Eadric with a look of bewilderment. "You do realise that I'm more than 1,500 years older than you?"

"Ah, it's not the age, lad, it's how you carry yourself," Eadric answered. "You walk like my son, Dabney, used to. Strong, confident and full of life. Me? I'm an old man, past his prime, who tries to be 'one of the boys' by drinking the night away while telling one of a hundred stories of my life as a Knight of the Round Table."

"You speak too harshly about yourself, Sir Eadric," Feredir said. "You have lived a long and fruitful life, serving the people of Avalon with honour. You have nothing to be ashamed of."

"He's right, Sir Eadric," interjected one of the other knights. Your presence means a lot to young men like me." The other men nodded their heads in agreement, chiming in to support the aged warrior.

Eadric said nothing in reply. He just leaned against his halberd and sighed. Feredir saw that something was on his mind. "Is something bothering you, Sir Eadric?"

"My son, Dabney," Eadric said, his voice turned solemn and sad. "I haven't thought about him for over a year before now, not even speaking his name."

Feredir jerked his head, unsure of where Eadric was going with this. The old man continued. "Dabney died last year at the battle of Idlehorn Mountain. We were defending the right flank when a Drow Strider came right at us. I got under the beastie with my halberd while Dabney sliced it right between its eight eyes. The Drow fell off the spider's back, so I ran it through with the pike.

"We turned our back on the spider, thinking it was dead, but it had a little bit of life left. It grabbed Dabney and ran him through with its stinger. Some lads carried him to the rear while I continued to fight. When the battle was over, I went to find Dabney but…"

His voice trailed off, not finishing his sentence, but Feredir understood and finished the thought. "They had to burn his body because Drow spiders lay eggs inside their victims when they die. The only recourse was to burn the bodies before the eggs could hatch. I'm very sorry, Sir Eadric."

Eadric wiped the tears from his eyes and took a deep breath to regain his composure. "That's all right, lad. We all have to go sometime. I'll see my son again one day; that's what keeps me going."

The two remained quiet for almost half an hour until Eadric finally broke the silence. "Do you remember a Storm Giant by the name of Boras?"

"Boras? I remember when he came down from Merlin's Pinnacle to raid cattle and sheep farms," Feredir recalled. "His people were starving because they didn't stock up enough for the winter, so he took it upon himself to get some provisions, as it were. I heard it took more than 100 knights to finally bring him down."

"101, actually," Eadric said slyly. "Let me tell you about it, you see—"

"Oh no, Eadric, not the Boras story again!" interrupted a voice from behind. The men all turned to see Sir Hunter and Chancellor Beauchamp walking toward them. Hunter was carrying a Lancer, as if he was ready to fight while Henri carried a teapot.

Eadric walked up to Hunter and greeted him like a brother, embracing him enthusiastically. "What are you doing here, Sir Hunter?" Eadric asked. "I thought you were in Alfheimer?"

"I finally got a clean bill of health from Doctor Bonapat, so I took the first flight back here. My mother was driving me crazy!" he joked. "Actually, I'm just escorting Chancellor Beauchamp out here. Henri thought you all could use some efion tea."

"*Mais bien sûr*," Henri said, as he began pouring tea for each of the men. "I wanted to bring you some of Chef Manfred's world famous Cioppino, but he would not let it out of his sight. *De toute façon*, the Gil-Gamesh always said that everyone needs a little something to keep them going until morning, *n'est ce pas?*"

Sir Eadric greedily took the cup from Chancellor Beauchamp. "God bless you, Chancellor, this is just what I needed!" He took a big sip of tea, savouring each swallow with a soft moan. "Ah, a Christmas Hot Toddy! Just the way I like it!"

Efion tea was an Elvish drink that provided nourishment to Elves when they travel away from Alfheimer. For humans, its effect was like that of an energy drink on steroids. A unique quality of the brew was that it reflected the drinker's taste desires, ranging from sweet to savoury.

Henri offered a cup to Feredir, but the Elf politely refused. "No thank you, Chancellor Beauchamp. I had some before I came on watch. I am perfectly…fine…"

His voice trailed off as his eye caught something different on the horizon. Hunter knew how keen the eyesight of an Elf was and tried to see as well. It was a clear night, the moon waning as a small sliver of a crescent high in the sky.

"What is it?" Hunter asked. "What do you see?"

"There's a new ship out there, one I've never seen before."

"Are you sure, Feredir?" Eadric asked. "Those metal contraptions look all the same to me."

"I have observed all the same ships for the past few weeks, that one is new."

Try as he might, Hunter could barely make out the ship in the darkness. "Can you describe it?" he asked. "Do you see any writing on it?"

"It looks like the other large warship…the aircraft carrier, I believe your father called it, but the front of the ship is curved upward like a ramp," Feredir said. "There is some writing on the side of the main structure but I'm not familiar with the language."

"Show me!" Hunter demanded. Feredir took a dagger and wrote a few letters in the dirt next to the fire. Hunter didn't understand the words, but he recognised the language. "That's Russian, I think," he said. "It must be a helicopter carrier of some sort."

"Are those the machines with the spinning blades on them?" Feredir asked.

"Yes, why?"

"Because there are four of them headed our way!"

Feredir drew his bow. Hunter turned to two of the younger knights standing with them. "Pass the word down along the coast that invaders are coming toward Avalon," he commanded. The two men took off in opposite directions to warn the other outposts. "Henri, go tell my father what's going on! We need him here immediately!" Henri dropped the teapot and he took off running toward the main encampment.

Hunter reloaded his Lancer with two new spellshots as he and Sir Eadric crouched low behind the protection of some rocks. Feredir acted as lookout.

"How far out are they?" Hunter asked.

"Three of them are holding their position about six furlongs off shore," he said, scanning the horizon. "I've lost the fourth one."

"What?" Hunter exclaimed and jumped up to look. Eadric followed suit.

"Where did it go?" Eadric asked. Before Feredir could answer, the three men heard a whirring sound from just off the cliff. From below the edge, a helicopter rose up in the air in front of them, threatening them with a rotary mini-gun.

The three took cover as the helicopter opened fire, pelleting the ground around them with rapid-fire spray. Feredir notched an arrow and readied himself. The firing stopped for a moment and the Elven warrior stood up and fired off an arrow. The aim was true, a perfect shot at the helicopter pilot, but it ricocheted off the front windshield. Feredir got a second arrow off, but it had the same result. He dove behind the rock just as the pilot began firing again.

Feredir cursed. "My arrows won't penetrate that infernal machine!" Hunter weighed all the options and he came up with an idea.

"I think I can help you there," he said. He pulled up his Lancer, ready to fire. "After I shoot, hit him again. Your arrows should penetrate this time."

Hunter took a deep breath before he popped up and fired his Lancer at the helicopter. His spellshot—a combination of magic and alchemy loaded into a cartridge the size of a shotgun shell—fired a freezing spray at the helicopter, coating the front of the aircraft in a layer of frost. The windshield froze instantaneously, and the pilot stopped firing.

Feredir quickly popped up and fired another arrow at the windshield. This time, his arrow shattered the glass and pierced the pilot through the chest. The aircraft pitched to the side and the co-pilot tried to regain control. Feredir didn't give him a chance and he fired another arrow, killing the co-pilot instantly with an arrow through the throat.

The helicopter spun out of control as it flew over the three warriors and careened toward the ground. The engines shut down just before impact, then it crashed, exploding in a giant ball of fire. Sir Eadric and Hunter roared loudly at their victory. Feredir just stood there silently; there was a hint of a grin on his face.

"Now that was teamwork," Eadric cheered. "Well done, lads; well done to both of you!"

Hunter looked closely and calculated the distance from the cliff to where the helicopter crashed. His face turned sour.

"The barrier has shrunk even more," Hunter surmised. "It reaches almost 500 feet away from the cliff."

"We should order the outposts to move in," Eadric said. "Otherwise, their weapons can reach us."

Feredir concurred. Suddenly, the sound of engines filled the air. The three warriors turned around to see two more helicopters rising above the cliff and moving towards them. The copters opened fire, tearing up the ground as they strafed toward the men.

With uncanny reflexes, Feredir grabbed Hunter and threw him to the ground behind the outcropping of rocks. Sir Eadric was not as fast. The spray from the mini-guns ripped his body apart, killing him before he hit the ground in tatters.

Hunter cried out in sadness as he looked at Eadric's lifeless form. Feredir lowered his head for a moment. Then something strange happened to Eadric's corpse. "Feredir, look!" Hunter said. The two watched the body glowed briefly as Eadric's spirit rose from his body. It hovered over the corpse for a moment as it transformed into a wraith—an armoured warrior with a ghostly visage for its head. The energy from his spirit absorbed into the heart stone on its chest and pulsed to life.

Once fully formed, the wraith let loose an unearthly shriek before it flew into one of the helicopters. The pilot panicked and swerved into the other helicopter. The collision forced the blades of the copters to shred one another into pieces. The two helicopters fell straight down to the beach below, exploding on impact. The wraith that was Sir Eadric was gone.

The last Russian helicopter was not deterred by the destruction of the first three. It hovered back from the cliff and fired a pair of assault missiles at the two hiding behind the outcropping. Hunter saw the missiles being launched from the aircraft. He grabbed Feredir by the arm and pulled him away from the rocks as quickly as possible.

The missiles hit the rocks, causing a massive explosion that hurled the two warriors through the air. They crashed into the ground hard and had the wind knocked out of them. The helicopter moved in closer. Its mini-gun whirred to life and started firing.

"*Acheron Draconis!*" shouted a voice from behind them. The Gil-Gamesh summoned his dragon form, erupting with magical energy as it formed around him. "*Defendo!*" he chanted, as the dragon's wings folded down in front of Hunter and Feredir, protecting them from the gunfire.

"*Infernus!*" Bryan commanded. The dragon form reared back and breathed fire, blasting the helicopter with full force. The helicopter exploded almost instantly, dropping down on top of the other two wrecked aircraft.

Bryan dismissed his dragon form as Rhona and Amelia rushed to check on Hunter and Feredir. The two men were mostly unharmed, just bumped and bruised from the explosion. Bryan ran over to Hunter, concerned for his safety.

"Hunter, are you all right?"

"We're fine, Dad, but Sir Eadric was mowed down by those bastards and then something weird happened."

"What? What happened?"

"It was like his soul left his body, but it reformed into a ghostly knight. It destroyed two of the helicopters, but I've never seen anything like that before."

"I have," Feredir interjected. "The *Hîldrägo Boquè* once ventured into purgatory and were met by the Wraith Legion. Sir Eadric was tormented by not being there for his son at the Battle of Idlehorn Mountain. His self-doubt caused him to become a wraith, but I've never seen one outside of purgatory before."

"Nor I," Rhona observed. "If the Wraith Legion has left purgatory, who will hold back the demon horde?"

"That's not our concern right now, Rhona," the Gil-Gamesh affirmed. "Henri said you saw a Russian carrier off the coast, Feredir?"

"Yes, milord," he said, looking out over the horizon. "It's maintaining a position with the other carrier."

"I want you to go to the other *Hîldrägo Boquè* and let them know what to look for," Bryan ordered. "We need to keep a close eye on them. Amelia, go with him."

Before the two took off to carry out their orders, Hunter stopped them. "Father, we also need to move the outposts back from the coastline. When the first helicopter crashed, its engines didn't shut down until they were overhead. The barrier is still shrinking."

Bryan sighed in frustration but knew that Hunter was right. "Amelia, tell the outposts to move inland another 300 feet. Rhona, get some replacements out here as soon as possible. Hunter and I will stay until they get here."

Amelia just bowed politely before taking off with Feredir to warn the other outposts while Rhona headed back to the encampment. Bryan wrapped his arm around Hunter as the two walked over to tend to Sir Eadric's body.

The two pulled his body over next to the remnants of the outpost before Hunter draped him with his cloak. The two men said a small prayer for the deceased knight, both knowing it was probably in vain after hearing Feredir's story of the Wraith Legion.

There was profound silence between them until Hunter finally spoke up. "Dad, what the hell's going on? There is something more here than Outlanders and a shrinking barrier."

"I know Hunter, I know. I just don't have time to worry about anything else right now.

"The real danger is out there," he said, pointing out toward the ocean. "We can deal with whatever menace is scheming—whether it's Abdel Ben Faust or wraiths out of purgatory—once the barrier has been restored."

"By then, it may be too late," Hunter said. "You're taking too much on yourself, Father. You're the Gil-Gamesh, but you can't be in every place all at once."

Bryan took his son's words to heart. He was right, and Bryan knew it. "All right, Hunter, I'll have Ocwyn investigate this wraith phenomenon. In the meantime, we'll get the men ready for the next incursion. Sending helos at us was just the beginning."

Hunter nodded his head, then added, "Oh, and do me a favour. Please don't tell Mom about the missiles and gunfire. She'll never let me leave her sight again if you do."

Bryan couldn't help but laugh. "Okay, Hunter, not a word."

***

Secretary Barry threw the binoculars across the bridge of the Russian aircraft carrier Admiral Kuznetsov. He hoped the Russian's would have had better luck than the US Navy since they didn't have the trepidation that held the Americans back. The Russians were aggressive, but that didn't work either. The Gil-Gamesh and his forces brought down the helicopters with relative ease. That frustrated him to no end.

"Calm yourself, Mr Secretary," General Garasimov stated through a thick Russian accent.

"Calm? How can you expect me to be calm when your inept and ineffective strategy produced the same results as ours?"

General Garasimov frowned, his disposition soured by Barry's assertions. "It is common courtesy for guests to refrain from insulting their hosts, Mr Secretary, especially when your personal reputation is at stake."

"My apologies, General Garasimov, but you can't be happy with results like that!"

"On the contrary, Mr Secretary, I am very happy with the results," he asserted, confusing Secretary Barry even more. "Please understand, the pilots will be revered and honoured as heroes of the Russian Federation. Their sacrifice will help us get the upper hand on these medieval dogs."

General Garasimov escorted him over to a radar console to explain his strategy. "This is where we lost contact with the first helicopter," Garasimov said, as he pointed to a single marker on the screen.

"I'm sorry, General; I don't follow you."

"Look how far inland it is. The last flyover the American aircraft did was here," he continued, pointing at another marker on the screen, well short of the current one. "This barrier that is preventing our machines from operating over Avalon is shrinking at an accelerated rate. Our best estimate is one month, maybe two, until it is completely gone. We should be able to land an assault force and slowly push our way in with aircraft to cover our incursion."

"Not bad. But we may not have one to two months," Barry said. "The UN. General Assembly is moving to legitimise Avalon's claim as a sovereign nation. Once they do that, the President will not allow any further actions against them."

General Garasimov smiled at the thought of beginning his operation. "Well then, let's get started."

Chapter 8
The Invasion of Avalon

Of all the magical places on Avalon, Excalibur Cove was the most sacred. It was where Merlin took Uther to receive the sword *Excalibur* from the Lady of the Lake. It was also where Arthur drew the sword from the stone to become King.

The King's Stone sat in the middle of the cove. *Excalibur* rested in place in the stone, returned there over a year ago when the Gil-Gamesh brought the shattered pieces of *Twilight* and *Dusk* to the Lady of the Lake. His original swords were forged from the pieces of *Excalibur* until Morgana destroyed them with the Dark Tides. The Lady of the Lake reformed the broken pieces into *Excalibur* and drove it into the King's Stone. Now, it waited for the King to draw it when he was ready.

On the shore just off Excalibur Cove, as the first light of dawn broke over the calm waters, stood a dark, robed stranger. He stared at *Excalibur*, as if it were calling to him. His machinations were coming together, piece-by-piece. He had his allies, his general and his army. Now, he needed one more thing to assure his place on the throne of Avalon.

He reached inside the folds of his robe and pulled out a crystal globe filled with a smoky mist. He held the orb up to his mouth and whispered an incantation to it.

The mist from inside poured out of the glass orb, spreading across the water from the shoreline to the King's Stone. The man placed the orb back in his robe as he stepped out onto the mist, crossing the lake as if he were walking on stepping stones.

He paused at the King's Stone, examining the sword very closely. He tentatively reached out for the handle, but then pulled away, hesitant to touch the enchanted blade.

"It will not come to you," a voice echoed from beneath the lake. Rising out of the water was the Lady of the Lake, eternal guardian of Avalon. She was a beautiful woman, garbed in glittering, golden chain mail. Her long, blonde hair fell effortlessly across her shoulders from underneath a light-golden helm.

The stranger shielded his eyes from the brilliance of her presence. He couldn't bring himself to look at her directly, so he stared at her reflection in the water, and watched as it came closer

"Why did you come here?" the Lady asked. "You must know that *Excalibur* could never be drawn by the likes of you!"

"I am the rightful heir to the throne of Avalon," the stranger cried. "The sword will be mine!"

"No, it will not!" she exclaimed. With a simple gesture of her hand, the stranger's hood flew from his head, revealing his face. He was ageless, still young and beautiful thanks to the enchantments placed on him by his mother, Morgana le Fay. His hair shined like flecks of gold, flowing around his face. Though he looked to be a mere teenage boy, he was more than 3,000 years old. He was Mordred, immortal knight, sorcerer and bastard son of King Arthur.

"You will never wield *Excalibur*, Mordred. Resolve yourself to that!"

"Resolve myself? I have waited for 3,000 years to take my rightful place on the granite throne of Avalon. My mother's spell has kept me young, beautiful and nigh-immortal. I will not be denied from taking what is rightfully mine!" Mordred lunged at the Lady of the Lake, but his hand passed through her. The Lady was unfazed.

"Your threats are useless. No mortal hand can touch me, Mordred. You cannot harm me in the same way; you cannot draw the sword from the stone."

An evil grin appeared on Mordred's face as if he already knew all of this. "No mortal hand, eh? Well, what about an undead one?"

From beneath the water, two wraiths arose and grabbed the Lady of the Lake by her arms. Then, without warning, Abdel Ben Faust dropped in through a demon hole and wrapped a heavy iron chain around her. The Lady collapsed as if all her strength had been drained by the massive chain.

The two wraiths carried her to the shore and dropped her to the ground. For the first time in a millennium, the Lady of the Lake was outside of her watery home in the lake. Mordred walked back across the mist, grinning proudly at the success of his scheme.

"Don't you recognise them? These are the Chains of Tartarus, forged by the blacksmiths of Atlantis to hold any man, woman or beast captive by reflecting its own power back against them. The stronger you are, the heavier the chains become."

He leaned down so the Lady of the Lake could see the smug expression written all over his face. "Not so powerful now, are you, dear Lady?" The Lady looked up at him defiantly and rose to her feet.

"It doesn't matter what you do to me, Mordred. You may take the throne of Avalon, but the people will not follow you as long as the Gil-Gamesh is there to stop you. Even then, I know of three who will rise to oppose your reign of terror.

You have come back only to fail again, Mordred!" she finished before collapsing again as the chains continued to take hold. Mordred's smug expression turned sour at her premonition.

"Take her to her new home in Purgatory," Mordred ordered. "Let her discover the meaning of pain and torment, as she watches her beloved Avalon fall before me."

The wraiths picked her up and carried her away as Faust kept a close eye on Mordred. The ageless sorcerer walked back across the mist toward *Excalibur* and the King's Stone.

"This is the second time I've heard someone speak of 'three' opposing you, Master. What does it mean?" Faust asked.

"I don't know, Abdel, and I don't care. Once I have *Excalibur*, no one will deny my right to rule Avalon."

Mordred reached down and grabbed the sword by the hilt, but *Excalibur* wouldn't budge. He pulled on it with all his might, but the sword remained secured. He screamed, as he placed both hands on the hilt and tried to pull even harder, but it failed to move.

He released the sword, frustrated and angry beyond measure. "No! I will have you!" he screamed, as he kicked the stone, his voice echoing across the water. His breathing was heavy and laboured by his unsuccessful efforts. He stood there with his fists clenched.

"*Pedere Confringes Lapis!*" Mordred bellowed, hurling deadly bolts of magical energy at the King's Stone. The water surrounding the rock turned to steam from the intense heat. When the fog cleared, the *Excalibur* still rested in place within the King's Stone.

This was the first-time Faust had seen Mordred angry and it troubled him. He knew that anger could turn even the most powerful men into simpering idiots. He decided to test and see if Mordred was falling prey to that. "Are you sure it was wise to capture the Lady of the Lake like that, Mordred? She is the heart and soul of Avalon. The people will not follow you once they've learned what you've done."

"I care not for the mewling masses, Faust!" Mordred screamed. "Those sheep will do exactly what I say once I am on the granite throne. They will follow me, or they will die, it's as simple as that."

Mordred spun around and walked away from the King's Stone. With the wave of his hand, he dispelled the mist. Abdel turned to leave but Mordred stopped him with a hand to his chest. "I know what you're thinking, Faust," Mordred asserted. "I am not going mad. I have spent the last year planning every facet of my return. I will not be undone, not by the Lady of the Lake, not *Excalibur* and certainly not by you."

"I meant no disrespect, Master," Faust said. "I just wanted to be sure you were not falling as your mother did. She let her anger and hatred of Arthur, Merlin and others consume her, blinding her to her failings. I had yet to see that in you, Mordred, until today."

Mordred thought for a moment. "That is why I have you by my side, Abdel," Mordred contended. "I know that you will not let me falter, will you?"

Faust smiled, his fanged teeth adding an intimidation factor to his grin. "No, master, I will not."

"Good, then have the wraiths remove the King's Stone and keep it hidden," Mordred commanded. "I may not be able to draw the sword, but neither will little Bowen or anyone else. If I can't have *Excalibur*, then no one can!"

***

At the first light of dawn, the Russians began their invasion of Avalon. With military precision, the invading forces of Russian soldiers along with a company of Spetsnaz troops began landing on the beaches of Avalon. By boat and by helicopter, the set up a beachhead on the shores of Avalon.

From atop the cliff overlooking the shoreline, the Gil-Gamesh watched as the enemy forces began to establish a hold on the beach. It was a sickening sight, a vendetta by Secretary Barry for Lord Moondrake's attacks against him. Bryan knew that Barry was trying to save face by getting the Russians to do his dirty work for him. Eileanora and Hunter watched alongside Gil-Gamesh, the former clearly agitated.

"I must object once again to your strategy, milord," she said. "Why are you letting these Outlanders get a foothold on our sacred lands?"

"I know it's hard for you to understand this, Eileanora, but with the barrier shrinking at a rapid pace, we cannot hope to withstand their firepower," he explained. "We have to contain them here, keep them engaged while we have the high ground. If we stop them here, then they will be forced to retreat."

"By forcing them to fight on our terms, we maintain our advantage over them," Hunter added.

Bryan smiled at the continued growth of his son into a warrior and a leader. "Exactly Hunter, keep their forces pinned on the beach, and their only option will be to retreat back to their ships."

Eileanora pondered the Gil-Gamesh's strategy. Though sound in its appearance, the thought of these Outlanders invading Avalon troubled her.

As quick as the wind, Maverick flew in and sat on Bryan's shoulder. He spoke in a series of chirps and gruff noises—nonsense to Eileanora—but perfectly spoken dragon tongue to the Gil-Gamesh and Hunter too.

Bryan gave the little faerie dragon a scratch on the head then motioned for Maverick to leave. The familiar flew off in the same direction he came from, disappearing in the blink of an eye.

"Edan's ready to go, now we just need some cover," Bryan said, turning back toward one of the outposts and signalling them to move in. The ground shook as a group of Storm Giants stepped toward them. They stood between ten to fifteen feet tall. They wore only simple loincloths as their skin was as hard as plate mail armour. Their skin was a soft, bluish-grey, a distinct trait of this group of giants, or Jotunn as they were better known.

They were led by Pasha Bataar, the Chief of the Jotunn. Though they had been enemies of Avalon in the past, the Jotunn came to terms with their evil ways and joined the rest of Avalon in the battle against Morgana le Fay over a year ago. They reclaimed their honour and intended to keep it that way.

"It's time, my friend," Bryan declared. "We need some rough seas and heavy fog if you please."

"By your command, Gil-Gamesh!" Pasha Bataar acknowledged. The mighty giant motioned to his Jotunn brothers and they began to do what Storm Giants do best—control the weather.

The three Jotunn cupped their hands together and blew into them like horns. A fog flowed out from their hands, spreading across the land and down the cliff to the beach below. Soon the fog covered the entire shoreline, blanketing it in a dark, dense cloud. The mist rose higher into the sky until they began to rumble and build into a powerful storm.

The seas began to swell as the storm tossed the boats around. The dense fog grounded their aircraft, stranding them on the shoreline. The sudden storm caught the Russians off guard as they tried to protect themselves and their equipment.

Bryan felt like gloating. Things were going exactly as planned. Eileanora was still not convinced.

"Now what?" she asked cynically.

"Now, it's show time!" Bryan yelled and pointed across the water. Moving down from the clouds, gliding between the cloud cover and the rough seas below, was a pirate ship, floating effortlessly above the waves. Unlike the other airships of Avalon, this one had no wings, and what appeared to be torn and tattered sails in the rigging. The skull and crossbones flag was quite visible, flying from the main mast, but this one had a snake wrapped around the crossbones its head was coming out of one of the skull's eyes.

"Is that the *Flying Fancy*?" Hunter asked.

"It was, but Edan renamed her," Bryan explained. "She's now the *Black Adder*, the pirate ship of Avalon. They cast an illusion spell on the ship, hiding its wings, giving it tattered sails and hiding the crew. To them, it'll look like a ghost ship."

"Dad, I swear, sometimes you really scare the hell out of me with these ideas of yours," Hunter said with a smile.

The gun ports on both sides of the ship opened and the cannons stuck out, one by one. The fired off a myriad of spellshots, ranging from dragon nails to exploding fireballs. In one pass, the Russians lost men, boats, helicopters and other equipment. Boats floundered in the water while explosions and fires raged across the beaches.

They were all sitting out in the open, just as the Gil-Gamesh wanted, making them vulnerable to the volley of cannon fire from the *Black Adder*. The Russians fired back with what weapons they had left, but they were ineffective against the ghostly airship.

The *Black Adder* rose back into the clouds above as the storm subsided and the fog disappeared, leaving a decimated Russian invasion force, trying to pick up the pieces. Eileanora was quite impressed.

"I will be the first one to admit when I am wrong, Lord MoonDrake. You are indeed a general among men. However," she said, gesturing to his ears, "it was clearly the Elven part of you that made your stratagem work. Well done, milord!"

Bryan was bemused by the backhanded compliment, but accepted it all the same and bowed politely to Eileanora. "Hunter, let's keep a close watch on them. I doubt they have the capability to regroup anytime soon, but we need our forces ready in case they make any moves. Get with Rhona to bring up suitable forces on the ready."

"Yes, Father," Hunter said and took off to carry out his orders.

"Thank you, Pasha Bataar, please return to the encampment for now. We may need your Storm Giants again."

Pasha Bataar and the other Jotunn bowed to the Gil-Gamesh. "We are at your service, Gil-Gamesh!" he said, as the giants departed. Bryan turned his attention to Eileanora.

"Eileanora, I need you to make your way into their camp and evaluate what forces they have, fighting capability, any intelligence on what they're planning. Think you can do it?"

"Of course, milord. It will be done." The Elf gave a quick, courteous bow before heading off for her assignment.

Bryan looked over the remains of the Russian forces and watched as they picked up the pieces of their invasion force. They still had a formidable force on the beach below. Bryan's little trick with the *Black Adder* may have scared them a little, but it wouldn't last. He needed help. Not from Avalon, but from out there. He needed to talk to Captain Rich and find out why they were being so aggressive.

***

Captain Rich watched the ensuing invasion from the captain's chair on the bridge of the *USS Theodore Roosevelt*. He stared through his binoculars, trying to catch every aspect of the battle. Rich warned Secretary Barry against the Russian's invasion plan—a sentiment echoed by many of the Joint Chiefs—but it fell on deaf ears. Barry convinced the President that this was the option with least liability to the United States while still taking advantage of the receding magical barrier, and the plan moved forward.

Barry and the Russians considered the people of Avalon a bunch of backward, medieval savages, but Rich knew better. The Gil-Gamesh was a United States Navy Chief Petty Officer, a capable leader with the knowledge of modern military equipment and tactics. Rich was afraid that Secretary Barry's overconfidence would be his downfall.

He watched as fires rage on the beach from destroyed Russian aircraft and floundering amphibious craft. "Officer of the Deck, signal the *Admiral*

Kuznetsov and tell them we are standing by to assist with recovery operations and provide medical assistance."

The OOD acknowledged the order and began to relay it to CDC and the signal bridge. Warrant Officer Lucas stepped onto the bridge with an armful of documents requiring the captain's signature. Rich didn't pay much attention to her as she placed the folders and papers in an inbox sitting next to the captain's chair. Rich continued to observe the aftermath of the invasion, when out of the corner of his eye, he noticed Ladonna was still standing there, waiting for him.

"You're hovering, Ladonna, what is it?"

"Sorry, sir, but I think you should look at the top folder; it's quite urgent," she said, her voice quivering with trepidation. Rich looked at her with concern. This was out of character for her, so he knew something must be wrong.

He put down the binoculars and grabbed the top folder from the inbox. He opened it and read the single piece of paper inside. His eyes grew wide. "Where is he?" Rich asked quietly, so as not to alarm the bridge crew.

"In the inport cabin, Captain. He's waiting for you."

"You haven't told anyone else?"

Ladonna just shook her head. "I didn't want to raise the alarm, sir. I thought that would do more harm than good," she whispered back to him. "Besides, I don't think he's here to hurt anyone. He said he just wanted to talk to you, Captain, and, well, I believe him."

Rich knew how much care his Ship's Secretary took when it came to people wasting his time. She was a great judge of character and he trusted her completely. Rich jumped out of his chair and headed down to his inport cabin with Ladonna in tow.

Rich opened the door and saw the Gil-Gamesh, sitting comfortably in a chair, sipping on a cup of coffee. The hole Bryan cut in the bulkhead to escape the last time he was here was covered with plywood and wood shores. Rich motioned for Ladonna to stay out as he closed the door behind him. Bryan noticed the Captain enter the room but just sat there, quietly sipping his coffee.

"You're taking a big risk coming here," Rich stated. "This better be important."

"I wouldn't be here if it wasn't," Bryan replied. "I just have one question. Why on Earth would the United States allow and support one nation invading another?"

Rich sighed. "I'm a bit at a loss here too, Bryan. Secretary Barry can be very persuasive. He convinced the President that letting the Russians try to force you back to the negotiating table was worth our ignorance."

"Force us back? Do you think the Russians will stop once they get a foothold on Avalon?"

"The Secretary has the word of General Garasimov that once you agree to come back to the negotiating table, the Russians will leave Avalon."

"I doubt that will be the case. And where is Secretary Barry? He's on the Russian carrier, isn't he?"

"He's there as an observer, yes."

Bryan shook his head in disbelief. "This is madness," the Gil-Gamesh grumbled. "That man will do whatever it takes to get his way, even it means forgetting every oath he swore to uphold."

"Well, you didn't help things by attacking our ships and bringing down our aircraft!"

"We were defending our home!" Bryan screamed and leaped to his feet. "What were we supposed to do? Just let you continue to bombard my island until there was nothing left?"

The two men stood there staring at each other, not wanting the argument to escalate any further. The silence was painful. Rich finally broke the tension. "Look, Bryan, I'm not blaming you for defending yourself; you had that right. But maybe if you come back to the negotiating table, things can even out."

Bryan considered it. They were well past that point. "Tell me something, Larry, what did Secretary Barry tell the President to convince him that the only recourse was to attack Avalon?"

"Exactly what I told him. That you were evacuating the floating island but were ready to defend yourselves. Why?"

"Do you really think the President and the Joint Chiefs would have approved the attack on Emmyr if Secretary Barry told them exactly what you said? I may have been out of the loop for the past few years, but I don't think any administration would risk an all-out attack against a people trying to evacuate women and children."

"Are you saying he lied just to get back at you?"

"All I'm saying, Captain, is that you should find out why your country started a war with Avalon. Was it justified or was it revenge? The Gil-Gamesh gave the Captain a cold, hard stare. "*Migro-transit Avalon!*" he shouted, and with a wave of his hand, was gone in a flash of magical energy, leaving Captain Rich with nothing but questions. He picked up his telephone and quickly dialled a number.

"Ops, Captain. Is that old girlfriend of yours still assigned to the Joint Chiefs? Think you could reach out to her for me? I need some information, but let's keep it quiet, okay? Yes, I'll make sure your leave gets approved, no questions asked."

Captain Rich hung up the phone, waiting patiently for the Operations Officer to call him back, knowing that the path he was pursuing could lead to inquiries, investigations and maybe even Congressional hearings, but he had to know the truth.

***

Eileanora couldn't believe how easy it was to infiltrate the Russian camp. A simple glamour spell hid her Elven appearance, an unconscious soldier provided a uniform and she made her way around the camp with relative ease. The Outlanders were easily distracted by a flirtatious glance or a sway of the hips; they were just men, after all.

What Eileanora didn't expect was the amount of military personnel and weaponry at their disposal. She counted more than 1,000 soldiers, armed with a wide variety of modern, technological armaments. Most of their aircraft, vehicles and small boats were destroyed by the *Black Adder*, leaving them scrambling to bring in replacements. She's counted more than 10 equipment and vehicle drops within the past hour alone.

Thanks to a translator crystal, she could understand and speak their language. To her, their words were barbaric, and not unlike like speaking goblin. The sounds were harsh and guttural, not smooth and free flowing like Elvish. It was demeaning for her to speak in their tongue, but quite necessary for her infiltration.

The men were quite superstitious, just as the Gil-Gamesh predicted. Many were worried that their childhood nightmares were waiting for them somewhere out there. Others seemed more interested in gold, gems or other treasure they might find.

As she started to head back to report her findings to the Gil-Gamesh, something caught her eye. One of the boats—she recalled Lord MoonDrake called them amphibious landing craft—had come ashore, and from inside it stepped Secretary Barry and General Garasimov. They were greeted by Colonel Vitor Rusev, the commander of the invasion force.

The Russian Colonel looked like a model Soviet—tall and muscular with chiselled features framed under a flat-top buzz cut. After a customary salute to General Garasimov and an introduction of Secretary Barry, the Colonel escorted the two men to the command vehicle. Curiosity got the best of Eileanora, so she followed close behind.

Getting into the command vehicle was a problem. Access was limited to senior officers only, but she had an idea of how to get past them. Eileanora knew that the fastest way to any man's trust and confidence was through his stomach. She swung by the kitchen and talked her way into delivering a tray of food and drink to the command vehicle for General Garasimov and his guest.

Eileanora rarely got to use her feminine wiles like this. Her normal repertoire hardly ever called for such elaborate infiltration. She found this outing tremendously satisfying and hoped to do more like it in the future.

The command vehicle was a modified tractor-trailer bed. Inside was a variety of communications and surveillance equipment. The senior staff hovered around a table with an enlarged overhead photo of this section of Avalon, showing the relative positions of the Gil-Gamesh's forces and the Russian forces.

The guards saw Eileanora carrying a tray of food and drink and automatically assumed she was ordered to bring it to the commander. She slipped past them with ease but walked carefully through the command vehicle. She didn't understand a lot of the equipment, with their bright screens and electronic lights, but she understood surveillance and stratagem.

As Eileanora approached the command table, she saw that Colonel Rusev already had started his briefing. She quietly stepped behind them, setting up the service while listening in to their conversation.

"We have control of the beach for one mile in each direction," Colonel Rusev stated. "There is a small gully to the south that gives us access to the meadow above, but it is too small for our vehicles and the narrow pass makes us vulnerable to attack."

"Where are they at?" Secretary Barry asked. "Are they making any moves toward your position?"

"No, Mr Secretary, they are maintaining a defensive position about 1,000 meters from the cliff edge," Rusev said, as his pointed to positions on the map. "Their main encampment is another 1,000 meters behind their outer defences."

"And what is the complement of their forces, Colonel?" General Garasimov asked.

"Satellite imagery is getting better but unfortunately, it is still unable to penetrate the veil of their, uh, 'magical barrier' as it were," Rusev said with obvious distaste for such words. "We hope to have our scouts move in and get a better idea of their numbers."

"Well, what do you know so far?" Secretary Barry snapped impatiently. Colonel Rusev didn't like being questioned like this, but a quiet nod from General Garasimov quelled his anger.

"Mr Secretary, they have outposts along the entire coastline at 3,000-meter intervals," the Colonel said. "Each outpost has anywhere from five to ten knights. These knights vary from men and women and from Elves, Dwarves, giants and centaurs.

"These are creatures I only read in stories as a boy, and we are seeing them in flesh and blood for the first time," Colonel Rusev continued. "I don't know the exact number of their forces, Mr Secretary, but there must be from 3,000-to-5,000 strong. They are heavily armed, wielding powers that we have no way of knowing the extent of nor how to defend against them. In my opinion, they are trying to contain us on the beach here.

"If we don't move inland soon, we may find ourselves trapped here forever," he concluded. The room was silent as the men took in all the information. General Garasimov sighed loudly, shaking his head as he looked over the map.

"When will we have all the replacements brought ashore?" he asked.

"General, we should have all the necessary equipment brought ashore by tomorrow."

"All right then. First, we will have our demolition team blast the gulley wider, so our equipment can move inland," General Garasimov said. "I want us off this beach within the next few days. Once we force them back, they will come to us to negotiate a peaceful settlement. Don't you agree, Mr Secretary?"

"Yes, General, of course. The sooner the better," Barry said with a half-hearted smile. He was not convinced that going with the Russian stratagem was a good idea, but it was his only option.

"Then let's toast to our success!" the General shouted, as he stepped over to the table where Eileanora was setting up the food and drink. "*Milaya Devushka*, would you be so kind and bring us a bottle of vodka, *pozhaluysta*?" The General stroked her gently on the chin.

Eileanora said nothing. She just smiled politely and resisted the urge to cut him open for touching her. She finished setting up and turned to leave, but not before she overheard a conversation in Russian between General Garasimov and Colonel Rusev.

"You have two days to get us inland, Colonel. Can you do it?"

"We will do our best, General, but may I ask why?"

General Garasimov looked sideways toward Secretary Barry. "In two days, there will a vote in the United Nations. We must have a foothold on this land or else all our efforts will be for naught. There are riches here for the taking, and thanks to our foolish American ally, we are the first and the only ones here.

"Once we have a strong foothold on the island, we will be able to negotiate with these Cossacks from a position of strength, not cowering behind us like these American buffoons," he concluded.

"Then I will make sure we push back the barbarians, General," Colonel Rusev assured and the two men shook hands. As Eileanora left the command vehicle, she was afraid. These Outlanders were relentless in their pursuits and, as the barrier shrank, their technology would eventually overpower them. Something had to be done soon or else all would be lost.

***

Avalon wind patterns were usually predictable, but since its return to the outside world, no one could predict or manage to fly through the new currents effectively. What once took hours took days to get around Avalon, with ships flying miles off course just to find a patch of wind that would take them where they wanted to go.

However, it was still relatively easy for a single airship to hide within a slow-moving cloudbank to quietly observe the ground below. It also helped if you had a powerful wizard aboard to keep the winds at bay, but the *Hood's Revenge* was no ordinary airship, nor did it keep an ordinary wizard.

This was the personal airship of Jaeger Nottingham, son of Sir Cuthbert Nottingham, the Earl of Nottinghamshire, and was unlike any other on Avalon. The wooden hull was reinforced with steel plating, making it virtually impenetrable. It carried more than 30 cannons, double stacked from stem to stern, and unlike the airships made on Emmyr, this was designed with a magical engine to make it fly.

The ship was designed by the Master Tinker Edwyn Broadfoot, a gnome machine-smith. He relished the chance of showing up the Gil-Gamesh and his 'old-fashioned' airships ever since he refused to allow Edwyn and his gnomes the opportunity to learn about the modern machinery used in their design. Mordred turned Edwyn's greed into his own, giving the gnome tinker the chance to build his own warship.

Hood's Revenge had an engine powered by Dwarfish lodestones—a magnetic ore found deep within the mines under the Gilded Halls. Edwyn found a way to harness the powerful mineral outside the Dwarfish homeland in his new machine. Though they could not sustain flight for as long as the airships of

Emmyr, they were quite formidable. This was the first of many secret war machines being built by the allies of the son of Morgana le Fay.

Mordred stood on the bow of *Hood's Revenge*. He peered down at the Outlanders encampment. He watched them scurry about with all their technological war machines as they prepared to move inland.

Jaeger stepped up behind Mordred, greedily chomping on an apple. He was considered a brute by most, more brawn than brain. He stood an imposing six feet five inches, carrying more than 300 pounds of solid muscle. He carried a large mace, harnessed across his shoulders. He preferred crushing his opponents with heavy weapons rather than cutting into them with a sword. To him, it was more merciful to kill them instantly than let them slowly bleed out.

He took another bite of his apple, crunching it loudly between his teeth. Mordred was quite agitated by his uncouth manners. "If you're going to continue to eat that, Jaeger, I suggest you do it elsewhere before I throw you off this ship."

Jaeger took the hint and tossed the rest of the apple over the side. He sidled alongside Mordred and looked over the edge. "Why are we watching them, Master Mordred? We should be kicking their *arses* off Avalon, not watching them from up here. The *Hood's Revenge* can wipe them out in an instant!"

Mordred was quite annoyed with the young noble, but needed these allies to ensure his plan came to fruition, so he tolerated them for now.

"You fail to grasp the plan once again, Jaeger. If we attack them with our new warship, then the Gil-Gamesh will know who we are and what we're up to. It's best to let Faust and the wraiths handle them for us."

Jaeger tried to wrap his limited intelligence around Mordred's plan and failed. "Of course, milord, I see it now," Jaeger lied. "But then what are we doing here?"

Mordred smiled, as he turned to his young charge. "We're here for the entertainment, of course."

Just then, a demon hole opened, and Abdel Ben Faust stepped through. He bowed to Mordred but ignored Jaeger completely. The young knight felt slighted but knew better than to challenge a sword master like Faust.

"It is done, my master," the half-demon said. "We are ready to attack!"

"And the Gil-Gamesh's forces, where are they?"

Faust pointed out across the meadow. "They are back well enough," he asserted. "They will hear the attack, but they will not see us. We will be finished before they could even react to it."

Mordred smiled. He knew he picked the right man to lead his army. "Then by all means, General Faust, let's teach these Outlanders a lesson and add to the ranks of the Wraith Legion. You may commence your attack!"

Faust smiled, his fangs showing prominently in his gleeful grin. He opened another demon hole and disappeared as it closed behind him.

"I don't trust him, milord," Jaeger complained to Mordred. "With that army at his command, he could threaten you and your rule with a single word."

Mordred did not show any emotion, but inside, he was delighted that young Jaeger was bold enough to stand against Faust. He knew that pitting his minions against each other was a good way to cull the weak and reward the strong.

"I'm thankful that I have you to look out for me, Jaeger," Mordred said, masking his sarcasm. "But you need not worry about Faust. He has no desire to rule, only to conquer those beneath him. He loves war, conflict, chaos… It's what feeds his passion, his drive.

"He is a master of conflict, and he will bring order to Avalon—driving the engines of war to crush our enemies," Mordred concluded with an evil grin. "With the Wraith Legion, he will cleanse Avalon for me."

The attack was swift and brutal, just the way Faust wanted it to be. The wraiths rose from beneath the ocean waves as the moonlight shimmered across the water. The soldiers were caught off guard as the wraiths stormed through them. The Russians fired blindly at them with automatic weapons, but their bullets had little to no effect on the wraiths.

The wraiths struck down one terrified soldier after another, cutting through their ranks with blade and axe, but these were no ordinary weapons. The wraiths wielded Phantom Blades, weapons forged in the fires of Purgatory. These ungodly relics were designed to cleave through the natural magic of demons. Against humans, the wounds festered and spread through their bodies like a deadly poison. Death was almost instantaneous and quite painful as the poison forced the blood out through every orifice until there was nothing left but a desiccated husk.

For the Outlanders, their worst nightmares came to life right before them and soon their ranks were culled. As soldiers fell, their spirits rose from within and were encased in ghostly armour and joined the ranks of the Wraith Legion.

Faust revelled in the slaughter. He couldn't believe how easily the wraiths responded to his command. They were his thralls, their every action controlled by the mere sound of his voice. He relished in the power he wielded, but even he knew his limits.

Faust heard the muffled cries from inside one the Outlander's machines. He cut through the metal with ease, thanks to the fiery edge of his cursed blade. Inside, he found Secretary Barry, cowering in fear as he pleaded for his life. "P-p-please, don't k-k-kill me!"

A wraith moved in to silence him, but Faust stopped him with the touch of his hand. "No, leave this one alive," he commanded. Faust leaned down, his face mere inches from Barry. The frightened diplomat turned his head, closing his eyes so as not to look at the demonic visage that hovered over him.

"You will tell the rest of your world what happens to those who step foot on Avalon, Outlander," Faust whispered through fanged teeth, grinning from ear-to-ear as he brought the tip of his sword next to Barry's cheek. The cursed blade seared his flesh, causing him to scream in pain until Faust removed his blade, branding his cheek with the tip of his sword.

"Death to all who enter here!" Faust crowed.

Within minutes, the beach fell silent and the battle was over. The screams, gunfire and explosions could be heard from the outposts above, but no one knew who was attacking whom. The confusion among the ranks of the knights of Avalon helped the wraiths finish their attack in such a short period of time and they disappeared just as fast, not leaving a single trace of their presence.

***

The Gil-Gamesh couldn't sleep. Eileanora's report was as dire as he thought. If the Russians had planned to push inward and get a foothold on Avalon, he had to stop them while they remained on the beach. He tried to focus on the myriad of options before him as he glared over a map of the island.

Rhona and Eileanora stood across from the Gil-Gamesh and stared at him, worried about the burden weighing him down. Rhona was equally concerned about Eileanora's report, but for the first time in her life, she didn't know what to say or do. This was far and above anything she ever experienced as a Shield Maiden of Avalon.

"Milord, perhaps Pasha Bataar could bring some Stone Giants here to help block the passage from the beach?" she suggested.

"No, it would take them nearly a week to get here," Bryan replied. "They can't teleport due to their nature and they're too massive to bring in via airship. Besides, I'm sure the Russians have demolition experts with them. They would be able to blast through anything put in their path.

"My biggest concern is what their weapons will do to an armoured knight," the Gil-Gamesh continued. "I don't know if mithril will repel armour-piercing rounds fired from an automatic weapon. They didn't seem to faze the dragons, but it could be different in this case. There are just too many uncertainties, and I'm afraid we may lose a lot of men and women before this is over."

"Is there anything from your experience as a warrior in the Outlander's military that might help us divine a plan?" Eileanora asked.

Bryan laughed, just a little, under his breath. "I wasn't really much of a warrior in the outside world, Eileanora," he explained. "I oversaw the sailors on the flight deck of an aircraft carrier, like the one out there. My job was to make sure the warplanes launched and recovered safely on deck, so they could take the fight to our enemies. I didn't engage in combat myself until I came to Avalon."

Both Rhona and Eileanora were shocked by the Gil-Gamesh's admission. "I didn't know, milord," Eileanora stated carefully, not wanting to seem insulting. "I assumed that you were a seasoned warrior by the way you've acclimated so quickly to the role as Gil-Gamesh."

"I had excellent teachers in Sir Thomas, Sir Charles and Eonis," Bryan replied, reflecting on his former friends and mentors. "To be honest, the first thing you know as a knight is how to be a leader, and that was something I learned in my military career as a Chief Petty Officer in the Navy. It was that leadership training that I fell back on when I accepted my responsibilities as the Gil-Gamesh. The rest just fell into place."

"You have led us this far, Lord MoonDrake," Rhona assured. "We know you will see us through to the end,"

Bryan was glad to hear this from his Captain of the Dragon Guard, but he still had his doubts. He looked at the map one more time and decided on a strategy.

"I think we need to deliver a little shock and awe to the Outlanders," he said. "For starts, I want the Storm Giants to make their lives miserable with constant rain, heavy seas and high winds. That should bring their morale down a few notches. Next—"

Just then, Hunter and Amelia stormed into the command tent, out of breath. "Father," Hunter said, wheezing for air. "There's been an attack at the beach."

"What? Who attacked? The Russians?"

"No, milord," Amelia said. "Someone attacked the Outlanders, but we don't know who."

"What? How is that possible?" Rhona asked.

"We checked all the outposts near the beach and no one knows who attacked whom," Hunter explained. "There were sounds of gunfire, explosions and then silence."

The Gil-Gamesh was worried that someone might have jumped the gun and started a war or, by chance, someone else had joined the fight. Either way, he had to find out.

"Eileanora, assemble a company of *Hîldrägo Boquè*, Rhona get the Dragon Guard and meet us at the gulley heading toward the beach," Bryan ordered. "Hunter, Amelia, with me!"

Rhona and Eileanora ran off to get the troops together while the Gil-Gamesh raced toward the coast. Within minutes, he was at the gulley, which sloped toward the beach. The three drew their weapons as the slowly made their way down. As soon as they peered around the rocks, they saw the horror of the battle. The Gil-Gamesh and Amelia were seasoned veterans and Hunter had seen his share of combat, but nothing they'd seen previously compared to the horror before them.

Bodies were strewn across the sand as the blood washed out to sea in the rolling waves. Equipment, tents and other machines were demolished and burning; charred ruins of the mechanical might of the Outlander's forces. Nothing was left alive or left standing. It was a husk of the military encampment that was here hours ago.

Behind the three, Rhona and Eileanora arrived with the company of troops. "Spread out and search the area," Bryan ordered. "Look for survivors or clues of who or what did this."

The two women relayed the orders as the knights and Elves began to search through the remains of the encampment. Bryan slowly walked through, trying to comprehend what had happened.

"I've never seen anything like this, milord," Amelia said with a hint of fear in her voice, something Bryan rarely heard from her. "What could have done this?"

Bryan knelt next to one of the bodies. Blood was forced out through its eyes, ears, nose and mouth, yet no real wound was visible. The skin was sunken, desiccated from the lack of blood. It reminded him of something from a horror movie. Hunter squatted down next to his father, examining the corpse himself.

"This is so weird," he said, as he looked closely for wounds. "Is this a new magic? Or something else?"

Bryan lifted the dead soldier's shirt and found what he was looking for. "It's something else." he said, exposing the only wound on the man. It was a slit in his skin, caused by a sword, but the wound festered, as if it had been rotting for weeks. The area around the wound was blackened, diseased and putrid, spreading under his skin and through the veins of his body like a dark poison.

"A phantom blade," Bryan said with cold certainty. "These wounds were caused by a phantom blade."

"What's a phantom blade, Dad? I've never heard of it before."

"That's because they're not supposed to be on Avalon," Bryan said, as he stood up and looked around at the death and destruction. "Phantom blades are wielded by the Wraith Legion of Purgatory."

"A wraith? You mean that thing that Sir Eadric turned into?" Hunter asked.

"Yes, Hunter, but somehow they've abandoned their post in Purgatory and are now fighting on Avalon. That's not good."

"Why, Dad? We need all the help we can get against the Outlanders. It seems to me that these wraiths are doing us a favour."

"You don't understand, Sir Hunter," Amelia said. "If the Wraith Legion has abandoned Purgatory, then the way is open for demons to leave the Netherworld and come into our world. We will be overrun!"

"Yeah, but that's not the worst of it," Bryan added.

Amelia looked confused. "Worst? What could possibly be worse, milord?"

"The Wraith Legion is commanded by one of the Archangels," Bryan began. "So, either we're caught in the middle of some 'holy war' between Heaven and Hell or someone else has command of the Legion. I don't want to think about that army in the hands of some evil, power-hungry madman."

Just then, a knight ran up to Lord MoonDrake. "Milord, we found someone, a survivor," he said, pointing down the beach. The knight ran off and Bryan and the others quickly followed him into the encampment.

Eileanora and Rhona were standing next to the command trailer, looking over a rather pathetic sight. Secretary Barry sat quietly on the sand, his knees pulled close to his chest, rocking back and forth. He was shaking violently as he mumbled to himself. Bryan saw a severe burn on his face.

Bryan stepped up slowly, knowing that his presence might frighten him even more. "Has he said anything about who attacked him?"

"Not much we can understand, milord," Rhona answered. "He said something about a demon with a sword that burned his face."

Hunter took the Secretary by the chin and tilted his face, so they could see the wound better. It was a serious burn, welted up as if he was branded. The burn mark took the shape of the tip of a sword, with one edge jagged. "Faust!" Hunter shouted.

"Now you know my worst fear," Bryan said. "God help us if that murderer has control of the Wraith Legion."

"What can we do?" Amelia asked.

"We return Avalon behind the barrier, then deal with Faust," Bryan said. "There are forces taking advantage of the situation and we cannot allow their evil to spread into the outside world. Millions of lives are at stake. We may not like the Outlanders, but this is going to drive them to war with Avalon even faster."

"It may start sooner than you think, milord," Eileanora said, her gaze focused not on the Gil-Gamesh but out towards the ocean. "There are several boats approaching fast from the Outlander ships. They are filled with more soldiers like them."

She began shouting orders in Elvish to the *Hîldrägo Boquè* as they lined up and drew their bows. Bryan immediately stepped in between her and the Elves. "Do not fire on them, Eileanora. We don't need any more bloodshed here!" he commanded.

"They are armed to attack us, milord. We must defend ourselves!"

"If we start firing on them, they will have no choice but to call in a live fire on the beach. We will be slaughtered where we stand. No, I will not lead us into more death and destruction, so stand down and do not fire unless I give the command!"

Eileanora stood frustrated by the Gil-Gamesh's lack of inaction, but she resolved herself to step back. She gave another order to the *Hîldrägo Boquè*. With precision and discipline, they sheathed their bows and arrows, standing ready for the next command.

"Captain, pull the Dragon Guard behind the *Hîldrägo Boquè* and stand ready," Bryan commanded. Rhona quickly shouted orders and the knights of the Dragon Guard fell in behind the *Hîldrägo Boquè*, arms at the ready.

The boats, which Bryan recognised as Rigid Inflatable Boats, or RIBs, landed down from where the forces of Avalon were gathered. Sailors jumped out of the RIBs and pulled the crafts ashore. Bryan saw that they were all US Navy sailors, though heavily armed as they took up defensive positions as the last boats landed on the beach. He watched patiently for any sign of aggression, but thankfully, there was none.

The Gil-Gamesh was relieved when he saw Captain Rich getting out of one of the boats. He knew he wouldn't be here if they planned any kind of assault. Surrounded by a slew of armed sailors, Rich made his way down the beach to where Bryan waited for him.

Lord MoonDrake stepped up to greet him, keeping his hands on the hilts of his swords just in case. "I'm surprised to see you here, Captain. I thought you were staying neutral in this."

"We are, Lord MoonDrake. We only came to collect the Secretary of State," Rich answered. "I just wasn't expecting this."

"I can assure you, Larry, we didn't cause any of this," Bryan insisted. "There are darker forces at work here."

"Yes, I know!" Rich said. Bryan and the others were shocked by his revelation. "My lookouts watched as these ghostly figures rose up out of the water and attacked the Russians. It was over before we could warn them or do anything. Once I saw you and your knights arrive on the beach, I knew it was safe to come in. Again, my main purpose here is to collect Secretary Barry and place him under arrest."

"Arrest?" Bryan asked.

"You were right, Bryan. The Secretary lied to the President and the Joint Chiefs. He told them you were gearing up for war. That's why they ordered the attack. They asked me to offer their utmost apology for what Secretary Barry caused."

Bryan was glad to hear that. The war may be over sooner than he thought. "Apology accepted, Captain, although I don't think you need to punish Secretary Barry," Bryan said, motioning to the traumatised diplomat. "He will be suffering in his own personal hell for quite some time."

Captain Rich motioned for two sailors to pick up Secretary Barry and help him back to the RIBs. "The Russians are also sorry for their aggression. They just want to collect their dead and what remains of their equipment."

"You may tell the Russian commanders they have 24 hours to clean up the beach," the Gil-Gamesh acquiesced. "After that, the same rules apply. No one in or out."

"I understand." The Captain held out his hand to the Gil-Gamesh. "This will probably be the last time we see each other. I would like us to part as friends, Bryan."

Bryan reached out and took his hand, before pulling the Captain to close to hug him. "We *are* friends, Larry, thank you." Bryan released Captain Rich, as he shook his hand one last time. "I wish you all the best, Captain. I wish there was time to show you more of the wonders of Avalon."

"What will you do now?" Rich asked. "The UN is still planning to vote on the legitimacy and recognition of Avalon as a sovereign state."

"If we're still here by the end of the week, then I may have to take them up on that," Bryan said. Captain Rich nodded his head and ordered his men back to the boats. Within minutes, they left the beach and headed back to their ships.

"What did you mean when you said you'd take them up on their offer by the end of the week, milord?" Amelia asked.

"It means, Amelia, that if we don't restore the barrier by the end of the week, we will be stuck here forever," he stated quite plainly to his shield maiden. "The magic will be gone and life, as we know it, will never be the same again."

Chapter 9
The Ascension of the Elves

The Kingdom of the Elves shined brightly in the morning sun. Alfheimer was unlike any city in all of Avalon. The city itself was carved out of the stone face in a massive valley between two peaks. The white marble statues, columns, buildings and bridges glistened in the sunlight, if not from the magical glow of the Elves themselves.

As the Elves went about their daily activities of music, poetry, magic and philosophy, a new activity could be seen and heard within the walls of the sacred city…preparations for war. The Shield Maidens of Avalon, normally at home in their convent in the Glennish Hills, had taken their young charges to Alfheimer while their warriors helped man the defences along the coastline.

The women of the Order of Shield Maidens were made up of mostly orphans, but some had decided to join the convent. These women devoted themselves to God, Avalon and the monarchy. Young women began their instruction in the ways of the shield maiden as young as seven-years-old. While other young girls learned needlepoint, gardening and sewing, these young girls were being instructed in wrestling, fencing and other fighting arts.

In an open courtyard, Lady Stephanie MoonDrake sat quietly on a marble bench as she watched as her daughter, Rose, son-in-law, Andrew, and her grandsons, young Thomas Forest and King Bowen, received the same training as the young girls. Today's lesson was fencing. They were paired off as instructors took them through the paces with wooden practice swords.

Rose had been trying to sharpen her fighting skills and often visited Sarafina at the convent to further her training. Andrew was trying to improve his fighting techniques, something he rarely could do in the outside world.

The boys were doing what boys normally do as young nobles—knighthood. Though Stephanie wished that they could grow up and play games like children instead, she knew these were necessary lessons for life on Avalon. She watched as her own son, Hunter, went from playing baseball and video games to sword fighting and archery practice. She was used to the life, but she wasn't always a fan of it.

She looked down at her granddaughter, Meriel, playing innocently at her feet. Though only a year old, she was growing up so fast. Her curly blonde hair and deep blue eyes reminded Stephanie of what Sarafina must have looked like as a child. Her adopted daughter was off with the other shield maidens on the coast, but she checks in on her children every chance she gets. Though duty bound to the order, her first priority was as a mother to her children.

Sarafina entrusted her mother to watch over her children while she protected Avalon from the Outlander threat. Lady Stephanie was very good at waiting while the ones she loved risked their lives. It was part of her life, being married to the Gil-Gamesh. She had hoped that someday, there would come a time when Avalon was a peace and she and Bryan could enjoy the life they built here. Sadly, she knew that day might never come.

"I never thought I would see the day when the 'Shining City' would be filled with the sounds of war," said Lady Lyllodoria, surprising Stephanie, who stood quickly, out of respect for the Queen of the Elves. Lyllodoria quickly motioned for her to remain seated.

Stephanie smiled graciously. "I would think you have heard these sounds before, milady. The Elves have always been some of the finest warriors I've ever seen on Avalon," she replied.

Lyllodoria scoffed softly under her breath. She did not want to insult her guest, but she was truly ignorant to the ways of the Elves. "No, Lady Stephanie, we do not aspire for war," she explained. "The 'way of the sword' has never been the path of the *Ljósálfar*. The Elves have always sought enlightenment, knowledge and wisdom. We do this through the study of music, prose, magic and even through the fighting arts.

"The *Hîldrägo Boquè* are some of those, selected at birth, to become the protectors of Alfheimer," she continued, "but they do not train like this, out in the open for all to see."

"You make it sound as if they are ashamed of being soldiers instead of philosophers," Stephanie asked. Though slightly offended by what she perceived as cheekiness, Lyllodoria attributed it to innocent ignorance to the ways of the Elves and ignored it.

"Not hardly, Lady Stephanie. The *Hîldrägo Boquè* are the most honoured, most revered of the Elves of Alfheimer, for they will lay down their lives to defend us, no matter what the cost."

Stephanie knew that tone, one she heard from her own mother on many occasions, when she would interject herself into a conversation that she knew nothing about. "I apologise if I have offended you in any way, Lady Lyllodoria. I appreciate you providing refuge for all of us at these dire straits."

"No, dear lady, there is no need for apologies," Lyllodoria said, as she sat down next to Stephanie. "We do not normally discuss these matters with outsiders, though many have tried to gain such insight. Your husband, on many occasions, tried to learn as much as he could about the Elves of Alfheimer. Sadly, it is hard to put five millennia of history into dinner conversation, as it were."

The silence hung in the air between the two. Stephanie looked at Meriel and smiled, as she marvelled at the innocence of her granddaughter. She then looked across the courtyard toward her family, and she smiled again, filled with pride at these how they a growing into young men and women.

"Tell me, Lady Stephanie, how many people know that King Bowen is your grandson?" Lyllodoria asked. Stephanie was shocked, unsure of who told Lyllodoria about Bowen and she stuttered to find an answer.

"You need not worry, your secret has not been compromised," Lyllodoria assured. "I see a lot of your son and your husband in the young King. It was quite easy to distinguish his lineage."

"Please, milady, we have not told any of the Lords of Avalon," Stephanie explained. "We weren't made aware of it until the night of Ashley's wedding. We were waiting until Bowen was older and came into his own, as the King, before we would reveal it."

"You do not owe me any explanation, Lady Stephanie. "I consider it a personal matter between the King and the people of Avalon. The Elves are on a different path."

Stephanie did not like what she was hearing, and her smile turned inward, as her thoughts grew more and more troubled. Lyllodoria noticed the change in her demeanour.

"What troubles you, Lady Stephanie?"

"I am worried about our future, here on Avalon, if Bryan can't restore the barrier," she said. "Though there are many dangers here, none of those can compare to the evils of the outside world: Terrorism, drug abuse, mass shootings, gang violence, natural disasters. After all the years I've spent on Avalon, I can't imagine raising Meriel or any of my grandchildren in that world."

"There are many evils in both worlds," Lyllodoria said. "When greed, corruption and lust for power take over the hearts of men, there will always be some who fall prey to their ill will. It takes but the strength of character, heart and mind to defeat them.

"Such courage is found in your husband," she continued. "I have no doubt that he will find a way to resolve this."

"If you truly believe that, then why do you oppose him at every juncture, hiding behind your magical barriers in Alfheimer, removing yourself from life on Avalon?" Stephanie demanded. "Ever since Idlehorn, you've drifted further and further away from us, with no rhyme or reason, as if you blame Bryan for what happened to Eonis and Lord Baldrid—"

She paused, realising she may have overstepped her bounds by addressing the Elf Queen in such a manner. She stood and curtsied, bowing her head as she spoke. "Please forgive my outburst, Lady Lyllodoria," Stephanie apologised. "I get emotional when it comes to my husband, and often my emotions get the best of me."

Lady Lyllodoria nodded her head, accepting her apology. She motioned for Stephanie to return to her seat. "Do not mistake my lack of cooperation with the Gil-Gamesh this past year as a sign of condemnation against your husband. What I do is necessary to prepare for the coming days, when Avalon will be tested by more than an Outlander invasion."

Stephanie was taken aback. "Is something going to happen, milady? Have you foreseen some grim future for us?"

Now it was Lyllodoria's turn to be silent as she stood to leave. "Not for you, my dear Stephanie," she said with soft undertones. "I have been preparing my people for the *Ørientür*."

"*Ørientür*? What is that?"

Just then, Lady Lyllodoria saw Stephanie's daughter, Ashley, running towards them. "I will let your daughter explain," Lyllodoria said calmly, as she ignored Ashley and walked away.

"Mother, we found it," Ashley said. "Merlin found the spells to restore the barrier, but there's one problem."

"The *Ørientür*?"

Ashley paused in surprise, then nodded.

"What does it mean, Ashley?"

"*Ørientür*, it means the 'ascension'. The Ascension of the Elves."

***

After a lengthy conference with Captain McLoughlin on the fortification of the shore defences around Avalon, it took the Gil-Gamesh three days before he reached Alfheimer. He travelled to the Elven city aboard the *Black Adder*, along with the remaining complement of *Hîldrägo Boquè*, Eileanora and his son, Hunter.

He tried to understand what Ashley told him about the *Ørientür*, but he still didn't fully comprehend the meaning behind 'The Ascension of the Elves' and how that would restore the barrier. As much as he trusted his daughter in her studies with Merlin, he wanted to hear it from the wizard himself.

The airship circled above the city as it descended toward Lake Ouroboros, which was nestled just above the waterfall that separated the Elven city. Bryan looked down from the bow, with his shield maiden Amelia beside him. As he stared at the ancient city, he noticed something very strange. The walkways, bridges, balconies and courtyards were practically empty. The normal glow emanating from the 'Shining City' was dull and lifeless without the presence of the multitude of Elves normally found there.

"Are you all right, milord?" Amelia asked him.

"I've never seen Alfheimer so quiet, Amelia. Have you?"

Amelia leaned over the railing to get a better look. She was as stunned as the Gil-Gamesh. "No, milord, I haven't. It's as if they're all inside their homes."

"Ashely did say that Lyllodoria has been preparing the Elves for the *Øriĕntür* for the past year," Bryan said. "She must have known that this was going to happen, that this was the only way to save Avalon."

"Then why didn't she say anything? She could have prevented all of this from happening."

"That's the trouble with foreseeing the future, Amelia," he explained. "If you try to change things out of their intended order, there's a chance you could make things even worse."

"I don't understand, milord. If you can't change things, then why look into the future in the first place?"

"I didn't say you couldn't change things, Amelia. A good soothsayer can divine the threads of time like strings on a tapestry. They know which ones to pull and which one to leave alone so as not to upset the future.

"That's why Lyllodoria kept to herself this past year, ordering all the Elves on Avalon to return to Alfheimer," he continued. "She must have known what was going to happen and had to ensure things were done in the proper order to ensure the future for Avalon and the Elves."

"It's still so confusing to me."

Bryan laughed. "Now you know why I never use my dragon sight to see into the future if I don't have to. You remember the Manticore of Merthyr Tydfil?"

"How could I forget it?" she said scoffing. "That's the last time I let you use me as bait."

"Well, that's exactly my point. I used my 'dragonsight' to try and see where the Manticore would strike next," he recalled. "I saw him at the barn, stalking the young girl. I thought replacing you with the girl was a reasonable bet."

"Then why did he try to kill me?"

Bryan sighed loudly in exaggeration. "The other girl was blonde, you're a redhead." He threw up his hands in mock exasperation. "I guess you weren't his type." Amelia didn't appreciate the joke, but Bryan laughed so hard, she couldn't help but laugh herself.

Their laughter subsided as the *Black Adder* glided in for a landing, breaking through the water on Lake Ouroboros. Captain O'Brien piloted his ship next to the *Avenger*, moored at the Elven piers along with the *Aerdrie Faenya*.

Bryan was expecting a welcoming party, even just his family or even Chamberlain Ocwyn. Yet, the only one waiting for them on the pier was Rose. Bryan knew that she was most likely here to see Edan, but still, it all unnerved him.

As the ship was being moored, Hunter and Eileanora joined them on deck, as the four were ready to depart. "Amelia, let Rhona know we arrived safely and tell her to follow on as quickly as she can with as many of the Dragon Guard as she can spare. Then, contact Sarafina and tell her to bring the shield maidens to Alfheimer."

"How many of the shield maidens, Gil-Gamesh?" she asked.

"All of them," Bryan said without skipping a beat.

"By your command, milord!" she replied with a quick bow before taking off to follow orders. The sailors quickly lowered the gangplank as Bryan ran down to meet Rose. She gave her father a quick hug and peck on the cheek, but she knew he was in a hurry.

"They're waiting for you in the Great Hall of the Vanir, Father," Rose told him. "Everyone's there, including Lady Lyllodoria and her council."

"All right sweetheart, why don't you go say 'hi' to Edan before joining us? He's missed you." Rose smiled and hugged her father one last time before going up to see Edan. Bryan knew better than to stand between two young adults in love.

As he walked through the 'Shining City' with Hunter and Eileanora, it was like walking through a ghost town. There wasn't an Elf to be found, except for the occasional *Hîldrägo Boquè* on their way to and from the outer defences.

The Great Hall of Vanir was the main meeting place for the Elves. The walls were decorated with elaborate mosaics and murals depicting consequential moments in the history of the Elves, from the birth of the *Ljósálfar* and Døkkálfar (light-Elves and dark-Elves), Ólafr the Elf of Geirstaðir, the story of Thorsten, Beli and Angantyr retrieving magic ship *Ellida* and many more. Around the hall were various statues of Elven Lords and ladies, including a recent addition of Lord Baldrid and Eonis.

They were all there, as Rose said, except for Chamberlain Ulric Ocwyn. Though the absence of his old friend bothered him, Bryan immediately went to his family. It had been weeks since he saw his wife and even longer since he had seen his grandchildren.

The boys ran up to him first. Though Bowen was his King, formalities were set aside as he reached out for his Grandpa. Thomas jumped up too and Bryan picked both up in his arms. With a kiss on their cheeks and a tight squeeze, all was better in the world again.

After releasing the boys, he walked over his wife, waiting patiently with little Meriel in her arms. Bryan kissed his little granddaughter on the forehead before reaching in and kissing his wife lovingly. The Gil-Gamesh reached out to greet Ashley and Andrew before he turned to Lady Lyllodoria.

Bryan dropped to one knee, in respect of her royal highness, and bowed his head. "*Salüs dai Tulafáir*, Lady Lyllodoria," he said, as he placed his hand over his heart before extending it to the Queen of the Elves.

"*Salüs dai Atrémar* Lord MoonDrake," she said, as she extended her hand and helped him to his feet. "We welcome you home to the Shining City, Gil-Gamesh, and I must apologise to you if I was distant to you this past year. It was not meant to hurt you, but rather to prepare my people for this moment."

"No, I am the one who should apologise, milady. I was brutal and harsh toward you and I see now how wrong I was to think you would ever abandon Avalon, but surely there has to be another way," Bryan pleaded. "No one in Avalon wants the Elves to sacrifice themselves to restore us behind the barrier."

"It is not a sacrifice, Lord MoonDrake," Lyllodoria corrected him. "The *Øriĕntür* was conceived by our Great Father Freyr since the dawn of our birth.

He knew there would come a time when the sun would set on the *Ljósálfar*. That time is now."

"But why, Lyllodoria? Why must the Elves 'ascend' now?" Stephanie asked. "You've contributed so much to the peace and enlightenment of all races on Avalon."

"That's just it, Mother," Ashley said. "They have achieved the *Entôn ære* or the 'Glorious Finish' for lack of a better translation. This day was set by Freyr as the last day of Elves in the realm of men."

Lyllodoria nodded her head toward Ashley, a rare compliment from the Queen of the Elves. "Your daughter has a wonderful gift of knowledge, Gil-Gamesh, and she is correct. Our time on Earth has come to an end. It is time for us to join our brethren in *Vídbláin*."

"Excuse me, Lady Lyllodoria, but what is *Vídbláin*?" Bowen asked innocently as seven-year-olds do.

"It's what the Elves call Heaven, Your Majesty," Hunter explained. "It's the afterlife, like the Fields of Elysium or the Halls of Valhalla."

"And we must ascend to *Vídbláin* as one people," Lyllodoria interjected. "That is what we've been preparing for since the Battle of Idlehorn. We will not abandon any of our people to remain behind. We will commensurate the *Ørientür* with Merlin's spell of first magic. As we ascend to *Vídbláin*, our magic will spread across Avalon and the barrier will be restored.

"This is how it must be done, Gil-Gamesh. For Avalon to survive, this must be done."

Bryan stood there silent as he stared at Lyllodoria. He saw the truth in her eyes and realised that this was the fate of the Elves, as predetermined by Freyr, and everyone knows you can't argue with a God. He walked over and clasped his hands and hers, holding them as lovingly and tender as he could. A tear welled up in his eye as he kissed her hand.

"I will miss your counsel, your insight and your wisdom, Lady Lyllodoria," he said. "You helped me accept my life here on Avalon when I was lost and confused. Thank you."

Lady Lyllodoria smiled and reached out and kissed the Gil-Gamesh on the forehead. They both respected the duty and sacrifice they have made for the safety and security of the enchanted island.

"Now, what can we do for you, milady?" he asked, quiet and sombre.

"Once we begin the *Ørientür*, Alfheimer will be vulnerable to attack," she explained. "If anything disrupts the spell, it could mean disaster for both the Elves and Avalon."

"We have additional forces coming in from the coast," Bryan assured her. "They should be here in a few days."

"I have one last request of you, Lord MoonDrake. After we are gone, I want you to make Alfheimer your home."

Bryan was stunned, as was Stephanie and the others. "Your home on Emmyr has been lost to you," Lyllodoria continued. "We do not want Alfheimer to become a hollow ruin, torn apart by treasure hunters and looters. You and your family will forever be the protectors of Alfheimer, of its beauty, its knowledge and its secrets."

Bryan bowed to Lady Lyllodoria. "We would be honoured to care and watch over Alfheimer, milady," he said, as the others followed suit and bowed and curtsied in respect to the Elven Queen.

"Now, while you prepare our defences, we will continue our preparations for the Øriĕntür," Lyllodoria said with a bow of her head, as she turned to leave. As her attendants and council followed close behind, she stopped and turned back.

"Eileanora, please join us," she said.

Eileanora turned away from the Queen as if she was ashamed. "I'm sorry, Your Majesty, but I did not think you would allow me to take part in the Øriĕntür."

Lyllodoria stepped forward as Eileanora turned away. She reached under her chin and turned her face to hers. "My dear Eileanora, you are a daughter of Alfheimer. You have done all we have asked of you without question. Now take your place with us in *Vídbláin*."

A tear rolled down Eileanora's cheek as Lady Lyllodoria wiped away her tears and kissed her forehead. Eileanora always thought she would never be welcome in *Vídbláin*, but now she had been redeemed by her queen. As they departed Vanir Hall, Eileanora turned back to the Gil-Gamesh. He just smiled at her and nodded his head in approval. Bryan was happy that maybe, just maybe, Eileanora will know peace for the first time in her life.

After their departure, Bryan turned back to his extended family with some more questions. "First things first, where is Ocwyn?"

"He went back to New Camelot," Stephanie said. "The other Lords of Avalon were heading to New Camelot, for better security and protection from the Outlanders. He went there to ensure they didn't—and I'm using his words—ransack the place in the King's absence."

"All right, Sarafina and Captain McLoughlin should be arriving in a couple of days with the remaining shield maidens and Dragon Guard to protect the Elves during the Øriĕntür."

"Mommy's coming home?" Thomas asked excitedly. Bryan reached down and picked his grandson up.

"Yes, your Mommy will be here in a few days, and I'm sure she'll be just as excited to see you," he answered with a quick kiss on the cheek before he set him down. "In the meantime, I'll have Captain O'Brian take Andrew and Ashley back to the coast. We'll send word to Captain Rich to come in and pick you up, so you can return to the United States after Avalon's disappears from history yet again."

"Actually, sir—" Andrew started.

"We're not going back, Dad," Ashley said with abrupt certainty. She took Andrew by the arm. "Andy and I have decided to stay on Avalon."

"What? Why?"

"They already know who we are and who we're related too," Andrew said. "We could be persecuted or hunted down again if word gets out."

"Besides that, Merlin has asked me to become his apprentice," Ashley added. "I can't say no to him after all he's done for me."

"Ashley, do you realise what that entails?" Bryan asked angrily, having been caught off guard by this new information.

"I do. We've been discussing it for the past few weeks. Merlin said he could never find a more competent and capable apprentice to pass on all his knowledge, so he may finally know the peaceful sleep in the arms of death."

Bryan looked over at Stephanie, livid that these decisions were made without him. "Did you know about this?"

"I did and no, Bryan, I didn't tell you because you have the weight of Avalon on your shoulders right now and you didn't need any more stress," she snapped back, putting him in his place as only she could. "Besides the fact, they are adults, Bryan, and are capable of making informed decisions on their own."

The Gil-Gamesh sighed, knowing full well that he was not going to win this argument, no matter how mad he was.

"You can't take care of all of us on your own, Grandfather," Bowen said. "That's why we're a family, we look after each other."

Bryan couldn't believe the wisdom coming out of this little boy. And it was all it took to set him straight. "As always, I defer to your wisdom, Your Majesty," he said and bowed to the King. Bowen nodded his head and smiled. Hunter placed his arm around his son, reassuringly and with pride.

***

The streets of New Camelot were sparse these days, especially at night. With most of the Knights of the Round Table manning the defence of Avalon along the coast, the vibrant life of the capital of Avalon was diminished.

The city's defence was left to the Armiger Corps. These were knights who attained knighthood but have not yet attained rank in the Knights of the Round Table. The sole purpose of these knights was to protect New Camelot, roaming the streets and manning the ramparts, in defence of the capital.

Though the streets were practically empty at night, the Armiger Corps carefully patrolled them, keeping a watchful eye out for anyone trying to take advantage of the absence of the Knights of the Round Table.

As a patrol walked by the *Merry Widow* pub, they were carefully watched from the upstairs window. Tomas Elderson looked nervously down at the passing guards. The young man was thin, almost gaunt, which made the trembling of his body to be quite visible. The sweat trickled down his forehead as he failed to stop it with a handkerchief. He stuffed it back into his coat pocket before taking another peek out the curtain.

"Come away from there Tomas before you give yourself a heart attack," Finnick scolded. "Have a glass of wine; it'll calm your nerves."

Tomas turned back to the private room, one of many in the *Merry Widow* for those customers wanting time away from the bar to indulge in whatever vice they may have. He was joined by the rest of the first-born of the Lords of Avalon:

Finnick Devereaux, Jaeger Nottingham and Bree Olafdotter. The four were sitting around the room in comfortable, plush chairs, drinking wine and eating a small feast of assorted delicacies.

"We shouldn't be meeting out in the open like this, what if the guards find us here with him?" Tomas worried.

"They're not going to, you little piss-ant, unless you keep looking out the window and attracting attention to us," Jaeger teased.

"Knock it off, Jaeger, he's just concerned, and so am I," Bree said, as she walked over to calm Tomas down. "We've never met like this before, so why now?"

"Because our time has come," came a voice from across the room as a demon hole appeared and through it stepped Abdel Ben Faust, Artūras Blackstone and Mordred. The others quickly got to their feet and bowed to the immortal sorcerer.

"Please, my dear allies, sit," Mordred said, motioning toward them. "Let's have some more food and drink while we wait for our remaining guests."

"Guests? But milord, who else is coming?" Finnick asked. As if on cue, there was a knock at the door. Mordred motioned for Blackstone answer it. Once he opened the door, in walked a gnome, Master Tinker Edwyn Broadfoot.

He was shorter than a dwarf, less than three feet tall. His head was quite bulbous, matching his nose, with thinning, grey hair and beard. Atop his head was a leather skullcap with a pair of thick goggles attached, covering his eyes. Gnomes were unaccustomed to bright light and needed protection when above ground. Affixed to the goggles were a pair of optics, comprising a variety of lenses that could be shuffled in place, depending on the situation. He wore simple leathers, including a leather apron. Around his waist hung a tool belt filled with a variety of tools, from wrenches and screwdrivers to hammers and hand drills. In his hand was a massive iron wrench, which he used as both a walking stick and a weapon.

"Well, don't look all excited to see me," the diminutive gnome said sarcastically. He gave a quick nod to Mordred before helping himself to some wine.

"Well, then," Mordred said, "now that we're all here, let's begin, shall we?"

"But what about Miss Minna?" Tomas asked Mordred. "Won't she be joining us?"

"Unfortunately, Minna Oddbottom refused our invitation," Blackstone answered for his master. "Her loyalties to her father and the King were unshaken by our arguments."

Minna OddBottom was the daughter of Master Dinius Oddbottom, Lord of the Gilded Halls of the Dwarves of Avalon. Her fiery disposition and tenacious loyalty made her both friends and enemies in the royal court. Tomas' confidence shrank when he heard that she wasn't joining them.

"But, she could warn her father about us, about the plan," he stuttered out, fear quivering in his voice. "They might warn our fathers and the Gil-Gamesh and—"

"Calm yourself, Tomas," Mordred said. "Artūras took the necessary precautions, as he did with Princess Amira of Togo, and all of you. Miss Minna forgot about their conversation once she refused our offer. No one in Avalon knows about me or my plan."

"I'm sorry, Master Mordred, it's just—" Mordred placed his hand on Tomas' shoulder.

"You have nothing to fear, Tomas. In a few days, all of Avalon will know of my return and you will be there by my side…all of you will!" Mordred looked fiercely into the eyes of his young charges trying to instil confidence in them.

"And what about Sir Hunter MoonDrake," Bree interjected coolly, "did you approach him as well?"

Mordred didn't like the tone of her voice but continued. "I never considered asking the son of the Gil-Gamesh to join us," Mordred answered diplomatically as possible. "The Outlander and the rest of his family have no place on Avalon. They will be dealt with when the time comes."

"Don't mind her, Master Mordred," Jaeger said. "She has feelings for the little runt, that's all, like a little lost puppy." He nudged Bree. She didn't take his insult lightly, drawing her sword as she spun around and placed it right at Jaeger's throat.

"If you speak to me that way again, Jaeger, I'll gut you like yesterday's catch!"

Jaeger threw down his goblet and went for his weapon, but Finnick and Tomas separated the two. "Enough of this!" Blackstone shouted, as he stepped between them. "You shall act like Lords and Ladies of Avalon in the presence of Master Mordred!"

"Let them be, Artūras," Faust said, as he poured himself a drink. "They need to harden their hearts and toughen their spines for what's ahead."

"There is a time and place for everything, General Faust. Now, we must have calmer heads about us if we are to succeed," Mordred added. "Sheathe your weapon, Brigda Olafdottor, you need not waste your energy on trading blows with this one.

"And you," he continued, as he turned to Jaeger Nottingham, "you will keep your comments and jokes to yourself while in my presence, or you may lose your tongue in the process." Jaeger swallowed hard and nodded his head, not wanting to incur Mordred's wrath.

"So, Tinker Broadfoot, how goes our new fleet of warships?" Mordred asked, as he turned his attention to the gnome.

"We're on schedule, Master Mordred, thanks to the shipbuilders provided by young Master Nottingham," he said with a toast toward Jaeger. "I'll have seven more dreadnoughts ready by the end of the week. Along with *Hood's Revenge*, *Fafnir* and *Maleficent*, that makes a total of ten in your fleet. I'm still fine-tuning the engines to extend the flight time, but still, they're more than a match for any of the Gil-Gamesh's airships." He chuckled under his breath and took another drink.

"Excellent work, Master Tinker," Mordred praised his associate before turning back to the others. "Within the next few days, the Elves will initiate the Øriĕntür. Once the ceremony has begun, Alfheimer will be defenceless. That's when General Faust will attack with the Wraith Legion, wiping out the Gil-Gamesh, his Dragon Guard and the shield maidens."

"Why must you attack them, Master Mordred?" Bree asked. "If we disrupt the Øriĕntür, won't the barrier remain open and Avalon will be overrun by the Outlanders?"

"My attack will be against the Gil-Gamesh and his forces," Faust answered. "I will let the Elves finish their accursed ceremony, so we can be rid of them, once and for all."

"With the Elves gone, the Gil-Gamesh dead and the barrier restored, Avalon will be ours for the taking," Mordred interjected. "I will ascend to the throne of Avalon and take my rightful place, removing the bastard grandson of the Gil-Gamesh from it. For now, I have just one final task for each of you."

Mordred reached into his robes and pulled out a dagger. Blackstone held out a wine goblet as Mordred cut his hand let a few drops of blood fall into the wine. "We will make the 'fatal bond' for the last step to prove your loyalty to me." Mordred handed the dagger to Finnick. "When the attack begins, each of you will kill your mother and father and take their place as a Lord, and Lady, of Avalon."

The four young nobles were shocked. None of them expected to have to kill their own parent. Mordred could see the unwillingness in their faces. "You all agreed to this, did you not?"

"Well, yes, but I thought that Faust or Blackstone would carry out the deed, not us," Finnick said softly.

"So, you're okay with your parents being murdered, as long as you don't have to do it yourself," Faust said with a sneer. "What a bunch of cowards, all of you!"

Jaeger took offense to being called a coward. He snatched the dagger from Finnick and cut into his palm, squeezing the blood out over the cup, as it dripped from his fist. "No man will ever call me a coward!" he snapped, much to the delight of Mordred.

Finnick took the blade and cut into his hand, keeping his palm open as the blood trickled down his hand and into the goblet. Once he pulled his hand away, he wrapped the wound in a handkerchief and handed the dagger to Bree.

Bree was hesitant, but realised she had no real choice. She took the dagger and cut her hand, holding it over the cup to drop into the mixture of wine and blood. "What I do, I do for the sake of my people, not for myself," she said, as if to justify her actions to herself and the others.

All that was left was Tomas, the youngest of the four. Bree held out the dagger to him, but Tomas shied away. "You're committed to this, Tomas, as are the rest of us," Bree assured him. "There is no turning back now!"

Tomas stared at the cup and the dagger. He scanned everyone in the room, all staring at him, waiting for him to decide. He reluctantly nodded his head as he took the dagger from Bree. Unlike the others, he pricked his finger with the point of the dagger and squeezed it over the goblet until a single drop fell into the liquid.

Tomas was about to hand the dagger to Tinker Broadfoot, but the little gnome refused to take it. "Unlike you four, I'm getting paid for my assistance; I don't need to make a pact."

Mordred laughed as Blackstone handed the metal goblet to him. The immortal held his hand over the cup and began to invoke the Fatal Bond—a spell used by wizards to compel people to do their bidding. Once accepted, the task must be completed, or they would die a horrible death.

Mordred finished the spell and took a sip of the mixture. "By my hand, you four have sworn to me to complete this task," he started to say. "You will kill your mother and father at the apex of the *Øriĕntür*, so you swear."

He handed the cup to Jaeger. One-by-one, they drank from the goblet and each one vowed to uphold their pledge to Mordred. With each passing of the cup, the magic of the Fatal Bond flowed from the cup to each of them, binding them to Mordred. Tomas took the last drink and the spell was complete.

Mordred smiled, as he clasped Jaeger and Tomas on the shoulders, looking happy and proud of them. "We will reign in a new era on Avalon, removing the old ways and ushering in a new order. It will begin in a fortnight, so steel yourselves, my Lords of Avalon. Our time is now."

***

The Gil-Gamesh wandered through Alfheimer with a newfound appreciation for the fabled city. He had visited so many times before, but he never took the time to really see the beauty and grace of this ancient wonder. He always found himself so wrapped up in other duties that he could never take in the sights like he could today.

With Stephanie on his arm, Bryan walked down the marble walkways and across granite bridges, enjoying the view of what will soon be their new home. "This will take some getting used to," he said coyly.

"What? A floating island wasn't enough for you?" Stephanie retorted. "This is tame compared to seeing Emmyr for the first time."

"I just can't believe that they're really going to do it. The Elves are leaving Avalon, leaving our world, forever."

"You were the one who told me that you cannot deter from prophesies," Stephanie argued. "This is something that has been set for more than a millennium. They must go through with it."

"I know, I know, it's just…I've lost so many of my friends over the years, but this is the first time I've lost an entire race."

"You're not losing them, Bryan," Stephanie explained, as she tightened her grip on his arm, to comfort him. "They aren't dying from a disease or being wiped out by genocide. They are moving on to somewhere some of them have been waiting thousands of years to see.

"I've learned so much since I've been here," she continued. "I can't tell you how sad it is for me to see them go after they've done so much for us, our family, for all of Avalon, but this is something that is completely out of our hands."

The two of them sat down on a marble bench within view of the majestic waterfall that cascades down from Lake Ouroboros between the valley walls. "It's incredible how much beauty and life are within the walls of this valley," Bryan said. "I don't know how we are going to survive without them. They've brought so much to the people of Avalon, some of which won't even know of the sacrifice the Elves are making to save our world."

"They will know, Bryan, because when they come to Alfheimer, to see you, we will make it our solemn duty to make them aware of everything the Elves have done."

Bryan was glad to hear such encouragement from Stephanie. At first, he wasn't sure that she would adjust to our life on Avalon. She has done so with the vigour and enthusiasm of someone who's lived here their whole life.

"It'll be wonderful to have the whole family here, together," Stephanie continued. "Maybe after all this is over, we can finally have that peaceful life we hoped for."

Bryan shook his head and chuckled. "I wish that were true, Steph, but this is Avalon. There's always something afoul here. Abdel Ben Faust is on the loose, killing indiscriminately and seemingly controlling a ghost army, the gnomes have been causing trouble in cities, and Keane Foley and his band of thieves are taking advantage of the whole Outlander situation by robbing people blind."

"And that goes to my point earlier about carrying the weight of Avalon on your shoulders," she interjected. "You have to let the local magistrates take care of some of these burdens. You can't be at everyone's beck and call every time there's trouble."

"They depend on me, Stephanie," he replied. "I have responsibilities to—"

"You also have responsibilities to me and your family, Bryan. Don't forsake us for duty. How many families were torn apart by sailors more concerned with duty than family? Do you remember?"

Bryan did remember the many men and women he counselled when he was a Chief Petty Officer. He listened to their woes of being separated from spouses and children, and time-and-time again, and he told them to find the balance between duty and home. Maybe now he needed to take some of his own advice.

"You're right, Steph, as much as I hate to admit it, you're right."

"Well, hallelujah, hell is freezing over! The Gil-Gamesh admitted he was wrong."

Bryan laughed at his own expense. He pulled her close and kissed her, proving to her even more that he conceded to her wisdom, but then reality of another sort sank in as she leaned her head against his chest.

"What about Ashley?" he asked. "Becoming Merlin's apprentice is a big step. I don't know if she can handle all that power and the responsibility that comes with it."

"Bryan, if Merlin thinks she can handle it, who are we to dispute the all-powerful Wizard of Avalon?"

"Wow. Two admissions in one day that we don't know everything. What is the world coming to?" Bryan joked. Stephanie laughed.

"Yes, well, don't tell the kids that. They still have to believe that Mother and Father know everything."

They laughed again, and were beginning to believe that maybe this was the beginning of a better life for them. Bryan wanted to be optimistic, for Stephanie's sake, but it was difficult. He had seen too much evil in Avalon to hope for peace in his time. To the Gil-Gamesh, peace usually meant darker forces were planning something. He knew evil was patient.

"*Bon après-midi,* Lord et Lady MoonDrake!" came a voice that broke the peaceful silence. Stephanie recognised it immediately and cringed. Bryan turned to see Chancellor Henri Beauchamp walking briskly toward them.

"What in God's name is he doing here?" Stephanie quietly asked.

"I don't know. In any case, we'll need Henri to get things organised here in Alfheimer, and there's no time like the present."

Stephanie nodded her head and begrudgingly agreed with Bryan. As much as she hated Henri's pompous attitude, he was the best at what he did. As Henri approached the two, he removed his oversized feathered hat and bowed politely to Lord and Lady MoonDrake. Bryan reached out to his chancellor and greeted him with a firm handshake.

"It's good to see you, Henri. Is there anything wrong?" he asked.

"*Non, non...rien du tout,* Gil-Gamesh," Henri replied. "I came as soon as I heard we would be making Alfheimer our home. There is much to do if we are to bring the people of Emmyr here*, n'êtes pas d'accord*?"

"Well, I'm not sure if we will be, Henri. I don't want to turn Alfheimer into another Port Charles, with its taverns, brothels and warehouses. That's not what the Elves would want."

"I agree, Bryan. There'll be none of that here," Stephanie interjected, as she agreed with her husband. "Alfheimer means much more than that to turn into a carnival sideshow."

"*Mais bien sûr*, Lady Stephanie, I did not mean to insinuate anything of the sort," Henri apologised immediately. "I merely wanted to convey the hope of everyone from Emmyr."

"What do you mean?" Stephanie asked.

"The people of Emmyr, they are all looking forward to being together again," he explained. "After all, we are family, *sommes-nous pas*?"

Stephanie choked up as a tear welled up in her eyes. She realised her error in dismissing the feelings of the people she has come to know and love over the past ten years. She went over and hugged Henri, something she had never done before. It caught Henri and Bryan both off guard. Bryan couldn't help but chuckle at the irony of it all while Henri reciprocated as politely as he could.

"Thank you, Henri," Stephanie said, as she released him. "Thank you for reminding me about what's most important to us all—family!"

Henri smiled. "*Ah oui, chère madame*, that reminds me, I arrived with some very special guests," he stated, as he motioned behind him. Bryan and Stephanie turn to see Sarafina and Rhona McLoughlin walking toward them.

They hadn't seen their adopted daughter in months and were elated to see her in Alfheimer. While Stephanie reached out to hug Sarafina, Bryan welcomed his Captain of the Dragon Guard before the two switched to greet the other.

"I am so happy to see you, daughter," Bryan said, as he hugged Sarafina. "We've missed you."

"And I've missed you, Father," she said with a smile. "I've brought every available shield maiden with me, more than 1,000, along with another 100 of the Dragon Guard with Captain McLoughlin."

"Excellent, we will need every one of them," he said. "Rhona, you and Henri go up to Vanir Hall. Amelia can get you and your troops settled. We'll discuss the security plan later."

"I should assist with getting the shield maidens situated, Father," Sarafina implored.

"Oh no, you have something more important to do first," Stephanie contended as she took Sarafina by the arm and led her away. "I know two children who are dying to see their mother. That, my dear daughter, is your first task."

Sarafina didn't dare argue with Lady Stephanie and followed her to see her children. Bryan was glad Stephanie had that in hand and started toward Vanir Hall with Henri and Rhona.

"Any further incidents with the Outlanders, Captain?" Bryan asked.

"None, milord. The ships have maintained their distance off shore since they removed all their men and equipment from the invasion," Rhona replied.

"And the Wraiths?"

"There have been no reports of any sightings, Gil-Gamesh," Henri said. "*Son très étrange*, they disappeared as quickly as they appeared."

"Don't count on it, Henri. They're out there, with Faust as their commander. I'd bet 20 gold sovereigns they'll be here when the *Øriĕntür* starts."

"Did you foresee it in your dragon sight, milord?" Rhona asked.

"No, but I've got a bad feeling about this. Anyone know how to kill these things?"

"Only theories, Gil-Gamesh. No one has ever fought them before," Henri explained. "*Le spectre* is said to be vulnerable on the 'heartstone' on their chest. *Il est dit* the source of their power."

"That's only a legend, Chancellor, we don't know if it will work," Rhona added.

"Legend or not, it's all we have to go on, Rhona. We'll brief everyone before we position them around Alfheimer. Once our forces are in place, I want Lady Stephanie, King Bowen and any other civilians taken aboard the *Black Adder* and the *Avenger*. I don't want any of them in the line of fire just in case."

"In case of what, milord?" Rhona queried.

Bryan stopped and looked at her with cold, hard determination. "In case any of this goes wrong."

***

It had been days since Captain Larry Rich heard from the Gil-Gamesh or anyone on Avalon. The aircraft carrier continued to carry out its duties of reconnaissance flights over and along the coastline of Avalon as the magical barrier continued to recede deeper into the island. Things remained tense among their forces, the Russian Navy and Avalon, but the recent UN vote condemning the Russians' invasion and acknowledging Avalon as a separate and sovereign nation seemed to mellow things out.

"Permission to enter the bridge," came a voice from behind the skipper. Ensign Longwood stood just off the bridge in her flight suit, waiting for permission to enter.

"Permission granted," replied the OOD. She stepped in and walked immediately over to Captain Rich.

"Permission to speak with you, sir."

"Yes, it's all right, Ensign. Commander Johnson said you wanted to talk to me before you left," he said before he looked at his watch. "Your COD is almost ready to launch. You should be down in control."

"Yes, sir, I just wanted to thank you for getting those orders to Bethesda cancelled. I really didn't feel like having any more poking and prodding done by doctors."

"Well, you can thank Commander Gerwien for that," Captain Rich explained. "She gave them all of your test results, including some extra vials of your blood, to satisfy the folks at Navy Medicine. Besides, with everything that's being argued about the actions of Secretary of State Barry, the Navy doesn't want to add to it by going after a young Ensign with a new lease on life. Speaking of which, what are you going to do now?"

"I've been emailing with my fiancée back home and we're both very excited about the chance of having kids," she confessed. "We're going to move up the wedding, so we can get started as soon as possible."

"Well, I'm very happy for you, Ensign Longwood. Congratulations," he said, as he extended his hand to her. The two shook hands and the Captain turned back to his work. Then Longwood turned to leave but stopped short and turned back around.

"Excuse me, sir, but have you heard anything from the Gil-Gamesh, Lord MoonDrake?"

"No, no I haven't. Why do you ask?"

"I just thought that if you have the chance to speak to him, please tell him I said thank you, for giving me this opportunity."

"Well, if he sends anything my way, I will be happy to tell him, but I don't think…"

The Captain's voice trailed off as he looked over to the outboard hatch to see the tiny faerie dragon, Maverick, hovering at the window, waiting for him. Rich leapt out of his chair and went over to open the hatch. As soon as he did, Maverick flew inside and landed on his chair. He set down a rolled piece of parchment and nudged it toward the Captain.

"What is that?" Ensign Longwood asked.

"It's the Gil-Gamesh's pet, kind of a medieval courier pigeon." When he said that, Maverick growled at him, pulling the parchment away, but it came out more like purring. "Sorry," the Captain corrected. "His familiar, I believe he called him." Rich raised his eyebrows at the dragon. "Is that better?"

Maverick nodded his head and nudged the message back to him. Captain Rich picked it up, broke the wax seal and unrolled it. "How I long for the days when I didn't have to reason with dragons as part of my job," he mumbled to himself. "If you want to get a message to the Gil-Gamesh, Ensign, you might as well tell him. He can deliver it for you."

While the Captain read the message, Ensign Longwood leaned into the tiny dragon and whispered to him. "Can you give Lord MoonDrake a message for me?" she asked. Maverick just nodded his little head. "Please tell him that Ensign Longwood said thank you very much for saving my life." Maverick nodded his head. The Ensign leaned in and kissed the nose of the little dragon, causing it to swoon and purr in delight.

Captain Rich ignored the antics behind him and read Bryan's message:

Captain Rich,

We have discovered a way to return Avalon to its previous position, hidden from the outside world. If all goes well, we will fade from existence at dawn tomorrow. I would advise you to move the fleet farther away from the island and suspend all overflights as we don't know what effect it will have on all of you once the spell is complete.

I just wanted to say I'm sorry for not trusting you when we first met. I should have tried to reason with you better and, perhaps, we could have spared all the unnecessary bloodshed and death. I guess part of me did not want to bring you into this new world of mine because I knew the danger it represented.

In any case, I know you didn't mean to put Ashley and Andrew in danger. Though Stephanie has a hard time forgiving people who attack her children, I can be a little more understanding. As for Ashley and Andrew, they have decided to stay with us on Avalon. If you could, please let his parents think they died in that cabin fire. It's for the best that they don't know the truth.

Well, this is goodbye, my friend. I will say it this time, for the last. I hope I haven't damaged your career. In any case, my best to you and your family and your crew. Fair winds and following seas!

Lord Bryan MoonDrake, Gil-Gamesh of Avalon

He rolled up the parchment and turned back to Maverick. He thought for a minute how to respond, then reached into small desk area at his chair and grabbed one of his Captain's coins. It was a small coin with the ship's emblem on one side and the eagle insignia of a Navy Captain with the words 'From the Commanding Officer' on the other. It was given to sailors who had performed above expectations in their duties. To him, it was a message he knew Bryan would understand.

"Please give this to the Gil-Gamesh," he said, as he handed Maverick the coin. The little dragon took it, but looked puzzled when his eye met the Captain's. "Go on, get out of here, you flying iguana!"

Maverick huffed and growled again, before flying out of the hatch as quick as he came in.

"Officer of the Deck, inform all ships to move two more miles away from the coast of Avalon, then set course appropriately," he ordered. The officer answered back and immediately took actions to follow his orders. The Captain then went over to the call box to call up to the tower. "Boss, recall all aircraft and then secure the deck immediately after the COD launches."

Through the box, the Air Boss relayed the order. Captain Rich watched, as his ship began to move away from Avalon.

"What's happening to Avalon, sir?" Longwood asked. "Where are they going?"

"Home, Ensign," he said quite plainly. "They're going home!"

Chapter 10
The Battle of Alfheimer

The morning haze gave way as the sun began to rise over Avalon. Twinkling lights from lanterns could be seen from the four corners of the city as thousands of Elves took their last steps on this earthly plain. They were all dressed in long, white, hooded robes, their heads bowed in reverence. A soft, hypnotic chant echoed throughout Alfheimer as they walked, shuffling their feet in succession.

Since before sunrise, the Elves marched in quiet procession into the Temple of Eternal Starlight, the most sacred place in Alfheimer. The temple consisted of a circular amphitheatre with trees and rock formations surrounding it at the top. Inside, the seats were formed from the rock itself that descended into a small, circular open area. In the centre of the temple was a small, rock pedestal with inlaid silver, gold and mithril that formed an ornate basin.

It was here that the Gil-Gamesh received his ultimate honour when he was magically transformed into a Half-Elf. Now, it would serve as the focal point of the *Øriĕntür* as the Elves crossed over to *Vidbláin*, restoring the barrier around Avalon in the process.

Bryan patiently waited at the entrance to the temple with Amelia and Captain McLoughlin. Stephanie and the others were already airborne, and the remaining shield maidens and Dragon Guard had been assigned defensive positions around Alfheimer. His heart ached as the Elves walked past him. He understood that this was their destiny, as well as the necessity of it all, but mourned the countless lives that would soon be sacrificed so that Avalon could exist beyond the reach of the outside world once again.

As the last of the Elves entered the temple, Lady Lyllodoria approached with Eileanora and several members of the *Hîldrägo Boquè*, who were dressed in full armour and armed. The Gil-Gamesh though it an odd sight after seeing thousands of Elves enter wearing nothing but white robes.

Bryan bowed politely to Lyllodoria before turning his attention to Eileanora. "Going to the afterlife armed for war, Eileanora?" he asked.

"To use one of your human vernaculars, Gil-Gamesh, I feel naked without my sword," she replied with a small smile. Bryan chuckled softly. "I and these members of the *Hîldrägo Boquè* have decided to leave this world as we came into it—as warriors!"

Bryan bowed to Eileanora before turning his attention to the Lady Lyllodoria. "I cannot thank you enough, dear lady, for all you have done for me and for what you are about to do for Avalon. The sacrifice of the Elves of Alfheimer shall be forever remembered as the greatest single act of courage in our history."

Lyllodoria reached out and took Bryan by the hands, holding them close to her chest. "I thank Freyr for bringing you to us, Gil-Gamesh," she said, as a single tear rolled down her cheek. "We were blessed that day and shall forever be in your debt. We will hold a place for you and your family in *Vidbláin*. I look forward to the day when we will see each other again." She leaned in and kissed Bryan on the cheek before turning to enter the temple, followed by Eileanora and the *Hîldrägo Boquè*.

"Eileanora!" Bryan shouted. The assassin stopped and turned. Bryan paused a moment to find the right words. "Say hi to Eonis for me…and remind him that he still owes me 20 sovereigns from our last poker game."

Eileanora smiled at the Gil-Gamesh's poor attempt at humour, then nodded once before entering the temple.

Bryan walked outside the temple foyer with Amelia and Rhona and found Hunter, Sarafina and Andrew waiting for them. "Andrew? Why aren't you with Ashley and the others? You don't need to be here."

"With all due respect, milord, I am a knight," he replied, firmly standing up to his father-in-law. "I am more than capable to help with the defence of Alfheimer."

Bryan admired the courage of his son-in-law, while the others stood shocked and surprised to hear someone stand up to the Gil-Gamesh like that. "You're absolutely right, Andrew," he started. "You and Rhona take command of the southern flank. Hunter, you and Sarafina have the northern flank. Amelia and I will stay here to ensure no one enters the temple and disrupts the ceremony."

"You sound as if you're expecting trouble, Father?" Sarafina asked.

"He's always expecting trouble," Hunter chimed in, "It comes with the territory."

"This is no time for jests, Sir Hunter," Rhona said. "With Faust and the Wraith Legion just waiting to strike, who knows what to expect?"

"Captain McLoughlin is right," Amelia said. "Alfheimer will be vulnerable once the ceremony starts and we have to be ready for any contingency."

"And this may give us the opportunity to find out who's keeping Faust on a leash," Bryan added.

"Do you think someone else is behind Faust's attacks?" Rhona asked.

"Abdel Ben Faust is a brilliant swordsman but he's no General Patton," he explained. "Faust is just the puppet here, someone else is pulling his strings. This may be our chance to find out who the puppet master really is."

"In any case, these should help us against the wraiths," Hunter said, as he tossed a new spell shot to his father. Bryan caught the munition and studied it carefully. Unlike other spell shots, it was encased in silver and etched with various runes to collate the spell and alchemical mixture inside.

"What are these?"

"It's a new spell shot I call 'Uriel's Flame'," Hunter explained. "It fires a concentrated beam of light hotter than the sun. I had them consecrated with holy water and encased in a silver casing that's been blessed by Father Rochelle. It seemed like the right thing to do when you're fighting against the undead."

"Brilliant, Hunter. Absolutely brilliant!" Bryan commended. "Just remember, 'don't cross the streams'!" Hunter and Andrew laughed knowingly, while the others looked confused. "Have these been distributed to the troops?"

"The Dragon Guard has them, but the shield maidens refuse to use the GunStars." Bryan looked at Rhona and Sarafina for an explanation.

"With respect, Gil-Gamesh, shield maidens have a tradition we must uphold," Rhona stated. "We don't use magic in hand-to-hand combat. We live, and die, by the sword."

Bryan understood. It is hard to get people to accept change, especially people on Avalon. "Very well, Captain, but let's hope your reluctance doesn't sway the battle in their favour. This could very well be the most important fight of our lives. There's an endgame here, for Faust and his secretive master, and it all comes down to this," Bryan paused. "And, with the Knights of the Round Table and the remainder of our forces protecting the coastline, we are all that stands between the Elves and the completion of the *Øriĕntür*." Bryan walked over to Hunter and placed a hand on his son's shoulder. "But I, for one, am glad to be standing here, fighting alongside my family. I wouldn't have it any other way."

He looked in the eyes of everyone there, and they looked back at him. The Gil-Gamesh swelled with pride, as he never had before. Here in the heart of Alfheimer, as they awaited their destiny and the destiny of all of Avalon, he was content. Without another word, they each departed to take their positions. The chants from inside the Temple of Eternal Starlight grew louder and louder. The ceremony had begun.

The sound was a melodious tone, building slowly, flowing from their tongues in harmony in a single stream of pure thought. As the song grew, so did the light from the Elves themselves. They glowed brighter and brighter, until the Gil-Gamesh and Amelia had to avert their eyes from the temple.

The intense glow exploded into a beam of light that erupted skyward toward the sole star that was still visible the early dawn. Bryan watched as the tail of the beam disappeared into the atmosphere. Almost immediately, the beam returned and spread into a dome that encompassed the entire island of Avalon. Bryan could feel the connection between the light, the star and the island, and smiled and as the spell unfolded, the barrier being restored as predicted. They would soon return to that of myth and legend, away from the outside world. The war with Outlanders would soon be over and done.

Then he heard it—the faintest of sounds. A distinct 'pop'. Just once. Then there was another. And then another. Repeatedly, the faint popping could be heard, like the melodic beating of a drum, faster and faster. The Gil-Gamesh drew his swords immediately. He recognised that sound from before. It was the sound of demon holes opening.

From the highest points on the mountains flanking the two sides of Alfheimer, the Wrath Legion poured down the mountainside and into the city. Thousands of armoured wraiths ran down the sheer cliffs into the defenders below. The two sides clashed instantly, steel clanging against the phantom weapons of the wraiths.

The shield maidens held their own against the Wrath Legion, living up to their reputation as legendary warriors. The Dragon Guard matched well against the ghostly warriors. Hunter's spell shot proved most useful against the wraiths, breaking through their armour and shattering their heartstones with a blast of fiery light.

As the battle raged around them, the Gil-Gamesh watched and waited, looking for their leader to appear. The sound of a demon hole opening behind him assured him that his wait was over. Bryan spun around as Abdel Ben Faust lunged at him, bringing his broadsword *Deathsong* down at the Gil-Gamesh's head. Bryan crossed his swords and blocked his attack. Amelia stepped in and, true to fashion, used her shield to pummel Faust, hurling him away and to the ground.

Faust got up slowly as he ran his hand under his nose. He saw the dripping blood, caused by Amelia's blow, and it angered him even more. "You'll pay for that, you little bitch!" he cursed.

"Take another step closer, braggart, and I'll knock you down again!" Amelia jabbed back at him. The three circled each other, there in the foyer of the temple, and jockeyed for position.

"I don't know who or what possessed you to commandeer the Wrath Legion, Faust, but it ends today. You're putting all our lives at risk from the demon hordes of Hell, and for what? For some foolish master with eyes on the throne of Avalon?"

"You know not of my master, Gil-Gamesh, and when you do…you will only find your death!" Faust lunged at the two again, slashing wildly. Like a precision machine, Amelia and the Gil-Gamesh worked in unison, trading blow-for-blow with Faust. Amelia blocked his attacks with her shield while Lord MoonDrake struck back at Faust.

Bryan knew that the best way to take down a formidable swordsman like Faust was to keep him off balance. The Gil-Gamesh pressed his attack, keeping *Twilight* high and *Dusk* low. Faust swung mercilessly at the two of them, cutting out chunks of marble from the floor and columns with his massive broadsword.

When one such blow briefly lodged *Deathsong* in it, the Gil-Gamesh saw his opening. He leapt into the air and spun, his blades extended. Bryan sliced at

Faust's chest with *Twilight* and connected. The unearthly dragonfire of *Twilight* engulfed the broadsword's blade, hilt and beyond, burning away part of Faust's tunic, not to mention Faust himself. The half-demon stepped back and snarled in pain. It was then that Bryan saw the source of Faust's power.

The Gil-Gamesh looked at the heartstone attached to Faust's chest. It looked just like the ones on the wraiths and glowed with a heavenly light.

"You…insufferable bastard," he said. "You captured the essence of the heavenly host in that stone to control the wraiths, didn't you?"

Faust spat on the ground and smirked. "Nothing gets by you, does it?"

"But how, how can a lowlife half-demon like you get command of such magic?" Before Faust would answer, a phantom blade pierced the Gil-Gamesh from behind. Bryan fell to his knees as he dropped his swords in pain. Amelia tried to lash out at the wraith responsible for the attack, but two more appeared and grabbed her by the arms, disarming her in the process.

Faust smiled with utter delight as he walked over to the Gil-Gamesh. He motioned for a wraith to hold him steady and turned to face Amelia. "Well, shield maiden, it looks like you failed. You failed to protect your Lord, the Gil-Gamesh, the Knight Eternal of Avalon. It is the most solemn duty of the shield maiden and you *failed*, little one."

Amelia began to cry as she looked at Lord MoonDrake, helpless and dying from the festering wound incurred by the phantom blade. She felt guilt wash over her and screamed defiantly at the half-demon. Faust knew it was time. He thrust his sword through the shield maiden's stomach, eviscerating her through and through. Bryan cried out as the wraiths let Amelia's limp body fall to the ground.

Faust walked up behind the Gil-Gamesh and whispered in his ear. "Now watch this; it gets even better!" From out of Amelia's corpse, Bryan saw her spirit rise above her body and hover there as a formless ghost. In several quick bursts of light, pieces of armour flashed into existence and encased the spirit, a final flash locking her soul away in a heartstone. Amelia was no longer there, only another soldier in the Wraith Legion.

Bryan wept. Faust, on the other hand, revelled in the moment. "Pick those up and take them to my vault," he commanded the newly formed wraith. Without hesitation, the wraith gathered *Twilight* and *Dusk* it its spectral limbs and carried them away.

Faust turned back to Bryan and placed his sword under his chin. He smiled at the Gil-Gamesh as he forced his wounded foe to look at him. His was the last face Faust wanted Lord MoonDrake to see before he died.

"Your shield maiden is mine and your family and friends will soon join her," he gloated. "All will kneel before my master, the true King of Avalon."

"And who is this master of yours, Faust?" Bryan could barely choke out the words. "Who is this mysterious benefactor?"

Faust considered for a moment. "I will tell you, Gil-Gamesh, so you will know the depth of your failure. The one true King denied his birthright by your ancestor, Sir Percival. The one true son of Arthur."

Bryan looked at Faust in disbelief. "No, that's not possible. He died, killed by Percival in Blackbriar Forest. He—"

"He lives, Gil-Gamesh, Mordred lives!" Faust laughed. "Once we're done here, the Wraith Legion will take New Camelot and Mordred will take his rightful place on the Granite Throne. Your greatest enemy, the enemy of your ancestors, will rule Avalon. It's sad that you won't be around to witness his triumph, but I will make sure your wife and children are. They will serve Mordred and there's nothing you can do about it!" Faust reared back to strike the killing blow.

Then Bryan heard the faintest whisper of wind, and a moment later, a sword was protruding from Faust's chest, clean through his right clavicle and shoulder. He looked up to see Eileanora and the *Hîldrägo Boquè* charging out from the light of the temple and into battle.

They immediately dispatched the wraiths in the room and surrounded Faust. The wounded half-demon clutched his shoulder in pain and stared hatefully at the Elves, knowing his only recourse was to escape.

"This isn't over, Eileanora!" he cursed.

"Yes, it is Faust, for an Elf stands in Alfheimer again. And you and your wraiths are not welcome here!" She had barely finished speaking when a pulse of magical energy spread out from the temple to the very edges of Aflheimer. Every wraith was flung through the air like ragdoll until not a one was left within the city walls.

Faust was flung as well. High in the air, he opened a demon hole and vanished.

The Gil-Gamesh fell to the floor and the Elves rushed to his side to tend to him. Eileanora looked back as the Elves inside the temple transformed from corporal beings into pure starlight. "Can we go back in?" one of the *Hîldrägo Boquè* asked her.

"No, it is too late for us," she said. Light blasted from the temple and into the sky once more and extended across Avalon a final time. The barrier was being restored.

***

Captain Rich and his crew had watched light erupt and radiate from the island for the last hour. The final burst temporarily blinded them. When their eyes adjusted, the island of Avalon was gone.

Rich walked over to the radar to confirm what his eyes were seeing. What was once there was now gone again from the world. Suddenly, the sea rumbled, shaking the ship and everyone on it from stem to stern. The powerful vibrations lingered for just a moment, then were gone as quickly as they came. Within second, dark clouds rolled in and it started to rain. A storm swell began to rock the seas as hard as if the ship was caught in a hurricane.

"Captain, what's happening?" the OOD asked him.

"The world's returning to normal, Lieutenant," he said, as he stared out at the empty ocean where Avalon once sat. "The magic is gone. It's gone."

***

The elation of the knights and shield maidens upon seeing the barrier return and the wraiths removed quickly turned to fear as the entire island of Avalon was struck with violent earthquakes. The fear grew as the shaking grew worse, and quickly turned to terror as cracks began to form in the earth. The island was tearing itself apart. Landmasses split, buildings shattered and people and creatures alike fell into massive sinkholes and deepening chasms as the ocean poured in to fill the gaps.

The unforgiving tremors continued for more than an hour, the landmasses moving farther and farther apart. Avalon, once a great island, was now an archipelago.

The Fenris Mountains and Blackbriar Forest was the largest of these new islands. The breadth of the mountain range surrounded the forest like a ring, with the fishing village of Steinfisk and the North Highlands to the West with the Centaurs of Kéntauros and the Gilded Halls of the Dwarves to the East. Only Merlin's Pinnacle stood alone, giving the Jotunn an island unto themselves.

Like Merlin's Pinnacle, the magical tower of Strongürd Keep sat alone in the seas between the islands. It's an impenetrable fortress of magic, sealed off from the rest of Avalon, as was the island of Togo, once again. The same went for the sprawling city of South Essex, the farmlands of Eldonshire and the Port of Nottinghamshire. A few, small towns and villages, once scattered across the plains of Avalon, were now isolated from the main thoroughfares that once connected them.

New Camelot found itself adrift in the centre of these new islands. Its walls and buildings lay cracked and ruined from the earthquake. As people began to pick up the pieces and help each other, a more sinister deed was being carried out.

The Lords of Avalon sequestered themselves with their children inside the Great Hall of Castle Pendragon. As the tremors subsided, the children saw this as the opening Mordred had mentioned and they knew it was time to fulfil the Fatal Bond. Many of the Lords had been injured in the disaster and were unable to defend themselves.

The children acted swiftly and unmercifully, killing their parents with the ease of an accomplished assassin. Even Tomas, who could barely prick his finger to invoke the Fatal Bond, lashed out to do the deed as quickly as possible. He did so only to save himself from the possible death that awaited him should he fail to execute his parents. They didn't even attempt to cover up their crime. They knew that when Mordred took the throne, none would ever know of their deception and murder.

From his hidden quarters within New Camelot, Mordred watched as the people began to recover from their terrifying ordeal, yet he himself did not know what or how this happened. He did not plan for Avalon to be ripped apart by the *Oriĕntür*. His plan to rule Avalon was falling to pieces around him like the island itself.

There was a knock at the door before Blackstone entered the room. "Master Mordred, it is worse than we feared," he started, "Avalon as we knew it is no more. The island is now a cluster of islands, from north to south, east to west. There is destruction everywhere. What could have happened?"

Before Mordred could answer, the familiar popping sound of a demon hole came from the other room. "Perhaps we'll find out now that Faust is here," Mordred declared. He pursed his lips and calmed his anger before stepping into the other room, Blackstone close behind. They saw Faust wincing in pain as a wraith pulled Eileanora's sword out of the half-demon's shoulder.

"Faust, what happened in Alfheimer?" Mordred demanded.

Faust grabbed a bottle of brandy off the table and took a big swig before pouring it over his wound. He cringed as he sat down, his arm still hanging limp from the damage and drank some more brandy. "That damn she-devil, Eileanora, and the *Hîldrägo Boquè* jumped out of the temple and attacked me just as I was about to kill the Gil-Gamesh. Once they exited the temple, the wraiths and I, we were…expelled from Alfheimer. We were regrouping when the quakes started."

"So, the Gil-Gamesh lives?" Blackstone asked.

Faust shook his head and took another swig of brandy. "No, he was stabbed with a phantom blade. He'll die soon enough."

"And the swords, *Twilight* and *Dusk*?" Mordred inquired.

"Safely in my vault, Master Mordred. I still don't know how it all happened, do you?"

Mordred stepped closer to Faust, then reared back and slapped him across the face. Normally, Faust wouldn't take that from anyone, including Mordred, but he was in no condition to retaliate.

"You let the Elves leave the temple?" he screamed at Faust. "What were you doing, gloating over the Gil-Gamesh? Lauding over him like some back-alley thug? You were the one who told me that my mother made that same mistake all the time, and here you are, doing the same thing!"

"This happened because the spell was incomplete, you fool. The backlash from the spell had nowhere to go except down into the heart of Avalon, tearing it apart like a hammer to stone."

Mordred turned his back to them and whimpered like a spoiled child throwing a tantrum. "What is there to rule now but a shattered kingdom?"

Blackstone exchanged glances with Faust. "Perhaps not, milord? The people are scared, unaware of what has happened to them and why. We can use that to our advantage."

"What do you mean?" Mordred asked.

"No one knows what happened in Alfheimer. We can tell them the Gil-Gamesh failed to take certain things into account and that caused the disaster. He and his Outlander family will be hated and scorned and the people will need new leadership to guide them—yours!"

Blackstone continued to explain the prospects to Mordred whose fondness for the plan grew more and more. Just then, another wraith appeared and whispered something to Faust, giving him cause to smile. "What is it, Faust?" Mordred inquired.

"The ranks of the Wraith Legion have just been increased by nearly ten thousand strong," Faust explained. "It seems that when Avalon shifted, most of the coastline fell into the ocean along with the Knights of the Round Table, the Dwarves of the Gilded Halls, the Jotunn and the Centaurs. The protectors of Avalon have been decimated in one swift stroke."

Things were looking up for the three conspirators, but Mordred still saw some uncertainties. "We will need to rally the people behind their new King, and to do that we need political might as well as knowledge," he ascertained. "We have the young Lords of Avalon at our side, but we need someone the people already trust to legitimise my claim to the throne."

Blackstone understood. "I know just the person, milord," he said with an evil grin.

***

Hunter and Sarafina raced toward the Temple of Eternal Starlight at a furious pace. They thought their hard-fought victory was theirs once the wraiths were expelled from Alfheimer, but the violent earthquake indicated otherwise. Like the rest of Avalon, Alfheimer now stood alone on an island amidst the rest of Avalon. Lake Ouroboros was gone but the waterfall still flowed from the top of the city down into the valley. It seemed the source of its endless water was not destroyed and still circulated through the city. The mountains on either side of Alfheimer now protected them, making any entrance into the sacred land virtually impossible except by air.

Once they reached the temple entrance, they saw some of the *Hîldrägo Boquè* standing around, and were curious as to why they were still here. When they looked inside, they understood why. The Gil-Gamesh lay motionless on the floor, his head resting in the lap of Eileanora. His chest lay bare, covered only by the bandage where the phantom blade had wounded him.

The two rushed to his side, holding back the tears at the sight of their injured father. "Dad? Dad, are you—?" Hunter asked he knelt next to him.

"He mustn't speak, Sir Hunter," Eileanora explained delicately. "He is very weak and needs to preserve his strength until your family arrives,"

"What? What are you saying?"

"He was stabbed with the phantom blade of a wraith," she said, touching the young man's face to comfort him. "My magic is keeping him alive, but he's barely holding on."

"Is he going to turn into one of those wraiths? We can't—"

Eileanora raised her hand calmingly. "You have nothing to fear of that, Sir Hunter. The spell keeping him alive ties him to Alfheimer, not the Wraith Legion. He will ascend to *Vídbláin* as did my kin."

Just then, Captain McLoughlin and Andrew walked in to see the wounded Gil-Gamesh lying before them. Hunter acknowledged them and turned. "Rhona, signal the *Black Adder* and the *Avenger* to land immediately! Hurry!"

As Rhona ran off, Sarafina knelt directly across from Hunter. She reached out and held the Gil-Gamesh's hand. She fought back the tears, not wanting to show the pain and helpless feeling that overcame her. Bryan reached up and wiped the tears from her eyes.

"No tears, Sarafina, no tears," he mumbled. "Remember what I taught you?"

Sarafina couldn't help but chuckle at his attempt at humour at this dire time. "*'There's no crying in baseball'*," she said with a smile. He could always get her to smile. "You can't leave us now, Father. Thomas and Meriel need their grandfather."

"They have a wonderful mother to take care of them, daughter," sputtering blood with each word. The infection caused by the phantom blade was spreading.

Sarafina leaned down and kissed his cheek. "You saved me, Father, you saved me…"

Bryan smiled, as he looked back into her teary eyes. "No, daughter, you saved me."

"Gil-Gamesh, please, you must save your strength," Eileanora implored.

"I'm not going anywhere, Eileanora, not yet at least. Besides, they need to know."

"Know? Know what, Dad? What happened?"

Bryan slowly raised his hand and pointed across the room. The two looked to see Amelia lying motionless on the floor, her body covered by the cloak from one of the Elves. Both Hunter and Sarafina bowed their heads and said a silent prayer.

"Faust killed her in front of me, so I would watch her change into a wraith," he muttered. "She's one of his now. This…was his plan all along…" He coughed violently, and more blood spilled from his lips. Eileanora wiped it away as she gently cradled his head.

"Whose plan, Father? Did he tell you who's behind this?" Hunter urged. He didn't want to push his father, but he knew the Gil-Gamesh wanted to tell him as much as possible before he passed.

"Mordred… It's Mordred, Hunter. The bastard son of King Arthur lives again." Everyone who heard that name stopped and stared at the Gil-Gamesh in disbelief.

"But that's not possible," Sarafina said. "Mordred was killed by the first Gil-Gamesh more than 3,000 years ago."

"That's what we thought too, Dame Sarafina, but it seems it was only part of the story," Eileanora interjected. "Remember, Mordred was blessed with eternal youth by his mother, Morgana le Fay. When Sir Percival killed him, he took his soul into the soul reaper, *Dusk*, but Mordred's body remained young and beautiful, empty without a soul.

"When Morgana destroyed the original *Dusk* with the Dark Tides, the souls kept within the sword were released," she continued. "Most of the souls went to the afterlife because they had no body to return to, but Mordred did. He's been biding his time, waiting for the opportunity to strike."

"It doesn't matter how he survived, he's going to take the throne," Bryan said. "It's up to you to stop him, Hunter, and return Bowen to his rightful place as King." With the help of Eileanora, Bryan pulled his dragon stone pendant from around his neck and handed it to Hunter. The pendant was a gift from the Dragon Queen Nihala when he first arrived on Avalon.

Hunter took the pendant reluctantly in his hands. "I don't know if I can do this, Father," he confessed. "I'm not ready to be Gil-Gamesh."

"Neither was I," Bryan coughed again. "I had my friends to support me; you have your family to help you. I wouldn't ask this of you if I didn't think you were ready for the challenge, Hunter. You're ready, son. You're ready."

A tear rolled down Hunter's cheek as he placed the pendant around his neck. He leaned down and kissed his father on the forehead before touching his head to his. "I love you, Dad!"

Bryan reached up and wrapped his arms around his son's head. "I love you too, son," he whispered. The sound of running interrupted them as Rhona walked in with Lady Stephanie, Ashley, Rose, Edan and King Bowen in tow. They were all shocked and saddened at the sight of the Gil-Gamesh lying helpless on the ground.

Hunter rose to his feet and helped his mother kneel next to his father. Both Ashley and Rose stood back, comforted by Andrew and Edan respectfully. Hunter walked over to Bowen, taking his son into his arms. The little boy broke down and cried.

Bryan opened his eyes to see his family standing around him. He looked over at Stephanie and smiled. "Are you doing anything Saturday night?" Bryan asked. "I know a great place down on Atlantic Beach Boulevard that serves the best crab legs and beer in Florida!"

Stephanie laughed despite the situation. He was recounting their first date in Jacksonville, Florida, where they met. "I think I'm available," she said, before she fell onto his chest, crying uncontrollably. Bryan stroked her hair and quietly implored her to stop crying.

"It's okay, honey, you're going to be all right," he assured, but Stephanie was inconsolable.

"I watched you die once already, I can't lose you again," she cried, as she buried her head in his chest again. Bryan lifted her chin, so she would look at him.

"You haven't lost me, my love. I will always be with you, a part of the magic of Avalon. When you feel the sunlight warming your face, that's me looking at you. When the wind blows through your hair, that's me touching you. And when the rain falls on your lips, that's me kissing you," he concluded. "I will always be with you, Stephanie. I love you, wife." Stephanie smiled, as she leaned over and kissed her husband. Even in the face of death, he knew exactly what to say to comfort her.

"I love you, husband."

Bryan looked over at Ashley and Rose as he motioned for them to come closer. Sarafina stepped back as the two girls took her place next to the Gil-Gamesh. He took each one by the hand and kissed them softly on the forehead, grimacing in pain as he forced himself to sit up and reach out to them.

"You are my precious angels," he said. "I'm so proud of you, both of you, of the wonderful women you've become. I'm counting on you to help Hunter, to be his big sisters. He will need his family to support him as he takes on the mantle of the Gil-Gamesh, but, in all honesty, the three of you are more powerful when you are united."

"You have the mind of a wizard, Ashley, wise beyond your years. You have the heart of a dragon, Rose, strong and true. And you, Hunter, you have the soul of a warrior, brave and honourable to the end. Together, you are an unstoppable force that equals any power on Avalon."

"Daddy, I—" Rose began to say, but Bryan put his fingers to her lips.

"I'm sorry I won't be there to walk you down the aisle, Rose, but you and Edan have my blessing," he said, as he looked past the girls at both Edan and Andrew. "Protect them at all costs. I'm leaving that to you two now. It's your responsibility. I'm counting on you."

Both Edan and Andrew stood tall and nodded their heads to the Gil-Gamesh. He smiled, assured that he was entrusting his daughters in good hands. Both girls leaned in, kissed their father, and said 'I love you' before stepping away into the comforting arms of their men.

"My king," Bryan said, as he reached out for Bowen. The boy king knelt and took his grandfather by the hand. "I am sorry, Your Majesty, I failed to stop the evil that has taken over Avalon. Please forgive me."

"You did your best, Gil-Gamesh, you always do," the little King replied. "There is nothing to forgive."

Bryan coughed again, and more blood came up. His wound grew darker as the infection sank deeper into his body. "Listen to your father, Bowen. Let him guide you as I did him. You will be a better man for it."

"I already am, grandpa, because of you! Please grandpa, please don't leave us."

But Bryan could not hear his cries. He looked past all the people and sadness that surrounded him to see a familiar face walking towards him. It was Eonis, his Elven friend who died more than a year ago. He looked as he did the last time he saw him. His long, brown hair pulled back behind his pointed ears, his handsome face shining in the magical glow of Alfheimer, and his mischievous smile beaming brightly.

The ghostly image reached out to Bryan. "It's time, my friend, time for you to come home."

Bryan chuckled under his breath and reached out to him. "You still owe me 20 gold sovereigns, you little cheat."

Eileanora knew instantly whom he was talking to. She leaned down next to the Gil-Gamesh's ear. "Tell Eonis I love him," she whispered.

Bryan smiled, closed his eyes and nodded once. His arm dropped to his side. Everyone bowed their heads and prayed. The only sounds to be heard were the soft cries of his family. Lord Bryan MoonDrake, the Gil-Gamesh of Avalon, was dead.

***

Chamberlain Ulric Ocwyn paced frantically through Castle Pendragon. The reports he had received were terrible. Though the barrier had returned Avalon out of the reach of the outside world, the result was devastating. The entire island was shattered into pieces. There were thousands of dead. It was a disaster. He hadn't heard anything from Alfheimer so he had no idea what had happened, and that was the one thing Ocwyn hated—not knowing.

He entered the Great Hall to see if the Lords of Avalon had survived the ordeal. As he opened the door, his heart sank and his eyes grew in horror. The Lords of Avalon lay dead on the floor of the Great Hall, but their deaths were no accident. Ocwyn saw clearly that the Lords had been murdered. Their prodigy stood off to one side, standing firm and strangely quiet by the gruesome scene before them.

"What is going on here?" Ocwyn demanded.

"A coup, Brother dear!" came a voice from behind. Ocwyn recognised the voice and spun around as he drew his wand from within the folds of his robe. He pointed it directly at Artūras Blackstone, who in turn was pointing his staff at Ocwyn.

"You have no right to be here, Johann!" Ocwyn commanded. "What have you done to these children to cause them to kill their own parents?"

"Me? Why Brother, I have done nothing. They acted of their own free will, for their own purpose."

"Purpose? What purpose? Do you think killing the Lords of Avalon will give you the throne?"

"I have no desire for the throne, Brother, you know that."

"Stop calling me 'brother'. You gave that right up when you brought shame to our family by siding with Morgana le Fay."

"And yet, you gave up our family name years ago," Blackstone countered. "You reversed them, calling yourself 'Ulric Ocwyn' instead of 'Ocwyn Ulrich' am I not correct?"

"I did that to prove my merits on my own—not with my family name—and Father approved of it. You dishonoured the family and what, calling yourself Artūras Blackstone is supposed to make a difference? You're still the malevolent little brother I remember."

"We did not come here to quarrel with you, Ocwyn, but to make you an offer."

"We?" Ulric asked.

"Yes, we," came another voice, as a demon hole opened in the Great Hall and, through it, stepped Abdel Ben Faust accompanied by a young man that Ocwyn was horrified to recognise.

"No, it's not possible. You cannot be here!" he shouted.

"And yet here I am, Chamberlain. Mordred, son of King Arthur and rightful heir to the throne of Avalon. I have achieved in one year what my mother couldn't achieve in more than three millennia. Avalon is mine." Mordred walked over toward the new Lords of Avalon. They all bowed to him simultaneously, and with the touch of his hand, the pact was complete. The Fatal Bond was broken.

"Do you think for one minute that the Gil-Gamesh will allow you to take the throne?" Ocwyn asked. "He—"

"The Gil-Gamesh is dead, Ocwyn!" Mordred declared proudly.

Ocwyn shook his head, thinking it was a lie and a ruse. Faust motioned, and a demon hole opened. From it stepped a wraith, carrying the twin swords, *Twilight* and *Dusk*. Ocwyn couldn't believe it but there were the Gil-Gamesh's swords. Then he noticed something else. There, on the heartstone within the wraith, he saw the face of Amelia Pomodoro, Shield Maiden of the Gil-Gamesh, her face contorted in agony, as she struggled against the will of Faust.

"We need your help, Brother," Blackstone said. "We need you to help with the transition of power, to assure the people of Mordred's rightful claim as the King."

"And why on earth would I help you do that?"

"Because I will spare Bowen's life if you do," Mordred said flatly, walking over to Ocwyn and looking him straight in the eye. "I've heard how fond you've grown of Bowen, so I know his safety and well-being are important to you. If you agree to be my Chancellor, no…not Chancellor, my Magister; yes, Magister, is a more appropriate title I think… If you agree to be my Magister and help me, and the people of Avalon, through this difficult transition, I, nor none of my charges will take any action against the little prince. He can live out his days without a care in the world."

Ocwyn carefully considered Mordred's offer. With the Gil-Gamesh dead, Hunter and his siblings were no match for Faust or Mordred. Ocwyn knew that it was his duty was to protect the sovereignty at any cost, even that of his own soul.

"Will you consecrate your word with me?" Ocwyn asked.

Mordred scowled at the notion, but he saw this as a small sacrifice in sealing his place on the throne. He held out his hand to Ocwyn. "Of course, I will. Artūras, will you please do the honour?"

Ocwyn took Mordred by the hand as Blackstone held his staff just above them. "*Consecrare et Verba Mea!*" Artūras chanted. A silky ribbon of magical energy intertwined their hands before the bond connected to each of their hearts.

"I swear and consecrate that I will serve Mordred as his Magister, loyally and truthfully, from this day forward," Ocwyn swore.

"I swear and consecrate that I nor anyone loyal to me shall take any action that will harm or kill Bowen Pendragon, from this day forward," Mordred recited. Once they were finished, the spell was complete, and the magical energy left their hands and swirled around their hearts until the glow faded away. The bond had been set.

Ocwyn stepped back and knelt before Mordred. "Your Majesty, I am yours to command," he said, as he bowed his head. A single tear rolled down his cheek for the Gil-Gamesh. Ocwyn was glad he wasn't alive to see the sacrifice he made to protect his grandson.

Mordred couldn't be happier as he looked around the room. Soon, the rest of them followed suit and kneeled before him, as soon would all of Avalon. His victory was complete.

***

The rolling plains and dense forests that once divided the major cities of Avalon were now open seas. Avalon, now broken into hundreds of islands, would need to return to the sea and travel across the water for its trade and commerce, as Emmyr was now deserted and uninhabitable for people and no more flying airships would be built. Some of the islands were barren rocks, with barely a twig or brush on it, while others contained small towns and villages, some with just a single home.

In Alfheimer, there was a slow return to life within the city. The MoonDrake family and the remaining outcasts from Emmyr slowly adjusted to their new home over the next month. Though their numbers were few, they tried to start their new life here. The shield maidens returned to their daily exercise and training, along with the *Hîldrägo Boquè*, who began teaching them some of their own fighting skills. Henri was busy trying to organise the people of the city, being his normal, efficient self. Doctor Bonapat and his wife, Julianna, attended the wounded who needed long term care with the assistance of Stephanie, who felt the need to keep occupied.

The Gil-Gamesh and Amelia were laid to rest in the Tomb of the *Ljósálfar*, along with the shield maidens and Dragon Guard who died in the attack, next to the honoured dead of Alfheimer. Eileanora placed the two of them in marble sepulchres in the centre of the ancient necropolis. Their sacrifice to protect the Elves of Alfheimer had earned them this place of honour.

While Ashley retreated into her lessons with Merlin, Hunter waited patiently for word about the survivors and what Mordred was doing. He had sent the *Black Adder* and the *Avenger* out to scout around the new islands for information several weeks ago. The waiting frustrated Hunter to no end. His father had a viable network for communication from one end of Avalon to the other. With the island in shambles now, that network was broken. He felt utterly lost.

"Sir Hunter?" The voice startled him, breaking him out of his funk. He turned to see Eileanora waiting for him.

"Yes, sorry Eileanora, I was a little lost in my thoughts there for a moment."

"It's completely understandable, milord, it's been a difficult time for all of us. I just wanted to let you know that the lookouts received a signal from the *Black Adder* and the *Avenger*. They are approaching Aflheimer along with three other airships: The *Defiant*, *Sirocco* and the *Redwing*."

"Only three others? There were nearly twenty ships on patrol around Avalon when the *Øriĕntür* took place."

"Perhaps they met the same fate as the other Elven airships we had moored on Lake Ouroboros," she inferred. "Our ships fell into the rocks below when the earth split open and took the lake with it. From what we've been hearing, it's quite possible they met the same fate. In any case, they should be arriving in the next few minutes."

Eileanora motioned for Hunter to follow her and the two started to make their way toward the Great Hall of the Vanir. "There is still no sign of your father's familiar, Maverick?"

"No, nothing. I'm not sure if that's from the aftermath of the *Øriĕntür* or separation anxiety from my father's death," Hunter explained. "Merlin told Ashley that when a wizard passes away, his familiar can suffer severe trauma from the splintering of the bond between the two. I'm sure Maverick is going through hell right now."

"I will have some of the *Hîldrägo Boquè* perform a thorough search of Alfheimer. There is a chance he may have found his way into one of the many discrete, hidden areas of the city."

"Secret spots, huh? Anything I should be aware of or is this primarily on a 'need to know' basis?" Hunter asked.

Eileanora giggled at his coy attempt to pry the information out of her. "I assure you, milord, when the time is right, I will let you know about all the secrets of Alfheimer. It's really—"

"Eileanora, please," Hunter interrupted. "I'm a Knight of Avalon, not a Lord. I haven't earned the level of respect for you to call me milord."

"I understand, milord, but as Gil-Gamesh, certain protocols must be maintained. It's a matter of discipline."

Hunter thought about what she said and remembered something his father told him from when he first arrived on Avalon. "My dad told me that when he first met Sir Thomas Forest, he hated how this seasoned knight was calling him, a simple sailor, '*sire*' and 'milord' all the time. He made a deal with Sir Thomas that, when they were alone, they were on a first-name basis, and he only used the proper titles when in other company.

"So, let's make a deal, you and me," he continued. "When we're alone, you can call me Hunter. That way, we both don't have to have these awkward feelings about what to say and when, okay?"

Eileanora was impressed that this young man was already growing into the role of Gil-Gamesh. "All right Hunter, we can do that," she said and extended her hand to seal the pact. Hunter took it as a sign of great respect, something quite contrary to the stories he'd heard over the years about Eileanora.

Hunter shook her hand. "Thanks, Elle!" He hoped she wouldn't mind the nickname. Her laughter proved him right. "Oh, that reminds me," he said, unhooking his sword from his belt. "I want you to have this."

He gave his sword, *Fire Dance*, to Eileanora. The magical Elven blade burned with the blue flame of Volund, an ancient Elven master smith. The sword had once belonged to Eonis. Lord MoonDrake gave it to Hunter after Eonis' death. He was a mentor to the young knight and aided in much of his training.

"Hunter, I can't accept this. It was passed onto you by your father."

"Yes, I know, but my father told me how close you and Eonis were. You lost your sword when Faust was expelled from Alfheimer. You lost it, sacrificing your place in the *Oriĕntür*, and that means a lot to me and my family. Please, do me this honour."

Eileanora was again impressed with the young knight and knew she couldn't turn him down. She took the sword and bowed respectfully to him. "Thank you, Hunter, you don't know what this means to me."

"I felt the same way when my father handed it to me."

"But, what will you use for a weapon?"

"Oh, don't worry," he answered, as they continued their way to the Great Hall. "I plan to get back *Twilight* and *Dusk* from that half-demon son of a bitch as soon as possible. They're the legacy of my family, and as soon as I get them back, I'm going to kill Faust and Mordred with them."

Eileanora admired his determination, though she knew that now, it would be a hopeless endeavour. When they reached the steps of the Great Hall of the Vanir, the sound of horns echoed off the valley walls. They watched as the five airships slowly descended to the water below where temporary structures had been constructed to moor the airships.

Both Hunter and Eileanora knew why only three airships were found when they saw them entering Alfheimer. The ships were badly damaged as if they had been in a massive firefight. They looked on as skeleton crews scurried around the ships to get them down safely. It seemed as if half of the crew complement was gone on each ship.

Hunter and Eileanora waited until Edan, Rose and Captain Jasper Hawke made their way to the hall. Dressed in her leather jumpsuit, Rose looked more like a pirate than a lady of Avalon. Once they reached Hunter and Eileanora, the two captains bowed respectfully to Hunter, recognising his new position as the Gil-Gamesh.

"I've ordered the crews to receive food and medical attention, Gil-Gamesh. They desperately need it."

Hunter nodded his head in agreement, as he watched shield maidens help carry the injured crewmembers off the airships towards the makeshift hospital. "What happened to them?"

"It's best we go inside, Hunter, so everyone can hear about what we've found," Rose replied. Hunter agreed, and they headed into the hall. Once inside, they all had some food and drink while they listened to the report from Edan and

Jasper. They were joined by the others, including Lady Stephanie, Sarafina, Ashley, Andrew, Rhona and, not the least of which, King Bowen.

"It's a mess out there," Edan started. "We counted more than 140 islands, and I'm sure we missed a few along the way. All the major cities—South Essex, Nottinghamshire, Steinfisk, Eldonshire and New Camelot, are islands unto themselves. Plus, Blackbriar Forest and the Fenris Mountains, the latter of which became the largest of the new islands and Togo, Strongürd Keep and Merlin's Pinnacle along with a dozen other villages and towns. They're all on their own, for the time being that is."

"What do you mean?" Rhona inquired.

"We saw massive shipbuilding efforts going on in Nottinghamshire," Rose interjected. "They'll have a fleet of ships ready to sail in a couple of months, in addition to the other ships we saw."

"What other ships?" Sarafina asked.

"Warships, Dame Sarafina, ironclad warships sailing on the seas and flying through the air," Jasper said, as he took another swig of whiskey, straight from the bottle. "I've never seen anything like them. Iron plating on the hull, double the cannons and flying without wings or rudder."

"Is that what happened to our ships?" Hunter asked.

"Yes, they almost destroyed our entire fleet," Edan explained. "They were attacked just as the barrier was restored, as if they were waiting for us. The only reason these three got away was that the ironclad ships suddenly dropped down to the water during the pursuit as if they ran out of power or something."

"Where could they get such technology?" Stephanie asked.

"Edwyn Broadfoot," Eileanora said. "That little gnome has been tinkering about with airships, trying to replicate them without using the wood from Emmyr. He was behind the theft of an Elven airship two years ago. Lord Baldrid only wanted the ship recovered; he didn't want to create conflict between Elves and Gnomes. I should have cut that little thief's throat when I had the chance."

"Well, perhaps you'll get that chance again," Hunter acknowledged. "What about our friends? How are they?"

"Most of the Centaurs and Jotunn are fine," Edan said. "They're keeping to their home and rebuilding, for now, same with Togo."

"And the Dwarves?"

The three were silent before Rose finally spoke up. "The entrance to the Gilded Halls is completely caved in," she asserted. "Even the wolf statues that stood at the gates are gone. We don't know what happened to them or even if they're still alive in there."

"No, not Master Dinius. If anyone could survive this, the Dwarves could," Andrew asserted.

"Be that as it may, we'll have to try to contact them another time," Hunter added. "It may sound cold, but we are limited in their resources right now. What about New Camelot? Did you get close enough to see what was going on there?"

Once again, they three were silent, afraid to tell them the sad news. "New Camelot is being guarded by the Wraith Legion," Rose eventually answered.

"We couldn't get nowhere near there. It was far too dangerous, but that's not the worst of it."

"What could possibly be worst?" Ashley asked. Edan took a roll of parchment and handed it to Hunter.

"We saw this posted in Steinfisk," he explained. "We entered the city after dark, trying to keep a low profile, which was especially good after what we heard from the passers-by. It seems the Lords of Avalon are all dead, killed during the earthquake. Their heirs will be coronated as the new Lords in a ceremony, immediately following the crowning of Mordred as King of Avalon."

"On top of that," Jasper said, "they're blaming your father for the earthquake, the destruction of Avalon and the death of the other Lords."

"What? How can they blame him?" Stephanie asked.

"Because, according to what's being told, Lord MoonDrake's incompetence caused the spell to backfire and destroy Avalon. You see, that's what happens when you're in control; you can rewrite history to fit your needs. Mordred blames it on the Gil-Gamesh so his rise to power doesn't smell like a coup."

"On top of all that," Edan added, "they're also telling everyone that Bowen is your son and putting him on the throne was a ploy by the Gil-Gamesh to control Avalon."

Everyone was shocked at how Lord MoonDrake's name and reputation were being ruined by lies perpetrated by Mordred and his allies. Hunter shook his head and sighed.

"There's an even bigger problem here," he said. "If the heirs are being coroneted as the new Lords of Avalon by Mordred, then they had to be in on his plans. I wouldn't be surprised if they had to kill their own parents as part of some test of loyalty to Mordred."

"Do you really think they're capable of something like that?" Stephanie asked.

"Bree and Tomas, not really, no, but Jaeger and Finnick? Oh, absolutely," Hunter said. "All I've heard is those two complain about when they would take their father's place as a Lord of Avalon. I wouldn't be surprised if they convinced the others to join in on Mordred's plans."

"You're in for another surprise, little brother," Rose said and gestured at the parchment. "Look at who signed the announcement about the coronation ceremony."

Hunter unrolled the parchment and quickly scanned past the pronouncements until he saw the signature at the bottom. "Ulric Ocwyn, Magister to His Royal Highness, Mordred, King of Avalon. Ocwyn? It can't be?"

"Ulric Ocwyn would rather die than betray your father like this," Stephanie said. "I refuse to believe he had any part in this."

"Nevertheless, Lady MoonDrake, we must take into consideration that 'Magister Ocwyn' is now a loyal servant to Mordred," Rhona said. Arguments ensued on both sides of the issue, some chastising Ocwyn while others held out the mixed hope that he was being controlled somehow.

"It's my fault," Bowen proclaimed. Everyone stopped to listen to the little King. "It's all my fault. Chamberlain Ocwyn once told me that he would do anything to protect me and Avalon. Somehow, he's doing this to protect me, I'm sure of it. It's my fault he's there, now, with Mordred."

Hunter went over to his son and picked him up in his arms. "Bowen, this is not your fault. If Ocwyn joined forces with Mordred to protect you, he did it of his own free will. You can't blame yourself for what other people do."

"I know, but I just don't want anything bad to happen to him. That's all I'm saying, Father. I don't want you to have to kill him because of something he did for me."

"Bowen, no one's talking about killing Ocwyn," Hunter assured him. "Once we deal with Mordred, Faust and the rest of his allies, we'll discover what Ocwyn's true intentions were, okay?"

Bowen nodded his head and hugged his father, a simple thank you for the reassurance he gave him. "Speaking of intentions, what are we going to do?" Rose asked. "We can't hide in Alfheimer forever!"

"No, we're not, but first we need to learn more about Mordred and how to defeat him," Hunter said. "Ash, can you take me to see Merlin? He's probably the best one to talk to about this."

"Sure, but Rose needs to come with us too."

"Me? Why me?"

"Merlin told me that once you got back from the scouting mission, I was to bring you and Hunter to his library. He didn't say why, he just said the three of us are to come see him together."

Hunter set Bowen down next to his mother and gave him a kiss on the forehead before heading off with Ashley and Rose. The others dispersed to continue with their duties while Lady Stephanie sat in the hall with Bowen.

The little king looked up at his grandmother and saw a tear roll down her cheek. "What's the matter, Nona? Why are you crying?" he asked.

Stephanie dabbed the tears away with her handkerchief. "I'm all right, Bowen. It's just…I watched your grandfather go off on dangerous missions, time-and-time again. Now, I have to watch my children do the same thing. It's hard to watch the ones you love risk their lives when you know there's nothing you can do to keep them safe."

Bowen leaned in and hugged her tightly. "It's going to be all right, Nona! Grandpa may be gone, but he's still going to protect us, I know he is."

Stephanie smiled, as she hugged her grandson tightly. Just like Bryan, the little boy knew exactly what to say to cheer her up.

Chapter 11
The Three Dragons

The three siblings opened their eyes and found themselves in Merlin's library, their minds having been transported there through the magic of Ashley's pendant. Hunter and Rose had never been to see Merlin before, so the trip was a little disorienting to them. Once they adjusted to their new surroundings, they were both in awe.

"This is Merlin's Library? Wow!" Hunter remarked. "I can see why you spend so much time here, sis."

"Yeah, this is definitely your kind of place, Ashley," Rose added. "I can't believe we're inside a spellbook."

"Merlin collected every spell ever used in the history of magic," Ashley explained. "There's even a section on alchemy you can check out, Hunter." Her brother was rightfully impressed by Ashley's growing acumen in the magical arts. For someone who's only been studying magic, off and on, for the past year, she had really grown into her role as Merlin's apprentice.

"So, where is the old man?" Rose asked. Before Ashley could scold her for her disrespect, Merlin appeared.

"The 'old man' was getting a bottle of Elderberry wine, young lady. I hope your ill manners are not the product of your parents' teaching, but rather a reflection of your own misspent youth, as it were."

"Please forgive my sister, Master Merlin. She sometimes forgets her place," Ashley apologised before motioning to her sister to do the same.

"Sorry, Master Merlin," Rose said. "It's been a really hectic month and I didn't mean to be rude nor disrespectful."

The wizard could see the sincerity in her apology, and realised that this hasn't been easy for any of them. He set the bottle of wine down before walking over to Rose.

"It's all right, my dear," he said with a touch on her shoulder. "A great burden has been placed on the three of you, and though your spirit may be strong and your heart true, it's not easy for people so young."

"Ashley said you wanted to speak with all three of us," Hunter asked. "Why?"

Merlin laughed under his breath. "Just like your father, Sir Hunter, straight and to the point. I see a lot of him in you. In fact, I see him in all three of you, which is precisely why I asked you to come here, together.

"My greatest fear has come to pass. I thought when Morgana le Fay was destroyed, Avalon would be safe from her evil, but it has reached out from beyond the grave in the resurrection of her bastard son, Mordred. He has been a blight on this land, the same as his wicked mother, and now, I'm afraid, the task has fallen to you three to stop him, once and for all."

"But, Master Merlin, the spells placed on him by Morgana make him immortal and immune to harm," Ashley countered.

"Which is precisely why Mordred had Faust steal the twin swords," Merlin said. "In their current form, the Twin Swords of the Dragon Knight would break through those spells and kill Mordred."

"*Twilight* burns with dragonfire, capable of cutting through any enchantment," Hunter said, nodding.

"And *Dusk* destroys magic, so it would obliterate those spells and kill him," Rose added.

"Which is why you must find the swords. Without them, you have no hope of defeating Mordred," Merlin concluded.

"But that's not why you brought us here, is it Merlin?" Hunter asked. The old wizard shook his head before he turned and walked over to a small chest, sitting on top of a table.

"As I told your sister, my time on this world is at an end," he said, fumbling through his pockets, trying to find a key to open the chest. "My spirit has dwelled here long enough. It's time for me to get my reward in the afterlife, and hopefully find some relative peace and quiet."

"You can't leave now, Merlin, we need your help in defeating Mordred!" Hunter beckoned.

"I've already told you how to defeat Mordred," he professed. "Beyond that, there's nothing more for me to do. Ah, here it is." Merlin pulled a small, chunky key from his pocket and opened the chest.

"But Master Merlin, I still have a lot to learn from you," Ashley appealed to the old wizard. "There is so much more for you to teach me before I'll ever be ready."

Merlin smiled at his apprentice with a sly grin. "Ashley, my dear, before we are done here, you will have all my power, my knowledge and my wisdom at your disposal. You see, before he died, Hugo Courtland visited me. He told me his final prophecy, about the rise of an evil moon over the House of Pendragon, the destruction of Avalon, and with it, our salvation: The three dragons."

"Three dragons? You mean us?" Rose asked.

"Yes, of course, the three children of the DragonMage of Avalon, the Dragon Lord of Emmyr, your father, the Gil-Gamesh. You are the key to bringing down Mordred and his allies and taking Avalon back, but to do that, you're going to need weapons, powerful weapons indeed.

"Over the years, I have been asked to secure some of the most powerful magical relics in the history of Avalon," he continued. "And I can't think of a better opportunity to put those weapons to good use."

He reached into the chest with one hand and pulled out a long sword from within the small box. The sword was over three feet long with a bevel on either of the blade. A narrow fuller ran up the centre of the sword, inscribed with ancient Elvish runes. The guard formed an eight-pointed star with a glowing, blue stone in the centre. The hilt was long enough to use with two hands just as easy as one. The sword glowed like a comet in the night sky.

"Behold, the *Edenstar*, sword of the first high King of the Elves, Lord Dain, forged in the Lay of Volund, master smith of Svartálfar. The sword was made from a star that fell from the sky, or so the legends say. This weapon has no equal in combat and will become whatever the wielder wishes it to be."

Merlin placed the sword across his arm and offered the hilt to Hunter. "Take it, Sir Hunter, it is yours, until you recover your father's swords."

Hunter could not believe what Merlin was offering him. Tentatively, he picked up the sword and felt its weight in his hand. It took almost no effort to swing it. Just then, the sword changed its form, lengthening the hilt and reshaping the pommel into another guard and sword. Now, two blades extended from either end of the hilt. With just a thought of transforming it, the blade became an even deadlier weapon.

Merlin smiled that sly grin again. He knew it would be easy for Hunter to control. "You see? An alchemist with knowledge of reshaping metal through magic can easily control the *Edenstar*. You were born to wield this sword, Sir Hunter."

With another thought, Hunter caused the sword to return to its normal shape. Merlin handed him the scabbard to sheath the blade, which Hunter did fluidly. "Thank you, Merlin," he said with a bow.

Merlin nodded his head politely as he turned back to the chest. "As for you, my little hellion," he said, addressing Rose, "you have been, and always will be your brother's protector. Your training with the shield maidens has been quite appropriate, for now, young lady, you need to protect the Gil-Gamesh as Dame Sarafina once did for your father."

From inside the chest, Merlin pulled out an armoured breastplate. The armour was coloured a metallic green. Etched on the breastplate was a tree that formed a mask-like face with thorny branches growing out like hair to the pauldrons on the shoulders. He then pulled out a shield with the same colour and design as the breastplate.

"This is the armour of Bredbeddle, the Green Knight," Merlin explained. "His armour and shield made him invincible. So much so, that when he was decapitated by Sir Gawain, he did not die. Although, I wouldn't recommend testing that out anytime soon."

Merlin held out the armour to Rose, but she was reluctant to take Merlin's gift. "Merlin, I'm not a shield maiden, like Rhona or Sarafina. I can't accept this."

"My dear Rose, you have the courage and determination of the most experienced shield maiden," Merlin said calmly. "With this armour, you will be able to improve on those skills even more. In addition, you now carry your father's legacy as protector of the dragons of Avalon. They will now come to you, as they did your father. It is building on the bonds you have forged since your arrival on Avalon."

"He's got a point, Rose," Hunter added. "You are the absolute best when it comes to dragons, and I can't think of anyone else I would want to stand up for me as my shield maiden than you, sis."

Hunter's words of encouragement stoked the fire in Rose as she reached out and gave her brother a hug before accepting the armour and shield from Merlin. "Thank you, Merlin," she said with respect and a proper bow.

Hunter helped her put on the breastplate. Once fastened, the armour magically extended to cover her arms and legs in the same magical metal. It even extended upwards to form a helm, all decorated with in the same motif.

"Wow, I feel just like 'Iron Man'," Rose joked. Ashley and Hunter chuckled.

"Now, my dear apprentice, it's time," Merlin said, as he reached into the chest and pulled out the last item. It was a staff—twisted shaft of Wyche elm with three branches at its top, resembling a trident, with crystals of rose, smoky and white quartz embedded in them. It was the legendary Staff of Merlin.

"Merlin...your staff?"

"Yes, Ashley. I've kept it here, waiting for the day when I would find an apprentice worthy of it. That day has finally arrived," he said with all the pride of a master to his apprentice.

Ashley reached out to take the staff, but Merlin stopped her briefly. "Understand this, dear Ashley, that when you take my staff, I will give everything to you in that one moment. You must carry the mantle as sorceress and protector of the magic of Avalon. It is a burden equal, if not more, than that of your brother and sister. Are you ready to accept that responsibility?"

"You bet I am!" she exclaimed and grasped the staff confidently. In that moment, the room exploded in an eruption of magical energy. Ashley held onto the staff for dear life as the energy flowed from Merlin to her. She looked across to her mentor and saw him smile as he closed his eyes and his body began to fade. Ashley realised that, for the first time in thousands of years, the wizard was finally at peace.

Hunter and Rose shielded their eyes as the energy consumed Merlin and Ashley until it dissipated as quickly as it came. When their eyes adjusted, Merlin was gone. Ashley stood there, robed in the same ornate robes that he once wore. Her eyes glowed with magical fire until they slowly returned to normal. Ashley took a deep breath, bracing herself on the staff.

"Wow! What a rush!"

"Are you okay, Ash?" Rose asked, looking at her sister with the same concern as Hunter.

Ashley smiled, as big of a smile as she could muster. "I never felt better in my entire life!" she shouted with pure, utter joy. The three of them came together and hugged each other. They closed their eyes, as they embraced one another and bowed their heads.

"Thank you, Father!" Hunter prayed. "We will not forget your sacrifice you made for us, and together, we will avenge you! An eye for an eye!"

On that they let go and looked at one another, amazed and impressed at the transformation that happened before them. "So, what now, Gil-Gamesh?" Ashley asked her brother, not in a playful tone as she might have done before, but one that was serious and respectful.

"Now, we're going to crash a coronation!"

***

New Camelot was decorated in grand fashion for the coronation of Mordred. Though most of the city still laid in ruin, in some form or another, the people disguised its wounds with banners and flags in honour of its new King.

The red and gold of Pendragon were gone, replaced by purple and gold of Mordred, displaying for all his heritage as the child of both King Arthur and Morgana le Fay. The three dragons of the banner of Pendragon was replaced with a winged lion holding an eye in its claws, with a crossed sword and lightning bolt in the eye—the new heraldry of King Mordred.

While many remained uneasy at the thought of Mordred on the throne, there were some who relished in his return. Most, however, were only motivated by fear. On every street and on every tower along the walls, the Wraith Legion could be found. While their presence was sure to dissuade any attackers, it was also vital for keeping the population in check. Mordred did not want anyone loyal to Bowen or the Gil-Gamesh thinking that it would be easy to take back the throne.

The people gathered in front of Castle Pendragon. On a raised platform near the castle sat a single chair, burnished in gold with purple silk over lays, covered by a canopy, decked out in gold and flying the flags of the four Houses of Avalon and Mordred's banner. In front of the platform stood the new Lords of Avalon: Baroness Brigda Olafdotter of the North Highland, Earl Finnick Deveraux of South Essex, Duke Jaeger Nottingham of Nottinghamshire and Lord Tomas Elderson of Eldonshire.

On one side of the throne stood General Abdel Ben Faust and Artūras Blackstone, recently named the Minister of Magic to the new King. On the other side stood Cardinal Dominici Allistar Magelleon and Ulric Ocwyn, Magister to King Mordred. As the Cardinal placed the crown on Mordred's head, Ocwyn tapped his staff on the platform and proclaimed, "Hail King Mordred the First, ruler of Avalon! Long Live the King!"

The crowd chanted in unison, 'Long Live the King' to Mordred's utmost delight. He relished in the praise and adulation, though he could see some sombre faces in the crowd. His demeanour turned sour at the sight of his subject's unhappiness at his rise to power. He was determined to make them love him at any cost.

Mordred rose to his feet and raised his hand to stop the cheering crowd. He stepped forward until he stood directly behind his new Lords of Avalon. "Long have I waited for this day to come," he began. "Since my birth, I was groomed for one role…to one-day rule Avalon. Although that day is here, there are many among you who are sceptical. I can understand that, especially with all that has happened in the past weeks. I want to assure you that I will bring Avalon to a new age of prosperity and revolution. With the new Lords at my side, we will achieve a brighter, most glorious future for Avalon, but with newfound prosperity must come sacrifice.

"With the Gilded Halls of the Dwarves destroyed, the wealth of Avalon is now gone. We will need to raise taxes on all, to help bring about the restoration of our homes from every new island of Avalon. With the Wraith Legion protecting us from any potential threats, we can focus our efforts on reconstruction.

"Now, demonstrate your loyalty and commitment to your Lords and your King. Kneel before us!" he commanded. "Kneel before your King!"

Like a wave across the courtyard, everyone knelt to their new King. Except, in the centre of the courtyard, three cloaked figures remained standing. The people around them looked at them with disbelief, dumbfounded that they had any reason to disobey King Mordred.

Blackstone stepped forward and slammed his staff on the platform. "Who are you that would dare disobey your king?" he shouted. "Kneel!"

"No!" the centre figure shouted. "Because he's not my king!" The cloak dropped to reveal Sir Hunter MoonDrake, the Gil-Gamesh of Avalon. Hunter donned an armoured breastplate, carved with the coat of arms of the House of MoonDrake—a dragon over two crossed swords and a crescent moon. He wore a leather waistcoat, adorned with a collar of black fur and an armoured pauldron on his left shoulder, held in place with a heavy leather belt. Two GunStars hung from his waist, strapped to both legs like a gunslinger. His carried his sword on his back, the hilt just over his right shoulder.

Behind him, Ashley and Rose lowered their hoods. When the people around them saw who it was, they pushed back away from them, so as not to incur Mordred's wrath. Bree and Tomas feared for their friend's life, as did Ocwyn, while Finnick, Jaeger, Faust and Blackstone smirked gleefully, waiting to see what Mordred would do with them.

At first, King Mordred was furious that these Outlanders interrupted his coronation ceremony, but then he saw this as a wonderful opportunity to deal a final blow and end the line of the Gil-Gamesh once-and-for-all.

"I'm surprised to see you and your sisters here, Sir Hunter. Have you come to seek recompense for your father's failure?" he asked with undue sarcasm.

"We're here to let the people know what really happened during the *Øriĕntür*," Hunter accused. "How your pet demon, Faust, and the Wraith Legion attacked us, causing the disruption of the *Øriĕntür*, killing our father in the process and stealing the twin swords, *Twilight* and *Dusk*. It was your fault that Avalon was torn apart, not our fathers."

"Such a tall tale, Sir Hunter, but I really just see this as a poor attempt, by you, to put your bastard son back on the throne."

"The only bastard on the throne of Avalon is you, Mordred," Hunter snapped back. "I was the royal consort of Her Royal Highness, Queen Cadhla Edaline Raewyn Pendragon of Avalon. Our union was blessed by Cardinal Magelleon himself. Bowen is no bastard! He is the rightful heir of Pendragon, not you!"

"Please, Your Majesty, allow me to shut this traitor's lying mouth," Jaeger said, then drew his mace and charged at Hunter. In an instant, Rose threw off her cloak, displaying her bright-green armour, and brought her shield up in front of Hunter as the brute attacked. The magic shield absorbed the Jaeger's blow. Rose remained unfazed, and retaliated by slamming the shield into a stunned Jaeger, throwing him back into Finnick.

"The Green Knight?" Ocwyn murmured. "She's wearing the armour of Bredbeddle, the Green Knight, but how?" Mordred overheard this but ignored him. He glanced over at Faust and nodded. Faust drew his own sword and stepped forward.

"Wraiths!" he shouted. Immediately, the ghostly warriors moved in toward the three siblings.

Now it was Ashley's turn to drop her cloak and step forward in the robes of Merlin. She lifted the Staff of Merlin into the air. *"Vade Autem Spiritus!"* she shouted and slammed the staff onto the ground. A wave of magical energy erupted outward, pushing the wraiths away. The courtyard was then surrounded by a dome of luminescent energy, one that the wraiths couldn't penetrate.

"By Hades, she has the Staff of Merlin!" Blackstone cursed. "How can an Outlander wield the Staff of Merlin?"

Faust grew irritated and leapt off the stage at the three, his sword raised high above his head to strike. Hunter acted first, drawing his Gunstars and firing them at Faust with a new spell shot. Metal bolos—projectiles consisting of two balls connected by an iron chain—exploded from the weapons, spinning through the air until they caught Faust around his legs. He dropped like a rock, unable to teleport away via a demon hole due to being bound in iron.

Hunter holstered his Gunstars and drew his sword from its sheath. People were enchanted by its luminous glow, including Faust, who recognised the blade immediately. "The *Edenstar*," cried the half-demon from the ground. "The boy wields the *Edenstar!*"

Hunter ran up as Faust, laying prone, raised his sword to block him. He spun around and, as he moved past Faust's blade, he extended the *Edenstar* into a double-bladed weapon. In one swift stroke, he sliced off Faust's left hand. Faust dropped his sword and he screamed in pain, clasping his bleeding stump with his remaining hand.

Hunter held the tip of the *Edenstar* at Faust's throat. "That was for what you did to Amelia, demon," Hunter exclaimed. Faust scowled at him, defenceless.

"Enough!" Mordred shouted. "You three will not ruin my coronation! I will—" Mordred stopped. "You three…"

Hunter backed away from Faust to face Mordred. "Yes, Mordred, the 'three dragons' as the prophecy went, didn't it?"

"An evil moon rose over the House of Pendragon," Rose declared as she stepped up next to Hunter. "Only to be opposed at every turn by three dragons."

"We are the children of the DragonMage of Avalon, the Dragon Lord of Emmyr, Lord Bryan MoonDrake, the Gil-Gamesh," Ashley said, as she stepped up with Rose.

"You may have killed one Gil-Gamesh, Mordred, but now you have three to contend with," Hunter concluded. "We will continue to fight for and protect the people of Avalon, just as our father did. We are the Gil-Gamesh!"

The people of New Camelot were clearly gaining spirit and confidence as they spoke amongst themselves about the three children of the Gil-Gamesh. Mordred saw this and grew angry, his heart filled with contempt.

"Mark my words, Gil-Gamesh, this is not over!" Mordred scowled as he shook his finger at them. "You will rue the day you took up arms against me!"

"And you will rue the day you killed our father!" Ashley spat back.

"Or, better yet, to quote a Klingon proverb, 'Revenge is a dish that is best served cold'!" Rose shouted. "And you just walked into a blizzard, bitch!"

"We won't forget those who stood with you, against our father and against Avalon," Hunter said with a cold-stare at the new Lords of Avalon and Ocwyn. "I, for one, will never forget nor forgive."

With that, Hunter transformed his sword and sheathed. Ashley raised her staff. "*Migro-transit Alfheimer!*" she said, as she casted her spell and the three disappeared. The people of New Camelot whispered in awe of the children of the Gil-Gamesh, while Mordred and his allies are left to pick up the pieces.

"What do we do now, Your Majesty?" Blackstone asked the infuriated King.

"Do, Minister Blackstone? We do what we are meant to do. We will rebuild Avalon in my image and, in the process, step all over the people they hold so dear. The people will suffer until those three are dead and buried, and then they'll suffer some more.

"I will make sure they remember these Outlanders as the cause of all their pain and then? Then they will come to worship me. Then they will come to love me."

Mordred left the stage in a huff, leaving the others behind to clean up the mess. Ocwyn watched as the new Lords helped each other, and Blackstone went to aid the injured Faust. Never had he felt so alone.

"What have I done?" he whispered to himself, distraught as to what those three children he'd grown to love must think of him.

***

In the months that followed the coronation of King Mordred, Alfheimer grew into a bustling city once again. People who believed in the Gil-Gamesh and King Bowen came to Alfheimer, both for protection from Mordred and the Wraith Legion and to help their efforts to reclaim Avalon.

Though Mordred and his allies tried relentlessly to get into Alfheimer, they were continually thwarted. The Elves that stayed behind had restored the ancient magic that protected the city. As long as an Elf remained in Aflheimer, no one could enter without their permission.

Of course, Henri Beauchamp took it upon himself to organise the people according to their various needs and skills. Alfheimer was completely self-sufficient with fresh water, grazing lands for animals in the reclaimed land around the city as well as fully functioning workshops, blacksmiths and storehouses. He even convinced Eileanora to allow a couple of taverns to sprout up.

Due to the large numbers within their ranks, the shield maidens stepped into the new role as the Army of Avalon. With the Knights of the Round Table all but gone, these warriors now forged their own path in the fight against Mordred. They remained loyal to the House of Pendragon, the true rulers of Avalon. They would fight for the defence of the scattered lands.

Like the Knights of the Round Table, they wore the gold and red of Pendragon, emblazoned with the three dragons on their tunics. Their shields, however, bore the image of a castle tower to signify their strength and fortitude to defend Avalon. They resembled the Valkyries of legend, living amongst the people as their protectors.

Rhona stepped into the role of General, commanding the shield maidens. She was entrusted with this role by Bowen and the Gil-Gamesh, while Dame Sarafina retained her title as Headmistress of the Shield Maidens. This allowed her time to be with her children while focusing on training the next generation of warriors for Avalon. It was quite the contrast to see her go from stern taskmaster on the training ground to sweet, gentle mother when she was with Thomas and Meriel.

Eileanora and the *Hîldrägo Boquè*, as well as the remaining men of the Dragon Guard, now defended Alfheimer. They manned the watchtowers and parapets built to keep watch across the oceans that now separated them for attacks by Mordred's forces or anyone else. They vowed to never allow any of them to ever set foot in the sacred city again.

Edan and Jasper were slowly rebuilding the fleet of airships. They travelled across Avalon, finding whatever remains they could to help repair and rebuild their ships. Edan was also using his pull as the 'Pirate King' to bring other pirates to their cause. Though many didn't care for Edan nor the Gil-Gamesh, they disliked Mordred even more. With all the new taxes being levied against them, it was hard for a pirate to make a decent living. Edan promised them they could keep whatever bounty they get, so long as they stole from King Mordred and the other Lords and not the innocent people of Avalon.

Ashley spent most of her time in Merlin's Library, studying hard to perfect and improve upon her skills as a sorceress. Though her actions somewhat made

Andrew feel alienated, he had his own work to focus on. He worked with the blacksmiths, forging weapons and making improvements to old ones. He enjoyed being useful on Avalon, something he rarely felt before. He tried to keep Ashley grounded so she didn't lose herself in the magic, but it grew harder and harder with each passing day. His hope for them to start a family and settle down would have to wait yet again.

Lady Stephanie kept herself busy with the education of the children who now resided in Alfheimer. She was going to be a schoolteacher, at one point in her life, and now she was determined to ensure the children here had a proper education, including Bowen. She not only taught them the basics, but also focused heavily on the history of Avalon and of Alfheimer itself. It was a promise she made to Lyllodoria that she never forgot.

Hunter, though, was worried about his mother. He found her, late at night, sitting next to the tomb of his father. She would sit there and carry on conversations with him, from how the kids were doing to what new happened that day in Alfheimer. She sat there, holding his pocket watch as she carried on conversations with him. He made sure to keep a close watch, for her own safety.

Hunter paced himself as he walked through Alfheimer, watching the city grow more and more active with each passing day. Eileanora walked with him, going over information and issues within the city and Avalon. Though he was not a Lord of Avalon by title, he was treated as one within Alfheimer. She, on the other hand, found that going from the role of an assassin to an administrator was a difficult transition. She would have preferred to track a horde of goblins than have dealt with greeting new arrivals, and would have left it all to Henri, but she still didn't trust the man to adhere to Elven protocols in certain matters.

"We have another forty-people coming in at the end of the week aboard the *Sirocco*," she reported. "That's over two hundred in the past month. We must slow down the pace or there will be people sleeping in the streets."

"I know, I know. It's just so hard to say no to them," Hunter replied. "I know it's a slow process for you to sort through and catalogue items in the Elven homes before allowing people to move in. Is there anything we can do to help speed up the process?"

"I'm afraid not. Some of these homes contain artefacts thousands of years old. These are not just mementos, they're the heritage of entire Elven families."

"No, you're right," Hunter agreed. "I'll have Henri set up some temporary housing. The people will have to understand the fact that they are transitioning into someone else's home and we have to be respectful."

"Thank you, Hunter. I appreciate your sentiment," she acknowledged. "Besides, if I should hear Henri Beauchamp talk about 'speed and precision' one more time, I might just be forced to eviscerate that egotistical Frenchman!"

Hunter laughed, only because he knew how frustrating Henri could be. "Has Sarafina heard anything from Devil's Point prison?"

"Unfortunately, no," she answered. "All we can determine is that it's still operational. We just don't know if it's Mordred or if the trolls are still running it."

During the battle with Morgana le Fay, Sarafina recovered the Talisman of King Onkee, the first troll master. This gave her dominion over the trolls. She placed them in charge of Devil's Point Prison, where the most vile and evil prisoners in Avalon were kept. If any prisoners disobeyed the guards, they might find themselves on the dinner menu instead of a cell.

"We might have to make a special trip up there," Hunter interjected. "If Mordred frees those people, we'll have even worse problems.

"Speaking of Mordred, how's the connection with our new spy in New Camelot?" he asked.

"Perfectly," she answered. "Mrs Thurgoode is working for Mortimer Toadmier at the *Grinning Toad* tavern. She has a new name and a somewhat altered appearance. Are you sure it's wise to have her do this?"

"She practically volunteered to do it, especially once she heard about Dad's death and Ocwyn's betrayal. I was not about to stand in the way of that woman and revenge. The one thing I learned on Emmyr was to stay out of Mrs Thurgoode's way. Trust me, she's more than capable to carry this out," Hunter added. "I just don't want to see anything happen to her."

"I'll make sure to check up on her on a regular basis," Eileanora said. "She's our eyes and ears in New Camelot and I, for one, don't want to lose such an asset. Besides, she makes the best *Perfŭgio undá Dulcîse* I ever ate."

Hunter laughed again at her wit and humour. He was so surprised to find this unusually charming side to someone whose exploits could only be described as evil and quite frightening. "I have to admit, Elle, you are nothing like the stories I've heard. Nothing that I've seen in these past months even remotely resembles the *Dubh Bhean* I've heard so much about."

"I can understand that. I had quite the reputation," she started to explain. "I think my time with you, your father and the rest of your family made me appreciate the things I had never even hoped of having.

"I spent all my life being the best at killing things. It was what I was good at, but in doing so, I blocked out the important things in life like love, family, inspiration and hope. I thought I would finally have the chance of that with the *Øriĕntür*, but that too was denied to me.

"I could have drowned in the bitter anger that swelled up inside, but then I saw you and your family come together like you did," she continued. "You experienced the worst thing possible and yet here you are, optimistic that you can retake Avalon from Mordred's grasp. If you can have that hope for a better tomorrow, then why can't I?"

Hunter was personally moved by Eileanora's candid remarks, but before he could say anything, he heard the roar of a dragon from above. Dee Dee bellowed again and glided down to an open courtyard nearby. Rose was seated on the back of her dragon, still donning the armour of the Green Knight.

As Hunter and Eileanora approached, she jumped off Dee Dee, patting the dragon on her side as a way of saying thank you.

"Isn't it bulky for you to wear that armour while riding Dee Dee?" Hunter asked.

"Not really. It's amazing how effortless it is to wear!" she answered. "It protects me from the cold and wind better than my old flight suit used to."

"Well, did you find them?" Hunter asked. Rose scoffed, as if there were any doubt. "And?" he asked again, trying to pry the information from his sister. Rose just looked up skyward. Hunter and Eileanora looked up to see Gamorg, King of the Dragons, gliding down toward them. Once he landed next to Dee Dee, Gamorg let out a mighty roar of his own, announcing his presence to all.

The three bowed to him respectfully, and Gamorg nodded his head to acknowledge them. "It is good to see you again, Gil-Gamesh," he said to Hunter in dragon tongue. "Please accept the condolences of the Dragons of Emmyr on the death of your father. He was, and forever shall be, my friend."

"Thank you, Gamorg. I appreciate you coming to see us." Gamorg gruffed softly, scoffing at him the same way Rose did.

"It was no problem, Sir Hunter, as we were already on our way here."

As they spoke, a shadow fells across Alfheimer. When they looked up into the sky, Hunter couldn't believe his eyes. It was the floating island of Emmyr, former home of the Gil-Gamesh and his family. The dragon isle eased across the cityscape until it took position off the northern edge of the city.

"Emmyr, I can't believe it!" Hunter exclaimed. "So, you'll join us?"

"We will protect Alfheimer and do what we can to help you in your endeavours," Gamorg growled. "However, Emmyr remains off limits. I cannot allow my home to become the focus of another war. We cannot be responsible for human lives again. We must tend to our own needs."

"I understand," Hunter assured him. "Would it be possible to return to Port Charles to retrieve supplies and equipment that were left behind in the evacuation?"

Gamorg thought about it for a moment before answering. "You may, but it will be the last time. I give you 24 hours and then you must leave Emmyr, never to return."

Hunter bowed in appreciation to the dragon King. He quickly ordered Eileanora and Rose to get Henri, Edan and Jasper to fly back to Port Charles and scour the city for anything and everything they might need.

He turned his attention back to Gamorg, as his tone grew sombre. Hunter had a difficult question to ask. "Gamorg, I have to know. Did you foresee my father's death? Did you know it was going to happen?"

Gamorg lowered his head as if he was ashamed to answer. "I saw the pale of the reaper hovering over your father when we last spoke on Emmyr," he began. "I did not know how he would die, only that it would be soon. The one thing I learned from my mother was that you cannot outrun death. To do so would inflict considerable pain and suffering, and I would not wish that on my friend.

"I know he died peacefully, surrounded by the people who loved him. That is a good death, for any man," he concluded. Hunter understood and bowed again to the Dragon King.

"May I call on you for counsel, as your mother counselled my father?" he asked. Gamorg nodded his head, reassuring the Gil-Gamesh.

"I found someone hiding on Emmyr," Gamorg affirmed. "I thought he should be here with you." The dragon let out another tremendous roar. From somewhere on Emmyr, a blur zipped down through the sky. Maverick, Lord MoonDrake's missing familiar, whizzed through the air until he landed on Hunter's shoulder.

"So, there you are!" Hunter exclaimed, as he petted the little dragon's head. "We've been worried sick about you." Maverick appreciated the sentiment as he curled up in the fur on Hunter's collar and laid across his shoulders, his head peeking over his right shoulder.

"The death of the Gil-Gamesh was devastating to him," Gamorg explained. "I sensed his pain and found him in your father's room in the Dragon's Veil. My magic eased the pain of separation from the Gil-Gamesh. He may bond with you or your sister, Ashley, as a familiar, but he needs time to adjust."

"Don't worry, I'm sure Mom will fawn over him once she sees him again. Thank you, Gamorg, for everything."

The Dragon King bowed his head one last time. "I am at your service, Sir Hunter. After all, we are brothers, at heart." He roared one last time before spreading his wings and flying into the air, followed quickly by Dee Dee, returning to the dragon isle above.

Hunter turned his attention back to Maverick, giving the little dragon another scratch on his head. "Are you hungry, Mav? I think there's some fresh sardines down by the docks?" The little dragon cooed and whistled his answered, which Hunter understood as a resounding yes. The two started down toward the water's edge.

"We've got a lot of work ahead of us, little one. I hope you're ready for it!" Hunter asked. Maverick responded with some more clicks and whistles. The familiar was ready indeed.

***

The throne room inside Castle Pendragon was dark and eerily quiet. The statues of the past Kings and queens of Avalon were shrouded, by order of King Mordred so he did not have to endure the stares of the Pendragon legacy. He was King of Avalon now and he would not be influenced by anyone, including ghosts of dead relations.

Mordred sat on the granite throne, drinking wine as he stared into the darkness. The only light in the room shined on the throne, and he liked it that way. Mordred drank as his mood soured even more.

His perfect plans for ruling Avalon had gone awry. The island had splintered into thousands of smaller islands. He now had to expend resources into building boats, piers and other infrastructure to maintain commerce, communication and security with every new territory within the archipelago.

On top of that, the threat of the new Gil-Gamesh and his sisters, wielding magic more powerful than anything before, remained. The Wraith Legion, an army more powerful than anything before it, couldn't penetrate their home on

Aflheimer. More and more flocked to their side, turning Mordred's triumph into an all-out civil war.

Mordred gulped more wine, desperate for its intoxicating effect, but it wasn't happening as fast he wanted it. The King held out his goblet and waited until a servant girl stepped out of the darkness with a pitcher. She kept her head lowered to avert her eyes, so she would not stare at him, as ordered. By Mordred's command, none may look at him unless directed to by the King himself. She filled his goblet before stepping back from the King. Mordred waved her off as he drank some more. The servant girl curtsied before disappearing back into the darkness.

From the other side of the throne, Ocwyn stepped forward toward the King. He was followed closely by a scribe, carrying an armful of parchment rolls and a small table with ink and quill pen. The scribe set up his little table, awaiting to dictate anything said by the King or Magister Ocwyn.

Ocwyn bowed to the King before speaking. "Your Majesty, we have issues that require your attention, if you please."

"I'm really not in the mood for this, Magister Ocwyn. Can't it wait?" Mordred replied, as he swallowed another mouthful of wine.

"We've put it off twice now, Your Majesty. We cannot put it off anymore," Ocwyn said, but Mordred still sat there, drinking his wine. "This is part of being King, Mordred, whether you like it or not. Now, you'll forgive me, but I am not here to make these decisions for you. You must rule on them, drunk or not. You are King now, Mordred, so start acting like it!"

Mordred stared at Ocwyn with undeniable contempt that he would speak to him in this manner. The scribe just looked away, hoping that whatever Mordred did to Ocwyn wouldn't hurt him as well. Mordred stood up, his fist clenched as he stood over Ocwyn.

"You dare speak to me this way!" he shouted. "I am your King!" He threw the wine goblet, causing it to clang as it bounced across the floor.

"Yes, you are, Your Majesty, but even Kings need to be reminded of their duties. That is why you kept me here, isn't it?"

Mordred thought carefully about what Ocwyn said. He sat back down on the granite throne, wrapping his cape around him. "Tell me, Magister, did you ever speak to Bowen or Lord MoonDrake this way?"

"All the time, *sire*. It's why I'm so damn good at my job!"

"Very well, Magister Ocwyn, you may proceed," Mordred said, as he motioned for more wine. The servant girl brought a fresh goblet and handed it to the King while Ocwyn began his dissertation.

"We've received responses from 58 of the magistrates from 120 of the known villages still standing," he began. "They have all pledged their support for Your Majesty's rule. The others, I must presume, do not."

"Give the names and locations of those unresponsive magistrates to General Faust," Mordred commanded. "I'm sure he will be able to persuade them."

Ocwyn nodded his head and motioned to the scribe to make note of the King's command before continuing his report. "The first ships have started sailing between the major cities over the open waterways," Ocwyn reported. "The currents and new wind patterns are causing some delays. Duke Nottingham says he has his best captains working on mapping out routes, both sea and air, that will provide optimal speed and less delay."

"And has Master Tinker Broadfoot improved on the flight time of his ironclad ships?"

"I'm afraid not, Your Majesty. He says he needs more loadstones from within the Gilded Halls to continue making improvements to his engines."

"And where do we stand with the Gilded Halls, Togo and the other occupied islands?" Mordred asked. "Any progress?"

"Togo remains inaccessible, as does Strongürd Keep and the Gilded Halls. Dwarf Master Sempir Dwallis estimated that the cave in goes down deep into the Gilded Halls. He said it may take more than a year to open the way in."

"Inform Master Sempir Dwallis that he has six months to clear a path into the Gilded Halls or I will find someone else who can do the job," Mordred said, as he took another drink. "If he needs slave labour, start sending him prisoners to do the job.

"And tell Jaeger to set up a blockade around Strongürd Keep. They can't lower their defences to bring in supplies without letting us in, so we'll starve them out, bring them begging to us.

"As for Togo, we'll let them be, for now, but tell General Faust to send some wraiths to patrol around their island. We may not be able to get to them, but I don't want them helping the Gil-Gamesh's children either."

As before, Ocwyn nodded to the scribe to write down the King's instructions. "Ailbe Dufaigh, Queen of the Dökkalfar, has claimed dominion over Blackbriar Forest and the area of the Fenris Mountains around the forest," Ocwyn noted. "I recommend we have one of the new lords pay her a visit to negotiate her tribute to Your Majesty."

"What happened to the goblins? I thought they held that territory?" Mordred inquired.

"Since the death of the Goblin King, they have been leaderless, save for a Brood Goblin named D'Legg," Ocwyn replied. "Rumour has it he's forcing their warlocks to breed more Brood Goblins in their breeding pits. He's trying to weed out the weak, leaving only the Brood as the inheritors of the Goblin legacy. Once he's done that, he'll surely attack the Dökkalfar to take back Blackbriar."

Mordred laughed at the audacity and resilience of the Brood. "Tell Blackstone to speak with this D'Legg and get him on our side. After that, we'll negotiate a settlement between the Dökkalfar and the Brood over who rules Blackbriar. I'd rather have them fighting with us than against each other. Anything else?"

"Just one more thing, Your Majesty," Ocwyn started to say, but first, he motioned for the scribe to leave. He bowed, picked up his desk and left as quickly as possible. Ocwyn waited until he was sure the scribe was gone before he continued.

"The dragon isle of Emmyr has been found, Your Majesty, and it's hovering in the air, just north of Alfheimer," Ocwyn stated. With that, Mordred spat out the wine in his mouth, coughing ferociously after all that. Once he regained his composure.

"Are they moving back to Port Charles?"

"No, Your Majesty, though reports stated a few ships docked at Port Charles then left shortly after that and returned to Alfheimer. No ships have returned since. In my opinion, they went up for some supplies or other materials and brought them back to Alfheimer."

"I'm not asking for your opinion, Magister, I'm asking for what you know!" he screamed, as he hurled another goblet clanging across the floor.

"My opinion *is* what I know, *sire*," Ocwyn replied, not even flinching at the King's temper tantrum. "The placement of Emmyr near Alfheimer adds to their defences but it is not being used as it previously was. I don't believe the dragons are allowing anyone back on the island to ensure it does not become a target like in the Outlander War."

"So, have the dragons joined with the Gil-Gamesh's children?"

"Yes, Your Highness, it would appear so. After all, Desdemona is the mate of Gamorg, the Dragon King. Her connection to Rose is unbreakable, so it definitely appears to be an alliance with Aflheimer."

"And what are your feelings on that, Magister Ocwyn," Mordred asked, as if to test his loyalty.

"My feelings are not relevant, Your Majesty. I serve you and you alone, so long as our contract remains intact," he answered without skipping a beat. "Will there be anything else, *sire*?"

Mordred shook his head and waved him off as he sat back in the throne. Ocwyn bowed before backing up and leaving the throne room. Once he was gone, a demon hole popped open and Faust stepped through.

"Have you found anything, General?"

"No, King Mordred. He's been keeping to his duties, no contact with anyone outside the castle. He doesn't even go near the *Grinning Toad*, where the Gil-Gamesh once kept his quarters in New Camelot.

"He's loyal to Your Highness…for now."

"No, he will remain true to his word, per the consecrate spell. If we don't harm little Bowen, he will remain my loyal servant."

"I wonder why he didn't include the Gil-Gamesh's children in that pact?" Faust inquired.

"Because, he knew they would oppose me," Mordred explained. "It was simply a matter of principle; save one if you can't save them all. However, I must find a way to bring the rest of Avalon to my side."

"The only way you'll do that is by pulling *Excalibur* from the stone," Faust answered. "That'll convince them that you are the rightful King of Avalon."

Mordred grinned, like a sly fox entering the henhouse. "Then that's just what I'll have to do!"

Epilogue
The Path to Nidavellir

The cave was dark and dank, without a single source of light, yet the Dwarves managed to make their way through the bowels of the Fenris Mountains. Master Dinius Oddbottom led his people through a vast network of caves as they escaped the cave-in that destroyed their home. With only lanterns glowing with magical gems of light to guide their way, the Dwarves marched on. They dropped deeper into the earth, following narrow ledges and tight caves, believing that Master Dinius would lead them to safety.

Minna, his daughter, followed close behind her father. Her dirty face and curly blonde hair demonstrated her tenacity and determination to fight her way through this disaster. She acted more like a fighter than the daughter of a Dwarf Lord. She had neither the time, nor the patience, for being dainty, and her gruff exterior proved that. It also put her at constant odds with her father.

"Where they hell are you leading us, old man?" she gruffed at him. "We've been walking for days. We should have stayed behind and dug our way out of the Gilded Halls, not following your nose on some wild, mole hunt."

"I told you before, daughter, the Gilded Halls was slowly filling with water," he explained yet again to her. "If we waited there any longer, we would have drowned before we dug our way out. I know what I'm doing, lass; now, for once in your life, do what I say and keep walking.

"We'll be there soon enough, and when we get there, all I want to hear out of you is an apology. It might be the first, and last time, you'll ever say that to me."

"I doubt it, you old cuss," Minna whispered to herself, as they continued their forced march. "Would you like to tell me where you're leading us, so I might have a reason to offer you this apology?"

"If I told you, you wouldn't believe me," Dinius snapped back. "You'll have to see it for yourself."

Minna complained even more as their march progressed until finally, a few days later, as Dinius said, they reached an enormous cavern with two large doors at the centre near the back of the cavern. The doors were massive stone doors with ornate carvings across each door front, from top to bottom. The carvings depicted the history of the Dwarves, including images of Austri, Vestri, Nordi and Sudri, the four Dwarves that were given the responsibility to hold up the sky, the Dwarf Alfrigg presenting the goddess Freya with the golden necklace *Brisingamen*, and the legendary blacksmiths Brokkr and Eitri forging the Spear of Odin, *Gungnir*. The doors were held in place with metal hinges and braces, etched with ancient Dwarven runes.

Some of the Dwarves fell to their knees upon entering the cavern, as if they stepped on holy ground. Minna just stood there and looked at the doors in awe.

"Are these…?" Minna stuttered. "Are we…?"

"Yes, daughter, this is the entrance to Nidavellir, the sacred home of the Dwarves!" Dinius answered, as he walked round the door as if he was looking for a keyhole.

"I'm sorry, Father, you were right; I had to see it to believe it!" she replied. Dinius smiled, as he realised he finally got his daughter to fall silent.

"It's all right, Minna, this old dwarf has to be right occasionally," he joked, as he continued to look for the keyhole.

"But, why didn't you ever tell me you knew the way to Nidavellir?" she asked.

"Because you didn't need to know," Dinius answered back. "The location of these doors was passed down to me from my father, from his father and so on down the line of Dwarf Lords since we came to Avalon. We swore never to return here until the beginning of Ragnarok, the end of days for the world."

"Are you daft? What makes you think that Ragnarok has begun?" Minna argued.

"Because the wolves are gone, daughter!" Dinius shouted, losing patience with her. "I was outside when the island started to shake itself apart and fall into the sea. The wolves that guarded the gates of the Gilded Halls, Sköll and Hati, were gone. Ragnarok has begun and we must prepare for war."

He turned back to the door and finally found what he was looking for. One of the metal plates moved to one side, revealing a giant, oddly shaped keyhole. It was thin at the top and triangular on the bottom, much like an axe head.

"Do you have the key?" Minna asked sarcastically.

"Aye, daughter, I do!" Dinius replied, as he placed the head of his weapon, *Steinknuse*, in the keyhole. He turned the handle, and all heard the door unlock with a distinct 'clunk' that echoed throughout the cavern.

They all stepped back as the doors slowly began to swing open on their own. When they looked inside, all they could see was eternal darkness.

"Pombur, give us some light, will you?" Dinius commanded. Pombur stepped up, giddy with excitement as to what awaited them inside.

"*Kveykva þúsand Stjarna!*" he shouted, pointing his staff into the air. Suddenly, the tip of the staff exploded with a thousand fireworks that streaked high into the roof like shooting stars. The lights stayed up there twinkling, illuminating the entire cavern.

It was the legendary city of Nidavellir, carved from the stone itself. The massive structures stretched from one side of the cavern to the other, from top to bottom. The buildings varied in size, shape and especially composition—the dwarves could readily make out the textures and colours of granite, marble, limestone and quartz. The walls reflected the light from Pombur's spell, illuminating the entire cavern. The Dwarves stared in awe at the place of their birth.

"We are here, at last, my friends!" Dinius exclaimed. "I don't know what happened to Avalon, but we will do all we can to ensure we are ready when the time comes. There are more than enough supplies here to relight the forges and make our weapons of war. Once armed, we'll march back to the surface and fight to save the world from Ragnarok. This is our destiny! This is our future! This is our home!"

THE END

The story of Avalon continues in THE PROMETHEUS ENGINE: BOOK FOUR OF THE FOREVER AVALON SERIES.